THE DEAT

To Danni
Hope you like it!
Love

Kristina
x

THE DEATH SWITCH

KRISTINA VIVEASH

M&D Books

First published in Great Britain in 2004
M&D Books, Reading, Berkshire

ISBN 0 9547759 0 2

Printed and bound in Great Britain by Antony Rowe Ltd, Eastbourne

Cover design by Alfredo Moya

Edited by Susan Collins

Acknowledgements

I would like to thank firstly my mum, for all the hours of careful editing she put in. I really appreciate it. I had never properly grasped the concept of punctuation before - forgetting that people do like to breathe occasionally, when they are reading! Thank you Dad for all your support and financial help. Without you both, I couldn't have got this far. Next, I really want to thank my husband, for being there for me all these years. He has had to endure my notable absence on many occasions, since I first started this book in 2000. It must have been especially difficult having to interrupt me during the editing months - not dissimilar to walking into a bear pit I would imagine. As any writer will tell you, the initial writing bit is fun, it's the subsequent drafts that you have to keep producing that drive you batty! Thank you Andy, for being the best bro a girl could have! Thank you Grandad, for your inspiration, you have always believed that people can achieve anything if they put their mind to it. I took this concept on board and decided to go for it. I would also like to remember my nan, who I know would have been so proud of me. I miss you.

Thank you to my stepchildren, Rebecca, Katie, Nathan and Sam, you have inspired me more than you will ever know - and to my beautiful baby boy, I can never thank you enough.

A big thank you has to go to Fredy for designing the cover for me. Without a cover, my book would have been extremely floppy and dull looking, so I am exceptionally grateful to you also. Not forgetting of course my friend Liz Harrison, who I must thank for her expert proof reading skills - no spelling mistake or general blooper is safe from your trusty gaze!

Lastly I would like to thank all my friends, who have supported and encouraged me over the years - you know who you are. Thank you for making me laugh and more importantly for keeping me sane. You did it!

*for my husband Ian and our darling son William ~
I love you more today than I did yesterday,
but not as much as I will tomorrow…*

Chapter 1

As the alarm pulsated in her ear, Courtney groaned inwardly and curled her body into a foetal position with her hands over her ears, trying to block out the sound, trying to pretend it wasn't morning, trying to pretend it wasn't *that* morning. Adam reached over and turned the alarm to snooze. He rolled over to embrace his young wife as he always did, their bodies curled together. She felt his warm naked flesh against her back as he slid his hands around her waist, venturing up towards her breasts. She stiffened and could feel the tears welling up in her eyes. To him it was just another day, but how could she act normally today? This was the day that her life was going to change forever.

'I'm sorry,' she tried to disguise the fact that she was crying. Adam knew his wife too well, he pulled her closer to him and they lay together drifting in and out of sleep, until the alarm again interrupted their slumber.

Adam was the first to get up; Courtney eyed his naked form as he searched round their room for his dressing gown. She loved to look at his naked body, which belied his age. Again she had to remind herself that he was now a man in his mid forties. His skin was still smooth, smoother on his body than on his face, which was a bit more defined. He always blamed these few lines on 'facial warming' as he called it and the ever-increasing hole in the ozone layer. She just thought they gave his face more character, and she had always envied his natural tanning ability anyway. She wished he hadn't got out of bed, she loved to snuggle up against him. He turned and smiled at her, laying there with the covers up round her ears.

'You can't be cold,' he laughed, 'it's May, the sun is shining, it's the weekend.' She wished she could share his enthusiasm. Usually she was the first out of bed at weekends, but today she wanted to stay there as long as possible; she wasn't cold, she just felt vulnerable, and the covers were now her only protection.

'What time are you going to the airport?' Courtney didn't really want to know, but at the same time felt that she had to try to pull herself together.

'Well, I guess around midday, their plane lands in about two hours from now,' he waited for her to respond. He knew this was hard for her, he didn't want to come across too excited as he didn't want to upset his wife any more than she was already. Of course he was looking forward to seeing his daughters again; it had been ten long years since he had last seen them, as they had been just eight years old when he had left their mother.

Courtney began to cry again, 'just promise me, when you see them, when they get here, you promise you won't start loving them more than me, because…' she buried her face in her hands.

'Hey, hey Courtney,' Adam sat on the bed next to his wife. He moved her hands away from her face, tilted it up so he was looking right into her eyes, and cupped her face in his hands. 'Listen to me,' he kissed her forehead, 'I love you, nothing will ever change that, not them, not anybody. I love you more than you will ever know, you're my life, I won't let them spoil that. I've told you before, they're both eighteen now, they're grown up.'

She gazed back into his deep brown eyes, 'but what if they want to stay with us, and don't want to find a place of their own?'

'They won't babe,' he answered, 'they went to boarding school, they must be very independent. I don't think they're going to want us cramping their style now are they. Smile for me.'

She forced a smile, 'now that's better,' he kissed her. 'Come on, get up, have a shower, you'll feel better. Just remember who's boss round here, that's me and you - it'll be fine.'

She wished she could believe him. She did in a way, but these twins were not like any other twins. She'd seen the photographs sent to Adam from their school in Philadelphia. They had both graduated now; they were young women, and had the kind of looks that Courtney knew she could only ever dream of having herself. She thought that it would have been easier for her if they were just plain looking and ordinary, maybe then she wouldn't be feeling so threatened by them or thinking that their impending arrival was going to render her presence and status in the house obsolete.

Adam left the room to go and get breakfast on; she could hear him whistling as he went down the stairs. She sat on the bed and stared at herself in the mirror, *what will they think of me?* She sighed as she tried to force her fingers through her thick mane of dark wavy hair. Her hair was shoulder length, and cut in a modern style. It was tangled from the nights sleep though, she could see bags under her eyes, but no wrinkles still, that was good she thought. *Maybe the girls might like me cause I'm young, maybe they might want to go out drinking with me, just maybe.* She smiled to herself; *maybe we could even become friends.* She certainly didn't want to be a mother figure to them; it would make her feel too old. Courtney leaned forward to look at her eyes up close. They were usually blue and bright, but today they were red from crying so she reached for her magic eye drops as she called them, to turn them back to white again. She tried to imagine what it would be like to come face to face with her husband's estranged daughters for the first time. She had dreamt about this day before, but never really thought that day would come, or if it did, she thought it would maybe be at one of their weddings in the future. She could go there wearing her best suit and hat, smile and act like the perfect stepmother for the day, whilst still remaining detached from the role. Then she could return to her life back in Florida unaffected, and forget about them all over again. As it was now, she was going to have to live with them for the foreseeable future. She was worried what it would be like when her forced smile began to make her face ache, what then? She couldn't risk being unpopular, she was nothing to them after all. *My face is too chubby*; she pulled at her cheeks and grinned at herself, accentuating her cheeks and revealing her straight white teeth. She had always thought that her face was too round, according to Adam that was 'all in her mind.' He had described her as having 'a heart shaped face with pronounced cheekbones and a perfectly proportioned and straight nose.' He's biased though, she concluded. *Mind you he isn't the first person who's ever said that to me, well not exactly that, but something similar anyway.* She then felt a sudden surge of energy, having finally managed to psyche herself up and break the introspective loop she had caught herself in. She pulled on her best pants, (snowboarding pants) and her latest designer T-shirt which had a scoop neck that revealed her cleavage, not too much but just enough for her to feel really feminine. She put on her make-up noticing that her usually fair skin was starting to develop a reasonable tan - her long afternoons sunbathing finally seemed to be paying off - and no pimples either. She usually got pimples from too much sun cream.

'Courtney!' Adam called up the stairs. 'I got your breakfast, I've got to go in ten minutes, I want to see you first though.'
She was forced back to reality by the sense of urgency that had now come over her. She ran down the spiral staircase to the hall, almost slipping on the wood tiled floor as she turned towards the kitchen, where she found Adam sitting reading the newspaper at the breakfast bar.
'Got you poached egg, and there's some pancakes if you want them, syrup's on the side.' He was busily cramming a pancake into his mouth, chewing and washing it down with a mouthful of coffee.
Courtney didn't feel like eating, she had started to panic again. The clock said 10.45 a.m., only fifteen minutes of happiness remaining.
Adam turned to look at his wife as she headed for the fridge to pour some juice; 'you OK honey?' he asked, to reassure himself it would be all right to leave her.
'Sure,' she replied.

As he closed the front door behind him, Courtney walked to the front window to watch him as he got in to their Space Wagon. He waved at her from behind the steering wheel and she waved back. She was crying again, but she didn't think he had noticed this time. He reversed out of the drive and sped off down the road. Silence.
Now she really was alone. She walked over to the drink's cabinet; she had wolfed down the juice, but now felt she needed something stronger, *this is crazy*.
She never usually drank in the daytime, but she needed to now. She nervously poured herself a large glass of white wine. It

wasn't chilled, but she didn't have time to worry about that now. She sipped it at first, then she picked up the bottle, and grabbed her pack of cigarettes and took herself out onto the patio in the back yard, where she sat in the morning sunshine.

She didn't have that long, the airport was not that far from their house in Kissimmee. He would probably only be an hour, but then they would have to wait for their luggage, so maybe she had an extra half an hour to play with. She certainly had enough time to finish her bottle of wine, and smoke all of her cigarettes. She began to daydream, and think some more, trying to prepare herself.

She hoped that Adam would stick up for her if the girls were rude - that was very important. She hoped he had meant what he said about choosing her over them if it ever came to that, and something inside Courtney told her that it just might.

Courtney began to think about the girls' mother. They had been eleven years old when she was killed in that car accident. Goodness only knows how something like that would affect the mind of a child, perhaps they were mentally unstable, that's all she needed. Adam had never talked about Sarah much, Courtney knew they had been very young when they met, and the twins were born about four years after they married. So if Adam was forty-five now, he must have been twenty-seven when the twins were born. Courtney counted on her fingers, and that would have made him twenty-three when he married Sarah. Apparently she would have been forty last week had she survived. A shiver went up Courtney's spine; she poured herself another glass of wine, and lit another cigarette.

She started to wonder why it was that the girls were sent to boarding school in Philadelphia. Why hadn't Adam taken them with him down to Florida when their mother died? Then she remembered Adam once saying about their grandparents, Sarah's parents, being nearby. She thought that maybe Adam had not wanted to take them from their hometown, as he had left them anyway for a new life in Florida when the girls turned eight years old.

Courtney thought about the letter that Gabrielle and Alicia had sent to their father, just after they graduated. They hadn't invited him to their graduation, they just decided after leaving school they wanted to go and live with him in Florida, until they found a place of their own. They wanted to get bar jobs, and go to the beaches, after all Philadelphia's weather doesn't compare with the sunshine state. She expected they had men on their minds as well, she remembered what it was like being eighteen years old, it wasn't that long ago since she had been that age herself. *Why did they have to write to him? Why couldn't they have just stayed where they were?* She began to cry again. *This is stupid, Courtney pull yourself together.* The sun was getting hotter, she felt very warm, and the mixture of the alcohol and the heat was making her eyes heavy and she started to feel like she was back in bed again. She was snapped back to reality by the sound of the neighbour, Mr Fraser, cutting his grass as he did on every weekend. He peered over the fence as he cut near the borders by Courtney's garden, turned off his mower, and leaned precariously over the fence. Courtney was sure that one day it was going to collapse under his weight.

'Mornin Courtney, what's this sunbathin this early? You won't get a tan that way, and what's with the wine, you celebratin?' Mr Fraser had always had a way with words.

'Not exactly Ted,' she sat up on her sun lounger and shielded her eyes from the sun as she tried to see him properly. 'No Ted, I certainly am not celebrating.'

'You oughta watch this mornin drinkin young Courtney,' he continued in his thick southern drawl. 'Next thing you know you'll be pouring it on your breakfast cereal instead of your milk, then AA 'll be callin you up.'

'Well if my life gets any worse, I might just be doing that! Adam's daughters are coming to stay today - they're moving in with us.'

'Holy Moses,' he said, scratching his head in disbelief. 'But he ain't seen those girls for a good ten years, I remember him tellin me. You watch you don't take no cheek off 'em. I know what these teen age girls can be like - we had hell with our daughter, with her loud music, and men friends.'

'You're not much comfort Ted,' she half laughed. You could rely on Ted Fraser to always speak his mind, one of his mottoes was 'say it how it is.' That was probably something to do with his being a retired police officer.

'Now you listen to me young Courtney,' he continued, pointing his finger and waving it about to make his point. 'You just remember, this is your house, and if they start causing trouble, you give 'em hell you hear me?'

'Yeah I'll remember that.' She started to feel a bit stronger now. He was right, they were still children after all, and what trouble could a couple of adolescents possibly cause that she couldn't handle?

'You just come 'n see me if you need anything,' he added. 'By the way, when are you two gonna open that pool of yours?'

'I don't know Ted,' she replied, 'but Adam was talking about calling the pool cleaners in a couple of weeks, so should be by beginning of June, I hope.'

'Glad to hear it.' He turned on his heel and started up his lawn mower. 'Catch ya later,' his voice sang out over the sound of the mower, and then he was gone heading for the back end of his garden.

Courtney went back into the house, feeling a little stronger, but she was a bit unsteady on her feet because of the wine. She headed back upstairs to check on her tidying one last time. She had cleaned the house the day before from top to bottom and had booked off a long weekend from work to get ready for the impending arrival. They had an impressive house in an affluent area; both of them together possessing a sizeable combined wage. Adam was the principal wage earner of the two as he was now a high-ranking consultant at the Florida Hospital in Kissimmee. She also worked in the same hospital on the reception desk, which had been how they had met six years ago in Leesburg. He had been working as a doctor in the hospital there; she at the time was in the hospital records department working as an administrator. Leesburg was her hometown. She had been born and raised there, and both of her parents still lived there, in the same house that she had grown up in. She had been happy there growing up, but it was a much sleepier town than

Orlando and as she got older she soon realised that there wasn't nearly enough to do there, especially for the younger generation. Orlando on the other hand was the complete opposite with its theme parks, countless restaurants, bars and night clubs. Adam had first moved to Leesburg when he separated from his wife, in search of a less hectic lifestyle. He had originated from Philadelphia, and was tired of big city life. He lived there in hospital apartments sharing with friends for the first four years, then he met Courtney. She at the time had just turned twenty-two and he was thirty-nine. She had never dated anyone as old as him before, and it was the talk of the hospital for a long time, what with the age gap and the fact that she worked in the office filing hospital records, and he being a well thought of doctor. They married after a two year courtship and had both decided to pursue their careers, rather than start a family. Shortly afterwards they moved to their current home. Courtney still felt too young at the present time to have children, even now four years later, and what with the twins moving in, that was sure to put paid to any plans she may have had in the near future.

Courtney dreamily made her way back up the spiral staircase, her feet cautiously treading up each wooden stair, holding tight to the bannister rail for fear she might fall. Her head was swimming. As she rounded the corner, she looked first into the box room on the left, which currently housed all their junk, but what would now be their only spare room. Straight ahead of her was the main bathroom with its navy tiles still gleaming from yesterday's scrubbing. She nodded to herself as she eyed the interior of the bathroom; everything seemed to be in order there. As she turned to her right, the upstairs corridor now loomed ahead. On the left was the third bedroom, it was kind of an ensuite, with an adjoining door to the bathroom. The second was directly opposite, and at the end of the corridor was hers and Adam's room.

She wandered down to her bedroom, which was easily her favourite room in the house, well second to the lounge anyway. She considered this was a good thing, as she felt this room might become her only sanctuary once the twins arrived. Courtney had decorated their room in a rustic orange and terracotta patterned paper that they had both liked, and the theme of the room was distinctly Mediterranean, with furniture to match. They had holidayed in Spain the last two years - it was one of their favourite countries to visit. They had two paintings on the back wall of Spanish views, and a photograph of themselves on holiday in Spain, looking so happy together at a restaurant by the sea, in Marbella. That was her favourite photo of them both, apart from their wedding photos. She walked over to the bedroom window, there were two, and both had chequered white squared panes, with white shutters on the outside. She opened the nearest window and craned her neck out to look down their road. They lived in a very quiet suburban area in Kissimmee. Their road was tree lined, and all the houses were detached, only residents usually drove up the road as it was private. She couldn't hear any cars approaching, she exhaled with relief, she still had time.

She walked back down the corridor and turned to enter the bedroom on the left. She leaned up against the wall, and stared down at the beige carpet, which was long overdue a change in colour. She thought though that there would be no point in changing the carpet, or decorating the hall until after the twins had moved out again. With her life no longer on hold, it would be a welcome new start for her then, unlike this current phase of her life which she felt had been imposed upon her. *What if they never move out? What if they want to stay forever?* As she leaned back against the wall she closed her eyes, her head was spinning; her whole world was spinning. *This is a nightmare; I'm wishing them gone before they've even moved in.* Panic gripped her again which was heightened by her increasing drunken state. She opened the door to the bedroom, the décor was light blue and it contained matching light pine furniture. She sank to her knees and sobbed, 'paint it all black, paint the whole house black.'

Suddenly the door flew open. Courtney's heart missed a beat; she let out a cry and spun around to see Liza her friend standing in the doorway.

17

'God Liza you scared me half to death,' she said breathlessly. She pulled her hair away from her face, and knelt there in front of her with her other hand now resting on her chest - her heart pounding beneath it.

'Jeez, Courtney, I didn't think you were so nervy,' her friend half laughed, 'don't you remember, I said I'd come round today before lunch, to help you get everything together before they arrive.' Courtney nodded slowly in recognition, still a little dazed.

'I knocked the door for about ten minutes,' Liza went on in her matter of fact way, 'but you didn't reply, so I let myself in through the back. What's happened to you? You're a wreck. You promised me the other night you wouldn't get like this.'

'God I know,' Courtney said, struggling to her feet. 'What time is it?'

'It's midday - I'm late. What time did Adam leave?' Liza replied.

'About an hour ago.'

'And in that time, you've managed to get yourself in this state.' She put her arms round her friend and gave her a hug. Liza was shorter than Courtney, she was 5ft 6in, two inches shorter to be precise. She had short bobbed dark hair, a young looking face, and the biggest brown eyes. She pulled Courtney's head up off her shoulder and looked into her eyes, 'and you're drunk missy,' she said shaking her head, 'I don't know, what am I gonna do with you?'

'Make me a coffee?' Courtney smiled. Liza laughed, took her friend by the arm and led her out of the room.

'Liza,' Courtney said as they rounded the corner to start down the stairs. 'I'm so scared, they're gonna take over everything, my whole life'll be ruined, I just want it to be me and Adam, like it's just you and Grant.'

'You listen to me Courtney. You're a strong girl, you don't take any crap from anyone, least of all any teenage girls, so why should these two be any different? You have to take control of the situation. You can cope I know you can, just don't give up on yourself.'

'I know,' Courtney steadied herself as she walked down the stairs, holding tight to the handrail. 'You're right, you're always right, but it's OK for you, you don't have to deal with anything like this.'

'And,' Liza said starting to get annoyed.

'- And,' Courtney interrupted, 'your life is so damn perfect, you've got everything.'

'Oh and you haven't?' Liza retorted. 'Listen I didn't come here for a fight, I came here to help you.'

Courtney wasn't listening to reason now, and just carried on arguing with her friend, 'oh and I suppose you'd be so fucking great at coping with this. You wouldn't get drunk would you, oh no, you'd be totally calm wouldn't you?' she bellowed.

Liza grabbed her arm, 'I don't know what I'd be like Courtney, but I think I might try to be a bit more positive about the whole situation.'

'Oh of course you would Liza,' Courtney screamed. 'You'd probably be looking forward to it wouldn't you, and you wouldn't need me to come over to your place the day they arrived. Oh no, you'd be hanging the fucking welcome flags out in the drive way.'

The two stood in the hallway, Liza still trying to calm Courtney down. 'What you don't even begin to think is, that you might even like these girls.'

'Yeah right,' Courtney continued to rant, 'little Miss Perfects coming to stay, the apple of their father's eye! Don't you see, Liza, I don't need this, I've been off the medication now for six months, six months.'

'You mean the Prozac?' Liza recalled.

'Yeah I mean the Prozac, and I can see myself having to go right back on it again.'

'But try Courtney, please try to look on the positive side. Maybe just maybe, they might even make your life better.'

Courtney put her hands on her hips and leaned menacingly over Liza, 'Bullshit!' she yelled.

Liza had had enough of Courtney's mouth. She shouted back at her, 'well at least you'll have something else to talk about now instead of just you and Adam this, and you and Adam that, which frankly can get real boring sometimes.'

'Oh it does, does it!' Courtney screamed. 'Well why don't you go screw yourself.'

Liza struck her friend across the face. Courtney sprawled to the ground, and lay there motionless. Liza reeled back covering her mouth to suppress the scream that was welling up in her throat; she was so shocked at what she had done.

She and Courtney had been friends ever since she had moved to Kissimmee. She and her husband Grant lived across the street - they all worked in the same hospital, she as a doctor, and her husband as an anaesthetist. They had keys to each other's houses, and did everything together.

She fell to her knees next to Courtney, 'Courtney I'm so sorry,' she started to cry, 'I didn't mean to hurt you.' She felt her head, which luckily had just missed striking the doorframe. She had landed on soft carpet, which was an added blessing under the circumstances. She could tell that no major damage was done, and Courtney's eyes were open, just staring at the ceiling in disbelief. She rolled her head to the side to face Liza, and blinked slowly,

'I deserved that,' she said calmly, almost as if the blow had sobered her up.

'What did you drink?' Liza asked incredulously.

'A big bottle of wine,' Courtney groaned and held her head, 'one of those party sized ones.'

'Oh God you didn't did you?' Liza replied. 'At least I know that all this abuse was just drunken talk then.'

'What about what you said about me going on about Adam then?' Courtney said.

'I didn't mean it I swear. You know you're my best friend,' she smiled at Courtney, 'after all you know I'm just as bad if not worse, going on about Grant night and day!' The two laughed.

'Don't make me laugh, it hurts when I laugh,' Courtney moaned.

'Hurts where?' Liza said, beginning to panic again.

'Only joking,' Courtney grinned. 'Get me up Liza, I need the bathroom, I think I'm gonna throw up.'

The two women staggered towards the bathroom door with Liza supporting Courtney, who was leaning up against her. It wasn't too far, it was just under the stairs, but to Liza it seemed a long way having to support an almost dead weight. She kicked the door, which swung open; it was only small, and there wasn't a lot of room to manoeuvre. She was afraid that Courtney might hit her head on something, so she lowered her gently to the ground with her head in position, and closed the door to the sound of her retching. Luckily because of her job, she was used to coping with situations like this, so didn't find it too off putting.

Liza went into the lounge and turned on the TV. Just as she sat down on the couch the phone rang, it was a loud shrill ring, it made her jump, she answered it.
'Hi Mary,' she sang out, it was Courtney's mother phoning from Leesburg. Liza had met her and her husband on many occasions. Courtney's parents always took their holiday in Florida, and stayed at their house.
'Just wanted to see how she's coping today,' Mary said, she had already spoken with Courtney several times that week about the twins impending arrival.
'Well they haven't arrived yet Mary,' Liza said, 'but she's not coping too well at the moment.' Just then Liza heard the toilet flush, and Courtney pulled open the door, 'Is that Mom? Don't for God's sake tell her about the drinking.'
'I didn't,' Liza said covering the receiver, 'I only told her you're not coping too well.'
'Can you get me something Liza, some coffee and a couple of tablets?'
'Sure,' she replied handing her the phone.

Liza left Courtney discussing the potential horrors of the twins' arrival, and ventured into the kitchen. Upon opening the door, she let out an ear splitting scream…
'God Liza, what's happened?' Courtney shouted from the lounge.
'It's your damn cat, he's gotta bird.'
'I'll be right there,' she called back.

Sparkey, Courtney's very spoilt, fat ginger cat, stood proudly on the mat, licking his whiskers, and pushing his offering towards Liza with his blood soaked paw; the bird lay twitching on the mat, still in its death throes, and Sparkey had ripped its head clean off.

Liza moved towards Sparkey who began to bat the bird with his paw, and pounce on it playfully.

'You bad, bad cat,' Liza shouted at Sparkey, who looked almost surprised, as to him it was a present to his owner, a display of his hunting prowess.

'Get out, go on get out,' she shooed the cat back through his cat flap.

Just then Courtney appeared at the door, 'oh no,' she exclaimed. 'Not again, last week it was a mouse, and I don't know where it came from. I found some rat poison in the cupboard and put that down, in case we get infested.'

'I wouldn't worry about that,' she retorted, 'I'm sure Sparkey has all the rodents in the neighbourhood well under control.'

Courtney went over to the window, she could see Sparkey slinking round the back door looking sorry for himself, but Liza had flicked the switch on the cat flap to stop him getting back in.

'Go on, shoo,' she banged on the window. Sparkey shot off over the neighbours' fence.

'Liza, look you've frightened him now.'

'Well he should have thought of that before he killed this poor bird,' Liza said unrepentant. 'You're too soft on that damn cat anyway.'

Courtney wrapped the bird in an old cloth and they took its body down the garden to give it a little burial.

Another half an hour passed, with still no sign of Adam or his daughters.

'I best be going,' Liza said. 'You make yourself another coffee, sober up, and remember what I've told you. I don't wanna hear anymore of this scared talk, do you hear?'

'OK Mom,' Courtney joked, she was certainly feeling a lot better than earlier. She gave Liza a hug, 'I'm really sorry about earlier, I can't understand what came over me, I'm so glad you're a good enough friend to stick by me when I'm acting like such an idiot.'

'What are friends for?' Liza flashed a smile, and then left out the back door. 'Just call me if you need me.'

Courtney watched her as she walked out from the back, down her drive and across the road. She waved after her, and smiled to herself. She couldn't believe what had happened, but in a strange sort of way, she felt as if she had got rid of some of the anger and frustration that had been building up, even if it had been directed at totally the wrong person. Her head was starting to clear; the tablets had started to take effect. She looked at the clock, it was nearly 1.30 p.m. and still nothing. She walked away from the window, thinking to herself that she'd just go and have a little relax in the garden, and read some more of her book. She moved towards the back door, and opened it, to the sounds of a warm spring day. She took a deep breath of the sweet flower filled air, and felt content for a moment. She looked down the garden, it was so lush and green, and the flowerbeds were brimming with colour, even Adam's old shed looked brand new in the sunshine she thought. The pool was the centrepiece, not yet open but would definitely be the finishing touch. As she looked to the right of the pool, she saw a flash of ginger out of the corner of her eye. Sparkey was back in the garden again, and this time was trying to catch a goldfish in their pond right at the far end. He was scooping his paw in the water, and darting round the edge like a thing possessed.

'*Sparkey!*' Courtney hollered at him, he leapt back, and went trotting over to her, all innocent and wide eyed. She scooped him up in her arms, and rubbed his head with her fist, which he hated. He was a vain cat, and seemed to hate having his fur ruffled out of place. 'If you don't *stop* trying to fish and catch birds and mice all the time, I'm gonna keep you locked up in the house, do you hear me?' she said, sternly this time like she meant it. 'Now just behave.' She put him back down firmly and turned on her heel, to go back in the house to make another coffee. When she looked back, Sparkey had gone again. She rolled her eyes in despair.

The kettle had boiled, she made the coffee, and was really starting to enjoy the peace and tranquillity of the empty house; she sipped from her steaming mug and walked back towards the lounge. Just as she reached the doorway, she heard the sound

that she had been dreading - their car rolled into the driveway. Engine Off. Silence. Doors slamming. Footsteps.
The key turned in the lock.

Chapter 2

Courtney suddenly felt herself coming back to reality, she could hear voices calling her name, she was becoming aware of her body again, somebody was squeezing her arm, and somebody else was stroking her forehead. She groaned inwardly. She tried to open her eyes, they felt heavy, her whole body felt heavy. As she opened her eyes slowly, she could see three shadowy figures standing over her. She tried to focus, the fuzzy image started to become clearer. She focused on two of the figures, they were both identical in size and shape, then she could see colours again, she could see blonde hair, and two sets of the bluest eyes looking at her inquisitively, blinking slowly. She had never seen such perfect faces before; their skin was radiant, almost glowing. For a moment, in her confusion she thought that they must be angels. 'Have I died?' she said quietly, struggling to get the words out. The two girls laughed, then the other figure standing next to them suddenly came into focus; it was Adam.

'Honey it's me, and this is Alicia and Gabrielle, we just arrived, and you were slumped on the floor, in a faint.'

The reality of the situation was starting to dawn on her, 'oh God, she moaned, 'I feel such an idiot, what must you think of me?'

'Don't worry,' Adam said softly smoothing back her hair from her forehead. 'I saw the empty bottle on the side, and almost tripped over the mug of coffee you dropped all over the carpet - so I put two and two together, I think you'd best get some rest, I've checked you over, there's no damage done.'

He lifted his wife back up off the couch, and helped her up the stairs. He lay her down in their bed, and kissed her tenderly. 'I should have taken you with me, I'm sorry,' he looked at her with concern in his eyes. 'I didn't think you were that scared about meeting them, I should have known.'

'It was the sun,' she tried to find an excuse, 'I was drinking the wine outside, and the heat, and I felt so woozy and I…'

'Shhh now,' he put his finger over her lips, 'get some sleep I'll check on you later, you just need to sleep it off.'
He left the room. She curled back up into her foetal position, and felt the tears rolling down her cheeks again.

The next morning, Courtney was up and about early. She felt fully refreshed and strong enough to face the day ahead, and even the two girls who were now living in her house. After all, she had already seen them, and they had already seen her. Adam had said to her before he'd left for work that morning that they hadn't said anything disparaging about their stepmother, at any point during the day, or evening of their first day. They had, he said expressed concern for her, and had been asking lots of questions, but nothing else.

Courtney opened the bedroom door, hair freshly washed, make up perfect and with her new slacks and shirt on, especially picked by herself to impress the girls, on this their second day living in her house. She took a deep breath and walked down the corridor with her head held high. She slowed down as she passed the first bedroom on the left, she wasn't sure at this stage which of the twins was in which room. She could hear girls' voices talking rapidly, and then she heard laughing. She stopped outside the door and listened.
'So do you reckon she's an alcoholic 'Licia?' Courtney bristled as she immediately realised they must be talking about her.
'I'm not sure,' Alicia replied, 'but she must have drunk a hell of lot yesterday, to get in that state.'
'Yeah well,' Gabrielle continued, 'I spose it's better than living with a teetotaller, there'd be no liquor in the house at all then.'
The two girls then burst out laughing again.
Courtney felt an intense rage surging through her body. She straightened up, composed herself, and knocked loudly on the bedroom door, at the same time as opening it.
'Hi girls,' she sang out, the two twins jumped as the door rebounded off the wall. They looked startled. She now had the problem of trying to tell them apart.
'So which one of you is Alicia and which one is Gabrielle?'
They just stared back at her, and each pointed at the other one.

'Well that's no good,' Courtney continued in her dominant tone, 'I still don't know which is which.'

'I'm Alicia,' said the one on the left. She looked the more surprised of the two, and had a guilty look on her face. However Gabrielle just glared back at her, seemingly unrepentant. Courtney felt she now knew what she was up against. First impressions were very important to her, and she had formed an impression of Gabrielle. She was the troublemaker of the two, that was clear. She was the one, who she'd have the problem with. Courtney knew that straight away, but for some reason, she was no longer afraid of them. She had confronted her fear head on, and she felt that she had the power to command respect from them. She felt glad, because she realised that she was her true assertive self once more, she was being herself still in her own home, and she wasn't about to take any crap from any eighteen year old, least of all her new stepdaughters.

There'd been a long silence, where the three women were eyeing each other suspiciously, almost sizing each other up. Courtney was standing in the doorway in a confident stance, and the two girls were sat on the bed shifting awkwardly from side to side.

'So how am I gonna tell you apart?' Courtney broke the silence.

Alicia again was the one to speak, 'Well I've got about five small freckles on my nose, but Gaby hasn't got any.'

'That's a good start,' Courtney forced a smile. 'Have you had breakfast yet?'

The girls shook their heads.

'Right then, if you two get dressed, I'll fix you some.' Courtney turned on her heel, and walked towards the door. She stopped halfway, and turned back,

'By the way, I'm not an alcoholic,' she said, 'I just enjoy a drink now and again, bit like you two I expect!'

Alicia again looked shocked, and lowered her head in shame, Gabrielle, just stared back at her defiantly.

Courtney left the room and shut the door with a bang.

She listened at the door, and could hear who she knew must be Gabrielle, speaking again in a low whisper, 'Stupid bitch,' she said, 'shouldn't be listening to our conversation anyway.'

Courtney burst back through the door and shouted at the girls, looking directly at Gabrielle, 'Don't you dare ever insult me in my house. You can say what you like out of here, but in this house, you'll respect me, or I'll send you back where you came from, do I make myself clear?'

'We're sorry,' Gabrielle said with a sarcastic smile.

'You had better be, because I'm not gonna take any shit from you - you'd better believe it.'

She noticed a sudden change in the girls' attitudes, it was as if it had dawned on them in that split second, that she was serious, and that she would have a lot of influence over their father. They wanted to stay in Florida, after all, and realised they'd better start again, or risk ruining everything before it had even started.

They apologised to Courtney, and this time really seemed to mean it. 'Can we start again, and pretend this never happened?' Gabrielle said, with an almost genuine look in her eyes. 'You won't tell our dad, will you? We're truly sorry and promise never to be rude to you again.'

Courtney nodded, 'OK, let's forget this ever happened, so let's have breakfast and start again.'

The two girls smiled cautiously back at her.

This time when Courtney left the room, she didn't listen at the door, but strode confidently down the corridor towards the stairs. She was smiling to herself and she felt strong, really strong, and was relishing the sudden rush of adrenaline that had been triggered by her own new sense of empowerment. She felt all of her anxieties melt away and started to think that maybe Liza was right in what she had said, maybe this experience would enrich her life, maybe she *was* going to have some fun.

Over breakfast Courtney tried to engage the girls in some light friendly conversation. Although she had felt her confidence returning to her she still felt a little overwhelmed by the situation she now found herself in and when her mind stretched forward to the future her panic returned, *what if they stay forever?* She blocked the thought out of her mind and snapped back to reality again as she heard the kettle boiling in the

28

kitchen. The two girls sat quietly on the patio in the morning sunshine, faint contented smiles on both their faces.

'You want more coffee?' Courtney turned back as she stepped back into the kitchen, forgetting almost that it wasn't just going to be one or two cups of coffee anymore.

'Yes please,' Alicia replied timidly.

'Not for me thanks,' came Gabrielle's reply.

As Courtney poured the boiling water into the mugs so many thoughts were racing through her mind, there were so many questions she wanted to ask, but she just didn't know if she should, or if it was the right time. She realised how little she really did know. She and Adam had barely talked about them, she knew nothing of their past, or their mother for that matter. Courtney didn't really like to think about their mother, it upset her that somebody had been there before her, that Adam had had an intimate relationship before he'd met her. There was no escaping it now, she thought, the evidence of that relationship was sitting out on her patio.

She opened the fridge and reached for the milk, she still wasn't feeling too well, her head was aching, she didn't really feel herself completely.

She walked back outside. The sound of birdsong filled her ears, and the smell of the spring flowers filled her nostrils, lifting her spirits again.

She sat down on her recliner placing the mugs down on the garden table next to her. She looked down the garden and breathed slowly and deliberately, she tried to relax as she had always been able to do before, so easily.

'You're not allergic to cats are you?' Courtney finally said. She had seen Sparkey slink out from under Ted Fraser's fence and then dash across the garden in his usual clumsy erratic style. The two girls laughed at the sight.

'No,' Alicia replied, 'I don't mind cats, they're OK, and he's a beauty.'

'Yeah,' Gabrielle piped up, 'cute, fat and ginger, is he tame?'

'He's a bit nervous around strangers,' Courtney replied. 'I'm sure given time he'll come around, he's got a funny personality,' she laughed taking a sip of her coffee. 'He can be very prickly sometimes, usually he likes to be cuddled and stroked and other times he doesn't want to know you. He tried to scratch me the other day because I tried to pick him up and he wasn't in the mood. I swear he should have been born a female.'

The girls both laughed again.

'We used to have a cat when we were young,' Gabrielle said. 'He was a skinny cat, brown with white patches, funny looking actually - Rolo, do you remember him Licia?'

'Yes,' she replied dreamily, 'that was when Mom was alive, Mom never liked him much, don't know why we had him really.'

'Dad bought him for Mom didn't he before he left,' Gabrielle recalled.

Courtney felt a pang of jealousy mixed with panic; this was what she had not been prepared for, hearing about the past she had denied for so long.

'Oh yeah it was for her birthday wasn't it,' Alicia added.

'I don't know why he did?' Gabrielle looked quizzically at her sister and then glanced over at Courtney to see her reaction.

Courtney composed herself, wanting to get one up on them.

'Funny present for a birthday,' she interjected, 'your dad always buys me jewellery or something like that.'

Gabrielle gave a wry smile at her reply.

'Especially seeing as Mom never liked cats anyway,' she laughed, 'oh well at least it shows that Dad thinks more of you than he ever did of Mom.'

Courtney had not let her guard down yet, but she concluded in her mind, having gone over every word again in her head, that it was all right.

'Oh I didn't mean it like that,' she quickly added placing her coffee back down on the table. 'I'm sure your dad thought a lot of your mom.' *Your dad* that was her husband she was talking about - it seemed so strange and very uncomfortable. Courtney smiled back at them.

'Don't worry about it,' Gabrielle replied flippantly, 'she's dead anyway, so no competition there hey.'

Courtney was shocked by Gabrielle's tone, but wanted to keep the situation and atmosphere friendly, so decided to change the subject.

She reached for her cigarettes, 'do you smoke?' she said hesitantly.

'I'm afraid so,' Alicia responded, 'do you mind?'

'No, sure you take one,' Courtney replied, extending the open packet to her stepdaughter, 'just so long as you buy your own when you get a job.'

'No problem,' Alicia replied, I have some money saved anyway. We had jobs before we came here. Well I had to quit mine - well working at night.'

Gabrielle shot her sister a warning glare. Courtney read this as meaning that Alicia had said too much already, and that she should stop now. Alicia just waved her sister away like she would a marauding mosquito.

'It doesn't matter Gabrielle,' she said annoyed, 'it's up to me who I tell, not you.'

Courtney frowned and took a deep drag on her cigarette.

'What is it?' she asked concerned.

'Oh, I got raped that's all.' Alicia turned to her new stepmother, disregarding the event with a tut and a downward flick of her wrist. Her eyes told a different story though and had become moist with emotion.

'That's all!' Courtney said aghast, 'I didn't know, your dad never said.'

'Oh he doesn't know, nobody does really, not the sort of thing you want to broadcast.'

'Yes, but he's your dad,' Courtney reached forward and touched Alicia's arm lightly, as a gesture of solidarity and concern, Alicia didn't flinch.

'Well he is, and he isn't,' Alicia said in a matter of fact tone. 'I hadn't seen him for ten years remember, and when something like that happens to you, you turn to the people around you who you're close to.'

Courtney felt sorry for her. It suddenly struck her, that she had always known her father, and been assured of his love for her, although they had had their differences, she just took it for granted that it was like that for everybody.

'So how long ago did it happen?' Courtney pressed her further, not wanting to change the subject.

'A couple of years,' Alicia took a drag on her cigarette, 'I'm over it now though, lost my virginity to that sonofabitch.' Her voice although still confident didn't disguise her hurt and anger. 'Where, how?' Courtney continued, her gaze fixed on Alicia.

'I was walking late at night, it was stupid, but hey, you learn by your mistakes,' she glanced sorrowfully at Courtney.

'Course I had a bit of counselling, Aids test all that crap, but I'm OK, I haven't got HIV, so I'm not going to die because of it, which is a bonus.' She smiled sarcastically. Courtney noticed how her tone and personality had completely changed, she was no longer the shy one, she was strong. Maybe that was because she was recounting how she had triumphed over adversity; she had experienced something that her twin had never had to cope with.

'Did they catch him?' Courtney asked deciding this would be her last question on the matter.

'No,' she answered dully, 'No, they never did, I don't really remember much about him. I did once, but I've managed to block it out now - I used to have nightmares.'

'I'm not surprised!' Courtney shook her head in disbelief. 'I can't understand why there are so many sick twisted people in this world.'

'I guess you just have to try to focus on the good ones,' Alicia replied. Courtney was astounded by her positive attitude. She seemed mature beyond her years.

'You won't tell Dad will you?' Alicia then asked Courtney, her eyes pleading.

Courtney felt uncomfortable about this. She and Adam had never kept secrets from each other, they had always been a trusting unit, they shared everything. She thought about it though, and on this occasion she would relent. She wanted to stay on favourable terms with the girls and rape was something so personal, she couldn't possibly break her trust.

'It's just that I want to make a whole new start here,' Alicia said looking down the garden with such excitement in her eyes. 'If Dad knew, he might look at me in a different light.'

Courtney felt uneasy, she was in a dilemma. In her mind's eye she saw on her left side Adam smiling with his arms outstretched, and their cosy exclusive happiness surrounding him. On the other side stood the two girls, alone like orphans, their innocent faces thin and troubled. She didn't want to let them into her world, but as she stood between them she took one last look at her previous white picket fence existence, and mentally took a step to the right.

'OK,' she sighed, 'I promise I won't tell him.'

Life at 240 Bay View Grove started to settle into a new routine over the next few weeks. It was now June, and Courtney had been back at work at the hospital for a couple of weeks. She had taken another few days off when the twins had first moved in. However, getting back into her work routine she managed to achieve with relative ease. She enjoyed being back with her colleagues, and had found that at home the atmosphere was not nearly as oppressive or as tense as she had anticipated that it would be. The pool had been cleaned and officially opened the last weekend in May, which pleased the twins no end. They would spend endless days sunning themselves in the garden, and lazing around by the pool. Courtney didn't have any problems disciplining the girls, after the incident on the second day, and at least to her face they were always courteous and respectful. Courtney even started to get the impression that they liked her, and if it wasn't her, they certainly seemed to like living in their new home in the Sunshine State.

Alicia was still the quieter of the two twins despite her opening up to Courtney when they had first arrived. They had never spoken about the rape since. Although Courtney was beginning to enjoy life again, more than she could ever have hoped for, the secret she was keeping from Adam weighed heavy on her mind. She tried to forget about it, but she felt an overwhelming sense of guilt deep down inside of her. Adam seemed so happy, she couldn't tell him now when everything seemed to be going so well.

Gabrielle and Alicia were very open about sex, and Gabrielle especially used it to tease her father. One time when the pool was first opened they had all been outside watching the sun go down. They had been having a barbecue, and were all sat down, their stomachs groaning with food, sipping their drinks. Everything was quiet, apart from the sound of the crickets, and the faint sound of Ted Fraser's TV - he always had the volume up too loud. He was watching one of those early evening cop shows he liked. Gabrielle lit a cigarette, and then sat back in her recliner, without saying a word. Alicia who was sat next to her sister followed suit, and reached for the cigarettes. It all seemed so peaceful and relaxed, right then. Courtney looked at Adam, he smiled back at her with this self-satisfied look on his face. He looked almost regal in that moment, like a king surveying his castle, and grounds.

Just then Gabrielle decided to break the silence. She turned to her father and with a seeming serious expression on her face said, 'would you mind if I invited some men round for an orgy, while you're both at work?'

Adam started to choke on his beer, which had gone down his windpipe with the shock of what he'd just heard. The two girls fell about laughing, and when Gabrielle managed to regain her composure, she winked at her father 'only joking,' she said 'just wanted to see your face Dad.'

Adam however was not amused. Courtney just sat there, smoking her cigarette, trying not to laugh herself, after all it had been the last thing either of them would have expected to hear. Courtney could see the funny side. Maybe if they had been her own daughters she may not have done, but with them she didn't feel a motherly protectiveness, probably because she was so close to them in age herself.

'I should hope so,' Adam finally said sternly. He didn't see the funny side. After that the pleasant family scene by the pool could never return to how it had been moments before. Adam was now too on edge. He got up and went inside, banged about a bit, and then put the TV on and slumped in front of it.

Gabrielle and Alicia had got waitress jobs in a local Jamaican restaurant. They had been hired by the end of their first week in Kissimmee, and only had to look for a day before they were offered their positions. They had visited four other restaurants in that day, all of which had been extremely keen to hire the twins, as their looks could potentially attract more customers. In the end they chose the waitress positions in the Jamaican restaurant, as the wages were slightly higher and the staff were all younger. The restaurant always had a party atmosphere, and was one of the most fashionable places to eat in Lake Buena Vista. The girls would catch a bus from Kissimmee to Down Town Disney, every night except Sundays, and then the restaurant would pay for their cab back home again. Adam liked this arrangement, as right from the offset he was constantly preoccupied with his daughters being propositioned by members of the opposite sex. Of course they would regale him with stories of being chatted up and propositioned at work, even being offered large sums of money for sex by some customers. The girls however said that they would never go through with anything like this, and that it was strictly against restaurant policy. Courtney knew this was true, as she knew they were far more mature and cautious than they would have their father believe. They were also both effectively grown ups, and there wasn't an awful lot either Adam or her could do to control their behaviour outside of the house. She knew that both girls were drinking alcohol, three years before the legal age, as they would drink with the restaurant staff after hours. There had been more than one occasion when the girls had returned home from work drunk, in the small hours of the morning. One night Alicia had passed out on the stairs, with her slacks soaked in urine, where she'd lost control and Adam had had to carry her up to bed. Two days later Gabrielle had vomited on the front lawn on her way up the drive, just as her cab pulled away from the front of the house.

Adam, although alarmed by these events, just said that he thought they'd soon get bored of the alcohol, and tired of the late nights. He'd threatened to go down to the restaurant on more than one occasion, to have words with the owner. Both girls protested though, telling him not to get involved, and that they were old enough to look after themselves. In return they agreed to cut down on the liquor drinking after hours. Courtney knew better, knowing herself what it was like to be an eighteen year old girl struggling towards womanhood, and these girls were no different to many other girls the same age. They were not interested in doing what their father wanted them to do -

they wanted to push the boundaries as far as they could, and as young women, she considered they were entitled to, as she herself had done when she had been their age.

Although Courtney wanted to give the girls the benefit of the doubt, so far as the liquor drinking went, she was sure that this was just the start. Courtney was trying to work everything out. She was in one of her thoughtful moods, looking out of her bedroom window at the clear night sky. The house was empty apart from her and Sparkey, who was hiding somewhere. She looked at the stars above her. She had always been a deep thinker, she thought too much which had been her problem before. She took a deep breath to try to cope with the onslaught of words and pictures that had yet again invaded her crowded bustling mind. As she stood there the still night air enveloped her cooling her slightly, and in that split second she had become aware of her surroundings again and was able to look out of herself for a moment. Her head had cleared - she thought of nothing. She longed to have that feeling back again permanently, the way she had felt before when she had been on Prozac. The freedom she had felt, freedom from fear, freedom from obsessive thoughts. That had been living she thought. That was the period in her life when she had really enjoyed every day for what it was and not for what it could be or should be. She had been torn, however. Was that really her true self, or was it a chemically altered self, somebody who didn't really exist at all? Since she had stopped taking the tablets, after a period of time of withdrawal, where she had convinced herself that she couldn't function normally without them, she slowly forgot, and was able to carry on again in her new vein. It was as if in the period of time that she had been taking the drugs, they had somehow mended some loose wires in her brain and apart from the occasional flashback, she managed very well and functioned how she believed other *normal* people did. The exception to this rule was undoubtedly stress; any form of stress or anxiety or change to her routine. This was her greatest fear of all, losing it, becoming a gibbering drooling wreck. It would be so easy, if she let it, but she knew she had to fight it, if it took all the energy within her she would beat it. She stared straight ahead of her listening intently to the sounds of the night, the distant wailing of police sirens, the ever vocal crickets rubbing their legs together vigorously in the grass and hedgerows. She could hear music too, people having fun, laughing. It suddenly struck her what a truly amazing place it was that she lived in. This was the holiday capital of America, the place families across the world saved up to go to. She had all of this but she would trade it in, in a heartbeat, to have a sound mind. Adam always talked about the time when he had fractured his arm when he was younger; he'd been in a motorcycle accident. Courtney thought to herself then that she would rather that had happened to her, after all a broken bone will always heal.

As she began to talk herself round as she always did to try to make sense out of her confused thoughts, she realised that she must deal with the issues head on to get back to the place she had been at before the twins' arrival. She knew in time she would adapt, but since they had first arrived and the revelation about Alicia's rape, which had led to the secret pact being made between her and the girls, she had started to resent them more and more each day. They were laughing and joking and truly Alicia did seem to have recovered from her ordeal; this was old news to her and a fresh start, but the news to Courtney had placed a huge millstone around her neck. She had started to feel also that the girls had done this on purpose. Whether this was really the case or just more of her nonsensical paranoia she wasn't sure; but what she did know was that this secret had given them power and had already sought to drive a psychological wedge between Courtney and Adam.

She looked back up at the stars again and where her mind had seemed to have been coaxed back to emptiness, she felt all of a sudden as if she had glimpsed the future. There was a foreboding almost an unwritten destiny in the night sky, one that made her shudder. She had the feeling that she was going to have to battle on, but no longer against herself, she was going to have to channel this strength elsewhere if she was going to survive.

That night was the same as any other for the girls. Alicia and Gabrielle had caught the bus to Down Town Disney, and had walked to the restaurant where they both worked. Carlos the manager was in a dismissive mood that night. As they walked through the door, into the kitchen, he threw a tea towel at them, and shouted at them for being late, two minutes late to be exact. They had now been working at the restaurant for three weeks.

'C'mon girls, it's Saturday night, it's the busiest night, I needs your butts in here on time.'

Alicia went to say something but he cut across her, 'I don't want no excuses, just get your skirts on and then get back out here.'

They went to the locker room. They would always travel to the restaurant in their slacks, because the skirts that they wore were so short that they weren't allowed to go to or from work in them. It was another of the restaurant's policies. Alicia quickly changed. She put on her low cut white top, with the restaurant's motif written across the chest in blue, the skirt was blue, and only reached down to the top of her thighs. Her father had never seen it - it was probably just as well the restaurant kept the uniforms there. She moved over to the mirror where her sister was already dressed and applying her lipstick, which was dark red. She pouted at herself in the mirror, and smiled at her sister, who was laughing at Gabrielle's blatant vanity. They both tied back their long blonde hair in high ponytails, and then they were ready.

Melanie, one of the other waitresses walked into the locker room, she flung her bag down and swore, she was also late.

'Did Carlos rip into you too?' Gabrielle said, as she stuffed her slacks and Reeboks into her locker.

'He sure did, the bastard! Ya know, I feel like quitting this joint when he's in a mood like that.'

The twins both agreed, and left the locker room to start work.

There was a steady stream of customers coming through the door, most of them were attempting the limbo under the beam, which was one of the things that all customers were encouraged to do, in order to get a free beer. Alicia and Gabrielle always found it funny watching the people, especially the large ones. They would have such trouble. One night they'd seen this one man fall down on his backside, but he got up and tried again, and he did it, eventually.

Gabrielle, went off onto the deck outside to see to the customers out there, whilst Alicia was charged with waiting on a young family who she discovered were on holiday in Florida, and lived in Kansas. Most customers would always ask what the waitresses recommended they should eat. Alicia would always recommend the jerk ribs, which were a speciality of the restaurant, and were wood smoked by one of the chefs on an open barbecue, inside by the bar. The flames would always shoot up high when he first lit it and everybody in the restaurant would turn and look, thinking he was about to set the place alight. The staff were forever having to reassure customers that in fact the chef did know what he was doing, and that that was supposed to happen.

Both of the twins were extremely busy that night, hurrying backwards and forwards, fetching drinks and taking food orders. They usually got given generous tips, which they were all allowed to keep for themselves. The theory behind this was that it would encourage the staff to do a better job, and it worked to a large degree, as they would compete with each other, to see who could get the most money each night.

It was now eleven o'clock, although it only seemed like an hour had passed since they started at five thirty.

Alicia snatched a quick break, and went to the locker room to reapply her lipstick and brush her hair.

When she got in there, one of the older waitresses, Tina, came in. She looked tired and harassed and flopped down on the bench, by the lockers.

'How ya doing gorgeous?' she said to Alicia, who was just about ready to go back out again.

'Oh, I'm fine thanks, bit tired, but I'll survive.' She smiled back at Tina, who had always been so friendly to her and her sister ever since they started, and had given them valuable help and advice with regard to dealing with customers, and the restaurant politics and protocol.

'Hey Alicia,' Tina called after her as she opened the door to the restaurant. 'Be careful, one of the blokes who's just come in, the blonde one over there with the grey shirt, sat with the other three guys, you watch him, he's a bit of a pervert. I guarantee he'll proposition you - just report him straight away to Carlos.'

'Will do.' Alicia thanked her, and returned to the restaurant.

She had been asked to wait on this table, but she wasn't afraid, she quite enjoyed the banter with the male customers - it always gave her an ego boost. Sometimes they'd try to touch her behind, or her breasts when she leant over the table, but that was about the worst that she'd ever experienced.

She got the order from the table. All four men were remarkably well behaved, the blonde one had winked at her, but that was all. They all ordered beers, which Alicia had to get from the outside bar on the deck. When she got outside, she found Gabrielle, leant over the bar, chatting up the barman Matt. She always found her doing this between orders. Gabrielle apparently fancied him like crazy; he was also pretty smitten with her, but was spoken for already.

Alicia got the beers and returned to the restaurant. She again had no problems with the men, and after their food, and about five more beers, they left when the restaurant finally shut.

Alicia was feeling tired now, and wanted to get home to bed. She looked for Gabrielle, who was laughing with Matt, and was helping him wipe down the tables.

'Licia, we're staying for a late one,' Gabrielle sang out, 'I've checked with Carlos, he says it's OK. He's in a good mood now, he says he's gonna get laid tonight!' she laughed, and then Matt started to laugh uncontrollably.

'Not by you I hope,' Alicia replied.

'Do me a favour,' Gabrielle retorted, 'credit me with some taste.'

Just then Carlos's voice boomed from the deck, 'I heard that you dirty dog.'

'*Joke* Carlos, joke, funny ha ha,' Gabrielle replied sarcastically. She and Matt were still in fits of laughter.

For the first time since they started, Alicia didn't feel like staying and getting drunk that night. She had a couple of beers after she'd got changed, but then decided she wanted to go, as she was getting bored with her sister and Matt's relentless flirting.

'I'm going,' she announced.

'Whatever,' Gabrielle said dismissing her out of hand.

Alicia got up and walked to the back of the restaurant - it was now past midnight.

'I'll get a cab from Down Town,' she said taking twenty dollars off the side of the bar.

Nobody heard her. Carlos was in the kitchen preparing a quick snack, and Gabrielle was deep in conversation with Matt. She knew that it was against restaurant policy to walk from work, but she was only going to walk down the road a mile to Down Town Disney, and the streets were well lit. After all, she felt like some fresh air, and a chance to be by herself for a change.

She opened the back door of the restaurant, and shut it behind her. It was dark outside, very dark. She walked past the lake to the main road. There were lakes everywhere in Florida, and there were about four in this street alone. She paused by the lake to light a cigarette. There was a faint breeze in the air that made the water on the surface ripple slightly, and the moonlight was catching the resulting peaks and troughs, causing them to glisten with an almost magical silver hue. Her attention was suddenly diverted as a lizard darted out in front of her across the sidewalk, making her jump. She was annoyed at herself for being so nervy. She reminded herself then that she was quite safe, she was in a new town, the holiday capital, where everybody went to forget their stresses and strains and just have fun with their families. She smiled to herself, realising how stupid she had just been.

As Alicia rounded the corner, into the last main road she had to travel down, she found herself following the path away from the roadside, and back onto a darker section of the sidewalk that seemed to stretch on endlessly and forebodingly ahead of her. It was partially concealed by large looming, almost menacing trees, which were casting black spider like shadows on the ground all around her. With her senses now heightened, she suddenly became aware of the footsteps behind her. For the first time, and in the heady dread filled moments that followed, she was taken back two years. It was as if a key had unlocked the dark dungeons of her mind. She was back there again, and the footsteps, which she was now sure were following her, were the

41

same footsteps that she had heard *that* night. Heavy quickening footsteps, the rapid lust filled breaths of her attacker still ringing in her ears.

She walked faster her heart thumping in her chest, so hard that it took her breath away. She knew that again she had made the same terrible mistake. The fear that had taken hold of her was like nothing she had ever experienced, worse than the night of the rape, she hadn't known then what was about to happen to her.

As she speeded up, so the footsteps behind her too gathered pace, images raced across her mind - the face of her attacker who she had managed to forget before, now flashed before her eyes. She wished that she had stayed at work and endured her sister and Matt. She hated her sister in that moment for letting her go, for letting her put herself in the same situation again. She hated her for being so selfish that her desire for a man outweighed her love and concern for her sister. She hated him too for enticing her away, for liking Gabrielle more than he liked her. She hated herself for being so afraid, for having allowed herself to be spoilt for all eternity. In her eyes she was now dirty and worthless.

The footsteps were right behind her now, too close. It was happening again.

Then she felt someone grab her around the waist. She was expecting it, but still her intake of breath was so sharp that she felt as if she might die from the fright.

'Hey Barbie two,' the man laughed as he spun her round. She looked at him and recognised him - it was the blonde guy Tina had warned her about earlier.

'Why the fuck did you have to creep up on me like that you shit? You could have killed me.' Alicia screamed.

'Hey,' he smiled, 'I saw my favourite waitress and I figured my luck was in.'

He gripped her tighter and pulled her close to him, which made her feel physically sick, as he reeked of alcohol and cigarettes. Alicia recoiled from him; he wouldn't let go of her, so she smacked him hard across his unshaven jaw.

'Get off me - you stink! I'll tell Carlos about this - he'll bar you.'

'Hey I'm scared angel,' he laughed, his dark wanton eyes fixing on hers. 'Have you seen how many bars there are in town? If I can't go there I'll just go some place else.' He shrugged his shoulders with disinterest. He released his grip on her then and she turned to run.

'Hang on a minute,' he said annoyed grabbing hold of her arm, almost wrenching it out of its socket.

'You know what I hate most about stuck up pretty bitches like you?' he wheezed. Her fight had gone; she fought back the tears not wanting to give him the satisfaction.

'No, but I bet you're gonna tell me,' she said half laughing half crying.

'It's that you think you're so fine, I mean look at you, you thought I was gonna try and get it on with ya,' he laughed pushing her away from him.

'You're so full of it,' he said spitting onto the sidewalk just in front of her. 'You've been smiling at me all night, giving me the come on.'

'I was just doing my job,' she hollered. 'I'm a waitress, I'm paid to smile and be *friendly* to all my customers.' The words almost choked her as they came out of her mouth, and then the realisation hit her that she wasn't going to be raped after all, and this man was just making fun of her. She felt a strange feeling inside her, almost like a feeling of rejection. She felt panic come over her again. She reeled forward to push him, to get some reaction from him. He pushed her back; she stumbled to the ground, spilling the entire contents of her bag. He just stood there and laughed, lighting up another cigarette.

'Don't worry honey,' he said drawing on his cigarette, 'you're not my type anyway.'

He turned to leave. Blinded by tears she bent forward to gather her things back into her bag, as she did he turned back, 'Hey,' he yelled, 'I wouldn't lean down too low in that top, I can see right down your bra.' This was his parting shot, and with that he sauntered back up the road in the direction he had come from, not looking back once.

Alicia got back up and managed to stand shakily. A car stopped and an elderly man yelled across to her asking if she was all right, and if she needed a lift home. She couldn't trust anyone, it was as if the last two years had just melted away. She felt as if she was back to square one again. The humiliation and hurt she felt overwhelmed her. She told the man 'no I'm fine, leave me alone please.' He relented and drove off. She staggered to the roadside, crossed to the other side and walked along dazed, not really registering anything around her, even the traffic. Her face was streaked with makeup, her slacks were spattered with mud, but she didn't care right then. She didn't care if she never got home at all, and she hoped that if by some unhappy miracle she did, that she would be spared the indignity of being seen by anybody else that night.

Chapter 3

Courtney and Adam had been asleep the first time the doorbell rang. It rang again. Courtney surfaced from sleep. Their bedroom window was slightly ajar and she climbed wearily out from under the covers, trying to focus on the digital display on the alarm – 1.30 a.m. She leaned out of the bedroom window, as the doorbell rang for the third time.

'Hello,' she sang out. 'Who's there?'

By this time Adam had finally woken. She turned sharply and cast him a disparaging look.

'Adam, there's someone at the door, go down and see who it is.'

'Oh babe,' he said still half asleep, 'can't you go, I'm tired.' His head was still half obscured by the covers, which he had pulled up around his ears.

'For God's sake Adam!' she said whipping the covers off him, 'you're the man of the house that's your job, it could be anyone.'

He reluctantly rose to his feet and hunted for his dressing gown. Whoever it was outside was impatient and it would appear also deaf; they rang the doorbell a fourth time as Adam and Courtney ventured down the hallway towards the top of the staircase.

'Hang on, hang on,' he bellowed.

He opened the door to find Alicia, sat on the mat her head in her hands, crying.

'Alicia,' he said shocked, 'God what on earth has happened to you?'

He rushed forward and helped her to her feet. Courtney took her arm as he led her through the doorway towards the lounge. Courtney was surprised to find Alicia in this state but at the same time not, it was almost as if subconsciously she had been expecting it.

Adam sat Alicia down on the couch. 'Now just tell me what happened, are you hurt?'

Alicia shook her head. Courtney and Adam stared intently at her as she slowly began to compose herself - willing her to speak.

'I walked back on my own - I had a scare. This drunk guy grabbed me, that's all,' she said shakily, blowing her nose as she spoke.

'That's all!' Adam's voice rose to a crescendo. 'Who was it? Right - that's it,' he yelled jumping to his feet. 'And where the hell is your sister?'

'See I knew you'd be like this,' Alicia cried, thumping her fist down in frustration. 'That's why I didn't want to tell you.'

'Well, you shouldn't have rung the doorbell if you didn't want me to know. Where's your key?' Adam boomed.

'I lost it!' she shrieked back.

'What do you expect me to say Alicia?' he bellowed, 'just pat you on the head, say there there and tell you to be more careful in future? What *do* you expect?'

She began to cry again.

'Adam, calm down please, this isn't helping anyone,' Courtney said, despairing at her husband's insensitivity.

'Of course I'm gonna be angry,' he continued unabated, 'of course I'm gonna want to get the sonofabitch that did this, it's only natural.' He began pacing the lounge floor.

'He was drunk Dad,' Alicia sobbed, 'you don't understand, he didn't hurt me really, you don't know, OK?'

Courtney knew. She wished she didn't. She would have to persuade Alicia to tell her father, she couldn't keep this secret any longer. It wasn't fair to her or him - she had to reconsider on which side her loyalties lay.

Courtney looked knowingly at Alicia, who had decided not to say anything further on the subject.

'Where's your sister then?' he asked again.

'Still at work,' she relented.

'Right! That girl is in big trouble.' Adam stormed out of the room. Courtney presumed he was going to dress and go out in the car to look for Gabrielle. She didn't think to follow, but stayed in the lounge with Alicia. The two women sat in silence for what seemed like an age, neither one daring to speak. Courtney felt exhausted from the stress that she was now under.

Her shoulders ached from the heavy burden she was carrying. The sound of the front door slamming and the car engine starting not only broke the silence but the deadlock too. Courtney got up from the couch and walked towards the lounge door, still in her dressing gown. She tied the cord tighter around her middle.

'Do you want a coffee?' she asked hesitantly.

'Please,' Alicia had almost an apologetic tone to her voice.

Neither spoke again until the coffee was placed down on the table, 'So,' Courtney finally said taking a sip from her mug. 'What did happen?'

Alicia raised her head slowly and deliberately. Her whole countenance had changed, no longer was she the strong confident girl talking about her rape as if it had been nothing. Her shoulders were rounded now and she looked young and vulnerable. Although Courtney felt very sorry for her, there was still that underlying resentment and annoyance that she would have to rectify if she was to forge any kind of meaningful relationship with her stepdaughter.

'Well,' Alicia began cautiously, 'I decided to walk home, stupid I know, but Gabrielle was all over Matt. It was making me sick and I couldn't bear to watch. I'd forgotten I'm in a new town, I'd left all that behind me.'

'Why did it make you sick?' Courtney asked looking questioningly at Alicia.

'Well the truth is, I've never had a proper boyfriend. I couldn't trust, I mean I can't trust any man, not after what happened. *She* can though,' Alicia's face twisted with resentment, 'she has them all round her like damn puppy dogs. '*Oh Gabrielle you're so wonderful,*' she said mockingly. 'I mean we look the same, what the hell is it that I'm doing wrong? She commands their respect, they buy her things and they don't ever treat her like crap.' She sat back and sighed as if she had just offloaded everything she truly felt.

'Well,' Courtney began slowly, 'it's not surprising after what happened to you that you have a problem trusting men.'

'Yes,' she replied frustrated. 'But they don't come near me, it's like I give off some kind of foul odour or something, or have I just got *abuse me* written across my forehead in big letters?

That man tonight spoke to me like I was dirt, and the sad part is, that's how I feel inside, so it must be what I am.'

She reached for her coffee and took a sip.

'Whatever this man said,' Courtney answered, 'you want to take no notice at all. Don't believe it, you were in the wrong place at the wrong time, he'd have said the same to any other girl he'd met in the street.'

'Believe me, I was followed.' Alicia looked up at her with desperation in her eyes, 'he was out to get me, but not to hurt me, just to get at me, just to make me feel bad. It was as if I'd really hurt him, or insulted his family or something, the rage inside him, and it was all directed at me.'

'I think you'll find Alicia,' Courtney said realising what was behind it all, 'that his rage is at himself. He's insecure, he sees a beautiful woman and he lashes out. It's like he could never have you, so he wants to abuse you before you abuse him, if that makes any sense.' Courtney looked at her waiting for her reaction.

'But he said I wasn't his type anyway,' she said casting her eyes downwards, almost in self-pity.

'I bet if I'd have been Gabrielle, he'd have been kissing my ass,' she added sarcastically.

'Hey,' Courtney said, 'you'll get over this, he's just one asshole, and for every asshole, there are at least ten great guys.' Alicia forced a smile.

'That's better,' Courtney smiled back, and dabbed at Alicia's teary eyes with a fresh tissue.

'Aside from what he said, you're covered in mud. Did he physically hurt you?' she asked concerned.

'He pushed me, and pulled my arm,' she replied shrugging her shoulders as if it didn't matter.

'Well that's still an assault! Do you want us to call the police?' Courtney said rising to her feet.

'No,' came Alicia's definite reply, 'I just want to try and forget about it.'

'But he pushed you down in the street Alicia,' she reiterated.

'I know, not hard though, my pride's hurt more than anything else. I can't go through all that again - please Courtney,' she implored, 'don't tell them.'

'Well I don't know,' Courtney replied reservedly. 'I don't know what your dad will want to do. You really must tell him about the rape Alicia. I've been thinking about it, I really can't keep it a secret from him, it's not fair for you to expect me to do that, really it's not.'

Alicia bristled at the sudden opposition and pulled back, 'no please don't, not yet, I can't deal with him finding out.'

'But I can't not tell him, he's my husband. We've always been truthful with each other.'

Just as she said this she heard the car pull back into the driveway.

'I'm gonna have a cigarette,' Courtney said moving towards the doorway. She walked back to the kitchen, not wanting to be in the lounge when Adam came in, knowing the mood he was in. Gabrielle would undoubtedly be with him and in an equally emotional state. Courtney could hear Adam's voice booming as she opened the back door to light her cigarette. She decided to retreat to the patio recliner.

The front door opened. Gabrielle was sounding off at her father, who had obviously been raging at her all the way home.

'Here she is,' he flung open the lounge door. 'Where's Courtney?' he shouted.

'I'm outside,' she replied, annoyed at his anger, and the fact that her peace was about to be disturbed so soon after finding it again momentarily.

'You're not going to believe this,' he hollered as he marched through the kitchen towards the back door. 'Gabrielle is completely drunk again, and guess what she said when I told her Alicia had been attacked on her way home. Go on guess!' he said almost mockingly.

'Don't know,' Courtney replied wearily.

'Oh, not again!' he replied in a sing song fashion, '*not again*, I mean I'm only her father. Obviously I'm not meant to be told anything, I'm just the walking wallet.' His hands were on his hips, and he was visibly shaking with rage.

Courtney suddenly felt the burden lifted from her shoulders and she sighed, with relief rather than surprise.

'Bitch!' she heard Alicia scream from the lounge where a cat fight had ensued. Adam ran back to the lounge, closely followed by Courtney, who had now stubbed out her half smoked cigarette.

'Quit it,' he shouted, dragging Alicia away from her sister - she was seething with rage ready to kill Gabrielle.

'I'm sorry OK,' Gabrielle slurred, 'when Dad told me, the shock, it just came out.'

'But you promised you wouldn't say. I wanted to make a fresh start,' she yelled back.

'I know, I'm sorry OK, I made a mistake,' she held her hands up in front of her.

'I'm going to call the police,' Adam said from the doorway.

'No,' Courtney stepped in, 'Alicia doesn't want them called, she wasn't hurt, it just gave her a fright.'

'I'm still calling them,' he said resolute. 'He attacked my daughter.'

'Adam leave it,' Courtney retorted, 'you don't know the whole story, and I really think you must trust Alicia on this one.'

Adam stood pensive, the room went silent; it was obvious that he was still reluctant to back down.

'Well, you girls can forget working there anymore, that's for sure,' he finally said, his arms still folded defensively.

'Oh *what?*' Gabrielle rebuked.

'Gabrielle, you can't be trusted can you,' Adam replied angrily. 'You stay out drinking till all hours when you're not even eligible yet, and your sister wanders the streets putting herself in danger. From now on you're staying here until you can prove that you are responsible.'

'You can't stop us,' Gabrielle said defiant.

'Well if you want to stay living under our roof, you will do what I tell you,' he replied, walking towards the free couch on the other side of the coffee table.

'This is all your fault,' Gabrielle hollered at her sister, pointing an accusing finger at her. She then ran from the room and upstairs banging her bedroom door shut behind her.

Courtney leant against the doorframe, emotionally drained. 'Talk to her,' she said to Adam, who was now sitting awkwardly on the couch staring straight ahead at his daughter who had curled up on the other couch like a little child.

Courtney closed the lounge door behind her, leaving Adam and Alicia in the lounge. The closed door she thought would force them to have a civil conversation finally rather than a shouting match. She smiled to herself. She was glad he had said, "under *our* roof." She felt her power returning again and she had got through her first night of domestic unrest relatively unscathed. She felt exhausted though.

When Adam finally came to bed about two hours later he was a lot calmer. Courtney had been drifting in and out of sleep since she had gone to bed and as he climbed into bed and she felt his warm body snuggle up against her, she woke, and turned round to face him. He put his arms round her; she felt happy again, as if all the tension between them had eased. She didn't need to tell him now because he already knew. She had intended to tell him anyway, so it didn't matter. She could forget about it, and ensure that she didn't allow the girls to come between them like that again. He kissed her forehead.

'Courtney,' he said softly, 'I don't know what I would do without you. The girls are stressing me out. It's like I'm their father but I don't know how to act with them, it's all new to me.'

'I know,' she replied squeezing him tighter. 'I'm finding it hard too, but it won't be forever. We just need to focus on us, and our life together, and not let them spoil it.'

'You're right,' he breathed.

'So she told you then,' she said trying desperately to stay awake.

'Yeah, I managed to get it all out of her,' he said with a sigh. 'I don't know if I've done the right thing telling them they have to quit their job.'

'I think you have,' she answered, 'Gabrielle needs to calm down a bit, and neither of them really have a clue what they want to do long term.'

'I know,' he said, 'but they will need to work at some point. They can't stay freeloading off us forever.'

Courtney didn't answer; she had fallen asleep. Adam kissed her again, and slowly drifted off beside her.

Gabrielle and Alicia both had difficulty getting over that night. Alicia was much quieter than she had ever been before. She and Gabrielle didn't speak at all for a couple of days after the argument. Courtney realised it was because she did feel guilty for letting her sister walk home by herself, but still she didn't want to admit to it. She was frustrated, because she had enjoyed working at the Jamaican restaurant and hadn't wanted to give it up; she blamed Alicia for that too at first. A month passed, and their life did start to return to an uncertain type of normality. The girls had spent almost the entire month at home, in the garden in the day, and watching TV at night. They were starting to become bored as time went by, the novelty of having nothing to do was starting to wear thin, and Gabrielle especially had had enough of being around the house all the time. Gabrielle suggested that Alicia and her should get a day job at one of the local cafés, just to get out. Alicia thought she could cope with a daytime job. Adam agreed to this, but only *if* it was just in the daytime. It would be much nearer than where they had worked before; they felt that they would be safe, just around the corner, and wouldn't be putting themselves in the same danger as they had been working at night. There were a couple of cafés round the corner from the house, and more in the main high street, so the girls just had to decide which one they would apply for positions in. Courtney was quite relieved that they had decided to get a daytime job. It was becoming a strain on her with the girls being around all the time even though she was at work during the daytime. They would do the bare minimum in the way of household chores, although they did wash their own clothes. Alicia was becoming more positive about herself again, and had said to Courtney one night that if she stayed indoors any longer it would be like her attacker from two years back had won after all, and he had succeeded in ruining the rest of her life as well. She was determined this wouldn't happen. She knew deep down that most people *were* decent, and that the second incident had also just been a case of being in the wrong place at the wrong time. The drunk man had brought all of the feelings back that she hadn't properly dealt with before - this time she was forced to face them head on, and try to put her rape to rest once and for all. Courtney hoped that maybe she would be able to start meeting friends again, and Gabrielle too, as they had both cut themselves off from the friends they had made at the restaurant.

'Courtney!' Nicky called out. 'Are you still with us?'

Courtney was gazing into space one day at work; her colleague was trying to alert her to the fact that there was a patient waiting to be admitted.

'I'm so sorry,' she said and took the patient's details.

Nicky and Courtney were firm friends, and Nicky had proved to be a tower of strength to Courtney in recent times. She had come around many evenings to talk to Alicia, as she herself had been raped when she was sixteen. Although not in the same circumstances, Alicia found she could open up to her. Nicky helped her to come to terms with what had happened to her, and gave her the hope that she needed by her example. She told her that it was possible to go on and lead a normal and happy life even after something dreadful like that has happened to you. Nicky herself now had three children, and had been blissfully happy with her partner Terry for the past twenty years.

'What d'ya fancy for lunch?' Nicky said to Courtney in her excitable, high voice.

'I don't know Nicky, I don't know what's wrong with me lately, I can't seem to face the thought of food.'

'That's cos you don't eat the right stuff, you just eat junk all the time,' she replied.

'Let me take you out to this restaurant I know for lunch - they do wonderful sushi.'

Courtney reluctantly agreed although she thought that possibly raw fish might just send her stomach over the edge. They enjoyed their lunch together, sitting outside on the terrace in the midday sunshine, watching the world go by. Courtney thought the sushi had an interesting flavour, and she did like it, however she thought that she would probably go back to eating burgers and sandwiches for lunch in future. She wasn't really a great fish lover anyway, but it made a change and Nicky's company was always worth it. Courtney had a glass of wine with her sushi, and Nicky chattered away as she always did about Terry and the kids. She was always interested in Courtney's news though, which made her such a genuine friend. Some people she'd met just talked about themselves and never let her get a word in edgewise. She didn't really care for people like that; they weren't true friends in her opinion.

They finished their lunch, and Nicky looked at her watch, 'five minutes to get back,' she grimaced, and quickly paid the bill.

The two women hurriedly made their way back to the hospital, where the relief reception staff were waiting to go back to the office.

'Hope you're not gonna make a habit of these lunch dates,' Mavis said sternly but the two friends ignored her and got back to work.

It was then that Courtney felt a strange sensation like a fluttering in her stomach, it was the first time it had happened, so she just put it down to the sushi.

About a week later, Courtney woke up one Saturday morning abruptly, as an overwhelming nausea had come over her. She ran to the toilet and promptly vomited. Adam was at work. She was ill a couple more times, and then the feeling passed and she got dressed as normal. She headed down the stairs and had her first coffee of the day in the garden sat in the recliner by the pool. Alicia and Gabrielle had not yet decided where they wanted to work, so were still at home every day, however, they very rarely got up before midday. So this was Courtney's quiet time to herself, in the early morning sunshine, and she loved it. She suddenly realised that Sparkey hadn't been over for his morning stroke. He was normally coiling himself around the legs of the recliner before she'd even sat down. She shielded her eyes from the sun, and craned her neck to look down the garden, but there was no sign of him.

She decided that Sparkey must have been detained somewhere else, almost certainly engaged in chasing another unsuspecting bird in a neighbour's garden. She sat back in the recliner and sipped slowly on her coffee savouring the aroma and texture as she had treated herself on this occasion to a dash of Adam's full cream milk.

She was still not feeling herself and at the back of her mind she was concerned about it. Various scenarios played in her head as she tried to work out what it was that had made her ill. She went through everything she had eaten the previous day and concluded that there was nothing particularly strange or unusual about any of it. She hadn't eaten any more sushi since her lunch with Nicky, it must have been the wine she thought. She'd had two glasses after dinner, obviously it just didn't agree with her. Perhaps she had developed a temporary allergy to alcohol - she'd heard of similar things happening to other people. It usually passed after a few weeks, giving the body a chance to recover. She'd have to lay off it completely for at least a week and see if that made any difference.

Around lunchtime Courtney heard movement upstairs, having gone back in to the house to start on some housework. She looked at her watch and smiled, as usual she could have set it by the time the twins had woken up. Only Alicia replied however, when she hollered up the stairs to ask who wanted coffee.

'Is Gabrielle still asleep then?' Courtney bellowed, not caring if she woke her up, as in her opinion it was high time that she dragged her lazy bones out of bed.

'No she's gone to the store,' Alicia replied, making her way down the staircase, her hair not yet brushed, her eyes still struggling to focus, and with her dressing gown tied haphazardly around her waist.

'What for?' Courtney asked, surprised.

'She had a really bad chocolate craving during the night, and there was none left in the fridge,' she said sleepily.

'Well that's because you both ate it all,' Courtney laughed incredulously.

The doorbell then rang. Courtney rolled her eyes in exasperation. 'When will you girls ever remember to take your keys with you?'

Alicia made a move towards the front door, but Courtney barged past her. 'No don't worry I'll get it,' she said with a sigh, so Alicia shuffled on past her into the kitchen.

She turned the latch and pulled the door open, to find Gabrielle standing on the doorstep, with a bar of chocolate and a magazine in one hand, and Sparkey's heavy round body lying limply over her other arm.

'Oh my God!' Courtney exclaimed stumbling backwards in shock.

'I'm sorry,' Gabrielle replied, her voice shaking, 'I forgot my key, I was going to put him out back, and then tell you.'

'Never mind that!' Courtney bellowed blinded by tears. 'Where did you find him?'

'By the side of the road round the corner. I was on the way back - I didn't notice him on the way. It must have happened whilst I was in the store.'

'He probably followed you that's why,' Courtney snapped back. 'Give him to me.'

She lifted the heavy dead weight that was her beloved cat, and cradled him in her arms, her tears flowing freely now. She pushed past Alicia in the kitchen who was daubing syrup onto a plate of pancakes. She put the knife down as she was jolted forwards. 'Is he dead?' she said, not really knowing what else to say.

'Just get me the cat basket, and bring it outside!' Courtney shouted. Alicia stood motionless by the breakfast bar. 'Like now!' she added in despair.

She couldn't believe what had happened. Their road was so quiet, she thought, but it happened on the main road. *Oh God no*, her head was spinning. The two girls quickly followed her outside and Gabrielle placed the basket down on the patio. Courtney lay Sparkey's body down in it tenderly, inspecting then properly the blood that was still seeping from his half open mouth. She could see that his chest area had been completely crushed by the impact, and she knew that the faint sound that she could hear was just a death rattle - he had gone. She wept with her face pressed against his injured body, his soft fur caressing her cheek for the last time. The twins stood behind her silently.

'I can't believe it,' she cried, 'I mean what's wrong with people that they can just run down someone's cat, and not even bother to stop.'

'Well in fairness,' Gabrielle replied. 'When I found him, whoever did it had moved his body onto the sidewalk, I guess to stop him from being run over again. They wouldn't have known whose cat it was anyway.'

Courtney sat back and wiped her eyes, realising that there was nothing she could do about it, and that it wasn't really anybody's fault. Sparkey had almost certainly darted out in front of the car in his usual erratic fashion.

'He always was a dumb cat,' she said then struggling to her feet. It was somehow symbolic for her - the perfect life that she had had before, the husband, the cat, the quiet life had all been turned on its head when the twins arrived. This just seemed to be the next thing in a long string of events that only sought to prove to her that the life she had loved so much was gone forever. She felt powerless again then in this new climate of chaos.

'Rolo was run over too,' Gabrielle then said passing Courtney her cigarettes, as she had guessed that that was what her stepmother was looking around for so anxiously.

'That was how he died.'

Reason came back to Courtney then. It must have been a traumatic experience for Gabrielle having found Sparkey like that.

She took a cigarette from the packet with a shaky hand, and lit it having fumbled momentarily in her pocket for her lighter. She took a deep drag on it, hoping to calm her fraught nerves, but it just made her feel light headed again for a moment.

'Thank you for bringing him back,' Courtney relented. Her words relaxing the atmosphere between them a little. Gabrielle smiled back at her appreciatively.

'Well I couldn't have left him there could I,' she said.

That evening when Adam returned home from work they held an impromptu funeral service in the garden, having laid Sparkey to rest not far from the body of his last victim. Gabrielle had made a small cross for him that afternoon out of some bits of wood that she'd found and nailed together in her father's shed, and they'd picked some flowers, placing them in an old glass jar filled with water on top of the grave.

'Well you can bet that all the birds and mice in the neighbourhood are going to be celebrating tonight.' Adam had said as they were making their way back into the house for dinner.

Courtney was being ill quite regularly now; she kept getting the same strange sensation in her stomach that she had first got when she'd eaten that Sushi. She now knew that it couldn't possibly still be that which was causing the problem. She arranged an appointment to see the doctor.

The morning came when she had to go. Adam got called to an emergency, so she had to go alone.

She arrived at the surgery early, and didn't have to wait long, before she was called into the light airy office of their family doctor, Dr Snelling. He was a kindly old white haired gentleman. He looked a bit like a little garden gnome, and always had a friendly disposition that set her at ease.

Courtney explained that since she'd eaten this Sushi, she'd had an upset stomach, and everything she seemed to eat now just made her vomit. He stroked his chin pensively.

'Now Courtney, do you use birth control?'

'Yes of course, that's why I never thought it could be *that*,' she retorted.

He took a blood sample from her arm, 'now I'll have to send this away for testing Courtney. I shouldn't worry though, once we know what it is we can treat you.'

'By the way,' he continued, 'had you vomited prior to eating the sushi, in the weeks before?' She looked confused, and then she thought about it, 'yes I did once about two months ago. I got a bit drunk you see,' she said apologetically, 'my stepdaughters had just moved in.'

'You do realise Courtney, that if you vomit you should use added protection when you have sex, as it can temporarily stop the pill from working.'

Of course, why didn't I think, but still it can't be that, it can't be.

'So, Courtney,' the doctor continued, 'you ring the surgery tomorrow and I'll hurry the tests through. I'll tell the receptionist to put you straight through to me.'

Courtney was dumbstruck. She just nodded, smiled nervously, and then left the doctor's office.

When she got outside she lit a cigarette.

Then she thought about what she'd just done and quickly stubbed it back out again.

She felt the worse panic she had ever felt, and every fibre and sinew in her body was crying out.

I'm not ready.

She hurried home.

The next day she rang the surgery. She could barely breathe she was so nervous.

The receptionist as promised put her straight through to Dr Snelling.

His jubilant voice chirped at the other end of the phone.

'I was right Mrs Buchanan - it's good news - I hope, you're pregnant.'

Courtney was numb, *what will Adam say? It isn't the right time - oh God no!*

'That's great!' was all that she could say in reply.

Chapter 4

The front door slammed. Adam had arrived home. Courtney felt a sudden panic welling up inside her. She could feel it tightening her chest; burning as it rampaged through her upper body and tingling across her shoulders as it moved higher. She tried to stifle it, whilst continuing to wash the dishes. She didn't look up as Adam walked into the kitchen.

'Hi darling,' he sang out. 'What a day!' He swiped at his forehead with his hand, 'it's so hot out there.'

Courtney didn't acknowledge him - she couldn't speak. She knew that she had to tell him, but she didn't know how she was going to get the words out.

'Courtney, what's wrong?' he said, putting his bag down and walking over to her at the sink. He slipped his arms round her waist and nuzzled her, planting a light kiss on the nape of her neck.

'I'm pregnant,' she stammered.

'You're *what*?'

His grip tightened around her waist and he turned her around to face him.

'I'm sorry,' she continued, 'it's cos I vomited and the pill didn't work, and I know it's not what we need right now but -'

'Hey hang on a minute, you're talking too fast.' He looked into her eyes. She expected to see a look of horror or of utter panic, but she didn't see either of these. She saw an unmistakable look of delight in his eyes, unlike anything she had seen in him before. He picked her up and spun her around.

'You mean, we're going to have a baby? But how?' he said, gazing at her in disbelief.

'How do you think stupid,' Courtney laughed.

'I can't believe it! I never thought - oh my God, this is *wonderful*.' He was like a child who had just woken up on Christmas morning to discover that his stocking had been filled with more presents than he could ever have wished for.

Then the tears came. 'That's so wonderful honey. Oh my God Courtney, I'm gonna be a dad.'

He danced around the lounge whooping and laughing. Courtney just stood still, with the dishcloth in her hand, her mouth gaping open. She couldn't believe his reaction, it was totally unexpected.

'What do you mean?' she said incredulously, 'you're gonna be a dad? You're already a dad, look out there.' She pointed out of the window at the twins, who were reclining by the pool in the afternoon sunshine.

He stopped suddenly in his tracks, realising what he had just said. He swallowed slowly and nervously, his expression changing fleetingly as his forehead furrowed into a frown. Then as quickly as he had changed he seemed to snap back out of his sudden serious mood and smiled anxiously back at her.

'Well you know Courtney, I'm just happy because it's our first child together. It's different, like starting over again.'

Alarm bells were already ringing in Courtney's head, but she was caught up in a whirl of emotions, her thoughts racing. Before she had time to speak again Adam had rushed up to her, and grabbed her by the hand. Courtney did feel happy, she was so glad that Adam was pleased. He threw open the back door, smiling jubilantly, 'let's go and tell the girls.'

She protested wildly, but he was already halfway down the garden by this stage with Courtney stumbling along behind him, her hand caught tightly in his grip. The flurry of activity stopped as they neared the pool.

The two girls were stretched out, their bronzed perfect limbs glistening in the sunlight, their blonde hair stretched out behind them. They hadn't even looked round to see who was there.

Courtney could feel the butterflies in her stomach again, that had momentarily disappeared in the mad dash.

'Lets sneak up on them,' Adam whispered in Courtney's ear. Her head was in a spin.

She looked around her at the lush green grass, the flowers swaying in the gentle breeze and she could hear the sound of birds and the distant hum of lawn mowers in the neighbourhood gardens. It was a normal day for everybody else.

He grasped her hand in his.

'Hey girls!' he called in a sing song boyish voice.

Gabrielle lifted her sunglasses and placed them on top of her head. She craned her neck, shielding her eyes from the sun and looked at them with a nonchalant matter of fact gaze.

'Yeah?' was all that she said.

'We've got some news for you both,' he said excitedly. 'Go on Courtney you tell them.' He pushed her forward.

'Did Jennifer call?' Gabrielle exclaimed.

'No,' was Courtney's response. 'I'm pregnant.'

There was an eerie silence - nobody spoke. Alicia decided that this news did warrant turning around herself, and both girls looked at each other and then at their stepmother and dad.

'My God,' Gabrielle said. 'So that must mean that you guys have *sex*.' The two girls laughed. 'You're too old for all that Dad.'

'Is that all you can say?' Adam stared back at the twins with a look of amazement on his face.

'Well I'm certainly not too old for *all that*,' Courtney retorted. 'Are you pleased? Happy?' she continued.

The girls got up from the grass and Alicia shook her towel down. 'So that means we're gonna have another sister or a brother - yeah that's cool - I like babies,' she beamed.

Courtney breathed a sigh of relief and Adam looked at her as if to say, I told you so, and Gabrielle, came over and gave her a hug.

'This calls for a celebration,' Gabrielle sang. 'What's for dinner?'

'We're not eating in tonight, that's for sure,' Adam said as he led Courtney back in doors.

'Get dressed girls, we're going out.'

The four of them decided to eat at a local Chinese restaurant. It was small with a friendly ambience, and the food was well renowned in the area for its high quality. Courtney and Adam had been there many times before, and were always recognised by the staff. Courtney had always liked the traditional Chinese décor in the restaurant; it made her feel as though for one evening at least she was somewhere else. It was sheer escapism, a change from the monotony of everyday life, and she had always thought the orient exotic. It was somewhere she had always dreamed of visiting one day. It was unlikely now, as everything had been turned on its head. Nothing that was happening to her in truth seemed real. It was as though she was sitting there discussing someone else's plans. She had never imagined having a conversation of this nature and it relating directly to her. It didn't seem possible that she was pregnant - that only happened to other women.

They were all getting on especially well that night, and were all chatting around the table excitedly. It was as though the whole atmosphere between them had suddenly changed again, and the twins seemed to be equally happy about Courtney and their father's life changing news. Gabrielle and Alicia were planning the nursery with Courtney, and Adam was buying drinks for everybody in the restaurant. He had telephoned work earlier before they had gone out and swapped his on-call with a friend for the night. He had been happy to oblige under the circumstances. As the evening drew on Adam became a little intoxicated, much to the amusement of the two girls, who had never seen their father drunk before. He was telling everybody who cared to listen how he was going to be a dad, and complete strangers were congratulating the family. Over the meal the subject of work came up again for the girls. They had been discussing getting a day job at one of the local cafés, but their plans seemed to have fallen by the wayside. They were slipping into a life of laziness, spending every day by the pool and doing little else. Courtney pointed out to them that with a baby on the way, they may not be able to support the girls financially anymore. They would need to find new jobs at some point anyway. Not only that, but she didn't think it was healthy or productive for them to be lying around doing nothing every day.

The waiter in the restaurant came over with a complimentary bottle of wine for the expectant couple. Adam sampled it, and gave him a thumbs up to continue pouring.

Courtney had only had one glass all evening. She knew, however, that she shouldn't now be drinking at all. It was going to be so hard to give up alcohol - it had become her safety net in recent times, and she didn't know how she would cope without it. But she resolved that she was going to try her hardest, that was all that she could do.

'The last thing I want,' she said to Alicia, 'is to cause any harm to our unborn child.' Alicia, who had just lit another cigarette, suddenly noticed out of the corner of her eye that Jennifer was walking towards the table.

She jabbed her sister hard in the ribs; Gabrielle was in mid conversation with her father and hadn't noticed. 'What?' she said, spinning around sharply.

'It's Jennifer,' Alicia said, in a stage whisper, which was loud enough for the whole restaurant to hear.

'Hi,' Jennifer smiled. 'Out for a family meal I see.'

Jennifer was the manager of one of the cafés where Alicia and Gabrielle had been offered a day job.

She had immediately, upon seeing the girls, wanted them to work in her café. She knew it would give her the edge she needed to attract customers from the rival cafés and restaurants in the area.

'Do you girls still need a job?' Jennifer asked.

'Yes they do,' Adam said loudly, slurring his words.

'Dad!' Gabrielle scolded, 'I think that's up to us isn't it?'

'Well do you or don't you? I gotta cab waiting outside,' Jennifer continued, in a matter of fact tone.

Jennifer was smartly dressed, wearing a short designer evening dress with an expensive looking handbag and shoes to match.

Her smart clothes detracted from her plain looks, but she had a certain charm. She was attractive, but in an unconventional way. Her long, light brown hair was well groomed, if a little dull, but trimmed to perfection. She could afford the most expensive hairdresser in town.

'Well,' Jennifer said impatiently, 'what will it be?'

The girls looked at each other; Gabrielle winked at her sister. Then turning back to Jennifer she said coolly 'when do we start?'

Jennifer beamed, 'how about tomorrow?' The girls both nodded.

'Right,' she said, 'be at the café by 8.30 in the morning sharp.'

She tossed her hair back as she turned to look outside. 'I'd better go,' she said worriedly, 'my boyfriend's waiting.'

She fumbled nervously with her handbag, trying to stuff her diary back in. 'Isn't it always the way,' she half laughed, 'you can get it out, but you can never get it back in again, if you know what I mean.'

Adam laughed loudly; his sense of humour had been seriously enhanced by his alcoholic consumption that night.

'Well I'll be seeing you guys,' Jennifer said as she turned to leave the restaurant. Her boyfriend was shouting something at her from outside, but they couldn't see him properly, or make out what he was saying.

'Isn't it amazing?' Courtney remarked after she'd gone. 'A girl like that with so much money, and her own business, lets her boyfriend speak to her like that. I guess that proves everyone has their vulnerable side.'

The waiter arrived with the bill and they paid up and left the restaurant, with Alicia and Gabrielle talking excitedly about their new job.

The cab dropped Jennifer and Matt off at her parents' house half an hour after leaving the restaurant. They had argued all the way back, so much so that the cab driver had asked them if they were sure that they wanted to go home together. Matt was impatient; the fact that Jennifer had not come straight out to the cab was enough to set him off. Then he would start on her again, how she was lucky to have him, and that she shouldn't piss him off too often or he'd leave her for good this time. Matt had an athletic, toned body and was heavily into sport. He was considered to be attractive, with his all-American chiselled features, but there was nothing unusual or unique about him. His looks had forged his popularity in high school. He had been part of the in-crowd at the same school where Jennifer had been part of the out crowd; she had always admired him from afar. Both had since left. Jennifer then met Matt in a bar; he had spotted her friend Miranda first, but when she gave him the brush off because of his obvious drunken state, he started coming on to Jennifer. In his own words he had said that that night he'd been 'looking for a lay' and didn't care who it was, as long as they were female. The next morning when he had woken in Jennifer's parents' house, he had suddenly seen the advantages of getting to know this 'one night stand' a little bit better. He saw Jennifer as a meal ticket, and she knew it. She, however, was completely infatuated with him; she had lost her virginity to him that night, at the age of twenty-one. Jennifer believed in Christian family values. She felt duty bound to hold on to him for as long as was possible, even if he did take her for a ride along the way. She didn't care, what was money anyway, compared to apparent happiness? Now two years on, Jennifer was twenty-three and she still had hold of her man.

'Jennifer for God's sake,' Matt snarled at her on the doorstep of her parents' mansion, 'I wish you'd get a bigger handbag! You spend your whole life trying to squeeze your hand in there to find your keys. I'll get you some string then you can tie them round your Goddamn neck.'

Jennifer said nothing; she found her keys and opened the door. She entered into the long entrance hall of her house. Matt eyed the gilt-framed paintings avariciously as they proceeded down the corridor, their footsteps reverberating loudly on the ornate marble tiling. He had seen these paintings a thousand times before, but he enjoyed the splendour and the feeling of importance that they gave him whenever he passed through this grandiose hallway. It made him more determined to fulfil his ambition, which was to one day own a house that was identical in every way. Jennifer Thorpe's parents were well thought of in the area, her father being the mayor of Windermere and her mother a successful businesswoman. Both parents had also inherited vast sums of money from deceased relatives.

As Jennifer and Matt approached the central staircase, they heard a noise coming from the downstairs kitchen.

'It must be Molly,' Jennifer whispered, 'she's finishing late tonight.'

Molly was the family's maid; she did the cleaning and most of the cooking. Jennifer's mother cooked very occasionally, but not if she could help it. Most of the time she would be away at business meetings and dinner parties.

Molly didn't live in the house though, as she lived two miles away from Windermere, with her husband and three small children.

'She must have parked her auto round the back tonight Matt, I never saw it, did you?' she mused.

'No,' he replied vacantly.

The master staircase swept majestically up the centre of the house; it was vast and had two statuettes standing either side of the bottom stair. Matt took his girlfriend by the hand and led her up the staircase, then down the upstairs corridor to her bedroom, which was at the North East corner of the house. She had an ensuite bathroom, her bedroom alone was the size of most apartment flats.

He flung open the door and carried Jennifer over the threshold.

'You should be doing that on our wedding night,' she laughed flinging her head back.

'No, I should be doing this for my lady now,' he said, 'hang the wedding night'

He ran and jumped onto the bed, and lay there, beckoning seductively to her. She didn't have to be asked twice. She ran and jumped on top of him, and they began to kiss passionately.

She ripped his shirt open. 'Hey, that was new,' he complained.

'Yeah but I bought it,' she replied smiling, whilst continuing to disrobe him as quickly as she could.

She began kissing him, all over his muscular body, and he let out approving noises now and then. They continued to pleasure each other orally for a while, until Jennifer decided it was time to take Matt - she couldn't wait any longer. She got on top of him, and when she had finished they lay entwined, both hot from their lovemaking. Matt was the first to break loose from the embrace. Sex was sex to him, and he didn't like all the flowery bits afterwards - all the 'I love you's, and the 'I'll never leave you's,' it was all just a well-rehearsed performance. Maybe it would be real to him one day he thought, but he doubted it very much.

Jennifer rose from the bed feeling happy, and feeling loved. She, unlike her partner, meant everything that she said when they made love; she was oblivious to what was going on in his head. She knew that he didn't want to commit, but she still thought that with time he would change, and that it would end with the fairytale wedding that she had always dreamed of.

'You wanna drink?' she said. Matt had already got up and was heading for the shower.

'What you got babe, any of that French white left?' he replied.

'I think there's some left in the cooler, there's another bottle in the refrigerator,' she sang out from the kitchenette.

'That's all right then,' he answered.

Jennifer busied herself in the kitchen, getting glasses from her spotless white kitchen units. Her father had had her room custom made, with everything she could possibly need to live an independent life in her own home. Her father and mother slept over the other side of the house, so it was as if she was totally self-sufficient, as she rarely ran into them. Her father was the constant in her life, he was the one she saw with the most regularity. Her mother, however, had always been an enigma to her.

Even as a child she didn't remember her mother ever being there. She didn't remember her nursing her or anything. Apparently she did, but that was what her father had told her.

Jennifer had always been a disappointment to her mother, or so she felt. She had never lived up to the image that her mother had had, not having inherited any of her striking features, and that was a disappointment in itself. Her father, however, had always accepted her the way that she was, and loved her just the same. She had always had a lot of problems growing up, especially with relating to her peers. She had been picked on at school quite brutally, and she never had the support of her parents to get her through. Even her father at that time, had been too busy to intervene. The teachers had done what they could, but there was a limit to what they could do, and as Jennifer had learnt to her cost, a bully who had been punished would only become twice as vengeful and make it their mission in life to single her out more frequently. Now the bully felt they had just cause for their actions, despising her for grassing up on them. She'd decided after this happened to say nothing more. It was better to draw minimal attention to herself and try to slip between classes unnoticed.

Jennifer didn't know how she had got through her school days; she had however lived to tell the tale, but her emotional scars remained, just below the surface. College had been easier for her, as bullying was no longer a problem amongst the more mature students. Despite this she had still been in the unpopular crowd, hanging out with all the rejects in society as she saw it. At the time they were the only ones who would pay any attention to her. She had always had money, but she didn't then have the inclination to buy fashionable clothes, as the confidence she needed was just not there. She had no desire to even try to make the most of herself. The fact that her mother had an excellent dress sense had also put her off, and her mother had always been too busy to encourage Jennifer or guide her in the art of dressing well. Few of her fellow students knew where she lived, or who her father was, and her low self-esteem had only resulted in her appearing more insignificant and colourless in the eyes of her peers. Jennifer had learnt early on that at school looking good was all that mattered and people's opinions were formed on just that distinguishing factor; nobody looked any deeper, personality counted for nothing. She had always hated the fact that friends of her father and mother were always saying 'well you have a great personality.' She would just smile faintly - her eyes glazed and distant, her mind screaming back at them that she didn't want to have a 'great personality,' she just wanted to be pretty. It wasn't to be. However, now, she was using the only power she had over Matt. He had ignored her at College, but now he was interested, and she knew it must be because of her money. Matt had encouraged her to buy more stylish clothes, and the confidence she had got from his interest in her had finally empowered her to go out and fill her wardrobe with the perfectly tailored designer clothes that she now had. Jennifer's best friend Miranda had also been a great influence and source of encouragement in her life. An awareness of wealth only develops in a person, when that person is old enough to understand what it is to be poor. Matt had reached that awareness. For all his looks and apparent charm with the women, he had no qualifications. He came from a normal family who just had enough money to get by. They had no dreams or ambitions, but then neither did he if it came to that. His only dream was not to be as poor as his folks and he would do anything he could, even if it was to take someone else for a ride to get what he wanted.

He did have a job, but it wasn't the kind of job that was going to get him a career or the type of status that he craved. He worked in another restaurant in Orlando, as a barman; with his qualifications, that was all that he could get.

Matt emerged from the shower, wrapped in one of Jennifer's towels, with water still dripping from him.

Jennifer smiled at him, 'got your wine, it's on the side.'

'Thanks babe,' he replied, sauntering over to the side unit where his large wine glass stood, filled to the brim with the most expensive wine, the one that he liked the most.

'Why don't we go sit on the balcony,' she said, wrapping her silk dressing gown around herself, 'it might be a bit cooler now, but we can look at the stars and drink our wine.'

Matt winced at the romantic notion but went along with it anyway. Jennifer had put down the deposit for his new customized sports car, which was currently still at the manufacturers, but which was due to be delivered to Matt's parents' house in four week's time.

They walked onto the balcony, and sat down. There was an unusual chill in the air. Jennifer shivered, and pulled her dressing gown tighter around herself. Matt glanced over at her, and took a sip of his wine.

'It's quite a clear night,' she said, 'bit cold though.'

She was trying to make conversation, which was always a bit hard with Matt; he usually only became animated if talking about money or American Football.

She took a few more sips of her wine, and then she summoned up the courage to ask him what she really wanted to ask him.

She hesitated for a moment, then spoke, 'Matt, you know this open relationship thing that we agreed to - well, I don't know if I can handle it.'

He looked up from the table, quite shocked by what she had said; this had been the agreement since the start of their relationship, that he would be allowed to see other women.

'The thing is Matt, it's difficult, because when I'm with you,' she continued, 'I'm always wondering if you're comparing me to those other girls - I mean, the other week you stayed at that girl Melanie's house, and I didn't see you until the next weekend.'

'But babe,' he said with an almost pleading tone, 'you know I can't commit to you, we've discussed this before. I'm too young to settle down.'

'I'm not asking you to settle down,' she retorted, 'I just want you to stay faithful to me. Is that too much to ask?'

Matt grabbed at her hand that had clenched into a fist on the table. She snatched it away from him and slammed her fist down so hard that the wine glasses toppled off the table, and smashed on the balcony floor. There was silence then. He had never seen Jennifer this angry before. Her eyes were wild and it frightened him, she was always so quiet and unassuming usually.

He needed to take control back as quickly as possible. 'Let's think about this for a moment Jennifer.' He leapt to his feet and began pacing up and down the balcony like a prisoner locked in solitary, desperate to break free. 'Let's just *think* about this,' he raised his voice, so abruptly that she jumped, and flustered, tried to compose herself.

'What about everything I've done for you?' he said, waving an accusing finger in front of her face. 'What were you that night when I first slept with you? You were *nothing*.' He leaned in to her and put his face in front of hers. She craned her neck back to escape from his wrath. 'All you turned out to be was a rich man's little girl. You had no money of your own, you just sat there and had it all handed to you on a plate.' His mouth had curled into a hateful snarl as he spat out these last remarks.

Jennifer got up from her chair to go back inside.

'S*it* down!' he yelled, pushing her hard back down into her seat, sending a shooting pain up her spine. 'You should have tried growing up in our family. My mom had to scrimp for everything that we had, my dad would work every hour God sent to feed us. I never got all the brand name sneakers that my friends got for their birthdays.'

'Yeah,' she interjected, 'but at least you were popular - you had the looks, you never had to put up with being teased like I did.'

'That's cos I wasn't weak,' he snarled, 'I'm not like you Jennifer. I'm not a pathetic loser, you're so stupid you don't even realise you're being used.'

Jennifer was so angry and so hurt that she felt like everything she had ever suffered was going to culminate at this point. It was time for her to exorcise her ghosts. She summoned up all of her strength and shoved him so hard that he overbalanced, and by the time he had steadied himself she was up on her feet and standing in the doorway. She stepped back through the open door and slammed it, locking it behind her. He ran to get back through the door but she was too quick for him, and he stood pounding on the glass. He was still shouting but she couldn't hear a word he was saying. She stood staring blankly at him, with her arms folded. She was numb, she had started to see him again for what he really was, just a gold digging bully. He didn't love her and he never would. She sat on the corner of the bed and just gazed past him at the black sky. She watched the clouds as they glided elegantly past her. Half an hour went by in a flash, as she went into a trance-like state. She watched fascinated as the moon disappeared and then reappeared again, when there was a clear patch of sky. A tear glided slowly down her cheek. She knew she was in pain, but it was as if she was immune to feeling anymore - only her body reacted.

She came to abruptly when he began knocking on the glass again. Her eyes met his for the first time since she had slammed the balcony door. He looked sorry, and then those same old pangs came like waves over her. Her heart was ready to forgive him - her head wasn't. She walked shakily over to the door and opened it a crack. He tried to prise the door back open. 'Just hang on a minute,' she snapped. 'I'll let you back in when I'm ready, but this time, you have to promise not to shout at me again. Also, if you don't agree to what I've asked of you, you can forget that new auto, and I won't give you *any* more money.'

He looked amazed; she had never denied him anything before. She meant it this time he was sure. Then came the charm. He smiled winningly at her, 'God I've been such a selfish bastard,' he said lowering his head in feigned shame, 'Jenny, I promise I'll try and change. I do love you - you know that.'

Those were the magic words. She opened the door and embraced him. 'Oh I love you too,' she breathed, 'I'm so sorry for shutting you out.'

As they were hugging she forgot everything that he'd just put her through. He was glad they were hugging at that moment, because she couldn't see the uncontrollable smile that had just spread across his face. *I'm still gonna get my new auto.*

Alicia and Gabrielle stood outside Jennifer's café; the time was 8.25 a.m., they were five minutes early. The sun was already up, but there was a cool breeze in the air. Alicia looked at her watch and then at her sister who was eyeing the large red lettering across the top of the shop front. 'Jennifer's,' she mused, 'I like that - I work in Jennifer's…'

Alicia's hands were shaking as she pulled open her handbag and fumbled for her cigarettes. 'Another one?' Gabrielle exclaimed, 'you won't be able to smoke once we start work.'

'I know, I know,' Alicia replied, 'I'm just nervous, OK?'

Her sister laughed at her; Gabrielle never got nervous about anything; that was another difference between the two of them. Alicia looked at her sister, who was now peering through the glass to see if there was any movement inside. 'I don't know if Jennifer will like the pants,' she exclaimed, 'they're not very smart.'

Gabrielle was wearing a short-cropped black cotton sleeveless top, khaki pants and sneakers. Alicia on the other hand, had dressed more conservatively, and had opted for a long pastel coloured floral summer dress, a lilac cardigan and cream sandals.

'So,' Gabrielle retorted, 'it's up to her to say what we should or shouldn't wear, not you.'

Alicia shrugged her shoulders and continued to puff nervously on her cigarette.

Gabrielle wandered out onto the sidewalk, and craned her neck to look down the street. The other restaurant and café owners in Kissimmee's Bermuda Avenue, were busy setting out their specials boards, and arranging their tables and chairs outside their shop fronts, ready for the morning shift. Most of the cafés were already open and serving their customers breakfast. Jennifer's café already had its tables and chairs outside; they were all ornate silver coloured garden chairs and round tables, with red and white parasols over each. All around the shop front were long wooden window box style flower trestles, which mostly comprised of red and white roses. Gabrielle wondered why the tables were already set up, but there was no sign of Jennifer, and the sign still said closed.

Just as the thought had gone through her head, the front door of Jennifer's opened and there stood Jennifer herself. She had on a red and white apron, with "Jennifer's" embroidered in the top left-hand corner.

'Sorry girls,' she smiled, 'I've been here since seven but had to pop out just now for some more supplies. We were very busy yesterday - should be better now you two are here.' She beckoned to them both to come in.

Alicia looked around for somewhere to stub out her cigarette. The terrace was so clean and unspoilt looking she didn't like to put it out there, so she went out to the street, and dropped it down a drain.

The inside of the café was smartly decorated; it was very fashionable the girls thought. The furniture inside was made of pine, as was the floor. The walls were painted red on two sides and white at either end, in keeping with the colour scheme of the café.

On the walls were black and white photographs in frames. There were pictures of old movie stars like James Dean and Clark Gable, and also a photograph of Ginger Rogers and Fred Astair dancing. There were various pictures of American City skylines, in particular one of Manhattan that caught Gabrielle's eye.

The café was a lot bigger than it looked outside; facing the entrance was the main counter, which had on it the cash register, coffee percolators and a glass display cabinet filled with all manner of fresh cakes and pastries. Next to the counter, but set further back, was a short corridor that led to the restrooms. At one end of it stood an ornate coat stand for customers to use.

Immediately to the right of the counter was a dividing wall and an archway that led into the second half of Jennifer's. Here there were more pine tables and chairs, each with a small crystal vase filled with summer posies and the condiments placed either side. At the far right hand side at the back of the café there was a bar, and to the left of it a swing door that led into the kitchen. The same décor was repeated throughout.

As the girls looked around, they remarked on how well organised everything seemed.

'I didn't realise you sold liquor here,' Gabrielle then said.

'Oh yes,' Jennifer replied, 'but we only stay open late at the weekends. I prefer to think of Jennifer's as more of a café or bistro - more of a daytime place.'

The girls smiled.

'So,' Jennifer continued clapping her hands together and turning to face them. 'I expect you want to know what you'll be doing here.'

Jennifer walked through into the kitchen and they followed.

'Here you go,' she said, as she took two aprons off the pegs on the wall, 'these are for you.'

'So, does it matter what we wear to work?' Alicia gave a knowing look at her sister.

'No, not really,' Jennifer replied, 'what you have on is fine. The apron covers up most of it anyway - so long as you both tie back your hair, for hygiene reasons.'

Gabrielle smirked at her sister, who had obviously been hoping that khaki pants would be out. 'All I want you both to do for the time being is provide a waitress service for me,' Jennifer continued, 'that will then free me up to tend to the drinks and the cash register, and Antonio, my chef, will no longer have to bring the food out himself.'

'Wow, you must have been busy before,' Alicia exclaimed.

'I did have a waitress for a while,' Jennifer replied, 'but she was no good, so I'm counting on you two.'

Just then there was a knock on the back door. Jennifer went over and let in Antonio, who was all flustered and apologetic.

'I so sorry I'm late,' he said in broken English.

Straight away though he noticed the twins standing in front of him and beamed at them. 'Oh Jennifer,' he smiled, 'you have got the girls - I so happy.'

Antonio was a very likeable person and the girls warmed to him straight away. He was in his early thirties, with the customary Mediterranean dark brown eyes and dark hair, which was slightly thinning on top. He talked to the girls and showed them the menus whilst Jennifer opened up. There was already a queue forming outside as the café always opened at nine o'clock sharp. Jennifer's breakfasts were well known and very popular. Antonio was an accomplished chef, fully trained and qualified, with three years previous experience working in another local restaurant. He'd told the girls that he'd taken this position purely because he had been working as an assistant chef before and wanted the opportunity to run his own kitchen.

Alicia and Gabrielle's first day at Jennifer's went by very quickly, with only a couple of minor errors. Their father popped in during the afternoon and had a cup of coffee - he too liked the atmosphere in Jennifer's. He concluded that it had been the best choice for his daughters' new place of work. At the end of the day Jennifer praised her two new waitresses, and as they were leaving, said that she was looking forward to seeing them again tomorrow.

The summer this year was hot, and both the twins' tans were well developed. Their golden brown skin complementing their long blonde hair. They had now worked at Jennifer's for a month, and were becoming firm favourites with the customers. They had attracted a different type of customer to Jennifer's. Before they had arrived, the main clientele had been families of holidaymakers, and the locals had stayed away for that reason. Now the holidaymakers still came, but the young Floridian males were starting to come in their droves; and local young females were then attracted to the café because of all the hot blooded males who had started to use it as their preferred place to hang out. Jennifer was delighted with the increase in profits, but also realised that she had to increase her staff to keep up with the demand. By the end of the fourth week Jennifer decided she should hold a meeting to discuss her plans with her staff and so on the Friday, as a one off, closed the café early.

'I'm so happy with what's happening to this place,' she beamed at everybody. 'However, I know that Antonio is struggling to keep up with the orders, and we need to find some more staff for the kitchen, to help him out.'

Alicia nodded, and then Gabrielle piped up, 'we want some more men!'

Jennifer laughed, 'I think you're right.   Poor Antonio is definitely outnumbered in here.'   She then sighed, and braced herself as she had something else that she needed to ask the girls.

'Now girls, I know that you specifically said you didn't want to work nights, and I quite understand why, however, do you think you may reconsider? The reason is that our new customers are very keen for this place to stay open later in the weekdays, and the potential business for us if we do that is enormous.'

Alicia's face suddenly dropped, 'I'm sorry Jennifer, I just don't think I could do it. I'm still too nervous about being out after dark - I just can't seem to get over it.'

'Well in that case, we'll make sure that you only have to work days.   That isn't a problem, you're far too valuable for me to lose you.'

Alicia sighed with relief, and Jennifer reached out for her hand and squeezed it affectionately. 'What about you?' Alicia then said turning to her sister.

Gabrielle had moved her chair closer to her sister's protectively, 'what do you think I should do?'

'I could pay for a taxi home for you after your shift's finished, if you did want to do it,' Jennifer interjected. 'I can assure you, you would never have to walk home alone.'

'Gabrielle, if you want to work a night shift, that's fine by me,' Alicia replied, 'and maybe after I've seen that it's quite safe, then maybe I'll reconsider.'   Gabrielle smiled and nodded in agreement.

Jennifer clapped her hands together, 'well that's settled then. Now the next thing is we need to hire the extra staff. I'm gonna need another waitress to work days and another one to work nights, and I'm gonna need a regular bar person.' Antonio went to interrupt. She anticipated what he was going to say. 'Don't worry Antonio, I'm gonna get two more people to work in the kitchen also.'

'Well I'll tell you what,' Gabrielle said excitedly, 'for the waitress positions, what about those two girls that come in to ogle the guys - they're both really bubbly and confident. Sadie told me the other day she needed a job. I'm not sure about Candy though, but I reckon it's worth a try.'

'Sounds great! Isn't Sadie the smallish brunette who goes out with that guy with the blonde hair and the great body?' Jennifer remarked, 'I can't remember his name.'

'Dan!' both the twins sang out in unison. They all burst out laughing.

'Yeah Jennifer, and we've noticed you staring at him!' Gabrielle added.

'Hey, excuse me, but I'm spoken for!' Jennifer retorted.

'Maybe, but you can still look at the menu,' Gabrielle replied with a wry smile.

'Anyway I'll have a word when I next see her,' Jennifer continued, 'wouldn't it be great if they say yes.'

Antonio had already got two friends in mind for the kitchen positions, so it was only the bar person left to find.

As Jennifer got up out of her seat, and everyone else started to prepare to leave, there was a sudden and loud screech of brakes outside. Jennifer looked out of the café's front window to see who it was. The sun was streaming in through the glass, and she had to shield her eyes to make out who it was.

'Oh God it's Matt!' she exclaimed, 'what the hell is he doing here?' Jennifer's assertive air, seemed to wither away in seconds, and the girls again saw that vulnerable side to Jennifer that they had last seen that night in the Chinese restaurant when they had first been offered their jobs. She scurried to the door and unlocked it. The twins had never met Jennifer's boyfriend before. They could now make out the car that he had arrived in which was a very expensive looking brand new sports car, that was silver in colour, and was gleaming in the early evening sunshine.

Matt stepped in through the open door. Gabrielle was instantly sure that she knew him, but she couldn't make out his face properly as he had shades on, and if it was the person she thought it was, then he had a completely different hairstyle from the one that she remembered. His dark brown hair was now cut short at the back but longer on top, and he continually ran his fingers through it, smoothing it back so that it fell forward in exactly the right position. At first he didn't seem to notice the other people in the café. He grabbed Jennifer and swung her around planting a big kiss on her lips. She giggled in response like a little college girl.

'Hi babe,' he said affectionately.

Upon hearing him speak both Alicia and Gabrielle knew straight away that it was him, but neither of them said anything.

'The Lotus goes like a dream, it's awesome,' he continued, 'I still can't believe that it's mine. I took it for a spin down to Key West today. It purrs, and the acceleration, oh boy is that amazing - nought to sixty in six seconds, man is it cool.'

'Matt,' Jennifer interrupted him hesitantly, 'you haven't met my new waitresses yet.'

He turned to face them, taking his shades off and planting them on top of his head.

His steely blue eyes fixed on Gabrielle, and her alone. Jennifer noticed the look of utter amazement on his face.

'Gaby!' he exclaimed, 'Oh my God, how are you? Alicia too, I can't believe it.'

'Hang on a minute,' Jennifer was starting to panic, 'you mean you know them already?'

Gabrielle, seeing the concerned look on Jennifer's face, decided she needed to clarify the situation, before Jennifer jumped to the wrong conclusion.

'Oh yes, we remember Matt,' she said casually. We worked in the Jamaican restaurant in Lake Buena Vista together - that was until...'

'Until I got attacked on my way home, and I had to leave,' Alicia said in a matter of fact tone.

There was an awkward silence.

Matt looked embarrassed. He edged a bit closer to them from the doorway. 'I was so sorry when I heard what happened to you Alicia,' he said, seeming genuine, 'we shouldn't have let you walk home that night.'

Jennifer sank into the nearest chair, at one of the tables, and stared blankly at the far wall. She looked dejected and despairing for a moment, and then turned suddenly to Matt again, who had pulled up a chair at the twins' table.

'I, I didn't realise,' she stammered, 'you never said anything about them to me before.'

'Well he wouldn't would he,' Gabrielle said quickly, 'we only worked in the same restaurant. There were loads of waiters and waitresses in there.'

'I can't believe I didn't ask you the name of the place you worked before. I should have asked you - I mean you could have been making it up when you'd said you'd got previous experience,' Jennifer then said, her eyes darting frantically back and forth from one twin to the other.

There was another awkward silence, much longer than the first.

After a while Matt stood up, scraping his chair, which broke the silence, and he walked over to the bar. 'Anyone want a beer?' he asked hesitantly.

'Please,' said Gabrielle, the situation had left her desperate for a drink. She kept looking over at her new boss, who looked as though she had had all of the energy sucked out of her. She sat, her shoulders hunched, her head low, like a plant that hadn't seen water for days. She was just wilting before their eyes.

'Oh Jennifer,' Gabrielle said getting up out of her chair, 'it doesn't matter does it that we worked there before and that we already knew him. We would have known him after today, even if we hadn't met before.'

'I know,' Jennifer replied in monotone, 'I just can't understand why he never said anything about you before that's all.'

'Well maybe he never thought that we were that important to mention,' Gabrielle continued. 'After all we only worked together, and not always on the same shifts either. I doubt he gave us a second thought.'

'He did say about a girl getting attacked on her way home,' Jennifer then said, looking over at Alicia. 'I never guessed that it was you though. I should have realised when you'd said about not wanting to work night shifts. I just didn't think.'

'Don't worry about it,' Alicia reassured her, 'how were you to know? I'm sure the same thing has happened to other girls.'

Out of the corner of her eye, Alicia caught a glimpse of Matt at the bar. He was stood out of sight of Jennifer shaking his head and rolling his eyes, annoyed by his girlfriend's paranoia.

Alicia was remembering all the nights that Gabrielle and Matt had spent drinking at the bar together after hours, and how it had been because of him that Gabrielle had not come home with her that night.

Jennifer managed to pull herself back together and rejoined the rest of the group. After having a quick beer together, the twins made their excuses and left as the atmosphere had remained distinctly awkward between them.

The twins had now seen another side to their new boss that disturbed them greatly, and that, unlike the vulnerable side to her nature, wasn't the slightest bit appealing. As Gabrielle had looked across that table into Jennifer's eyes she had seen two grey pools of loathing and jealousy staring back at her. She had never seen that so pronounced in a person before, and it had sent a cold shiver down her spine.

Chapter 5

Jennifer's heart was beating with nervous anticipation as Matt opened the passenger door of his Lotus and ushered her in.

'She's a beauty, don't you think?' he exclaimed, running his fingers through his hair, and gazing at his new car in adoration.

'Which one Gabrielle or Alicia?' Jennifer replied flippantly.

Matt rolled his eyes, and ignored her remark. Jennifer shrunk back into the seat; she didn't feel that she belonged in this car. It was much too stylish and expensive looking for her. She realised it was strange that she was thinking this way, especially as she had paid for it in the first place. She thought that Gabrielle would suit the car better; she just felt that she looked totally out of place in it. She tortured herself further by looking in the passenger mirror; her mousy brown locks were hanging untidily around her face and her make-up had all worn off. She felt alone then, trapped in her own mind, unable to look out of herself, unable to break the spiral of depression that was slowly suffocating her entire being. In the last four weeks since the incident on her balcony, she had started to feel a little bit better about Matt and the whole situation. He had started making a real effort to be more considerate. He had stopped seeing other women and had been behaving more like a model boyfriend. Now, however, it was as though she had been kidding herself all along. She could see him again for what he really was; her fantasy had come to an abrupt end. She had found out about Matt already knowing Gabrielle and Alicia, and having seen the look that had been in his eyes, everything was suddenly different again, everything was unsure and unstable once more. Her demons had returned.

Matt started the engine. It purred into life, and as Jennifer looked at him, she saw on his face, a look of self-satisfaction. She felt nauseous as she saw him preening himself in the mirror. He didn't see what she saw when she looked in the mirror, and was never likely to. Almost an irrational wave of hatred and fear came over Jennifer at that moment. Matt turned to her smiling.

'Back to your place babe?' he said.

'Go where you like,' she stammered, 'I just don't give a shit.'

'What's wrong with you woman?' His mood changed. He had no patience with Jennifer when she was feeling like this - he was too self-absorbed. He just wanted everything to go his way, and for nothing to rock the boat. He couldn't cope with what he viewed as being irrational displays of emotion.

As Jennifer sat in the passenger seat, she felt a panic attack come over her. She started to shake and sweat, and tears were rolling helplessly down her face for no apparent reason. She didn't know what she wanted to do. She didn't know whether she wanted to get out and run, or stay there with Matt, even though he didn't love her. She did want to die, but she was afraid of that as well - afraid of being alone, afraid of everything, even her own reflection in the mirror. She felt as though she was trapped in her useless mind and body, so wanting to break free, to be a different person. To be like Gabrielle. If only she could wake up one morning and go to the mirror to find *her* face staring back at her, imagine what her life must be like. She latched onto that thought. She could have any man she wanted for keeps, the way she looked. *Surely you can't have any worries when you look like her; she has the confidence too. Oh God why can't I be like her? He tried to disguise the look on his face when he saw them, but I know; I'm not stupid. He's been with her before, I'm sure of it. He can tell them apart, he called her Gaby; nobody else calls her Gaby...*

'Jennifer, hey dopey, where do you want to go?'

'Just take me home and you can then go and fuck Gabrielle for all I care! Oh and I want the keys back for the auto, I paid for it after all.'

'Right, fine!' he bellowed. 'I might just do that, seeing as you're an emotional wreck who's no good for anybody.'

He got out the car and slammed the door, throwing the keys at her so hard that they gashed the side of her face. He then started off down the road in the direction that the twins had taken.

Jennifer was crying, sobbing so hard she felt that her heart would break. She felt desperate.

'Oh and you can tell those two dollies that they're both fired!' she shouted after him, her voice breaking up with emotion.

'Tell them yourself!' he hollered back.

Jennifer pulled her hair back from her face and rubbed at her eyes, which were both stinging and red from crying. She now realised that she had to drive this thing and the gravity of the situation she had put herself into suddenly hit her. Her thoughts became coherent for a moment. She wanted Matt back now - she had to get to him quickly and apologise, before it was too late, and he took her up on her suggestion. She wanted to take him back to her house to try to explain her irrational behaviour, to try to make everything better again. She became aware of the pain from her bleeding cheek. People in the street were staring - she had to regain her composure, and fast, it might harm her business, and reputation. She struggled with the keys eventually finding the right one. The engine started first time, but when she tried to put the indicators on, the wipers came on instead. She then somehow managed to put the radio on, which drew even more attention to herself. In her increasing panic she finally flooded the engine.

Matt had stopped further down the road, hearing all the noise from the car, and turned to look. He saw the people gathering on the opposite side of the street watching, talking amongst themselves. He felt guilty for getting so angry with her, and for hurting her with the keys, and he set off back up the road. When he got to the car, Jennifer was still revving the engine furiously, tears were still streaming down her face. Her injured cheek was now streaked with blood, which had mixed with her tears to make it look a lot more serious than it actually was.

'Jennifer,' he leaned over the car, and turned off the engine, taking the keys back.

'Baby listen to me,' he tilted her face towards his with an affectionate stroke of his hand.

Her glazed swollen eyes focused on his.

'Why do you keep hurting me?' she cried. 'Everything you say, everything you do - you're killing me.'

He kissed her injured cheek, 'Baby I'm sorry. I'm always screwing up. I'm just one big screw up - please forgive me.'

'I need help Matt! I can't live with myself anymore, there's nothing to live for.' Jennifer clutched at his hand so hard that he pulled it away from her in pain.

He wanted to get them both out of there as quickly as possible. There were too many people, and some of them he recognised as customers from her café. Jennifer seemed oblivious to what was going on around her. She was far away, somewhere else, in her own tortured world.

She moved herself awkwardly back into the passenger seat and Matt got back in the car. He sped away as quickly as possible and it was only when they were back on the interstate that he began to speak to her again.

'I think you need to see a doctor,' he said putting his free hand protectively on her leg.

'I don't need a doctor, I need to have it out with my mother, that's what I need to do,' she snapped back.

'Your mother?' he said, surprised. 'What's she ever done?'

'Nothing,' she retorted.

'Well if she's done nothing, why have it out with her?' he said, trying to understand her argument.

'When I say nothing, I mean she's done *nothing* for me!' she screamed.

'Stop shouting! Oh God, you're not gonna go all weird on me again,' he said flippantly.

'She is the reason I'm like I am.' Jennifer then suddenly grabbed Matt's arm and yanked it, causing him to swerve abruptly and dangerously to the outside lane.

'What are you doing you stupid bitch, are you trying to kill us both or something?' He thumped her across the chest with his free arm. Jennifer was unmoved.

'I've realised that you see,' she continued.

'Realised what?' he shouted back.

'If she'd loved me, maybe I wouldn't feel so unworthy, and just maybe I might have some confidence in myself.' She began to cry again, putting her hands up to her face in shame and self-pity. He tried to calm down; his angry tone wasn't getting him anywhere.

'Jennifer, I thought you said it was me who was killing you,' he remarked.

'Well you're just a trigger for me,' she replied.

'What do you mean a trigger?' he questioned her further.

'What I mean is that I already had problems before you came along, and you just seem to make me worse,' she said with an air of desperation in her voice.

'Babe, but I thought you loved me.'

'I do, that's the problem, but I know you're not doing me any good.'

'I'm going to try harder I promise,' he resolved, 'I don't know how many other girls would buy me a new Lotus for a gift.'

'There you go again' she sighed, 'it's all money with you - it's not me you want.'

'That's not true Jenny.'

'Just shut up - please just shut up!' she shouted back at him, 'I want to go home. I need you there because my mother's gonna be there, and I'm gonna give her the surprise of her miserable, selfish life.'

As they continued down the interstate, the evening sun beat down hard on the silver car, and it glistened as it cruised along. The wind blew in their hair and Jennifer thought to herself that right now she should be feeling so happy. She should be feeling like she didn't have a care in the world. Instead she felt sick. She felt as though she was going crazy and just couldn't halt the constant stream of tears that were coursing down her cheeks. A wave of emotion so great had taken her over, and she no longer felt in control of her own body or her actions.

It seemed like an age before they arrived back at her home in Windermere; it was only then that she remembered she'd left her own car back at the café.

'Damn!' she exclaimed, 'can you stay over Matt? I need a lift back to work in the morning.'

'I don't know Jenny, I'm supposed to be taking my brother somewhere.'

'Tonight Matt, that's all I'm asking. Mom and Dad go away next week, you can come and go as you please then. I just need you to be there tonight because something is gonna happen, believe me, and it's not going to be very pretty.'

The car pulled into Jennifer's palatial driveway. There were about fifteen other cars all parked up, and they could hear faint laughter coming from within the house.

'Oh they have a dinner party,' Jennifer smiled, 'even better.'

She rubbed her hands together with delight and turned to Matt, her eyes wild with excitement.

'Jennifer, are you sure you're all right?' He began to feel scared again, like the night when he'd been shut on the balcony, unsure of what his girlfriend was going to do next. Right now she was capable of anything, he thought.

He swung the car round and then began to reverse into a parking bay.

'Jennifer, listen to me,' he turned off the engine and caught hold of her arm, 'are you sure you're making the right move here?'

'Yes I am Matt,' she replied, her tone becoming serious again, 'I need to do this. It's been a long time coming, and I think it just might make me happy - come on.'

She tugged at the door handle and climbed out of the car, brushing herself down. She was wearing her casual work attire - she certainly wasn't dressed for a dinner party.

'Don't you think you ought to clean that blood off your face?' he said cautiously.

'You don't get it do you,' she replied, 'this is perfect.'

'I want my mother and her friends to see exactly what she has done to me. It wouldn't work if I was all dressed up, now would it.'

She turned and motioned to Matt to follow, and proceeded towards the front door, but she suddenly stopped and turned back abruptly. It had dawned on her that she wouldn't be staying there that night at all, and probably never would be again.

'Second thoughts, you wait here,' she called back, 'I'll be needing a get away vehicle.'

Jennifer was humming a tune to herself as she put the key in the lock and then swung open the heavy front door of her mansion house. She stood motionless in the doorway for a second, listening, before stepping forward and closing it behind her with a bang that echoed down the entire hallway. Nobody heard, or if they did, they didn't bother to go to look to see who it was. *They probably think it's another one of mommy's guests.*

'Molly!' Jennifer called out in a hoarse stage whisper. The Thorpe's maid turned round at the end of the hallway, having recognised her voice, and smiled broadly. She was a warm and caring woman, the type of person who Jennifer had always wished she'd had for a mother.

Jennifer walked towards her, and as she got closer Molly gasped and put her hands up to her face.

'My God Jennifer, your cheek, it it's covered in blood,' she stammered.

'Oh it's nothing, just a scratch, auto keys, looks worse than it is.'

'Don't let your mother see you like that,' Molly then said frankly, 'you know what she's like, and she's got a dinner party tonight - it's her business associates. I think you might recognise a couple of them, as well.'

'Now Molly, I've known you a long time,' Jennifer said, 'and you're very dear to me, so can you please go back and busy yourself at the other end of the house for a while. Pretend you never saw me, that way, you won't get in any trouble.'

'Oh Jennifer,' Molly welled up, 'what are you going to do?'

'Now I can't tell you that can I?' Jennifer smiled. 'You haven't seen me remember.'

Molly shook her head in disbelief, and headed off back down the hallway.

'Is my father home?' Jennifer called after her.

'No sweetie he's gone. He didn't say where.'

Jennifer stood still for a moment longer, watching Molly as she disappeared out of sight; she listened trying to locate exactly where the dinner party was being held. It wasn't in the front dining room, it must be in the dining hall behind it. That was even bigger, and designed for even more guests. Well there were a lot of cars parked outside, she remembered.

She proceeded slowly down the hallway, stopping now and again to listen. She didn't feel afraid - she felt excited. She just couldn't wait to see her mother's face.

She passed the first dining room on the right, and then headed further down towards the entrance to the dining hall. The main dining hall was on the left hand side, and was the same length as the entire hallway. The dining room on the right was intended just for family and other smaller gatherings, and behind that on the right was the lounge.

To get to the door of the dining hall, Jennifer had to turn left at the end of the hallway, and then left again. The heavy oak door was closed. She put her ear to it, and could hear the sound of cutlery against plates, and glasses chinking against other glasses. She could hear a general clamour of voices - lots of different people talking at once, interspersed with the occasional peel of laughter.

She turned the handle of the door slowly, and let it swing open on its hinges. She stood in the doorway motionless. Her gaze was drawn to her mother who was bedecked with jewels - her long red hair artistically arranged on top of her head with two wisps of hair falling either side of her heavily made up face. She looked every inch the rich businesswoman in her black evening dress. She didn't notice Jennifer at first; she was in deep conversation with the man sitting next to her. Jennifer recognised him as one of the directors of her mother's company. Everybody had turned one by one, slowly and deliberately, to stare at Jennifer, their faces registering amazement and confusion.

'Francesca,' the director said, clearing his throat and setting his champagne glass back down on the table, 'you appear to have another guest.'

Jennifer's mother looked round, and seeing Jennifer's face, began to tremble uncontrollably. Raising her champagne glass hurriedly to her lips, she drank the glass dry and immediately went to pour herself another one. She knew that her daughter's untimely entrance had signalled the end of her dinner party.

'Evening Mother.' Jennifer spoke, in a confident and eloquent tone. 'Have you room for another person at the table? I'm so hungry.'

Francesca didn't reply, she just stared mesmerised by the figure before her.

'Don't you have anything to say Mother?' she continued, 'after all, I would have thought you would be proud to be able to introduce your daughter to all your business colleagues.'

Francesca winced, and then removed her gaze from Jennifer turning her attention back to her guests.

'I do apologise for this intrusion,' she said pointedly. 'This is very embarrassing.'

'That's right *Mother*, this is very embarrassing for you isn't it?' Jennifer raised her voice.

'Get out Jennifer!' Francesca yelled. 'Go on get out!'

At that point the stern looking, grey haired man sitting next to her mother, put his napkin back on the table, and made a move to leave.

Francesca grabbed hold of his arm and pulled him back down again.

'It's all right Bob, you don't have to go, she'll be leaving in a minute.'

'Well actually Bob,' Jennifer continued, 'I'd like you to stay, in fact, I'd like for you all to stay, because you need to hear what I have to say about *her*.' She paused for a moment, trying to recall everything that she had planned to say. And then she began.

'Now as you all know, my mother is a very rich woman, with a big house and expensive jewellery, and I see that obviously none of you are that short of money yourselves either. You wouldn't believe we were mother and daughter now would you - would you?' Jennifer moved closer to the table; her mother cowered in her seat and started to edge backwards.

'What's the matter Mother?' Jennifer taunted. 'Never seen blood before?'

She imitated her mother's voice, 'Oh how disgusting, how could anybody be seen in public looking like that.'

'Now Bob,' Jennifer continued, her voice returning to normal, 'didn't know your name before, but luckily Mom just let it slip. Great to meet you,' she sat on the edge of the table, clearing the plates out of the way, and leaning forward to shake his hand, which he duly did, very hurriedly and nervously.

'Would you say that my mother was every inch the perfect woman, I mean just look at her, she doesn't look bad for fifty.' Her mother gasped.

'You told me you were forty,' Bob remarked turning to Francesca, who was now becoming tearful.

'Jennifer!' she bellowed, 'you have said enough, I don't know what's got into you tonight, but I'd appreciate it if you left now.' Jennifer turned to her mother, and stared at her in disgust. 'Oh Mother, I've only just started.' She stood back up and started to walk around the table. 'Did you know everybody, Mother had a face lift last year?' Nobody spoke, they all sat motionless, with just their eyes following her as she went by.

'Yes, well, everything starts to droop a bit when you get to that age, and being the vain woman that my mother is, she certainly couldn't conceive of growing old gracefully.'

Jennifer saw a glass half full with champagne on the side table, and drank it. There was silence, apart from the sound of her mother's pitiful whimpering at the other end of the table.

'Do you know why she's crying now?' Jennifer asked them. 'Not because she's concerned about me, it's because she's upset for herself - the only person she truly cares about. She doesn't even love my father I don't think - he just gives her a bit more status.'

Just then a plump kindly faced lady at the opposite end of the table, suddenly spoke up.

'My name's Ruby,' she began falteringly, 'I work with your mother. I was just thinking that maybe you shouldn't be so hard on her, and try to focus on all the things she has provided for you. I mean, look at the house you live in.'

'Oh sure,' Jennifer said, 'she's given me lots of *things*, but never any love. I realised something today which I would like to share with you all. I have my own business. I have my own flat - it's actually in this house, it's custom built. I have expensive clothes and I have a gorgeous boyfriend, but guess what? I have no self-confidence. I hate myself and I allow people, including my boyfriend, to treat me like crap, because that's all that I think I deserve. I don't have looks either, but you can get over all of that if you feel loved and happy. I would trade everything I have to be a different person, to have been born into a different family, and to have grown up knowing that I was worth something.'

Ruby cast her eyes back down and then another one of the guests got up to leave.

Jennifer motioned for him to sit back down, which he duly did without hesitation.

'I'll be finished in a minute, then you can all carry on with your dinner party,' she told him.

She walked slowly back around the table and then leaned over her mother menacingly.

'I don't know how to love Mother,' she said. 'I guess that must be the only thing that I inherited from you.'

Her mother didn't answer; her ice blue eyes just stared back at her daughter with disdain.

Jennifer suddenly made a grab for her hair, and pulled it out of its clip so that it fell untidily around her shoulders. She then smeared her dirty bloody hands across her mother's face, who screamed out in anguish, 'get her off of me!'

Bob made a move. 'This has gone too far!' he yelled.

'Don't worry *Bob,* I'm leaving now,' Jennifer replied sarcastically.

She turned and began to walk towards the door, stopping just short of it.

'Now you know what it's like to be me Mother,' she said, turning back one last time to cast her a disparaging look.

She left the room to the sound of her mother's sobbing, closing the door slowly and carefully behind her. She walked towards the staircase and did a thumbs up to Molly who was passing. 'Can't stop!' she sang out. 'Got to get my things.'

Jennifer entered her flat. She quickly got a suitcase from her closet and crammed into it as many clothes, shoes and toiletries as she could. She cleaned her face in the bathroom, and hurriedly dried it on the nearest towel. She left by the fire escape at the back of the house, and ran across the grass at the side. She peered around the corner and noticing that the guests were already starting to leave, she signalled to Matt, who was still parked out the front and who luckily was looking in the right direction at the time. He drove over to where she stood, destroying a flowerbed in the process. She flung open the door and jumped in. They drove off at speed, the wheels spinning on the grass.

'Glad to see you've washed your face,' he said as they left the driveway. 'Where do we go now?'

'Take me to Miranda's,' she replied trying to catch her breath.

'Right,' was all that he said in response.

They drove out of the private road, out of Windermere, and back onto the interstate.

Jennifer leaned her head backwards. She closed her eyes and felt the wind rushing by, as the lotus sped along. They were heading for the city centre, which was where Jennifer's best and only true friend lived. She could always count on her in times of trouble, and right now, Jennifer knew that this was the most trouble she'd ever had. Despite this, she also felt content. She didn't know how long the feeling would last as it now seemed alien to her, but at that moment she was at peace with herself and with the world. Matt hadn't spoken a word since they'd left the house. He was agitated and nervous, as the day's events were proving too much for him to cope with. He felt afraid of the woman who was sitting beside him - one minute she was happy the next minute she was behaving like a thing possessed. She was too unpredictable, and he felt that he was walking on eggshells - not wanting to say the wrong thing at the risk of upsetting her again. So instead he said nothing.

'Matt,' Jennifer mused, 'I really whipped my mother's ass today, and I feel great.' He looked at her sternly; she laughed back at him. 'Oh sorry I forgot, you don't approve of that kind of behaviour do you? Showing disrespect to your parents that's a big no no.'

Matt coughed nervously, 'I just don't understand why all of a sudden you've decided to do this. I mean the other week, you were fine - you've always been fine, why now?'

'Ah but that's where you're wrong Matt, I've never been fine, I've just held it all in, too frightened to break out, too frightened to do or say anything wrong.'

'So what's changed then?' He looked at her questioningly.

Jennifer didn't answer, and just stared straight ahead.

'The only thing that's changed lately is that you have more staff at your café and your business has picked up. I mean for heaven's sake Jennifer, everything's just getting good, and you're gonna just screw it all up? For what?'

'Oh Matt, you wouldn't understand. You'll never understand so there's no fucking point even trying to explain to you, so I'm not gonna bother.'

'Right fine, be like that, I don't give a fuck,' he retorted.

Jennifer's expression was serene. Usually she'd have been in tears by now, but it was as if her emotions had all been anaesthetised. She changed the subject.

'Now Matt, I don't want to fight, it's not worth it. I'm gonna ask Miranda if I can stay at hers for a while. I can't work right now, I need to sort out what I'm going to do. I need you to oversee the café for me while I'm gone, just check it's locked up at night. Oh and you'll need to do the cash registers as well and take the money down the bank for me. I'll call you anyway and let you know.'

'Yeah of course I will, but I got my own job too remember.'

'Don't worry, I'll pay you for it, it'll only be for a week. Speak to your boss, it's important.' Jennifer put her hand on Matt's thigh and stroked it affectionately.

They arrived at Miranda's house. Her car was in the drive, and she could see her looking out of the kitchen window. Jennifer waved madly at her and leapt out of the car, swinging her bag over Matt's head from the back seat.

She ran round to the driver's side of the car and leaned over giving him a tender kiss, whilst running her hand down the side of his face.

'Honey, everything'll be fine when I get back, don't worry,' she said, gazing at him intently. 'We can move in together, get a house in Kissimmee.'

He smiled back at her nervously.

'I know what I want in life,' she continued, 'it's you, and I don't need anybody else. Now don't miss me too much! Here's my house keys, you can collect some more of my stuff for me. Damn, and my auto's still at the café! It should be all right there. I can get a lift back but if I can't I'll call.'

He started the engine. Jennifer was already on her way up the drive; she turned back.

'I'll call you,' she sang out.

As Matt drove out of the city, his heart was racing and beads of perspiration were springing up all over his forehead. *This is stupid, what's wrong with me?*

Courtney was walking down the staircase clutching a heavy basket of laundry, when she suddenly felt her unborn baby moving inside her. It was the weirdest feeling in the world she thought - another life growing in her stomach. It was something that her body was unconsciously assisting, but that she felt detached from. She felt as if she had no control over what was happening to her. She was now three months pregnant exactly to the day and it was only a few days until September. The time was just flying by, she thought. August had been especially hot this year, and she was willing the weather to become a little cooler. It would still remain hot compared to the Northern states, as it was hot almost all year round in Florida. Courtney had now got a good rapport going with her stepdaughters, and she had become accustomed to them sharing her house. Adam was particularly happy at the moment. He was working hard, but he had an unusual air about him. He didn't seem nearly as stressed as he had been and he was so excited about the new baby. The twins seemed to be getting on well working at Jennifer's and in her eyes had become much more responsible. Courtney was glad that Alicia was starting to gain her confidence back after the attack, and she didn't seem nearly so distant anymore. She would laugh and joke again now, and would very rarely mention it. She looked at the clock, it was getting on for eight, and the twins still hadn't returned from work. Just as the thought was passing through her mind, she heard a key turn in the lock, closely followed by Alicia's voice.

'Hello, is anybody there?'

'I'm in the kitchen.'

'You'll never guess what's happened at work.' Alicia flung her bag down by the bannister and proceeded into the lounge where she flopped down on the couch in her usual fashion, flicking on the TV with the remote. 'Cool! Springer's on,' she called out.

'What happened then!' Courtney hollered, (she could barely hear Alicia now over the sound of the TV.)

'Turn it down, you'll go deaf!' Courtney had now finished loading the washing machine, and the sound of that now churning round and the sound of the TV together made it impossible to hold a conversation.

She strode into the lounge, and grabbed the remote from her, jabbing the mute button.

'Oh Courtney,' Alicia whined.

'C'mon,' Courtney continued, 'I wanna hear what happened at work.' She sat down opposite her.

'Well,' Alicia had a broad grin on her face, 'do you remember Matt who used to work in the Jamaican restaurant? You know the one that took a shine to Gabrielle.'

'Yes,' Courtney said cautiously.

'He's only Jennifer's boyfriend!' Alicia's eyes were wide, 'can you believe it?' she laughed.

'Really?' Courtney was shocked; 'well there's a turn up.'

Alicia gave Courtney a knowing look. She had a wry smile on her face and Courtney could tell what she was thinking.

'Right, I see,' she said, looking disapprovingly back at Alicia. 'You're not gonna tell me that Gabrielle's gonna get up to something again. You two'll get fired if you try to steal the boss's boyfriend.'

'No it's not like that,' Alicia replied, her expression suddenly changing to a frown. 'She found out this afternoon that we knew him and kind of flipped out over it. It was really weird, she'd been OK up until then.'

'Where's Gabrielle?' Courtney interjected.

'Well we were walking back and we bumped into some friends. We went for a drink - she's still there. I got tired and came back.'

'Well, all I can say is that you two need to be careful, especially Gabrielle. I know what she's like, but I wouldn't worry about it, I expect Jennifer'll be back to normal by tomorrow.'

'Oh yeah, I should think so,' Alicia resolved. 'That was all anyway,' she said, picking up the remote and turning the volume back up.

Courtney sighed, 'yeah and I had a good day too, thanks for asking.' Alicia didn't reply, her gaze was fixed back on the screen.

Gabrielle didn't come home that night.

The next time that Alicia saw her was the following day; she was back with her apron on, back at Jennifer's. News had spread that Jennifer had gone away unexpectedly, and that Matt had taken charge of the café in her absence. It was Gabrielle who had passed the news on to Antonio.

'So where's Matt today then?' Alicia challenged Gabrielle, who was arranging the tables. She wouldn't stop and Alicia was following after her.

'Oh he's gone to get supplies. He should be back this afternoon,' she said indignantly, with her back turned to her sister, not wanting to meet her enquiring gaze.

'Oh right, and just how do you know all this? Antonio's always the first to arrive and he said that Matt hasn't been in yet today - so explain that!' Alicia's tone was becoming increasingly angry. 'You saw him didn't you, last night? That's why you didn't come home, and isn't it just so convenient that Jennifer has suddenly gone away!'

'You can think what you like,' Gabrielle retorted, 'I stayed at Candy's apartment, and that's all I'm gonna say on the matter.'

'Bullshit!' Alicia bellowed. She grabbed her sister's arm and spun her round, snatching the knives and forks out of her hand and slamming them down on the table. 'Candy wasn't even there when I left you.'

'She turned up after you'd gone,' Gabrielle replied, her eyes cast down.

'So did you tell Candy about the waitress job? When can she start? In fact I think I'll call her right now, and ask her myself,' Alicia said sarcastically.

'OK OK, I did see Matt! He was in a state. He'd just got back from taking Jennifer to her friend's and he walked into the bar. We all had a drink, but I swear to you I never stayed with him - I swear it!'

'So where did you stay then?' Alicia persisted.

Gabrielle was becoming more and more agitated; her eyes were filling with tears.

Antonio, hearing the commotion, pulled open the kitchen hatch and leaned through.

'Break it up girls,' he said despairingly, 'we open in ten minutes. This really isn't the place for your arguing,' he leaned back and closed the hatch with a bang.

Alicia glared at her sister who was still hanging her head to avoid eye contact. She maintained her tight grip on Gabrielle's arm and leaned in closer.

'I'm warning you, you better not be sleeping with him,' she then said, in a harsh menacing tone, 'cos if I lose my job because of you Sister, I will *never* forgive you.'

She released her grip on Gabrielle's arm, brushed her apron down, and turned towards the front of the café to finish getting the tables ready for opening.

Gabrielle ran to the restrooms crying.

Matt arrived at the café an hour after they had opened for business. It was unusually busy that day and Alicia didn't have time to contemplate what had happened that morning. She would speak again to Gabrielle when she had finished her shift. Antonio was rushed off his feet that morning as his friend Bernard, who was supposed to have started working in the kitchen that morning, had called in sick.

Gabrielle was quiet the rest of the day, she was very conscious of the fact that her sister was watching her every move, and watching every time Matt went near her - watching the body language, watching for secret looks and smiles. Matt was on edge. He seemed to jump every time anybody spoke to him, and he was constantly watching the door. He was waiting for Jennifer to walk through it; hoping that she wouldn't.

At the end of the daytime shift, Alicia got ready to leave. The café had started to empty, but the evening rush was pending. They would have a couple of hours to prepare and then the second shift would start to arrive. Alicia decided not to work the night shift, as she was still nervous about being out after dark on her own. She was torn, however, as she didn't want to give Gabrielle the opportunity to be alone with Matt either. She envied her sister so much, because she was able to trust men and risk getting close to them. Since Matt had arrived at the café the previous day it had brought all of her memories flooding back again - all the things that she had been trying so hard to forget. The night when her sister stayed with Matt rather than walk home with her; if she hadn't walked home alone she could have forgotten the rape forever, she had been doing so well before.

Alicia walked to the door with her jacket and bag. She was in a dream. There was a strange feeling at the pit of her stomach, an unsettled feeling. She turned, almost in slow motion, and looked long and hard at her sister who was over by the bar talking with Matt - laughing and flirting. She had never seen that in a man's eyes before, the way he was looking at Gabrielle. At that same moment she had another flashback of her attacker's eyes. They were hard, depraved, steely and cold. Matt looked at Gabrielle adoringly; his excitement and anticipation revealed plainly in his affectionate non-threatening eyes. Alicia could feel tears welling up in her own eyes then, and she felt a kind of jealousy that physically hurt her, racking her entire body.
She moved closer to the door; she needed to leave before she was completely overcome with emotion. She felt that all the progress she had made towards her recovery had been completely wiped out. She took a deep breath, and resolved that tomorrow she would try to feel differently, and ignore the flashbacks. She couldn't give up; she had to keep striving to get her true self back.

'Gabrielle,' Alicia called to her sister as she opened the door to the café. 'You take care now.'

Gabrielle looked back at her, 'I will, I'll get Matt to drop me back after closing.'

'Oh one last thing,' Alicia choked back her emotions, 'I'm sorry about earlier.'

She closed the door behind her. Matt and Gabrielle watched as she passed the window and disappeared from view.

Gabrielle let out a big sigh, took off her apron and slumped down into the nearest chair.

'I need a drink,' she breathed. 'Get me a glass of wine Matt.'

'We shouldn't really be drinking on duty,' he said with a knowing smile, 'but what the hell.' He walked over to the chiller cabinet and poured them both a drink.

'True, but we don't open again for another hour and I need it,' she said putting her feet up on the next available chair. 'Where's Antonio?'

'He's gone out for some fresh air,' he replied, as he pulled a chair from the next table to sit next to her.

For a few moments neither of them spoke. Gabrielle felt drained of energy. She was in a dilemma, not knowing what to do about her new situation.

The chemistry between them both was almost electric. She was trying desperately not to feel the way she felt, but the harder she tried, the worse it seemed to get.

After a time of serious contemplation, both of them went to speak at the same time. They laughed, and it broke the tension momentarily.

'What were you going to say?' she said hesitantly.

'No you first,' came his reply.

'Last night, it was wrong. It shouldn't have happened,' she blurted out, and then sat back.

His expression changed. He winced as though in pain, devastated by this sudden and unexpected revelation.

'But why Gaby?' he grasped her hand, and she pulled back from him.

'I can't, I just can't! It's for my sister, it's for Jennifer, it's for me.' She got up from her chair, thrusting it back under the table, and walked to the bar where she stood with her back to him, not wanting him to see the tears in her eyes.

'Gaby, I told you yesterday, I don't love Jennifer. You have to help me, she's crazy! She wants us to live together and I'm afraid Gaby; you promised you'd help me.' He left his chair, and ventured closer to her, his arms outstretched.

'I just can't. I'll lose my job, my sister will lose hers and I don't want to put myself in danger, especially if what you have told me about her is all true.'

Matt touched her shoulder. She struck out behind with her hand, and then hugged herself protectively.

'Gaby, listen to me. I got sucked in by the money. I'm in so deep now, I'm up to my neck in it. She paid for my auto, she's bought my clothes and she's paid for my parents' auto. If she took all that back, my dad would lose his job.' His voice was breaking up; he moved closer to her, catching hold of her arm. She cried out in pain and shook free from his grasp.

'Why should I believe anything you say Matt?' Her tears were flowing freely now. 'When I knew you before, you were with Jennifer, you didn't stay in contact with me after my sister was attacked. You're still with Jennifer now.'

'I was sucked in,' he pleaded, 'I could control her, even though I cared about you so much - I still do, but I was on an ego trip then. Jennifer would give me everything I wanted, but it's different now. I don't want that anymore.' He walked over to the window and stood staring blankly out at the busy street, shifting awkwardly from one foot to the other.

'What do you want then?' she broke the silence.

'I want to be in love, and to be loved,' he replied in a matter of fact tone. 'I want to make my own way in life, with somebody else. I want to make something of myself, not live off handouts.'

'Why have you suddenly changed?' she said pointedly.

'I don't know,' he replied flatly.

Just at that moment, they heard the back door to the kitchen open and then close with a bang.

'Hello!' Antonio sang out from the kitchen. He pulled open the hatch. Gabrielle busied herself arranging the chairs, and Matt quickly moved back over to the bar, where he started unloading the dishwasher and stacking glasses on the shelves.

Gabrielle looked at the clock and gasped, 'Oh God,' she exclaimed 'it's almost seven.' She looked back at Matt.

'We'll talk again later?' he said earnestly. 'Please.'

'We'll see,' she said coolly.

As night fell, the time passed quickly. It was almost a blur, and by midnight they had finally managed to get all the customers to leave. It was always hard to get some of the regulars to go as they would keep ordering more and more drinks, and just sit in a haze of cigarette smoke, conversing with their friends.

Sadie and her boyfriend Dan were the last to go. Sadie being the much drunker of the two. When their cab finally arrived, Dan had to help her into it as she was now incapable of walking by herself.

'See you tomorrow,' Gabrielle sang out after them.

The café was now empty; Antonio had already left. It was pitch black outside, and there was an eerie stillness. Matt had left the back door ajar, to let in some fresh air. He stood in the doorway, listening to the sound of the crickets for a moment. The air was quite humid, and although it was cooler than it had been, it was still quite oppressive.

Gabrielle had packed and was ready to go. 'Can I have a lift home then?' she asked.

'Please Gaby, can we just have one drink before we go? I really don't want to be alone tonight.' He moved from the kitchen back to the bar and began pouring the drinks, before she had a chance to say no.

She put her bag back down, resigned to the fact that she wasn't going anywhere at that moment, and pulled up a chair to sit down.

'I'm not sure if Sadie is going to take the job in here,' she mused, 'I don't really think she's up to it anyway.'

'Well,' he replied carrying the drinks over to the table, 'I think we can cope now I'm working here. So what about our conversation earlier?' he then said changing the subject.

'What about it?' she retorted.

102

'I know what I want now,' he continued, 'let's just get out of this place. We can start again, get away from Jennifer, just me and you.'

'You've got a nerve!' she snapped. 'You're assuming that I want to be with you and I might not want to be.'

'But what about last night?' he interjected. 'You wanted me then.'

'Have you never heard of a one night stand?' she hollered, and with that she got her bag to leave. He quickly sprang to his feet, and grabbed his jacket.

'It's all right I'll walk!' she bellowed back.

He ran to the door to block her exit. She began to beat his chest and kick out at him, but he was stronger than her. She didn't want to look into his eyes, because she knew she would lose her self-control again.

He managed to restrain her and gripped her in a hard embrace. She was crying and he cradled her in his arms raining kisses on her head and forehead. She couldn't fight him anymore. She didn't want to.

'Look at me Gaby,' he said softly.

'I can't,' she sobbed.

He caressed the side of her face, and gently tilted her head up so that her eyes would meet his. The moment that they did, she felt an intoxicating cocktail of emotions surge through her body. As Gabrielle looked into his eyes, she felt that she would die; she had never experienced such intense feelings for anyone before.

The back door creaked open, slowly, very slowly. The two lovers were unaware of anything around them, only each other.

As Jennifer stepped into the kitchen, her wild eyes looking around furtively in the darkness, she didn't hear anything at first. She was muttering to herself, her hair was dishevelled. She was looking for her car keys, and then she saw them over by the hatch, on the hook.

As she ventured across the kitchen towards the keys, she heard a noise coming from the front of the café - the sound of whispering voices; she had assumed that it would be empty by now as it was past closing. Things had not gone very well at

Miranda's; she would drive to Matt's house and wait for him to return. She had lost control there too - she couldn't be away from Matt, she had to come back. The realisation of what she was hearing suddenly struck her, and she began to hyper ventilate as this new wave of panic gripped her tighter and tighter. Something then snapped in her brain, like someone flicking a switch. As she opened the door a crack, she saw that her worst fear had been realised. Silhouetted in the moonlight she saw them. Matt and Gabrielle were unaware that they were no longer alone, their kissing was now so passionate. She watched heartbroken from the doorway as he began to unbutton Gabreille's blouse.

Jennifer went straight to the kitchen drawer, without hesitation, and pulled out the largest butcher's knife that she could find. All rational thought had now been banished from her mind, and like a thing possessed, she swiped at her hair, and waited a few moments. Her breathing was erratic. She stared at the knife, and then brought it down sharply on her arm. Blood spurted from the wound. She was ready.

She moved towards the door, raised her right leg, and kicked it wide open, roaring like an animal in its death throes.

She surged towards Matt. She raised the knife and plunged it deep into his back. She twisted it and gouged at his insides, cracking his ribs. He screamed in pain, and terror. Blood poured from him. Jennifer's tortured face looked on, shocked at what she had done, but her mouth had curled into a faint smile. Gabrielle fell to her knees screaming; she was covered in Matt's blood. Jennifer pulled the knife from his back. He was still alive, his whole body was convulsing, and he was groaning in agony.

'Please Jennifer, please!' Gabrielle cried. 'Don't, please don't kill him, please - oh God help us!'

She put her hands out to protect him, but as the knife came down again and again, in a stabbing frenzy, they too were caught by the savage blade.

She screamed over and over.

Jennifer did not stop, and would not stop. Matt was no longer breathing, and the pain that Gabrielle was in was so excruciating that she willed her death to take place quickly. She knew she would not get out of there alive. She felt as if she was fading fast; she didn't have time, to say goodbye. This was so unfair; it wasn't her time.

She was lying on top of Matt's still form, awaiting her execution. Moments seemed like hours, but it had all happened in a few seconds. She had already been stabbed five times.

'Die bitch die!' Jennifer screeched, raising the knife for the final blow.

With a searing pain that shot straight through her chest, Gabrielle finally left that place. Everything was now black.

Jennifer relished the unmistakable stench of death that filled her nostrils, and as the tip of her tongue caressed her lips she could taste it, so warm and sweet. She gazed feverishly at the two corpses that lay in an untidy pile on the blood soaked floor. She had destroyed her envy, her hatred and her own self-doubt. It was like a large dose of morphine had suddenly been injected into her tired veins. They couldn't hurt her anymore.

She could hear strange voices in her head; she could hear them calling her name. She dropped the knife where she stood; it clattered to the ground and slid across the wood panelled floor, coming to rest against Gabrielle's lifeless body.

She walked in a daze back to the corner of the room, and slid her back down the wall. She pulled her knees up protectively to her chest, and there she stayed staring at the bodies, waiting for one of them to move. She hummed a tune to herself, and as she rocked backwards and forwards hugging her knees, an uncontrollable grin slowly spread across her blood spattered face.

Chapter 6

The blackest of nights shrouded Bay View Grove. The Buchanans slept on; unaware of the horror and grief that was about to envelop them. There was not a sound. The road was still, the air stagnant and humid. The time was 2 a.m. Sleep, fitful sleep, Alicia's dreams were disturbed. Her sleep was not restful as she lay in her bed. Her covers had been tossed on the floor and she murmured in her sleep, her head rolling from left to right. She breathed deeply. Shadows danced across her room. The drapes moved slightly by the open window, but this only served to let in more warm air. Beads of perspiration sprang up on her forehead; she batted at them with her flailing arms.

'NO!' she cried, her eyes suddenly wide open. She sat bolt upright and looked nervously round to her right - there was nobody there. She was sure that she had felt somebody prodding her arm hard as if they had been trying to wake her. Panic gripped her as her gaze darted around the room. She had never felt so afraid. 'Gabrielle!' she called out. She suddenly thought of her sister, and a sick feeling welled up in her stomach. Something was wrong, something was very wrong. Although Gabrielle's room was across the corridor, Alicia knew that she wasn't home. She didn't know how she knew, she just did. She sprang from the bed and ran to the door turning the handle slowly. Her heart was beating so fast that she felt faint. She could hear it thudding in her chest. She swallowed nervously as she cautiously opened the door. It creaked slightly, making her jump. She walked to Gabrielle's door and, without bothering to knock, opened it and snapped on the light. Her bed was empty. She was not surprised; she was hoping beyond hope that her premonition had been wrong. She wouldn't even have cared if she'd woken her sister up, and had been given a mouthful of abuse; at least then, she could have gone back to bed and drifted back into a peaceful sleep. Her eyes were still stinging from the sudden onslaught of artificial light. She squinted and rubbed at them, hoping that maybe this had all been a dream and when she woke up her sister would be there. She pinched herself. It hurt - she was awake all right. She turned back, dejected, and left the room, turning off the light and plunging everything back into darkness again. She felt her way along the corridor, and almost fell through her open door. She staggered back to bed, picked up her bedclothes and lay down, resolving to try to get some sleep, as she had to be up again for work at seven.

She started to sink back into sleep, when suddenly, again, she felt somebody prodding her arm. It was so real this time that she couldn't ignore it, but she thought it must be a waking dream. She jerked her arm away from the side of the bed and pulled it under the covers. Her heart was racing now. She looked around, and still no-one was there. Her eyes had quickly become accustomed to the darkness - she blinked a few times to make sure she wasn't dreaming. Suddenly without warning a large shadow darted across the room, the drapes billowed, and a freak gust of wind blew her photo frame off the dresser. It flew through the air, hitting the wall. The glass in the frame smashed and it fell to the ground. She shrieked in horror and leapt from her bed fumbling for the light switch - finding it at last. The darkness now gone, she paused for a moment, unable to believe what had just happened to her. Her hand was shaking as she ran it falteringly through her hair, which was now knotted and dishevelled from her troubled and disturbed nights sleep.

She walked unsteadily over to the broken picture frame. Broken glass lay all around. She was barefoot, and due to her tiredness and confusion she stepped on a piece of the glass. She cried out in pain and fell to the ground, checking the sole of her foot. She found the glass had not punctured the skin, just grazed it, but she was shaken. She reached forward to salvage what was left of the photo frame; she carefully lifted it up, as it had landed face down. As she looked at the photo of herself and her sister, smiling radiantly at their graduation, tears fell uncontrollably from her eyes. The broken glass had torn the photo, obliterating Gabrielle's face. It was almost unrecognisable. *Oh Gabrielle, what has happened to you? Where are you?* She struggled to her feet, overcome with emotion. She felt exhausted, but she couldn't sleep, she was too afraid. She cleared up the glass, and wrapped it in old newspaper, throwing it all away, including the frame. She kept the photo, and tried to stick it back together.

She returned to her bed, taking the photo with her, cradled it in her arms, and wept. *You're with Matt, I know. I just have to accept it, it's not my business. I can't keep on blaming you and him for what happened to me.* She lay staring at the ceiling, her eyes blurred with tears. She could barely see but she kept the light on. She was too afraid to switch it off again. She turned on her side, and still clutching the photograph to her chest, she eventually drifted off to sleep.

Morning came abruptly. Alicia opened her eyes to the shrill sound of her alarm clock. She rose from her bed still clutching the photo - her mind a blank. She carefully laid the photo down on her bedside table. The previous night didn't seem real, more like a dream, although she knew deep down that all of those things had really happened. She had to try to calm herself, ready for the day. She would see Gabrielle at the café and she would try to forget her jealousy - move on, give her a hug, and then that night maybe sleep soundly again. She showered and dressed. Downstairs in the kitchen Courtney had put the kettle on ready for their morning coffee. She was also due at work in a short while.

'Morning sleepy head,' Courtney smiled as Alicia wandered aimlessly into the kitchen. Courtney thought that she looked spaced out, her eyes were staring ahead of her blankly. She turned and sat down at the breakfast bar. 'Are you all right Alicia?' she asked.

'I'm OK I suppose,' she said gloomily, 'but Gabrielle didn't come home *again* last night.'

'Where was she then?' Courtney said taking a sip from her mug.

'With Matt I think,' Alicia replied flatly.

'Oh,' was all that Courtney said. There was nothing that she could do. Gabrielle was nineteen and old enough to make her own decisions and choices, but she knew that it was hard for

Alicia. She didn't need to spell it out, it would only make Alicia's pain worse.

The two ate breakfast together. Neither really spoke after that, except when it was time to leave.

'I'll give you a lift if you want,' Courtney said in an upbeat tone, trying to cheer Alicia.

'It's OK thanks, I'll walk, I need some time to think, and I'm gonna be early anyway.' She gave her stepmother a kiss on the cheek, 'thanks anyway,' she said forcing a smile.

The walk to Jennifer's usually took about fifteen minutes. It was four streets away, in the busier end of town. Jennifer's café, however, was at the quieter end of the street. It was on the same side as all the other restaurants and bars but directly to its right was a discount designer store, and on the other side of the road was another cluster of discount and souvenir stores, which were always closed at night. Alicia chain smoked on the way to work that day. She always smoked on the way to work, but today she was lighting one after the other without really realising it. This was now the second time she had had to walk to work by herself. She and Gabrielle usually walked together and she realised how much she missed her. The journey seemed to take twice as long by herself. She was thinking, trying to sort her head out, trying desperately to forget about the previous night. She felt agitated, and something just wasn't quite right. She concluded that it must just be in her mind. After all, everything had seemed normal at breakfast - the same as it was every morning, apart from the fact that she had been particularly quiet that morning. Courtney hadn't spoken to her much either, but then she never did if Alicia was in a quiet mood. *Mornings are never the best time to have a conversation. Most people don't want to talk when they've just got up. Gabrielle always does, but then she's weird like that.*

Alicia rounded the final corner and turned into the main street. She was now just five minutes away from work. The road was unusually busy that morning and there seemed to be more people than usual up and about. It was only quarter to eight in the morning and Sizzling Jo's was already packed; there was a constant stream of vehicles, including coaches, pulling in and out of the car park. It was mostly holidaymakers that went there at this time and it was for a hearty breakfast that would set them up for the day. They could eat as much as they liked for a fixed rate and then leave, their stomachs groaning with food. They would then set off to that day's designated theme park, content that they wouldn't have to interrupt their day again to stop for any more food. Alicia glanced up the road. She could just make out the discount store next to Jennifer's. Jennifer's was set back slightly from the main road and it had tables and chairs out front. She noticed that there was a large group of people standing around in the street, right near the entrance.

This was very strange. She frowned and looked at her watch. *It doesn't open for another hour, what on earth are those people doing?* It didn't occur to her at that moment that anything could possibly be wrong. Just as she was puzzling about the sudden increase in customers waiting outside her place of work, two police cars sped past, sirens wailing. *NO, It can't be!* Alicia saw them screech to a halt next to the crowd of people. Tears sprang into her eyes. 'NO!' she cried out audibly this time. She began to run, barely able to see where she was going, her heart thumping in her chest. Her hair streamed out behind her. People called out after her and a man tried to block her way. She pushed past him, 'What's wrong, can I help you Miss?' he called out, but she didn't stop.

'Gabrielle!' she screamed. She was now just by the crowd. She burst through them and stopped dead.

Police patrolmen guarded the entrance; they had cordoned off the whole of Jennifer's. Suddenly time stood still. Alicia could see officers inside. There was a canvas shield covering something near the window. Men in white moved silently. Flashes went off as photographs were being taken. She ran to the door screaming. She was held back by one of the officers - everything was a blur. She kicked out and flailed her arms. 'My God!' the police officer exclaimed, visibly shaken, 'I thought I had just seen a ghost! Get her away from here, she mustn't see!' His words were suddenly curtailed by the booming voice of another officer. 'Can people please move on, you are not helping. Unless you are a witness or a relative, please can you clear the sidewalk.'

Alicia watched the young patrolman as he desperately tried to disperse the crowd of onlookers. It was as if everything and everybody around her was moving in slow motion. Then he came towards her.

'I've got a relative here Brad. Can you take her?' the officer restraining Alicia handed her over to the young patrolman, who put a protective arm around her shoulder, and led her back to the road side.

She stared blankly at him, she couldn't speak; she didn't want to believe that her worst fears were true. How could they be? Who could have done this? How did she know that it was Gabrielle? The patrolman turned her around gently to face him, putting his hands on her shoulders, and looking straight into her eyes. He took a deep breath, as if he didn't want to ask what he was about to ask her, and then he did.

'Miss, do you have a twin sister?'

'Yes,' she said falteringly. Terrifying realisation, confirmation. She felt a pain in her chest so great it was as if her heart had been ripped out. The patrolman could feel her going; he tried to hold her up but her legs had collapsed beneath her. She fell to her knees sobbing. She clutched at the police officer's legs for support and held on tightly her face pressed against his uniform. It did nothing to muffle her cries. She cried as she had never done before. The police officer bent down and with all his strength hauled her to her feet. She was like a dead weight and had begun to go into shock - she was shaking uncontrollably.

'I need assistance,' he called out to one of his colleagues. 'Get me another ambulance right away.'

He helped her over to his patrol vehicle and sat her down on the back seat, 'I'm so sorry,' he said, his voice breaking with emotion. 'The moment I saw you I knew you had to be her sister. I was the first to arrive on the scene.' He looked away, obviously moved by the horror he had witnessed, and visibly shaken, 'I was the one who found them,' he stammered. 'I'll have to ask you some questions Miss, but not now, when you're feeling better. Could you just tell me your name for now, and where you live?'

Alicia was now in a severe state of shock and just stared blankly ahead of her, the tears still falling from her eyes in a never ending stream. She was not really aware of anything around her. Everything was just a blur.

'Alicia Buchanan,' she murmured, '240 Bay View Grove.'

'Great, that's just great Alicia, well done.' He then relayed the information to one of his colleagues, using his radio.

He noticed outside two stretchers being carried into the café; he knew what was coming next. Alicia didn't appear to be registering anything visually, but he pulled her away from the window anyway. He drew her to him and covered her eyes with his hand. Alicia was now too weak to resist. He wanted to spare her the pain of seeing what was about to happen. The detectives at the murder scene were releasing the bodies to the ambulance men for transportation to the hospital mortuary; both Gabrielle and Matt had been certified dead at the scene. The stretchers were brought out through the front door of Jennifer's, each carrying a black body bag. As they went past the patrol vehicle window, the patrolman sitting with Alicia also looked away. Although he had seen death before, he had never in his career been witness to such a ferocious and bloody murder scene - it had shocked him to the core.

As the ambulance pulled away, another pulled up in its place. A grim faced ambulance man opened the patrol car door and helped Alicia out.

'This is Alicia. She's one of the victim's sister,' the patrolman said as he handed her over. 'Take good care of her. It was a tragic scene, worst I've ever...' he didn't finish his sentence, shaking his head in disbelief, he turned and walked away.

Antonio groaned as the nurse placed the line in his arm, which was supplying strong painkillers and sedatives to his injured body.

'Antonio, can you hear me?' the young nurse leaned over him. His eyes were open but he just stared blankly at the ceiling. He had a stab wound to the fleshy upper half of his right arm, which had not penetrated too deeply. It had torn mostly muscle - the bone had stayed intact. This had already been stitched and dressed. He also had a surface wound down the right side of his face where his assailant had slashed at his face but had only inflicted a minor wound.

He was going to pull through, but it was the more serious problem of the shock and distress that this had caused that would take longer to heal.

Antonio didn't have any family members living near by who could be reached. It had been difficult in the first instance for the doctors to get any information out of him, as he was too distressed on arrival at the hospital to say anything about what had happened. When he could bring himself to talk, his story began to unfold. He had raised the alarm himself, as he had managed to escape from the café before he too was killed. He had run as fast as he could back down Bermuda Avenue, and into a 24hour gas filling station, where the kiosk assistant called an ambulance. He himself had called the police on his mobile phone as he ran bleeding down the road. He was reported to have just said 'Help me I'm stabbed! Bermuda Avenue, Jennifer's café … she's gone crazy. She tried to kill me, come quickly!' and then the phone had gone dead. One thing that was evident from this was that he had not seen the full scale of the carnage. He had entered through the back door, which had been left slightly ajar, and had surprised his assailant, who had burst into the kitchen upon hearing him enter. She'd then picked up another knife and slashed at him with it repeatedly. He must have then struck her and knocked her out cold, because when the young patrolman then gained entry to the café through the rear, he had found Jennifer lying unconscious on the floor. The knife she had used to stab Antonio was lying beside her.

A doctor passing in the corridor outside stopped and leaned into the private room where Antonio lay.

'It's a real tragedy,' he said to the nurse who was tending to him. She nodded and lowered her gaze. Sara had worked at the hospital for five years. She had never experienced anything like this before either. In Orlando, there was crime and people did own guns. Tourists were occasionally robbed but the scale of this crime had shocked everybody. The seeming senselessness of it, and the waste of young lives, a murderess, who had killed two innocent people. She had cut them to pieces. She had wanted them to suffer. She was found covered in their blood mixed with her own. The police had surmised that the wound on her arm was self-inflicted, as the two victims had been unarmed. Everybody was wondering what could possibly make anybody commit such a bloody murder? Sara looked up at the doctor; he too was fairly new to the hospital and the area.

'Mike,' Sara called after the doctor as he turned to walk away.

'Yes?' He turned back.

'You do know who the victims are don't you?'

She moved away from Antonio's bedside so as not to distress him further.

'I know,' he breathed. 'Adam Buchanan's daughter, and a Matthew Scott.'

'I want to see her!' Adam cried as he was being ushered temporarily into a private room. Courtney was at his side. She was trying to stay strong for her husband but she was finding it impossible, when she had first heard the news, she hadn't believed it, she didn't want to believe it.

Alicia was already in the hospital and the doctor had said that she was under heavy sedation. They could go and sit with her if they wanted to, but Adam kept insisting that he must see Gabrielle's body first. Peter then appeared in the doorway. He was one of Adam's closest friends at the hospital - a fellow doctor.

He walked cautiously over to Adam, his expression grave, then he hugged him.

'Words can't express how sorry I am Adam. I don't know what to say. There's really nothing I can say.' His voice began to break, 'I can't believe something this terrible could happen. If there's anything I can do?'

'Let me see her,' Adam said again, his voice hoarse from crying. 'I need to see her.'

'Adam,' Peter put his arm around his shoulders, 'she was horribly injured. I just don't think you should be putting yourself through this.'

'I think that's for me to decide!' Adam snapped back. 'C'mon Peter, I work here for Christ's sake! I've seen every sight there is to see.'

'I know,' Peter replied softly, 'but it's your daughter, it's different when it's your own flesh and blood.'

'Well I think that's for me to decide, not you.' He turned to Courtney, who was crying again.

'I need to be with you then,' she insisted.

'Courtney,' he clasped her hands, his eyes full of pain, and blurred with tears. 'Are you sure?'

'Yes,' came her reply.

Peter relented, realising that there was no stopping Adam. They didn't have the authority to prevent him anyway.

'I'll take him,' Peter said.

He led them down the hospital corridor.

'The forensic pathologist wants to do an autopsy Adam,' he then said in a matter of fact tone.

'Well they're not going to!' Adam shouted back. 'We already know she was stabbed to death. Is it really necessary? They already caught the mad bitch that did this, I don't want her mutilated any more.'

'Well it's up to you,' Peter replied, 'you do have the right to refuse.'

The walk down the hospital corridor to the mortuary seemed to go on forever - the stark white walls, relieved by an occasional picture, the bare clinical floors. It could have been the best decorated hospital in America, but it would still at that moment have been the most desolate and cheerless place on earth. Not a sound could be heard as the group proceeded slowly forward; it was as though they were in the funeral procession already. Courtney held on tight to Adam's hand. She was afraid, terribly afraid, of what she was going to see, but she felt that she had to remain strong. She needed to hold herself together both for Alicia and for her unborn baby's sake.

Courtney saw the sign for the mortuary. She took a deep breath. She didn't want to breathe when she was in the mortuary - all that death around her. She didn't think she would be able to stay in there long, she just hoped that she didn't pass out.

As they neared the door they saw two men leaving the room. Courtney wondered if they were detectives. There was a high police presence at the hospital as Jennifer was also there being treated for her injuries.

It didn't seem fair. Why was she being treated at all, Courtney thought, when she had butchered her stepdaughter and Matt, and attempted to kill Antonio? Surely she should just be left to rot.

They turned and entered the room. It was not the usual place that relatives viewed their loved ones, which was in the chapel of rest, but Gabrielle had not been taken there yet. Adam and Peter were the first to enter the room. The two other doctor friends who had been comforting the couple, waited outside. Courtney hesitated, took one last deep breath and followed them into the room. The room itself was very large. There were six tables and a dozen or so mortuary technicians working in there - all in white coats. They were talking loudly. It was very formal, but not the kind of situation Courtney had expected. She had thought that she would walk in to find a very sombre atmosphere, but it wasn't. It was clinical, but to these people it was just their job. They didn't know the people whose bodies they were working on. Adam was ushered over to an adjoining room, which had along the far wall what looked like a large grey rack of filing cabinet drawers. She realised immediately what they contained and turned away quickly, not wanting to see any more.

She followed Adam and Peter over to the table where the pathologist stood; the body was covered in a white sheet. Courtney could feel the tears welling up again, and had to fight to control herself.

'John,' Adam said. 'This is her isn't it?'

'Yes,' came the pathologist's grave reply, 'it is I'm afraid. Now are you absolutely sure you want to go through with this?'

'Yes, I have to,' Adam replied, his eyes filling with tears.

'Now, Adam,' the pathologist continued, 'her face has not been injured at all, apart from an impact bruise on the side of her forehead, which was caused as she fell. This is the only saving feature I'm afraid. I advise you not to look at the rest of her body. She's horribly injured, you really mustn't.'

'John, before we continue,' Adam interjected, 'I'm not going to allow a post mortem. I will not have it. The police have all the information they need. They have taken fingerprints and photographs at the scene - it is *not* necessary.'

'As you wish,' the pathologist replied, 'it may be useful for further investigation, but we cannot force you.'

'Well I am saying categorically, that she is not to be touched, other than to transport her to the chapel of rest at the funeral parlour. We will be making the funeral arrangements ourselves.'

'The coroner should be satisfied with the information we have,' the pathologist replied nodding his head in agreement. 'Don't worry Adam, as a friend I will see to it that all your wishes are carried out.'

The pathologist leaned over the table, and took the top corners of the sheet between his thumb and index finger on either side. 'Are you OK?' he asked again.

'Yes, yes,' Adam stammered.

He slowly pulled the sheet down to shoulder level. Courtney gasped and clasped her hand over her mouth from the initial shock of the realisation that it was her; it was Gabrielle.

Even in death, Courtney thought, she still looked beautiful. There was no blood on her face. Her hair had flecks of red intermingled in it, but the gold shone through. She reached forward and stroked her long, flowing hair. The colour had gone from her face and lips, but it was just as if she was in a deep sleep. She looked like a waxwork model, Courtney thought. The essence of her had gone. The thing that made her who she was wasn't there anymore. Adam crumpled as he stood leaning over her, his tears falling down on the white sheet. He just kept on saying 'no, no!' over and over again. Courtney gripped his hand hard. Nobody spoke. The emotion of it all was too great. It was then that he began to sob. He lay his head down beside his dead daughter's and willed her to wake up. Courtney embraced him and cried with him.

'Please Gabrielle,' he pleaded, 'please come back, please! I love you.'

Peter could see that his friend was starting to lose control. The pathologist nodded to him and he helped Adam to stand back up and led him out of the room, with Courtney still clutching at his hand.

The pathologist covered Gabrielle again with the sheet, and two of the technicians came over to wheel the body back to its temporary resting place in the other room.

Peter led them back to the private room that they had been in before, where they could gather their thoughts and decide what they were going to do next. Adam's head was pounding. He couldn't think straight. Such grief had come over him that he could barely stand. He needed time to think, even though, he didn't want to have to be going through this at all. It was too difficult to comprehend everything that had happened. Yesterday his life had been perfect. He was happy, looking forward to his wife having their first baby and now his life had suddenly fallen apart. As Courtney and Adam clung to each other, Peter left them alone for a while, with the excuse that he was going to fetch coffee.

'Why has this happened to us? Why?' Adam sobbed as his wife cradled him in her arms.

'I don't believe in God,' he continued, 'there can't be one, because if there was, he wouldn't have allowed this to happen, and if there is one then he must be a complete bastard!'

'Adam,' Courtney hugged him tighter, 'I don't know why either my darling. We will never know will we? We just have to be strong for Alicia. She's left on her own now and we're all she's got.'

'But I can't be strong!' he cried. 'How can I be? My daughter's dead! What's the point, I might as well be dead myself.'

'But your other daughter isn't dead.' Courtney wiped the tears away from his eyes. 'Look at me,' she gazed into his haunted eyes. 'We will get through this, I promise. We have to fight back, that's what Gabrielle would do. She was strong, she always stood up for herself, and that's what we will do. Stand up for our family. I'm not going to let this tear us apart.'

Her voice was firm, and she meant what she said. She was holding on by a thread to everything she held dear. Her life too was falling apart around her ears, but she couldn't go to pieces as well. One of them had to stay strong. She was surprised by her new found inner strength. She felt she was discovering a new part of herself that she didn't know was there, a strong determined side of her that had never been there in the past. Then she had always had to turn to pills, drink and cigarettes to retain her sanity. She had only really begun to discover the strong side of her character since Alicia and Gabrielle had first moved into the house. Then she got pregnant. It was the baby she was being strong for - she couldn't think of anything else.

Jennifer's eyes rolled vacantly from side to side. She was sprawled on the hospital bed, not moving or speaking. She was under armed guard in a private wing of the same hospital; she was secured to her bed with straps, to prevent her from leaving the room - not that she could have, as she was heavily sedated and incoherent. The detectives had been in to interview her; she didn't answer any of their questions. When asked if she had murdered Gabrielle and Matt, Detective Owens stated in his report that she had just smiled faintly, but no words had issued from her lips. She had just let out the occasional gurgling sound. It was obvious to all the doctors that had seen her that she had severe psychosis, and they didn't know if she would ever recover. The detectives would have to glean their evidence from forensics, which was almost certain to prove conclusive, as only her fingerprints would be found on the murder weapon. The fingerprinting and other forensic evidence was going through fast track processing as it was a murder enquiry, and they expected the results within a couple of days. They would have to then gain the permission of the courts for Jennifer to be moved to a secure prison hospital for further psychological analysis. The doctors did not think at this early stage that she would be fit to stand trial, as they didn't expect her condition to improve. Her parents had been informed and her father was due at the hospital that afternoon. Her mother, when told what had happened, showed no interest and certainly wasn't prepared to visit her daughter in the hospital, 'I've washed my hands of that girl' was what she had said.

Peter returned to the room with a tray of coffee, closely followed by Adam and Courtney's closest friends and neighbours, Liza and Grant. Both also worked at the hospital. Liza was holding a bouquet of flowers.

'I'll leave you all to it,' Peter said placing the tray down in front of them.

'Oh Adam, Courtney,' Liza exclaimed, as she walked through the door. 'I am so, so sorry, for you. I don't know what to say.'

'Nobody does,' Adam replied flippantly.

'Thank you for coming Liza, Grant,' Courtney quickly interrupted. 'I know it's your day off.'

'I brought the flowers for Alicia. She's here isn't she? She's all right, that's the main thing.' Liza was flustered. It was very awkward and the room was highly charged with emotion.

'I'm going to miss her,' Liza continued, 'it won't be the same without the two of them.'

With that she broke down. Courtney also began to cry, and they hugged one another. It was all that they could do. Grant didn't know what to say. He just sat ashen faced, obviously deeply affected by what had happened, but unable to express his feelings in words.

After a time Liza picked up the flowers and asked if it would be all right to go to see Alicia.

'Oh God Alicia,' Courtney exclaimed, we haven't seen her ourselves yet! We've been too upset. We went to see Gabrielle's body and we just, well, we just don't know what to say to her.'

'Then don't say anything,' Liza soothed, through her own tears, 'just sit with her, and hold her hand. That's all you need to do. You're all hurting, just try to be there for each other.'

She took a handful of tissues out of the box on the coffee table, and dabbed at her best friend's eyes. 'We'll be there for you, won't we Grant,' she then said. Grant just nodded. 'Don't need to worry now, c'mon.'

Liza and Grant had proved just the tonic to give them the courage to move on out of that room and face their next hurdle. Courtney didn't feel so alone anymore. The fact that their friends had found the strength to face them under these circumstances meant everything to her. They truly were no longer on their own. As they left the room, Peter, who had been pacing outside deep in thought, suddenly started, having been jolted back to reality.

'Do you know where Alicia is?' Adam asked.

'Yes,' Peter replied earnestly, 'she's in one of the private rooms, over the other side, just outside the children's unit.'

'Thank you Peter, for everything,' Adam said, genuinely touched by his friend's display of solidarity and concern.

'Anything you need, just call me,' Peter then said.

Courtney and Adam entered the room together; Liza and Grant waited on some seats out in the corridor. A nurse sat by Alicia's bedside. She was a kindly faced, older nurse and as the couple entered she turned and smiled at them.

'You must be her parents,' she said beaming back at them. 'Hold on one moment, I'll just have a quick talk with you outside. We'll be back in a moment Alicia,' she continued in her upbeat tone.

Once outside her expression fell. 'I'm terribly sorry Dr and Mrs Buchanan. I know about your other daughter. I didn't want to say this in front of Alicia, we want to try to keep her from getting too distressed, so it's probably better if we don't mention anything until she's stronger.' She gazed at them intently, willing them to agree with her.

'Of course,' Adam smiled.

'Oh good,' the nurse smiled back, 'it's going to be very hard for her. She's been through probably the worst emotional trauma anyone can go through. She's a strong girl though, she'll pull through just fine.' She looked protectively back over her shoulder to check her patient.

'She's been on strong sedatives since she got here. She's not really aware of anything at the moment,' the nurse continued. Courtney noticed her name was Barbara.

'Sorry, my name is Barbara.' She had obviously seen Courtney glancing down at her badge.

'Now Dr Buchanan,'

'Call me Adam,' he said.

Barbara blushed at this, as she had always called him Dr Buchanan before. However, she relented all the same.

'Adam and?' she fixed her gaze on Courtney,

'Courtney,' she smiled back.

'Great. Adam and Courtney,' Barbara smiled broadly. 'Now,' she clapped her hands together, as if she was about to say something important.

'Right then, Alicia's fine. She is in shock but has no other physical problems.' Barbara spoke with her hands, as if she was compiling a list on her palm. 'Now she's not due anymore medication for another hour or so, so for now all she needs is plenty of TLC. That's what I've been giving her since she arrived - so I'll hand over to you both now. If you need me just ring the buzzer. She's drifting in and out of sleep, so just talk softly to her, and hold her hand. Barbara was so full of life that she inspired confidence in Courtney. Her positive tone and smiling face had started to help her to feel a little brighter, and seeing Alicia and hearing that she was going to be all right made a world of difference. Adam squeezed Courtney's hand and smiled back at her. She thought that he must have been feeling the same way.

Courtney and Adam walked hesitantly back into the small room. It had a large window facing out over the hospital's garden. The sun streamed in illuminating the pastel yellow walls. There was a small chair either side of the bed, so they sat down carefully, trying not to make any sound, as Alicia was still sleeping.

Courtney looked up at Adam who was looking down at his daughter. He was troubled. He couldn't speak as he didn't know what to say. Courtney found it hard to comprehend that half an hour ago they were looking at Alicia's identical twin. Only she was dead and this one was alive - but they still looked the same. It was unspeakable. She didn't know what to say either. They knew that Alicia had arrived at work that same morning only to find the horror of a murder scene. She subsequently discovered that her own sister was lying dead inside their place of work behind a canvas screen. Courtney thought about that morning and wished that she had insisted on taking Alicia to work. At least then she could have been with her. She wished that Alicia hadn't gone to work at all. She wished that the police had come to their house, that they could have been a family together supporting one another. She just wished that everything was different, that she could wake up and it would be yesterday again, that they had known what was going to happen, and they could have stopped it. Everything would still be the same. *Why did this have to happen?* Tears sprang into her eyes again and fell silently down her cheeks - a river of tears that just kept falling and falling. *Will they ever end? Will I ever feel normal again? Will we be able to start again, or will we just shrivel up and die too. I didn't think this kind of thing really happened to people, not in real life?*

Adam's pain was tangible. When somebody is hurting you want to make it better. When a child falls and grazes its knee and it cries, you can patch up the knee. You can kiss them and the hurt goes away. Courtney knew that there was nothing she could do to make it better. She felt helpless, useless and desolate.

It was still only morning. This had been the longest morning of her life. She felt so guilty that Alicia had been left on her own. They had failed her when she needed them most.

'Alicia, honey,' Adam said softly, stroking the top of her hand. She had a line coming out of her arm and the monitor beside her bed just beeped. She didn't stir.

Adam swiped at his eyes, trying to stem the flow of tears. They sat in silence for the next two hours, just looking at her, holding her hand. Liza and Grant crept into the room after a while, but they didn't stay long - it was a private moment for the family. Liza arranged the flowers in a vase. They hugged their friends and left. After a while Barbara came back into the room and changed Alicia's drip feed.

'I think you both could use some rest,' she said quietly. 'I'll take good care of her for you.'

'We can't leave her again,' Courtney said resolutely.

'My dear,' Barbara said catching hold of Courtney's free hand, 'I really think you need to go home, for a while at least. It's up to you, but I will call you I promise as soon as she wakes up.'

Adam nodded slowly; he stood up, leaned over the bed, and placed a gentle kiss on Alicia's forehead.

Courtney took one last look at her, and then turned and left the room silently.

Courtney and Adam were driven home by one of the other doctors who had just finished his shift. Nobody spoke during the journey.

As Adam opened the front door and entered, an eerie stillness filled the house. The same house that had been so full of life that morning had changed. It too seemed to be in mourning. Courtney didn't know what to do with herself; they stood silently in the hallway for a moment, holding hands. So much had happened that day, and it still wasn't over, it wasn't anywhere near over, it was only three o'clock in the afternoon. Courtney walked into the lounge. She looked out of the window into the garden, remembering the number of times she had looked out of that same window around this time to see the twins lying down by the pool together. *Sarah.*

'My God Adam, I just thought about Sarah.' Courtney whirled around and stared back at Adam who was still standing motionless in the hallway.

'What about her?' he said, his voice sounding uninterested.

'Gabrielle may have been reunited with her,' she said shakily.

'Shut up!' he hollered, not wanting to hear any more. 'Don't you think I know she's dead too? Don't you think this whole situation is bad enough, without you reminding me of her?'

'Oh I'm so sorry!' she screamed back. 'I forgot you were so in love with Sarah. It must be so painful for you!'

Adam launched himself at her and shoved her so hard that she fell backwards onto the couch.

'Don't, just don't!' his face had curled into a snarl, and he thrust his finger in front of her face. He was shaking uncontrollably.

Courtney struggled to get up. She felt another panic attack grip her, a wave of emotion was coming over her again. This was too hard to cope with. She ran past him and up the stairs crying. She lay on their bed, just staring at the ceiling; her eyes were stinging. She sat up to look out of the window and caught sight of herself in the mirror. *Oh God, my face is so pale, my eyes are red and my hair is such a mess. I look a wreck. God no wonder Adam idolised Sarah so much. I bet she wasn't a fucking mess like me. Oh and what about Gabrielle and Alicia, too perfect for words! Sarah must have been perfect too.* Her face crumpled again. *How selfish of me to think like this, but I can't help it. Gabrielle's dead. I wonder what she'll look like in a month's time? She'll probably have maggots crawling out of her eye sockets by then.* This thought made her curl into a ball. She hugged her knees and rocked backwards and forwards crying, feeling like she was going insane. Everything had been so right, but now it was all so wrong. She suddenly felt so isolated. There was something that had obviously been wrong from the start, but she'd chosen to ignore it. She wanted the happy family lifestyle at any price. Perhaps it was the age gap. Maybe it was the fact that she didn't want to be a stepmother because it made her feel old. Maybe if she'd waited a while and not married the first man who treated her with respect she would have found Mr Right, with no baggage attached. Then she really could have had the perfect life - the two children, the pet dog, the white picket fence, the leafy green perfect neighbourhood. There would have been perfect neighbours, not too nosey and not too friendly. As Courtney lay there, she tried to convince herself that everything she was thinking was normal at a time like this. Tomorrow was a new day, things still could be perfect maybe one day. She did love Adam after all, and she knew he loved her. Maybe that would be enough to get them through.

She rolled over onto her side, facing the open door; she looked at the laundry basket in the corner, which was brimming with dirty clothes. She wondered what to do next. Usually she would busy herself, get on with the chores, and not even think about it, *but how can I do the washing when my stepdaughter's just been murdered, I just can't! What do you do when someone's been murdered anyway? How are you supposed to act?* She didn't know.

She managed to summon the strength to swing her legs off the bed and stand back up again. She walked back down the corridor, slowly; she felt the hairs on the back of her neck stand on end as she passed by Gabrielle's room. She thought that maybe if she went in, she would be there, sitting on the bed, smiling, swinging her legs, saying 'huh fooled you!' She had been the practical joker of the two. Courtney shuddered at her latest thought and continued to the top of the stairs. She couldn't face going into Gabrielle's room today, she'd do it tomorrow. She knew however that she would probably put it off the next day too. Still it was better to try to convince herself that she would even though she knew that she wouldn't.

As she neared the top of the stairs she suddenly heard Adam's voice. *Who on earth is he talking to?* She hadn't heard the phone ring. Maybe it was Gabrielle's grandparents, but he'd said that he would wait a while to break the news to them, because he couldn't deal with them right now. Courtney would have to tell her parents too. She walked silently down the stairs, treading carefully, in an attempt to hear what he was saying, but she just couldn't make it out. As she walked into the lounge, Adam jumped, and instinctively slammed the phone down, without saying anything.

'I was err thinking of calling funeral homes. D'you think it's too soon?' he quickly said, Courtney eyed him suspiciously.

'I heard you talking Adam,' she said pointedly.

'I was talking to myself, I wasn't talking to anyone,' he replied angrily. 'God, what's got into you? First you accuse me of still being in love with my *dead* ex-wife, then I'm supposedly making secret phone calls. My daughter has just *died*. You don't even seem to care about that, you only seem concerned for yourself.'

'How dare you!' she yelled. 'You know I care! How dare you even suggest that, you bastard!' She began to cry again.

Adam flopped down in the chair, his head lolling back in exhaustion; he stared upwards vacantly.

'Come here,' he sighed putting his arms out in front of him, 'I'm sorry, I didn't mean it. I just feel so lost. I feel like my whole world is falling apart, it's not your fault.'

She sat beside him, and embraced him; she sobbed as he tenderly stroked her hair.

'We can't fight,' she cried, 'we're all each other has got.'

'I know baby,' he replied, 'I know.'

Just at that moment the doorbell rang. They both started at the sudden noisy intrusion.

'Damn!' he exclaimed. 'Who the hell is that?'

'Don't open it,' she replied vehemently.

He sighed. 'It might be something important though.' He got up and walked to the door.

As he opened it cameras flashed causing him to reel backwards in shock, and a reporter thrust a microphone into his face.

'Dr Buchanan, we just want to ask you a few questions about your daughter's tragic death.'

'Do you people have no soul?' he hollered back at them, and slammed the door.

The reporter then opened the letter box, and continued firing questions at him.

'I am not going to speak to you people!' He was beside himself with rage. 'Now get off my property before I call the police!'

They left. 'Oh God,' he knelt down on the floor in the hallway, holding his head in his hands. 'How did they find out where we live?'

'I don't know, I think we should call the police anyway.' Courtney got up to use the phone.

'Put the TV on,' he said, 'they must have it on the news. This is a nightmare.'

She flicked the switch. The local news was halfway through, it wasn't mentioned. Then the newsreader said 'and back to our main story of the day.'

The two watched in horror, as the story unfolded on live daytime TV. They had filmed at the murder scene. They had a reporter live giving out the latest information on the victims, whilst standing outside the hospital.

The phone rang, it was Courtney's mother Mary, crying down the phone. She had seen it on the local news in Leesburg.

'We're on our way honey,' she said.

'Oh Mom there's really no need,' Courtney protested.

'No buts,' her mother insisted. 'You need looking after at a time like this. We'll move in for a couple of weeks, do all the cooking, cleaning. You've got other things you have to take care of.'

Courtney smiled, she did need her mother to come down, it would help a lot. 'OK Mom, we'll see you and Dad later.'

A week passed, Alicia had woken the day after the murder and was getting stronger. She had been visited almost everyday by the patrolman Brad North, who had taken care of her at the murder scene. Alicia hadn't known who he was at first; she hadn't really registered his face properly at the time. He was young, only twenty-six years old. Courtney had seen him one day just leaving Alicia's room as she had been arriving. He had such a kind face, doleful brown eyes that lit up when he smiled, and short dark hair. Alicia liked him visiting, and all the gifts that he brought her. He would spend hours with her, talking to her, and had gently been able to tell her exactly what had happened. He was helping her to come to terms with it. He too had been deeply affected by what he had seen, and so could relate to Alicia, and the horror of that day. It had been the moment that Courtney and Adam had dreaded the most, having to go over the events of that day with Alicia, but he had lifted that burden from them.

Detective Owens had visited the Buchanans on several occasions at their home during that week. He was the detective in charge of the murder investigation. He was a very serious man, always formal, but at the same time he showed a deep concern for the family. He was an imposing figure, at 6ft 4in, an African American; he had very dark brown eyes that always seemed tinged with sadness. He came to keep them updated with the results of the forensic tests and other aspects of the inquiry. The forensic tests on the knives had proved conclusive; the only fingerprints found on both of the knives found at the scene had been confirmed as being Jennifer's. Antonio had been completely ruled out of any involvement. Although he had defended himself, and injured Jennifer in the process, he had not seen the bodies in the other room, so had been completely unaware that the murders had taken place. Forensic evidence too supported the fact that he had only been present in the kitchen area, and that he had not been present at all whilst the murders were taking place. Jennifer herself had been moved by ambulance to a secure prison hospital, pending trial. She was ruled unfit to stand trial by the court and taking into consideration the large amount of evidence against her, the judge ruled that she must remain in custody until such a time as she was deemed fit to stand trial. The motive for the killings was still unknown as Jennifer maintained her silence, and was unable to speak to anyone. However, Alicia had told Detective Owens about the relationship between Matt and Jennifer, and the suspected involvement of Matt and Gabrielle. Nothing however could be proved.

On the Sunday morning, Alicia had asked if she would be allowed to go home. Courtney had visited Alicia every day and taken in a bag of clean pyjamas and books for her to read, although Alicia didn't look at any of them. The media interest in the case had died down, as the public had satisfied itself that the murders had been solved. Although no trial had yet taken place, they knew that the suspect was in custody and that they were safe in their own beds at night. Alicia had been protected from it all as the strict security at the hospital had prevented any reporters from getting in. The television had also been removed from her room so that she couldn't see any of the news bulletins.

Courtney arrived at the hospital that sunny September morning clutching Alicia's bag as always. Adam was going to visit that afternoon. They tried to spread their visits so that she spent as little time as possible alone.

When Courtney walked in to Alicia's room, Barbara was there as usual. But today she wasn't fussing over Alicia, plumping her pillows or chatting away in her usual happy, positive tone. This morning was different. Alicia was up and dressed. She was wearing a pair of black ski pants and a pale blue scoop necked T-shirt.

'Whose clothes are those?' Courtney said surprised, as she put the bag down on the end of her bed.

Barbara blushed, 'well actually Courtney, they're my daughters. She's put on a few pounds over the Summer and they don't fit her anymore.'

'Oh that's very kind of you Barbara,' Courtney was a little annoyed, 'but if I'd known I'd have brought clothes in from home instead of pyjamas again. You only had to call me.'

'But I'm going to the chapel of rest today,' Alicia protested, 'and I thought that if I told you, you wouldn't bring any anyway, because I know you don't want me to go there.'

'Well we can't stop you Alicia,' Courtney's tone softened. 'I just don't want you getting unnecessarily distressed.'

'But I can't hide from it can I?' she continued. 'She was my sister, and everyone else has seen her. Besides, Brad is gonna go with me. He told me that they make the bodies look better before you're allowed to see them. They do their hair, and make-up.'

Courtney sighed, resigned; 'well you've obviously made up your mind. If you think it will help.'

'I just feel that I need to see her again. I need to say goodbye. I didn't get the chance. I know I'm never going to get over it, but the counsellors say that with time the pain will subside, and it will get better.' Alicia stood up and walked over to the doorway.

'Here comes Brad now!' she beamed. 'He's always early.'

Courtney and Barbara looked at each other, and Barbara gave her a knowing smile.

'Well, do you need me to come with you Alicia?' Courtney asked.

'No, I need to do this on my own. Thanks anyway. Can you get your mom to bake some more of her cookies for when I get home though?' she said with a cheeky grin.

Courtney laughed. 'Sure! You liked those ones I brought you then?'

'Just a bit.'

Brad entered the room. He had his uniform on today and he gave Alicia a hug.

'Hello ma'am,' he said to Courtney taking his hat off respectfully.

'Hi Brad,' she replied. 'Thank you for everything you've done.'

'It's been my pleasure ma'am,' he replied with a smile.

Alicia said her goodbyes to Barbara, and as they left the hospital, everybody seemed to turn and look. Doctors and nurses alike, as they passed on the way, all said goodbye, and wished her well. The murders had affected the hospital staff greatly, especially as it involved one of their colleague's daughters. It had been the main topic of conversation in the staff rooms all week.

Courtney left the hospital in their car, and Alicia headed off in Brad's patrol vehicle to the Chapel of rest, which was at the funeral parlour two blocks away. The funeral was scheduled to take place in two days' time, so for now Gabrielle's body was lying there, awaiting transportation to her final resting place in the churchyard.

Alicia was feeling very afraid at that moment. Brad kept looking over at her beside him in the passenger seat checking that she was all right. She sat rigidly staring straight ahead. She didn't speak. He felt nervous too. He wasn't sure if he was going to be able to cope with her reaction. He felt very protective towards her and a strong bond of friendship and trust was growing between them. Alicia had told him almost everything about herself over the week. She turned to look out of the side window as they neared their destination. Brad indicated left, and the patrol car pulled into a side road that led up a long dirt track. Alicia could now see ahead of them the funeral home, surrounded by lush grass and tall trees. Two chestnut horses grazed in an adjoining field, their heads down, their tails lashing at the air, as flies buzzed about them.

The patrol vehicle came to a stop outside the entrance to the modern brick building - a gold sign bearing the company name shone above the doorway, 'Elliott & Son Funeral Services.'

Brad stepped out of the vehicle and respectfully came round to the passenger door to open it for Alicia.

She looked up at him. His face was solemn, his eyes gazing down into hers; he looked so sad and concerned for her. She caught hold of his hand, she didn't need him to speak; she understood what he was saying to her.

'Brad, I'm gonna be fine, but thank you anyway,' she smiled.

They walked slowly to the entrance and were met inside the doorway by one of the morticians. He was dressed in black and was very sombre, in keeping with the mood of the occasion.

Brad explained why they were there and who they had come to see. Alicia clung onto his arm for support. She had been fine outside in the sunshine, with the surreal, non-threatening surroundings, but now the reality of the situation was starting to focus her thoughts. She wasn't sure after all if she could go through with what she had gone there to do.

The mortician was openly surprised upon seeing Alicia, although he didn't pass comment; Brad could see it in his face. He had obviously seen the bodies that were currently housed in the chapel of rest, and one of the visitors bearing such a striking resemblance to one of them was at the very least, a little unnerving.

The mortician ushered them down the corridor. The carpet was dark green with a velvet texture. The walls were covered in a strange patterned wallpaper that would have given anyone a headache had they stared at it too long. Gold plated light fittings jutted out from the walls. There were even paintings hanging at intervals along the entire length of the corridor. Alicia thought that it seemed more like a motel than a place that housed the dead.

They rounded another corner and the mortician came to an abrupt halt outside one of the rooms.

'Your sister's body is inside Miss,' he said gravely.

Alicia took a deep breath. She was afraid to enter the room but she knew she had to do it. She knew that she had to see Gabrielle so that she could know for sure that it was all true, and that she was really dead.

Brad stood nervously, clearing his throat suddenly.

'Alicia,' he said quietly, 'do you want me to come in with you?'

'No it's all right, I have to do this on my own,' she replied uncertainly. 'You won't leave me though will you?' she added almost pleadingly, taking one last look into his reassuring eyes.

'No of course I won't leave you,' he said squeezing her hand tightly. 'I'll be just outside if you need me.'

With that she turned and opened the door slowly. She could see the coffin at the far end of the small room. The lid was off and she could just make out some strands of blonde hair. She paused, took a shaky step inside and closed the door behind her. The room was dimly lit and had an eerie glow about it. White and mauve flowers were draped over the coffin and on the top of two ornate stands either side of it. Emotions surged within her like a relentless raging sea; disbelief mixed with the sheer horror of the room, the quiet cloying air, the strange smell of perfume

132

that wasn't the same perfume that Gabrielle had worn in life. She felt that this whole scene before her wasn't real and that if she closed her eyes and looked again, maybe it would have disappeared.

With her feelings now in turmoil again, and with trepidation, every step closer she took revealed more of her beloved sister until she found herself standing next to the coffin. She looked down not really wanting to, but knowing that she had to. Tears blurred her vision; she wiped them away in jerky nervous movements. Gabrielle was dressed in a pale blue gown; her mutilated hands and arms disguised by matching satin gloves. Her face had been made up with colours that she would never have chosen to wear in life - bright blue eye shadow and pink lipstick made a mask of her lifeless features. Her face wasn't racked with torture, as she had half expected it would be, and she looked too peaceful for someone who had been murdered. Alicia thought that it could so easily have been her lying there, her identical twin - the sight was too much to bear. Overcome, she felt she had to leave and she couldn't bring herself to say any of the things she had planned to say as she choked back her tears. She reached forward, her hand trembling, and lightly touched her cheek; it was ice cold. Her hair felt soft, but that too was lifeless - no longer the same. She withdrew her hand and turned to leave the room. She moved quickly as she felt an anguished cry rising up from way down in her stomach to her vocal chords. She clasped her hand over her mouth to stifle it, stumbling towards the door, her hand outstretched to reach for the handle. Upon reaching the door, she paused, turned to take one last look at her sister, then closed it quickly behind her with a bang.

Chapter 7

Tuesday morning the sun was shining, but in her grief and sadness there was no joy in the sunshine. It might just as well have been raining - in fact Alicia wished that it was raining. As she looked out of her bedroom window and contemplated the impossible task of getting herself dressed and facing the others downstairs, she thought that at least if it was raining it would mean that the heavens were sad too. There shouldn't be sunshine - not today.

She had no energy. She'd been like this since she came home from the hospital. Everything was an effort. There was a knock at the door; she didn't answer. The handle turned and Courtney stepped in.

'How are you feeling today Licia?' she said quietly.

'Like crap! Like every day I feel like crap, and probably always will,' she said slamming her hairbrush down on her dresser. Her upper lip began to tremble and the tears welled up. It was something she had no control over and she didn't have the strength to fight it.

Courtney walked over to her and hugged her, smoothing her dishevelled and unwashed hair with her free hand. 'After today's over with, things will improve I promise you,' Courtney said, desperately trying to console her.

'I doubt it,' Alicia replied hoarsely and without expression. It was as if she was just existing now, like the life had drained from her too. Courtney was so depressed. Everyone in the house felt as if they were walking on eggshells, nobody really spoke to one another. Everybody was trying so hard to hold on to the strands of normality that remained, and in doing so they had alienated each other. They tried to shut out the horror rather than deal with it. They would talk about TV and baking cookies, instead of mentioning grief, or death. Without realising it they were almost making matters worse, driving each other into isolation. Their silence disguised their real fear that if they did speak about it they would be letting the evil back into the house, and they couldn't let it touch them too.

Courtney flopped down on to the bed; Alicia sat back down on the stool in front of her dresser, staring blankly into the mirror.

'Do you know what?' Alicia said. 'I sit here for hours looking in the mirror. That's why I don't come down, and do you know why?' she said still sobbing.

'No why?' Courtney replied weakly.

'Because it's like I'm looking at her, and smiling at her, and she's smiling back.   Then in that moment she's not dead anymore, she's still alive. But I know it's just me deep down, she was nothing like me, not really.'

Courtney felt her heart racing, the tears welling up in her eyes. She had to fight it. The past two days had been hell since Alicia had come back. Whilst she was still in hospital, she and Adam had been so busy with visiting her and making the funeral arrangements, that reality seemed to take a back seat.   Her mother spent the days baking endless trays of chocolate cookies, to the point where it had almost become an obsession.   Ever since she'd found out that Alicia liked them, it had been the only thing she could provide for her that would make her feel just that little bit better.   Jim, Courtney's father, would potter round the house and sit in the garden for hours, just staring straight ahead, or reading his book. If Ted Fraser was in his garden, however, then the two men would often converse with each other. They were both around the same age and seemed to have a good deal in common. Ted had been very upset and shocked when he'd learned of Gabrielle's murder.

Courtney panicked again.   She couldn't go back on that emotional roller coaster today - she had to prepare herself and Alicia for the funeral.

She wiped her eyes, and stood up.

'Grandpa John and Grandma Thelma, are both arriving here soon, for the funeral,' she said as she turned to go back out of Alicia's room.

'Have a shower Alicia, it'll make you feel a bit better. Get dressed and we'll battle through the day together,' she continued, 'I'll be a shout away if you need me. Oh by the way, my mom's baked you some more cookies,' she half laughed trying to introduce a bit of humour.

Alicia didn't reply, but rose slowly to her feet, turning to get her dressing gown which was hanging up on the back of the door. Courtney was now satisfied that Alicia would be ready to go in an hour. She knew what time the funeral started, and Courtney was sure that she would not want to stay at home. She left her alone again and set off back downstairs. There was a hive of activity downstairs that immediately brought her back to reality - the reality of preparation and small talk with well-wishers, who were continually ringing on the doorbell. The neighbours had all been very supportive, especially Grant and Liza. They had been a rock since the day that it had happened. Courtney's mother was fussing over the food, which she had prepared for the wake. This was to be held in the back garden after the funeral. Jim just sat on the couch reading the paper, trying to stay out of all the mayhem. Adam was pacing the lounge floor like a caged tiger. He had been dreading today the most and he just wanted to get it out of the way and try to move on. He and Courtney had decided that once the new baby was born, they really would be able to start again. They felt that the baby was a blessing in all of this. Courtney was a great believer in fate anyway - getting pregnant when she did she felt was destined. There would be a new life - not to replace a life that's passed but to focus the mind on the living, and to be able to have fun and laugh again.

As Courtney looked out of the front window, she saw the funeral cars sweep majestically into the road. The funeral vehicles were like a flock of black crows, bringing the death and sorrow back to their doorstep. The coffin lay in the back of the leading car, swathed in flowers; its gold handles gleaming in the midday sunshine.

The crowd gathered out front. All the nerves came back, the sick feeling in the pit of Courtney's stomach and the permanent furrow deepened in Adam's brow. Alicia stood apart from the crowd, a serene look on her face. She gazed at the funeral vehicles, no emotion showed on her face. Her eyes blinked slowly and deliberately as her fine blonde hair was tossed wildly by the breeze. Hers was the only hair that moved. She was wearing a plain black trouser suit that she had found in Gabrielle's closet. It had been one of her interview outfits. Gabrielle had always preferred wearing trousers to skirts. Alicia had always been the more feminine of the two, but today she wanted to be more like her - her clothes and shoes were all that were left.

Walking now slowly, eyes cast down along the paved path towards the front of the church, painstaking steps, stifled coughs, sniffs, shuffling material, rustling skirts, throats clearing.
Steps now echoed and cold benches beckoned. A cross looming. Flowers blooming.

As they sat, Courtney looked around her awkwardly. Her neck almost too stiff to move, from the suppressed, deep down emotion. Her legs were trembling uncontrollably, but the overwhelming fear of her emotions spilling out and her losing control completely outweighed her feelings of sadness. *I mustn't let go, I mustn't,* she told herself over and over again. Alicia sat beside her, calm, motionless, but still alert, looking directly ahead. Then there was the coffin; Courtney looked sideways at the pallbearers, bearing their load, almost effortlessly. She suddenly imagined them dropping the coffin and the lid coming off and the body rolling across the aisle, people crying out in horror. She squeezed her eyes shut. She didn't understand why that bizarre thought had come into her head and she dismissed it from her mind as quickly as it had come.
They placed the coffin down gently and with such tenderness. Bowing their heads respectfully they then turned to walk back up the aisle of the church - their expressions grave.

There was no sound in the church for a few moments after they had left; everybody stared straight ahead at the coffin, which stood regally before the mourners. It was draped in flowers, with wreathes by the side of it, messages of condolence attached to them. Then the organist began to play. The music echoed around the building and it seemed to come from every corner of the high roofed, cold imposing church. Courtney fumbled for her order of service, which she had placed precariously on her lap. She turned to the first page of the flimsy white booklet to find the first hymn. The congregation stood as the priest stepped up to the pulpit, and they began to sing falteringly, hesitantly.

'Thine be the glory, risen conquering son, endless is the victory, thou o'er death hast won.' It was a hymn Courtney remembered from her youth. As she stared at the coffin her eyes filled with tears again, blurring her vision. She couldn't sing out loud, her voice had got stuck somewhere down the bottom of her throat - emotion was holding it back. The only voice that could truly be heard was that of the priest, as he sang out with great passion the words that were the cornerstone of his faith. Courtney wiped the tears from her eyes and turned her gaze away from the coffin towards this extraordinary man. He was no taller than 5ft 4in, but seemed so much more imposing standing there in the pulpit. He had short dishevelled grey hair and kindly, pale blue eyes. She watched him intently as he gazed with anticipation down at his flock, still singing with all his might.

The hymn finished. The congregation sat back down, people shuffled awkwardly on the dark wooden benches, and coughed nervously. Courtney looked again at Alicia who sat quietly next to her. Her eyes were slightly glazed, but she was composed. She sat up straight, still looking ahead. Her attention now shifted from the coffin to the priest in the pulpit.

'I'd like to begin by welcoming you all to St. Bartholomew's church. My name is Father David Price,' he began, his voice firm and commanding. He was not at all unnerved by the coffin that stood beside him.

'We have gathered here today to celebrate the life of Gabrielle, to draw together to comfort one another at this time of extreme sadness, and to offer one another hope for the future.' He held his arms wide open, as if to welcome everybody, and to draw people to him.

Gabrielle's grandmother Thelma could now be heard weeping audibly. She clung to her husband who had placed a protective arm around her shoulder.

The priest continued undeterred.

'The Lord said that he who believes in me, shall never die but shall have eternal life. This is our promise as Christians; this is our hope for the future. The problem for us at a time like this is that we want to know why?' He paused for a moment, and seemed to look at each person in turn in the congregation. 'I can't answer that,' he said with deep emotion in his voice.

'I do not know why Gabrielle has been taken from us at such a young age or why she had to die in the circumstances that she did. We will never know in this life.'

He looked down at the coffin, and looked back up again slowly.

'But what I can tell you, and of this I am sure, is that God's heavenly house has many rooms. He has prepared a room in his house for Gabrielle, ready for her, and she is with him now, in paradise.'

Courtney hadn't looked at Adam the whole time that they had been sat in the church. He was to her right. As the priest said these words Adam reached over to Courtney and clasped her hand. She squeezed it tight, and didn't let go until they stood for the second hymn.

The Lord is my shepherd now echoed around the church. The people sang out with more confidence this time.

After the hymn there was the bible reading, which was given by a middle-aged lady with dark curly hair. Courtney concluded that she must be one of the regular congregation, as she did not recognise her.

As Courtney's eyes followed the lady back to her seat towards the back of the church, her gaze fell upon a stout looking man with thinning hair and an unusually rosy complexion. His face was etched with grief.

He noticed Courtney looking at him and hung his head, almost in shame. She turned back to the front and decided that she would speak to him after the service. She felt strangely drawn to him but she wasn't sure why.

The priest began again.

'I did not have the pleasure of knowing Gabrielle personally, however, having spoken to her family, I have learned that she was an absolute joy to know. She was loved and is still loved deeply by her parents, her sister Alicia, and by all her friends. She was an extremely popular girl and I know that she will be sorely missed.'

He hesitated and looked back out into the congregation.

He motioned to Adam, who had agreed to say a few words about Gabrielle. 'I would like to introduce you to Gabrielle's father, Adam, who I'm sure you already know and who is far better qualified than myself to speak to you all about Gabrielle.'

Adam walked cautiously to the front of the church, a weary expression on his face. The grey circles under his eyes looked even darker today. As he stepped up to the pulpit he cleared his throat nervously.

'It's difficult to put into words the way that I am feeling today,' he began guardedly. Courtney noticed that his hands were trembling and his eyes were cast down trying to focus on the piece of paper he was holding in his hand.

She didn't know that he had made notes for his speech. She thought it a little strange, perhaps he just wanted to make sure he didn't miss anything.

He cleared his throat again before continuing, 'I have lost one of the beautiful rays of sunshine in my life that I had lost before, and had only just recently found again. She's been taken from us and I am very angry about it, but I can't change it.' His voice was very expressive. You could hear the anger in it but there was more a sense of his overwhelming desolation. 'She didn't even live to see her twentieth birthday. She could have done so much with her life and she will not be there to see her new brother or sister come into the world.' As he said this he looked up for the first time from his paper, straight at Courtney, who looked back at him her eyes full of tears. He jerked his head suddenly to face the front, visibly startled by something. He stared straight ahead.

'What the hell?' he suddenly exclaimed, his eyes wild with fury. The priest realising that the tribute was about to go horribly wrong, quickly stepped back up to the pulpit and stood by Adam's side.

'I told you, *not* to come,' Adam's hand was shaking with rage, clenched into a fist against the pulpit. His words were then suddenly cut short as Father Price grabbed at his arm and steered him away from the microphone as quickly as he could.

There were muffled cries from the congregation. People turned around to look at the back of the church. Courtney turned too, as did Alicia.

Just then the man that Courtney had noticed earlier stood up. He held up his hands apologetically.

Courtney was bewildered and upset by Adam's onslaught. Her face was burning and she had started to feel faint; panic and confusion surged through her body like a rip tide.

Adam's expression seemed to change to one of confusion as he looked at the man. His whole countenance was that of a man she no longer recognised as being her husband.

'I'm sorry for what happened to your daughter Mr Buchanan,' the man spoke hesitantly.

Adam didn't speak. He just looked on with the same perplexed look on his face, and then his expression changed back to one of anger again.

'I really just wanted to express my sincere sorrow to you,' the man continued.

'Get out!' Adam bellowed from the pulpit. Courtney couldn't stay in her seat any longer. She leapt up and ran to the front of the church.

Detective Owens and Officer North both rose to their feet. They had been sat in the back row of the church for the entire service. They took the man by the arm and ushered him out of the main door.

'For heaven's sake Adam,' Courtney blurted out. 'Please stop this!'

Adam turned and stepped down from the pulpit without looking at anybody. He walked back up the church aisle and out the open door into the sunshine.

Father Price gave a deep sigh, trying to regain control and restore some dignity to the service.

'Grief is a very unpredictable emotion,' he said, his voice still strong and commanding. 'It's like an untamed animal. It is fierce and wild and shows the pain of the loss that we feel for

141

someone we have loved so very deeply and will miss so terribly.'

There was silence again, an eerie sort of silence.

'Please turn in your order of service to page six,' he continued in a more positive tone. 'This hymn has very powerful words - words that should be spoken in our troubled world today. Let's stand to sing our final hymn then, Make me a Channel of your Peace.'

With that the congregation all rose as the organist began again. Still with stunned expressions on their faces they obeyed the priest like robots and began to sing.

After they had struggled through the first chorus, the pallbearers filed back into the church, sombre faced as before, and moved in two lines back towards the coffin.

Adam and Courtney stood next to each other at the church gates. 'So tell me Adam,' she asked again, more frantic this time, 'who was that man?'

Adam didn't answer. He just stared blankly over at the gravestones.

'For God's sake Adam,' she retorted, 'you weren't even looking at that man when you said those things - you only noticed him when he stood up.'

'Oh shut up Courtney!' he hollered, turning to her his eyes still livid. She had never seen him look like that before, apart from the time when she had mentioned Sarah's death. He had been furious then. She remembered how hard he had pushed her, causing her to fall down onto the couch. It could have so easily been a coffee table she had landed on, or a bureau. It was as if he was so full of hatred and loathing that even the sight of his own wife didn't quieten his spirit.

Adam stormed back up the path towards the church. Nearing the doors, he suddenly stopped dead in his tracks. The organist was still playing but the pall bearers were now leaving the church, carrying Gabrielle's coffin on their shoulders - four men dressed entirely in black. Following them, led by Father Price, was the rest of the congregation. Alicia followed behind the priest, walking on her own, having been deserted again by both of her parents. She was crying now. Adam ran up to her and took her arm. She snatched it back from him angrily as he tried to put his arm around her. She whirled around, 'get off me!' He hung his head in shame.

Courtney cut through the crowd and quickly drew level with her. 'I'm so sorry about your dad, Alicia,' she said softly.

'Why are you apologising?' she said indignantly. 'It's not your fault, he's a heartless pig.'

As they neared the empty grave, and the mounds of earth stacked up either side, Courtney could feel her heart racing again. Alicia reached out for her hand, she took it and squeezed it tight. How much more terrible must it be for her, Courtney thought.

It all seemed so final now. She was going to be buried. That was it - the end.

The mourners encircled the graveside and the coffin was placed on a platform above the grave. The pallbearers gathered the bouquets of flowers and placed them around the edge, to try to soften the stark, cheerless scene.

Father Price stood at the foot of the coffin, his arms outstretched.

'As we commit our sister Gabrielle's body to the ground, and her soul into the loving arms of our Lord…,' his imposing voice rang out.

Alicia's concentration was diverted. She leaned against her stepmother, whose arm lay protectively around her shoulders. She looked straight ahead. There was a large gap right in front of her where the mourners had parted. She could still hear the priest's voice in the background, but was no longer listening to his words; she rubbed her eyes to clear her vision. She looked again, thinking it must have been her imagination, her mind playing tricks on her. But she could still make him out in the distance, hiding amongst the trees, a shadowy thin-faced figure, and he was staring straight at her.

She froze, her eyes locked with his in that moment. He was some distance away, but clearly evident and tangible. She turned from his gaze and looked at her fellow mourners to see if their attention had been diverted away from the coffin, but they wept on - oblivious. Nobody else had noticed him; it was as though he was invisible to everyone but her. She shuddered then and felt an icy blast hit her full on - it enveloped her; she shivered although the sun was still shining and huddled closer to Courtney.

'Ashes to Ashes, dust to dust,' the priest intoned.

Alicia looked over at Brad, who stood, eyes downcast opposite her; he was wearing his uniform and held his hat in front of him, pressed up against his body, protectively. Detective Owens stood beside him in a smart suit and long black coat.

Brad looked up, as he could sense Alicia's gaze. Their eyes met and he smiled warmly at her. His eyes lit up and she felt alive again in that moment. It was as if all her troubles had suddenly disappeared. She didn't want him to look away from her; she wanted him to look at her like that forever.

Then as if waking from a dream, she snapped back to reality and instinctively looked back at the clearing, straining to see, willing her eyes to see him; she scanned the trees and dark shadows behind the mourners, but the thin-faced man had gone.

She felt almost disappointment, even though he had frightened her and although she didn't recognise him, she was sure that she knew him. She felt confused and unsettled.

The coffin had now been lowered into the ground; the grief-stricken had thrown trinkets and flowers in after it.

The ceremony was over.

Messages of condolence were passed between them, they shook hands with Father Price, and two of them even laughed, albeit a little nervously.

Alicia walked away from the graveside, still feeling cold; she pulled her black suit jacket together at the front, almost hugging herself as she walked towards the gate, towards her new life. Brad walked beside her. She could feel his warmth just from his presence. She wasn't sure if it was a physical thing or a spiritual thing. He was the only one who made her feel better. With him she had brief glimpses of happiness and possible hope for the future.

Courtney and Adam walked ahead of them, although they didn't speak to one another.

'How are you feeling Alicia?' Brad suddenly spoke as they neared the gate. She didn't have time to answer him.

A photographer was hiding around the corner, and as they stepped back onto the sidewalk and walked towards the waiting fleet of cars, he seemed to spring out from nowhere - his camera flashing as he took a series of pictures of Alicia and her parents. They held their hands up to try to shield their faces, and were quickly ushered into their respective vehicles.

Adam's temper flared again. 'Damn the press! I thought they'd let up, now that the case is closed.'

'Well it isn't closed though is it,' Courtney retorted.

'They know who did it though don't they? My God,' he mused, 'whoever that girl's parents are ought to be shot. They must be twisted themselves to have produced a daughter like that.'

'Well we can't really say can we,' she replied. He whipped his head round in annoyance.

'We don't know them, do we?' she added.

Adam sat staring sullenly out of the window, his bottom lip quivering. He looked for a second Courtney thought, like a spoilt child, feeling sorry for himself. Alicia had gone with Brad and Detective Owens, and it was just the two of them in the lead car. The grandparents were in the one behind.

'I don't know Courtney,' Adam sighed, suddenly changing his tone to a more affable one.

'Why is life so Goddamn hard eh? Why can't things just go the way you want them to go?'

'It doesn't work like that does it,' she said quietly. 'We could get run down by a truck tomorrow - you can never really plan for the future.'

'Oh depress me even more why don't you,' he half laughed.

'Damn!' he suddenly exclaimed, slamming his fist down on the inside of the car.

'So you're still not gonna tell me who that man was then?' Courtney changed the subject.

'Nope,' came his monosyllabic reply. 'Why?' she asked calmly, trying not to raise her voice again.

'Because it doesn't matter does it? Oh look we're back,' he started to stand up before the vehicle stopped, frantically trying to open the door. They were holding the wake at their home in Bay View Grove; they had laid some trestle tables in the garden

145

before going to the funeral.   Mary, Courtney's mother had prepared most of the food the day before.

The cars all pulled up one after the other; Adam rushed to the front door and disappeared into the house. Courtney wagered that he had headed straight for the drinks cabinet. She decided to stay on the sidewalk and greet the others as they emerged from the other cars, still tearful. Thelma supported by her husband John walked up to her.

'Oh Thelma,' Courtney said, 'this must be the hardest day for you.'

'I never thought I'd lose another one of my girls,' Thelma said with such sorrow in her voice.

'When Sarah died.'   She stopped and John shook his head slightly looking at Courtney, not in an unkind way, just willing her to change the subject.

'C'mon Thelma,' Courtney soothed, 'we'll go inside. We can sit in the garden if you want and have some food and then we can all talk about the future. We still have Alicia thank God.'

Thelma nodded and smiled; it was almost as if she had forgotten.

'Where is she?' she said, craning her neck round to look.

As she did, the unmarked police vehicle pulled up and Alicia and Brad got out of the back. The door slammed and Detective Owens, still looking serious and formal, followed them up the sidewalk.

Alicia flashed a smile at Courtney who returned it immediately. She felt a warm feeling pass through her entire body, just to see Alicia smile. Brad was talking to her, and she was laughing.

Perhaps the rest of the day will not be as bad.

Alicia caught hold of her stepmother's arm and led her up the driveway, following closely on the heels of Thelma and John. Ted Fraser was there and Liza and Grant were crossing the road having parked up in their own driveway opposite.

Adam had already positioned himself on a lounger in the garden. He had taken the trouble to arrange the rest of the chairs as there were other people arriving who had made their own way to and from the church.

'I wonder if Matt's funeral has taken place yet?' Alicia said to Courtney as she carried a tray of wineglasses into the garden. 'Help yourselves to food,' Courtney sang out from the doorway. The guests didn't have to be asked twice and were already queuing at the foot of the table where Mary was stood giving them their instructions.

Courtney really felt like having a drink that day. She felt she needed one so badly. It was hard enough to have quit smoking because of her pregnancy. She had vowed not to touch a single drop.

'One glass'll be OK,' said Adam who looked as if he was already on his third or fourth. Courtney thought then that he was definitely going to get drunk today and she just hoped that he didn't make too much of a fool of himself, and more importantly of her.

'I think his funeral was this morning too, wasn't it?' Courtney said, suddenly remembering that she hadn't answered Alicia's question yet.

'Yes I believe it was,' Detective Owens said as he walked past her with a plate brimming with food. 'It was at a church in Buena Vista I believe.'

Courtney shook her head remembering Matt. He had been so important to Gabrielle, but they hadn't even mentioned him in the service - perhaps they should have done. Then she thought about it some more. Maybe they were just assuming that Gabrielle had loved Matt, the Romeo and Juliet scenario. Maybe he had just been a sexual partner, or even just a friend. She wanted so much to believe that they had been in love, and that she was with him now, that she wasn't alone.

Courtney poured herself a glass of wine. She had reasoned that surely one glass couldn't do any harm, so long as it didn't lead to another, and then another, as it had done so many times in the past.

Alicia sat down next to Brad, who placed a protective hand on her leg. Detective Owens bristled and looked over, alarmed. Courtney seeing Detective Owens's reaction, sat down in the seat beside him and began to make polite conversation.

'I'm glad that's over with,' Alicia said with a sigh.

'I thought I was gonna pass out at one stage. I didn't think I'd make it through.'

'You did great,' Brad said with a proud smile.

He poured Alicia another glass of wine, as she lit a cigarette with her free hand.

'You shouldn't smoke ya know, it stunts your growth,' he said with a smile. They both laughed.

'You always make me laugh Brad,' she said. 'Aren't you gonna have a drink?' she then said, hoping he would say yes.

'Well I suppose there's no reason why I shouldn't. I'm not on duty today.'

He turned to Detective Owens who was deep in conversation with Courtney; 'Is it OK to have a drink Boss?' Brad called across, 'I mean I know I'm not on duty, but I have my uniform on.'

'Well um err, well I suppose,' Detective Owens was still frowning and mulling over the implications in his mind.

Brad sprang to his feet, rubbed his hands with glee, and said 'well that's good enough for me.'

He headed over to the table to fetch a glass, found one quickly and was back in his chair smiling broadly within seconds. He held out his glass to Alicia, who had already earmarked a whole bottle of wine for herself. She had placed it at the foot of her chair, reached down and then poured him a glass filling it right to the brim so that it spilled over the edge.

'Easy girl,' he said, 'are you trying to get me drunk or something?' He gave her a knowing look and they both laughed again. The others at the wake kept looking over, thinking it strange to see Alicia so happy on the day of her sister's funeral.

More people were arriving all the time. Courtney's mother took charge of the door, ushering all the new arrivals through the house and out into the garden. Antonio came round. He had now made a full recovery, but it was plain that he was still bearing the psychological scars of his attack. Courtney's friend Nicky from work came, with her husband, and a number of other doctors and nurses from the Florida Hospital also attended, including Adam's friend Peter. Towards the end of the afternoon, Alicia's friends Sadie and Candy arrived. They had

148

also been at the funeral, but had gone home immediately afterwards. Alicia seemed pleased to see them but was obviously distracted. Courtney noticed she kept looking over her shoulder checking to make sure that Brad was still there. Detective Owens seized his opportunity and moved over to sit beside him.

'Just how close are you to this girl?' he said sternly, but quietly so as not to alert the other guests to the conversation. His opening comment caught Brad completely off guard as he sipped at his fourth glass of wine. Brad stammered and didn't really answer.

'Just remember, she was Gabrielle's sister. The case has not gone to trial yet. The fact that we are certain in our minds who killed her is irrelevant,' Owens went on. It was as if he'd been rehearsing his speech for some time, and Brad couldn't get a word in.

'I know she's a beautiful girl - anyone can see that,' he continued unabated. 'She is, however, only nineteen years old, and given the circumstances of your meeting her, I consider it wholly unprofessional for you to be getting so involved with her.'

'Now hang on a minute!' Brad finally interjected. 'You're assuming too much.' Owens went to speak again but Brad continued in annoyance, 'I get on well with Alicia. She's a great girl, an awesome girl as a matter of fact. We're good friends that's all.'

'Oh C'mon Brad,' Detective Owens scoffed, 'I have eyes in my head. I'm not stupid, I've seen the looks between you.'

'That's none of your business!' Brad retorted angrily.

Detective Owens leaned in close. 'That's where you're wrong,' he said in a threatening whisper. 'You are getting involved with our murder victim's twin sister, who for all we know could be implicated somewhere along the line. This could seriously jeopardise your career and your reputation.'

'You know she had nothing to do with it,' Brad replied shaking his head in disbelief. 'There is absolutely no forensic evidence to support that.'

'It's true there is no evidence of her physical presence at the scene, but if Jennifer recovers from this temporary psychosis, we will have both sides to the story, and then hopefully the motive,' Owens replied. 'We can only speculate at this stage.'

'You don't know that she's going to recover for sure,' Brad then said. 'Jack Thorpe said that the doctors were hopeful, not definite.'

'Yes,' Owens answered nodding, 'but at first you remember they told him they didn't think his daughter would ever recover. It would appear all that has changed now.'

The detective then stood up and dusted himself down. 'Well,' he said in a matter of fact tone, 'I must be going. Got to get back to the wife and kids.'

Brad followed Detective Owens suspiciously with his eyes. He watched him go first to Courtney, and then to Adam who was now sat discussing work matters loudly with Peter. He shook their hands in turn and then left through the back of the house, closely followed by Mary who went to open the front door for him. Brad looked round at Alicia who was still standing with her friends. She looked over at him at the same moment and smiled - such a smile. It mesmerised him. She overwhelmed him completely. He quickly gathered his thoughts - fight or flee - this was the decision that he had to make, and he had to make it fast. He was a career officer. He wanted to move up the ranks, and the way he felt about her disturbed him - it was all consuming. It had taken him over - he couldn't even think straight anymore.

He drank the rest of his wine in a flash, and then stood up abruptly. Whilst still fumbling with his coat, he picked up his hat and set off after Owens.

'Wait,' Brad shouted after him. Owens stopped, and turned around. 'Just wait there a minute,' he called out again, 'I need a lift home.'

Alicia noticed Brad putting on his jacket to leave. She looked bewildered and signalled to her friends that she would be back in a moment. She went over to him as he stood saying his goodbyes.

'Brad,' she said quietly, 'you don't really have to go do you?'

He looked into her eyes; confusion took hold of him again.
'Yeah, I've gotta go. You know how it is,' he said awkwardly.
'Well I'll see you around then,' she said her voice dejected.
'Definitely. I'll see you around,' he smiled back. 'You look after yourself OK.'
'I will,' she replied with a sigh. 'I…'
'I what?' he answered.
'Oh it doesn't matter. I'll tell you next time.' She tried to force a smile.
'OK then.' He put his hat back on and turned to leave. 'See ya later then.'
Detective Owens waited in the driveway for Brad to emerge. 'Glad that you've finally seen sense,' he said with a pleased look on his face.
Brad wanted to wipe that triumphant look clean off his face right then. He felt now that maybe he had led Alicia on after all and that he was in fact entirely to blame for what had happened. He felt that he had let her down. All he wanted to do was to turn around and go back, but he knew that he had made his choice now, and that he had to stick with it.

Chapter 8

Alicia lay in bed that night feeling more alone than she had ever felt before. She stared up at the ceiling, blinking slowly in the darkness. Her thoughts were racing. She couldn't sleep and she still felt drunk from all the wine that she'd had at the wake. Every time she closed her eyes she felt a wave of nausea sweep over her. Everything would then start to spin and she had to open her eyes again, even though it was dark - she couldn't bear that feeling. She felt numb; her eyes were stinging from the constant stream of tears. She listened for noises in the house but all she could hear were the familiar creaks of the central heating system and the low hissing of the water tank in her closet. She usually didn't take any notice of these noises but tonight those sounds mixed with her troubled and obsessive thoughts were keeping her wide awake.

She sat up in bed, realising that this sick feeling was not going to pass. She considered trying to vomit, but she couldn't bring herself to walk down the corridor past Gabrielle's room. She had been in there that morning to find the suit and that had been hard enough. She had felt as if she was being watched the whole time she had been in there. She concluded that this had to be her paranoia kicking in again - Gabrielle was dead after all.

She swung her legs out from under the covers, and just sat, her feet now on the floor. With her head bent down and her chin resting on her chest she swayed gently from side to side, groaning. *It's too damn hot in here*! She stood up, unsteady on her feet, and made her way to the window. Her night vision was working well tonight - she had had lots of practice lately. This time she didn't collide with the dresser when leaning to open the window. It swung open, and a rush of air came in instantly sobering her a little, making her more alert. She walked round the dresser and up to the window ledge where she folded her arms in front of her and rested her chin on top. She closed her eyes and just let the breeze blow on her face. Her long fine hair, which would always take flight at the slightest breath of wind, began to move about, the individual hairs snaking forward haphazardly fluttering against her face. She reached behind her for her dresser stool and pulled it over to where she stood. She worked out that if she did sit she'd still be able to rest her chin on the ledge and get the breeze on her face. She sat for a while just day dreaming and had even started to feel a little cold - her pale blue silk pyjamas were not exactly warm. She had stopped feeling sick now, and that was her primary concern. Looking out the window into the shadows she could hear all the usual familiar night time sounds, the crickets mainly. She remembered how Jennifer had told her once before about the alligators in Windermere; she would always listen to them calling to one another at night time, with that familiar croaking sound, almost like a huge frog, but deeper toned. She wondered to herself what would happen if an alligator wandered into their garden one day, and decided to take up residence in the pool. She chuckled to herself, *just imagine Courtney going out for her morning coffee and seeing an alligator in the pool! She would freak.*

Alicia sighed, she was still wide awake. *I wonder how Matt's funeral went today?* She mulled over the day's events and thought about the man at the back of the church. The way her dad had behaved had made her so mad she hadn't spoken to him all day, and didn't think she would tomorrow either. She had seen him in a different light. There was something about him that she just couldn't figure out, something she didn't trust. Courtney on the other hand was different, she respected her. She had been up front with them from the start; her dad on the other hand had always tried to be nice, and to her it just didn't seem genuine. She wasn't really sure that he was being himself. Perhaps it was because he felt guilty about leaving them when they were so young, and was trying to make it up to them.

'Gabrielle are you with Mom now?' she whispered out loud. Even though she knew nobody could hear her she needed to break the silence, to prove to herself that she really was still awake and not just floating aimlessly in a fantasy world. Suddenly she felt very cold, colder than before, icy cold, like she had at the graveside. It was September. The weather was still mild outside and despite the fact that there was only a light breeze that night, she began to shiver uncontrollably. She had now become aware of another noise in the room - her clock on the wall, tick, tick, tick, tick. She felt as though somebody was watching her. Her heart beat in time with the clock and she felt paralysed with fear. She couldn't turn around, she was too afraid. The other sounds had melted away; all she could hear now was the ticking of the clock and her heart almost in competition with each other.

'Leave me,' she said her voice shaking with fear. She reached slowly towards her dresser for her hairbrush. It was the only solid object she could think of that was close enough to use as a weapon to defend herself. As she leaned over the dresser, groping in the darkness for the hairbrush, she felt the cold presence move to the right side of her. She was still too afraid to turn around. She knew though that by now if somebody really was there they would have made physical contact with her, or seeing her reaching for the hairbrush, would have grabbed her hand away. Then it did. She felt something jab her so hard in the ribs that she fell sideways onto her dresser, sending her beauty products and perfume bottles flying. She shrieked in horror. She landed heavily and, although in pain, knew that she had to move quickly. This thing was coming at her again. She leapt up and spun around, prepared to face her tormentor, knowing she had to defend herself. 'Aaaaagggggghhhhhhhh!' she screamed with fear and rage. It was almost like a war cry. Nothing. She looked furtively around her.

'Where are you, you asshole?' she cried. 'I know you're there! I'm not stupid, or are you too scared, you Goddamn chicken!' Tears were now streaming down her face, her eyes were wild. The room though was empty again. Tick tick tick tick went the clock on the wall.

The moonlight streamed through the window illuminating the familiar features of her room, her bedclothes were still in a crumpled heap on the end of the bed. The only thing that had changed was the top of her dresser; everything had been swept onto the floor. She still clutched the hairbrush in her hand. She held it so tightly that her knuckles were turning white, but still she looked around, breathing rapidly, her chest aching from the panic that had gripped her.

This was not over yet, and she was angry.

Brad, I need you so badly, why did you have to leave today? You're just a bastard like the rest of them. I hate you, I wish I'd never met you, you asshole!

Suddenly there was an almighty bang in the corridor outside her bedroom, and she instinctively knew that it was coming from Gabrielle's room. *My God her door just slammed! Fuck, her door just slammed.* Her nerves were at fever pitch. She stood quivering by the dresser, the breeze still blowing her hair. She faced the door, her eyes fixed on the handle waiting for it to turn, willing it to turn, but at the same time dreading it. She heard footsteps, loud footsteps, almost unnatural, like the sound of heavy shoes on wood panelling. It was not like the sound of someone walking on carpet. The noise surrounded her it was above her in front of her and behind her. *God help me, please if you're there please help me!* The footsteps stopped suddenly. She was shaking so uncontrollably that she could barely stand. It was then that she heard something that frightened her more than anything she had experienced up to this point. She heard crying, it was the sound of a young girl crying. The noise filled the room and echoed in the hallway outside. It was everywhere - the most desolate sound that she had ever heard. The pain and sorrow were palpable. She felt the pain in her chest more now, it was as if someone had taken a knife and slit her chest open. A wave of grief came over her, so powerful that it knocked her off her feet, and she collapsed onto the floor. She lay there still staring at her bedroom door, her eyes wide.

'Don't cry, Mommy's here!' she said, her voice now hoarse with emotion, the words just coming automatically from her mouth. The sound of the little girl crying continued as if her heart would break, but Alicia's face no longer registered any emotion. 'Mommy's here,' she kept saying the same words over and over again.

The door burst open. A figure loomed in the darkness. Then the light. Alicia squinted it was so bright. The figure stepped from the shadows and she leapt to her feet, running back to the window where she stood with her back to the breeze. She was still shaking, her eyes still straining in the artificial light.

A familiar voice spoke with concern and some annoyance.

'Alicia, what *are* you doing? You were making enough noise in here to wake the dead.'

'Gee Dad,' she retorted, 'how considerate and thoughtful of you to say that! You may remember it was my sister's funeral today and I am just a little bit upset,' her voice rose to a crescendo as her anger spilled over.

'God I'm so sorry,' Adam said putting his head in his hands. 'I always say the wrong thing. I'm hurting too you know. I just find it hard to express it, that's all; I'm frightened that if I start crying, I'm never going to stop - I can't afford to let that happen.' He sat down on the edge of her bed.

'Someone was in the room,' she said bleakly.

'What do you mean? Someone got in, where?' he said, jumping to his feet again.

'I never saw them, but I felt them,' she continued. She wrapped her arms around herself protectively.

'If someone's been in here, then I'm going to call the police,' he insisted, turning back towards the open door.

'You don't understand,' she replied frustrated. 'I didn't see them, but they were standing right next to me. I felt so cold, then I heard footsteps.' Adam turned back to face her.

'Well I'm not surprised you're cold,' he replied, 'your window's wide open.'

'This isn't the first time weird things have happened in here,' she continued relentlessly. 'I never told you before what happened to my photo. It broke the night that Gabrielle was murdered, but I never knew that at the time.'

'Alicia, enough!' he interrupted her angrily. 'I'm sorry, but if you're trying to imply what I think you are, then don't OK? I don't want to hear it.'

'But I'm telling you the truth,' she said with desperation in her voice.

'I don't want to hear it, now just stop! It's all in your mind, you had too much to drink today, as we all did. You're exhausted, now try and get some sleep.'

'I can't sleep,' she replied flatly.

'How about I make you a hot drink then?' he said trying to soften his tone.

'No, don't bother,' she replied indignantly, 'I'm going downstairs, I'm gonna watch the TV. I can't sleep and that's an end of it.'

Adam sighed, resigned to the fact that he couldn't talk her round.

Courtney was also awake. She had woken when she'd heard the door slam. She got up just after Adam and went downstairs - something wasn't right.

Alicia walked shakily out into the corridor after her father, who turned to go back to bed. The lights were all on. She ran past Gabrielle's room. The door was still closed and she could hear the kettle boiling downstairs. 'Courtney!' she called out from the top of the stairs 'is that you?'

'Yes Alicia it's me,' came her weary reply. Courtney's parents were sleeping in the spare room at the opposite end of the corridor and Alicia could hear movement in their room too - they had also been woken by all the commotion.

Downstairs Alicia flopped down on the couch in the lounge. Courtney came in with two steaming cups of coffee and some more of her mother's homemade cookies. Alicia looked at her. 'Did I wake you too?' she said apologetically.

Courtney sighed, 'I heard your door slam.'

'It wasn't my door,' Alicia replied.

Courtney sat down on the opposite couch, her face pale and wan.

Both women looked at each other. Courtney knew what Alicia was implying, but she wasn't about to explore the possibilities. She frowned back at her.

'Jennifer is getting better apparently,' Alicia said, quickly changing the subject. 'You know before they said that she'd never recover - well apparently she is.'

'What?' Courtney said perplexed. She continued to frown as she sipped her coffee. 'How do you know?'

'Brad told me today,' she replied.

'Well how does Brad know?' Courtney pressed her further.

'Jack Thorpe told him. Apparently he was the man they escorted from the funeral. You know, the one that Dad bellowed at.'

Courtney's heart had begun to beat faster; alarm bells were now ringing. 'Is that Jennifer's father?' Alicia nodded. 'Oh my God!' she exclaimed, the realisation suddenly dawning on her. 'I was right all along.' She felt that old familiar panic welling up inside of her again.

'What do you mean?' Alicia looked suspiciously over at her stepmother.

'He wasn't talking to him at all,' Courtney replied. Alicia was still confused.

'I asked your father who that man was, and he wouldn't tell me.' She placed her coffee back down on the table. 'God I need a cigarette,' she pleaded. 'Alicia, you have to give me one of yours.'

'But what about the...' Alicia was cut off before she could finish.

'I know I know, the baby,' Courtney said - she was pacing now as Adam had been before the funeral. 'C'mon, Alicia *please*.'

She walked over to Alicia her hand outstretched.

She gave into her reluctantly, almost throwing the cigarette at her. Courtney lit it eagerly and immediately took a long deep drag, savouring every moment. She sat down again, like an addict who had just had their first fix in weeks; she was calmer now.

'Your father doesn't know Jack Thorpe - he even said as much,' Courtney continued, willing Alicia to understand without having to spell it out to her. 'He can't have ever seen him before. He's never been on the news, well not that I've seen anyway, and your father watches far less TV than I do.'

'So who the hell was he yelling at then?' Alicia said, realising what all this implied.

'I don't know,' Courtney said wistfully, 'but I'm going to find out if it kills me.'

Alicia's eyes began to feel very heavy, her body finally giving in to her tiredness. She was too exhausted to talk any longer; she was still troubled by the night's events and terrified of what would happen next. She wanted to speak to Brad; her conscious world was turning into a waking nightmare that she was afraid she would never escape from.

'Will you stay down here tonight Courtney?' she asked quietly. 'I don't want to be on my own.'

'Of course I will,' she replied, her voice tinged with sadness, 'I don't want to go back to your father now either.'

Alicia could relax a little. She felt safer knowing that Courtney was there. She looked over at the clock on the VCR, it was now three in the morning.

'We'll leave the light on,' Courtney said as she lay down on the couch. As Alicia lay down on her couch she looked over at her stepmother, who was still awake. She smiled back at her affectionately, 'Night night Alicia.'

As Alicia drifted off to sleep she had another flashback. This time it was of the burial that day and it was then that she saw *him* again - the thin faced man, hiding amongst the trees on the far side of the graveyard. In her dream the mist had descended and swirled around him, obliterating his face, but she could still make out his eyes, dark troubled, empty eyes. Perhaps he wasn't real, perhaps she had just imagined him. Maybe he was there to forewarn her about something that was going to happen. 'Alicia,' he called her name and beckoned to her. She stepped forward. The crowd had dispersed. She moved quickly, floating above ground. The mist obscured everything and as she got closer to the dark shadowy figure he smiled seductively, willing her to come to him.

She faced him, and he reached out to touch her cheek. She recoiled. For some reason she was afraid that his hypnotic dark eyes could see deep into her soul and that he now knew everything. She tried to speak but couldn't. She had suddenly become aware of the moist cold earth beneath her and looking down she realised that her feet were bare - her shoes had gone. When she looked back up at his face it had changed. His eyes were now those of her depraved, triumphant attacker. She screamed but no sound came from her lips. She turned and ran, the wind in her hair, aware of the pain of her bare feet on the uneven ground. She could now see Brad up ahead, her saviour. He called to her his arms outstretched. Back in his warm embrace the horror around her finally melted away.

159

When Alicia suddenly woke she didn't want to open her eyes at first. Her dream world now was a lot safer than her reality. She kept them closed and tried to return to the dream that she had just been having; she had been on a beach in the blazing hot sun. Brad was lying beside her, resting on his elbow. He had picked up a handful of pure white sand and was trickling it onto her bronzed body - laughing as she tried to brush it off. She could hear the waves breaking on the shore and the children laughing and playing just a little way from them.

The sounds around her pulled her again back to reality. She could no longer ignore the fact that she was awake - raised voices were coming from the kitchen. The lounge door was closed but she could hear that it was Courtney and her dad arguing. She knew straight away what it would be about and groaned inwardly.

She sat up and ran her fingers through her knotted hair. 'Ouch!' she yelled. It was so tangled she knew she would have to go and find her hairbrush. She hesitated before standing up. The sun was shining outside and last nights shadows had gone. She felt she could go upstairs and back into her room, but she didn't know what she would do that night - she couldn't sleep in there again, not now.

'Why didn't you tell me Jack Thorpe was at the funeral yesterday?' Courtney raved at her husband who stood by the back door, his arms hanging awkwardly by his side. His face had adopted that same puzzled look that she had seen when he'd been standing in the pulpit.

'I thought as much,' she replied, her arms folded defiantly in front of her. Alicia walked straight past and upstairs, neither one acknowledging her. 'It wasn't him you were shouting at was it? You don't even know Jack Thorpe, you've never seen him.' There was an uneasy silence between them for a moment.

'I knew it was Jack Thorpe, of course I knew it was him,' Adam finally replied. 'I've seen him before. He is the mayor after all.'

'When did you see him? Because I sure as hell never saw him before.' she rebuked.

'At the hospital. I've treated him before OK.' He scratched at his head, nervously.

'Well why didn't you tell me that when I asked you?' she replied, still wild with anger. She slammed her fist down on the breakfast bar making Adam jump.

'Damn it Adam, you even made a point of saying to me about her parents!'

'I know,' he relented, 'that was stupid I admit it.' She rolled her eyes and shook her head in disbelief.

'Look, I remembered I'd treated him before, and when I saw him I recognised him,' he then said becoming angry again. 'Courtney, if you think I'm a lying bastard, then why the hell did you marry me?'

'Because I didn't know you were a lying bastard then, that's why,' she screamed back.

'Courtney,' he held his hands out and looked at her pleadingly, 'I saw him before. He *was* the one I was shouting at in the church.'

'Even though you weren't even looking at him,' she said sarcastically.

'Oh God, perhaps I've got a squint or something! I'll make an appointment to see the Goddamn optician if that'll make you happy!'

'Oh don't be facetious Adam, it doesn't suit you.' She sat down at the breakfast bar, feeling then as though all the energy had been drained from her. She didn't know anything anymore. She didn't even feel as if she knew her own husband.

'Look,' Adam sighed defeated, 'we're never going to agree. I've told you that I'd seen him before but I didn't want to tell you who he was because I thought it might upset you. I don't know why I said what I did in the auto; I was upset, I wasn't thinking rationally.' He stopped and waited for a response from his wife. She didn't answer - she wouldn't even look at him.

'C'mon Courtney,' he continued with desperation in his voice, 'haven't you ever made a mistake? Haven't you ever forgotten what you said or why you said it? I'm not a robot, I'm just some dumb guy.' He walked over to her cautiously, 'Courtney, I love you so much and you're having our baby in five months.'

'Well that's if all this stress doesn't kill it before it's even born,' she said gloomily.

'Oh don't say that Courtney please - you have to believe me,' his voice was now breaking with emotion.

'Please Courtney! Look at me. I'm sorry, I'm so so sorry.'

She looked up at him. She didn't want to fight anymore, she didn't have the strength and there was too much going on. She realised that she couldn't cope with it alone and that she needed the family unit to stay strong. She would have to accept his explanation and his apology or it would all just fall apart. But something deep down inside of her had left her uneasy and unsettled. Despite everything she knew that she didn't truly believe him. She didn't speak at first, she just stood up and walked over to him. He embraced her, kissing her fervently and nuzzling his face into the nape of her neck. 'God I love you,' he breathed in her ear.

'I love you too,' she answered bleakly.

Alicia was ready and out the house before the argument finished. She had called Brad from her mobile and arranged to meet him for lunch. He had sounded a little distant, but at least he had agreed - she needed to get to the bottom of what was going on. As she walked down her road she felt the usual butterflies in her stomach that she always felt around him, but today they were worse than ever. As she rounded the corner into the next street she reached into her bag for her cigarettes. She lit one, although she felt sick. She thought that must be partly due to the lack of sleep she'd had last night anyway. She was going to meet him in one of the café's on the main high street, the same road as Jennifer's. This was her usual walk to work. She didn't know when she would look for a new job, or if she ever would. She didn't feel strong enough yet. Jennifer's had been closed down for obvious reasons and the original owners didn't think they would ever be able to let it again. After all who would want to buy a property where two grisly murders had taken place.

Alicia's nerves were beginning to wear off a little. As she rounded the next corner she had almost forgotten where she was going and was just enjoying the warmth of the sunshine and the sound of birds singing. She had noticed a family of holidaymakers on the other side of the road and had to smile to herself. They were bustling along in their shorts, all wearing identical Mickey Mouse hats. There was a light breeze, which was catching her long mauve skirt. She wore sneakers and a short sleeved plain white T-shirt. She checked her watch, it was 12.20. She had to meet him in ten minutes so she still had plenty of time - she was almost there.

Brad sat at a table on the veranda of the Italia café bar, facing the way that he knew Alicia would be coming. She spotted him straight away and felt her heart start to race and her butterflies fluttering again. He watched her walk towards him, and although he tried to stifle it, a big smile spread across his face. He wasn't wearing his uniform but was in casual clothes and a pair of dark sunglasses. His short dark hair looked as if it had been cut that morning.

She stepped up to the veranda and pulled a chair out from under the table. It made a metallic scraping sound on the concrete, 'Aww that was a bit loud wasn't it,' she joked.

'Do you want a drink?' he asked looking round for the waiter, who was over by another table. Before she'd answered him he'd called him over.

'Oh I'll have a glass of wine please,' she replied with a smile.

She looked across the table at Brad, who just had a coffee. 'Aren't you gonna have anything a bit stronger?' she said with a smile.

She felt a little awkward as she sat back in her seat. It was a little disconcerting talking to someone who was wearing sunglasses. She ran her hand through her long golden hair and flicked it back so it hung straight down behind her.

Almost as if he could read her mind he took off his sunglasses and placed them down on the table next to his drink. 'You don't think this is just coffee do you? C'mon it's my day off,' he said with a wry smile. 'Try some.' He put his cup to her lips and she took a sip.

'Gross! That's got so much whiskey in it,' she said screwing her face up and recoiling. She didn't care for spirits.

'It's an Irish coffee,' he smiled back.

Her wine arrived at the table and she took a sip, lighting another cigarette. Brad signalled to the waiter again for an ashtray and he brought it over.

'Now then,' Brad said placing his elbow on the table and resting his chin on the back of his hand. He stared intently at her - his eyes lighting up with anticipation. 'So what did you want to talk about then?' he said.

She suddenly felt emotional. She had put all of the night's events behind her and didn't want to bring it up again, but she knew that she had to, because that night she was afraid that she may have to go through the same ordeal again.

The relief of seeing him, mixed with the stress that she had been under, just sent the tears rolling down her face. 'I'm sorry, I'm so sorry,' she kept saying.

'Hey,' he said tenderly reaching his free hand across the table and catching hold of hers. He squeezed it tight. 'What is it Alicia? Please tell me,' he was frowning now, still looking deep into her eyes.

'I don't know how to say this,' she finally managed to get the words out, 'but I couldn't sleep at all last night. *I think there's a ghost in our house,'* she lowered her voice to a whisper, not wanting anybody to hear.

'I can't sleep in my own room anymore and I don't know what to do. You have to help me!' He was dumbstruck and didn't reply at first. He looked troubled, and didn't seem to know what to make of what she had just said.

'What on earth has happened?' he said, still holding on to her hand.

'Well, first I felt the room turn cold, ice cold, then something struck me on my side. It felt like a hand - it dug into my ribs, but there was nobody there,' she spoke rapidly, not wanting to think about each event too deeply. 'Then I heard footsteps, all around me - they were so loud. There was a little girl, I could hear her crying.' She paused then and looked up to see his expression. His eyes were wide with amazement. He removed his hand from hers and sat back in his chair shaking his head in disbelief.

'My God!' he exclaimed. 'I don't know what to say to you.'

'Tell me you believe me,' she desperately needed him to.

'You've gone through a very traumatic time lately,' he replied formally. 'It's got to have had an effect on you.'

'Yes of course it has,' she replied, tears still welling in her eyes, 'but I haven't gone crazy - I'm not imagining it.'

He didn't reply but picked up his coffee and drank the rest of it down in one gulp. He then signalled to the waiter. 'Can I get a double brandy?' The waiter nodded and left them again.

'Alicia,' he said turning back to face her. 'What can I do? I'm not an exorcist or a medium - I'm a police officer.'

She felt so alone at that moment. He was reacting how everybody else would react - he was no different she thought.

'You're right. This was a mistake,' she said, picking up her bag, and standing shakily to leave.

'Wait!' he jumped up and caught hold of her arm, pulling her back down in her seat.

'Alicia, please don't go,' he said, his voice sounding anxious.

'I will try to help you.' He was resigned to the fact that he couldn't let her walk away from him. 'This is very hard for me Alicia. This case is ongoing and I'm involved because I was the first one on the scene. I'm going to be completely honest with you now.' He took a deep breath, the waiter returned with his brandy; he drank it straight down and ordered another one.

Alicia looked on in amazement.

'Would you like the same again ma'am?' the waiter asked.

'Yes please,' she nodded.

'I'm putting my neck on the line here,' he continued in a low whisper, 'I know I've gotten too involved with you. It's not your fault, it's my fault. It's the way I feel,' he held his hands up apologetically.

'Well, what's the big deal?' she said shrugging her shoulders. 'I'm nineteen but you're only twenty-six. It's not like you're forty or married!'

'I know, I know,' he said shaking his head again. 'The problem is that I've have been *told* not to get involved with you. Don't you see? I walked away yesterday but all I wanted to do was go back.'

'Hey,' Alicia said tenderly, putting her hand on his. 'What does it matter? I won't say anything to anyone.'

'But what if everything in the case came to a head? You are a potential suspect - you know that don't you?'

He looked into her eyes, trying to read her mind, trying to see if she was telling him the truth.

The waiter placed his brandy and her wine on the table and started to speak, but Brad waved him away.

'There's nothing to be suspicious about Brad,' she said quietly, looking straight back at him, 'I loved my sister. I didn't want her to die. I'm lost without her - you know that.' Her eyes blurred with tears again.

'I know,' he smiled, as if her words were confirmation that everything that Detective Owens had said was wrong.

He reached up and lovingly touched her cheek; she leant her face against his hand and closed her eyes for a moment.

She suddenly thought of Jennifer and remembered again what she had thought about the night before, about what Jennifer had said to her about the alligators in Windermere. At the time it had just been an ordinary friendly conversation with her boss. Perhaps that was why she had felt the presence in her room last night, she concluded, to remind her that she was supposed to detest Jennifer now more than anything else in the world. Perhaps it was Gabrielle trying to communicate with her. She wondered if it was her, why would she try to hurt her?

She opened her eyes again. They had only been closed for a couple of seconds. 'Are you gonna drink that brandy straight back too?' she asked Brad, who was resting back on his elbow again, looking out into the street at the passers by.

'No,' he said dreamily, 'I can drink this one slow, I've got all the embarrassing stuff out the way now.' He looked back at her and smiled.

'I saw this family on the way to meet you,' she said changing the subject. 'They were all in shorts and all had on the same Mickey Mouse hats,' she laughed. 'It's sweet though isn't it - a family all on vacation and excited about what they're gonna do that day?'

'You're not wrong there,' he agreed. 'Do you know I really wish I'd met you some place else and that I'd never been on patrol that morning.'

'I wish a lot of things too, but we can't change what's happened can we,' she said in a matter of fact tone.

She lit another cigarette and took another sip of wine.

'Brad,' she said, 'I want to go and see Jennifer.'

'No way,' came his immediate reply. 'That's a bad idea. Imagine what'll happen if she sees you! She's already unstable - it could push her over the edge.'

'Well what do we care!' she replied indignantly, 'I need to know why she did it.'

'No,' he insisted. 'Promise me you won't go there. It'll cause no end of trouble, believe me.'

She took another sip of her wine, 'OK,' she replied indignantly.

'We will find out why,' he affirmed. 'She'll have to talk sooner or later, don't worry about that.'

They finished their drinks, paid and headed off up the high street together. With the warm sunshine shining down on them Alicia felt safe now and also happy with the realisation that she hadn't lost Brad after all. Deep down she had probably known this all along, but had allowed her self-doubt to rule her head. She had suggested to Brad that they catch a bus to Down Town Disney for the afternoon. It was his day off and he agreed readily - seeing all the holidaymakers had inspired her. She wanted to feel at least for a short while as though she was on holiday too, and try and forget everything that had happened over the last couple of days.

When they arrived they had some lunch at one of the restaurants and more wine. They relaxed totally in each other's company and their new surroundings. Brad at one point was laughing so much at something Alicia had said that tears were rolling down his face. They finished their meal around four in the afternoon and then made their way to an open-air bar by the lake. The weather was cooling slightly but they were not in any hurry to get home. The bar was tiny and had small wooden tables with thatched parasols shading them. It was like a Caribbean bar, and as they sat there they both decided to have a cocktail, as it was more in keeping with the theme of the place. Alicia looked out over the lake to where there was a large boat on the other side. This was actually a sea food restaurant and she suggested maybe they should go there another night.

The conversation flowed so freely between them. Everything felt so natural and so comfortable it was as if they knew each other intimately already.

Although Alicia was now feeling quite drunk she felt all right and was determined not to go home early and spoil the perfect day. She leaned across the table. Brad sat looking out over the water with a faint smile on his face and a look of utter contentment. She planted a big kiss on his cheek. 'What was that for?' he said in amazement.

'For being the coolest guy I've ever met,' she said her voice slurring a little from the liquor she had consumed.

He leaned back across the table and held both of her hands in his. As their eyes met it was like an explosive chemical reaction. She felt a yearning in the pit of her stomach - the animal instincts within her had finally been aroused. He moved in closer to her face, almost in slow motion. He kissed her on the lips, such a tender kiss, and then he sat back. He took another sip of his drink and looked over at her, his eyes transfixed by her face, the face of his dreams; neither of them spoke. He couldn't help himself then. He was drawn back to her lips for more, but this time it was passionate and he pulled her to him. She put her hand around the back of his neck and ran her fingers through his hair. They finally stopped even though at that moment Alicia felt she could have easily made love to him there and then. It was as if everything and everybody around them had melted away, and it was just them sitting there by that lake. He put his hands either side of her face and kissed her gently on the forehead. 'Oh baby,' he breathed as he kissed her again. 'What are you doing to me?'

Alicia pulled back from him suddenly. As he spoke those words she had felt as if a wave of ice had washed over her, passing straight through her entire body. She sat hunched, shivering, her arms wrapped around herself desperately rubbing at her freezing limbs trying to get the circulation going again.

'What on earth just happened to you?' Brad said, a look of amazement on his face. 'What's wrong? I was told I had cold hands, but they can't be that bad!'

She breathed deeply, the warmth was returning again. The sun was beginning to set now, but on a warm evening like this the slight breeze coming off the lake would not have been enough to give anyone a chill like that.

'My God,' she finally said, 'I just felt that presence again! It was there, right next to me! It passed straight through me - lets get out of here!'

She jumped to her feet; Brad followed after her, catching hold of her hand as she walked up the two steps that led back to the sidewalk. They walked together back round the lake and she held onto his hand tightly, not wanting to let go. She felt her panic returning as the night was drawing in and she knew that she would have to go home at some stage - unless of course she got to stay at Brad's. She didn't, however, really want to risk sleeping with him so soon.

Then she remembered that Courtney and her dad were due to be going out that night for a meal. Now that Courtney's parents would have also returned to Leesburg by now, as they were going to leave before lunchtime that day - she would be totally alone if she went home now.

'Can we go for some more drinks?' she said.

Brad looked at her and smiled, 'Are you sure?'

Alicia knew that he was thinking that they'd had enough already, but she felt that getting drunk was the only solution to her problems right now - the real world was too frightening.

'I'm sure,' she said looking up at him earnestly.

He stroked the back of her hand as he held it in his, 'C'mon then let's go.'

They headed towards Pleasure Island and the bright lights and hustle and bustle. People were milling around everywhere - most still wearing shorts. No-one seemed to have bothered to dress up for the evening. Alicia didn't care about the crowd - in fact she liked it. This was the proper holiday feeling she had been waiting for - the fear had left her.

They walked together up the central high street towards the stage area where there was a live band playing. Even though it wasn't a particularly good one it didn't spoil Alicia's enjoyment as she continued to soak up the party atmosphere. They stopped at one of the outdoor bars where Brad bought them both a beer.

Wine, beer, spirits - Alicia had been seriously mixing her drinks. Although her head was swimming a little she didn't care. Anything that happened later would be a blur. Anything she said or did with Brad she could just blame on her intoxicated state.

Brad went and stood over by the side of the bar and leaned his back up against the wall. Alicia walked towards him and he looked at her appraisingly as she ventured nearer. She pressed herself against him; he slipped his arms around her waist and pulled her in close, spilling her drink.

'Watch the beer!' she said feigning annoyance.

'Don't worry babe, I can buy you ten more if you want me to,' he said his voice hoarse with passion.

'He buried his face in the nape of her neck and then slowly moved his head up putting his lips against her ear, 'I'd do anything for you,' he breathed. 'I want you so badly Alicia.'

'Don't make me go home then,' she whispered back.

He stood back up straight and tilted his head back, downing the rest of his drink.

'Ready for another?' He began to walk away.

'Lets go somewhere else,' she replied, hurrying to finish her drink. As he turned the corner and headed back down the Main Street she quickly caught up with him again. They decided to go into the Hawaiian Club. As they were walking up the stairs he pulled her to him and whispered in her ear, 'If you do get caught for that fake ID I will be in serious crap.'

'Don't worry,' she assured him leaning over laughing and kissing his cheek, 'I won't tell if you don't.'

They continued to drink and stood close together by the dance floor - lost in their own world. Alicia began to feel extraordinarily drunk.

'Do you want another?' Brad said, his voice distorted by the combination of loud music and the buzzing noise that had started up in her head. She looked up, trying to focus on his face. The ceiling was now spinning and she was completely disorientated; she reeled backwards. Brad caught her just before she fell. 'Get off me!' she yelled back at him. 'I think I'm gonna throw.' She ran blindly round the side of the dance floor.

Brad kept trying to grab her hand but she pulled it back each time. She was staggering now, aware of people staring at her; she somehow made it to the bathroom in time, flung open the cubicle door, and proceeded to vomit for the next twenty minutes. Brad waited for her outside, his head in his hands. He was sobering up fast now. *She's been in there for ages.* He decided that he would wait another five minutes and if she didn't come out then, he would have to go in and get her.

Just as he was preparing to march into the ladies bathroom, a bedraggled Alicia appeared at the door. She had washed all the make up from her face and cleaned herself up as best she could but she still smelt of vomit. Brad tried to ignore this fact, took her arm, and led her towards the exit.

'Where do you want me to take you?' he asked cautiously. Alicia just hung her head. She was still staggering and although the nauseous feeling had gone temporarily she felt more drunk than ever. Earlier on she had wanted to go back to his place, but now she just felt out of it.

'Just take me home Brad. I'm so sorry.'

He hailed a cab just outside Pleasure Island and they headed back to her house in Kissimmee. Brad sat in the back of the cab with Alicia slumped up against him. She had fallen asleep but he didn't wake her until they pulled up outside her house - he thought it best not to.

He paid the driver and asked him to wait. He then gave her a gentle nudge, helped her out of the cab and up the driveway. She fell to her knees just before the door and he had to haul her back up again.

'God I feel so ill!' she cried, tears streaming down her face. 'I'm so sorry Brad. I've ruined our perfect day - everything was going fine until I got sick.'

'Don't worry honey,' he said smoothing her hair back from her face. 'You'll have to try harder than that to put me off! Now where are your house keys?'

She fumbled in her pockets and eventually found them. She attempted to get them into the lock but the trouble was that now she was seeing two locks! She couldn't work out which was the right one.

Brad smiled to himself, reached out, took them from her and opened the door. The house was in darkness. Not having been there before he didn't know where to find the light switch, but once in the house Alicia found the light with ease.

'There weren't two of them then huh?' Brad laughed.

'Don't speak to me,' she groaned, 'I feel too bad.'

'All right sweetheart,' he replied. 'Do you want me to do anything else before I go?'

'No, just go,' she said waving him away. She could feel the nausea rising in her throat and didn't want him to see her throw up.

'OK babe,' he called from the door. 'I'll call you tomorrow.' With that he left, closing the door behind him.

She was alone. She took a deep breath and decided a black coffee might help. Then she would go to bed. She still felt drunk, so drunk that she had almost forgotten her anxiety about the night. She wandered into the kitchen and switched on the kettle. She positioned herself precariously on one of the breakfast bar stools and her head fell forward onto her folded arms. 'Don't fall asleep here Alicia - got to get up,' she said, and was then roused by the sound of the kettle boiling.

She lifted her head and summoning all of her strength she managed to slide off the stool into a standing position. On her way to the kettle she stopped to peer at her reflection in the mirror on the side of the grocery cupboard. 'Oh God,' she exclaimed, 'I look hideous!' Her eyes were bloodshot and her hair was matted.

She poured herself a coffee and then set off unsteadily up the stairs towards her bedroom. She kept lurching forward as the stairs seemed to pitch and roll before her. She spilt her coffee twice on the way up, and kept having to steady herself by grasping hold of the bannister.

She snapped on the light as she opened her bedroom door and proceeded cautiously inside. After struggling into her pyjamas she decided to watch a film - switching on her TV and flicking through the channels trying to find something worth watching.

She sat up in bed, the controller in one hand, her coffee in the other; she could feel her eyes drooping. She tried to keep them open but couldn't fight it any longer. She quickly put the coffee down on the side and threw the controller on the floor before slipping into unconsciousness.

Alicia was suddenly awake again; she had been asleep barely an hour when the noise of the TV blaring had jolted her back into consciousness. Confusion, *where am I?* She remembered then. She sat up, squinting in the bright light, her heart thumping in her chest. That familiar feeling of dread came over her again as she realised that the TV was getting louder and louder. Her immediate reaction was to cover her ears as the noise was deafening. She looked around frantically for the controller; she searched the bed, thinking it may be caught up in the sheets. Maybe she was leaning on the volume control, but it was nowhere to be found. Then she saw it. It was over the other side of the room, perched on the edge of her dressing table; the seat had been pulled out from underneath it as if somebody was sat there. She watched in horror, the infrared light at the end of the remote flashing by itself; the volume button was decompressed. She leapt out of bed and made a grab for it, but it flew out of her hand as if it were covered in grease. She went to pick it up again but as she reached it, it shot across the room, and disappeared from sight. She turned around and headed for the TV to turn it off at the switch, but as she reached it, it lifted from its stand and hovered above her head, before moving over towards the door.

'STOP!' Alicia screamed at the top of her voice. At this the TV switched itself off and fell like a stone, smashing to the ground. As it landed her bedroom light went out. She was in darkness. It was happening again. She couldn't take anymore; she stumbled over the remains of the TV and out through her bedroom door. Tears streaked her face. She was angry and she was more frightened than she had ever been before in her life. As she ran down the upstairs hallway the doors that she passed opened and slammed by themselves. She shrieked in horror. She had to get out of the house - she couldn't stay there any longer. She hadn't had time to pick up any of her belongings but she just knew she would be safe outside. As she ran down the stairs a vase of flowers suddenly took flight, smashing against the wall behind her - just missing her head. She didn't scream this time but just focused on the front door, getting to it as quickly as possible. She grabbed hold of the handle and frantically tried to open it. She kicked it and yelled but it wouldn't budge. She spun round and saw that the back door was open - she made it just in time. As she ran through it slammed behind her - her invisible assailant had not been quick enough. Up the side of the house she stumbled and into the street, the concrete slabs of the sidewalk were cold under her bare feet. Scattering the stray stones that littered the path she ran on, without looking back. She didn't know where she was going; she didn't care either, as long as it was as far away from Bay View Grove as possible.

She reached the main road and continued running down the sidewalk heading towards Highway 192. People noticed her but nobody tried to stop her. She was in a world of her own, and they were caught up in theirs. She thought about Jennifer. All this was down to her. Alicia hated her, she hated her so much that it was all consuming and she could think of nothing else.

Jennifer lay, drifting in and out of sleep, tossing her head from side to side, tormented by her dreams.

Her room was empty, the stark white walls reflecting the dim overhead lighting. The window at the foot of her bed was open, the navy curtain billowing in the breeze. She felt the cool air on her face as she drifted in and out of sleep. She was beginning to recover, slowly, but her psychological scars were deep.

As she lay on her side, muttering quietly to herself, she heard the sound of her room door opening. She didn't move. She just lay still her eyes fixed straight ahead, dull lifeless eyes that didn't seem to register anything.

'Jennifer,' the nurse called from the doorway. She didn't respond; the nurse busied herself in the room and then walked round to the side of the bed, picking up her empty glass.

'Do you want some more water Jennifer?' she said briskly. She wasn't the most appealing of nurses, a little rough around the edges on occasion.

Jennifer nodded her head once but didn't make eye contact with the nurse.

174

'I have to give you your evening injection,' she continued. 'Are you not cold with that window open? I know it's only pulled up a bit, but even so there's quite a breeze.'

The nurse went over to the window and unlocked the latch to pull it back down. Parallel iron bars on the outside of the window made escape impossible whether the window was open or closed.

'No, leave it!' Jennifer shouted angrily.

The nurse sighed, 'Whatever, you want.'

'My father's visiting me tomorrow,' Jennifer then remarked, perking up a little.

'That's true,' the nurse replied her voice softening a little. 'You look forward to his visits don't you?'

Jennifer didn't reply this time. She rolled onto her back, staring at the ceiling. Her dishevelled, mousy hair was splayed across her pillow and her face was pale with dark shadows under her eyes. She blinked slowly and deliberately, the corners of her eyes were moist but no tears formed in her eyes. She no longer expressed emotion. Since the murders she had retreated into herself, her feelings locked away, in denial.

The nurse administered her evening injection as she did every night, at the same time.

'I'll leave you then,' the nurse said from the foot of her bed. 'Sleep well.'

She turned on her heel and made her way to the door, switching off the light before she closed the door and locked it behind her. The room had a long window through which you could see into the corridor. Facing that window, on the opposite side of the corridor, was one of the many security posts, which provided round the clock surveillance for the maximum security hospital.

Jennifer's room now in darkness, she rolled back onto her side and closed her eyes. She let out a sigh, the injection starting to take effect, and she could feel herself drifting off into a natural sleep. Just as her conscious world began to fade she heard someone call her name, only this time it wasn't the nurse, and it wasn't in her head. The voice was coming from the doorway.

'Jennifer,' the voice spoke again. It was softly spoken, a female voice, non-threatening. Then it changed. 'Jennifer you bitch!'

In a flash the same voice had turned into a menacing, vicious snarl and was slowly moving closer to where she lay.

Jennifer began to shake and pulled her covers up around her ears, not wanting to look at the foot of her bed. She kept her eyes closed. The intruder grabbed at the covers and pulled them off in a flash. Jennifer curled herself into the foetal position, still shaking. 'Who are you?' she cried.

'I'm surprised you don't know who I am Jennifer,' the voice was relentless and angry.

'I'm your worst nightmare.'

Jennifer shrieked and reached for her panic button. Her hand searched desperately, clawing blindly at the wall, but it wasn't there - it had gone.

'You have ruined my life Jennifer,' the voice began to move closer still, around the side of the bed towards her.

'You have taken my sister away from me, now give me one good reason why I shouldn't kill you too.'

'Please,' Jennifer stammered.

'Open your eyes bitch and look at me!' The voice was now so close that it was an inch away from her face - so close that Jennifer could feel their breath on her face.

'Look at me!' the voice cried again, 'because I'm the last person you're ever going to see.'

'No I will not!' Jennifer screamed. As the pillow was suddenly yanked out from under her head she fell backwards. A hand went over her mouth to smother her cries as her limbs flailed in a vain attempt to fight off her attacker. The pillow was brought down heavily on her face; she gasped and choked beneath it.

'This is the only way Jennifer and it's what you deserve for what you have done to me and my family.' Now crying uncontrollably her attacker pushed down harder as Jennifer tried in vain to fight her off.

After a violent struggle all movement finally ceased. Jennifer's body twitched in its death throes and then lay still; it was finished.

Chapter 9

Alicia opened her eyes slowly. Pain racked her entire body; she felt freezing as the reality of her situation began to dawn on her. Instead of the usual feel of her soft mattress beneath her, she was sure she felt rough course grass. She felt as if she was naked. She tried to move her right arm but it felt dead beside her. It was icy cold and as she touched it with her left hand she jumped as it felt as if she were feeling somebody else's arm. Her eyes now fully open, she tried to focus on her surroundings. She was dazed and seeing the sky directly above her only served to confuse her more. S*urely not. God my legs - I can't feel my legs*! She reached down with her previously numb hand that she had managed to bring back to life. Shakily she slowly touched her legs. She could feel her silk pyjamas but no covers. W*here the hell am I?* She could hear voices in the distance but she knew instinctively that they were not near her and that nobody knew she was there. She had to get home. She struggled to her feet, and as she stood searing pains shot up each leg as she put the weight onto her feet. She looked down - her feet were dirty and swollen. She looked around nervously like a frightened animal and hunched over to try to make herself smaller, less significant. Terror took over now. As her eyes darted furtively around her new surroundings she deduced that she was in some sort of large garden. Grand trees loomed imposingly overhead and the garden stretched as far as her eye could see, lush and green. She had been lying next to a small bush like shrub, which had concealed her until now. There was little colour in the garden - just a vast expanse of lawn, interspersed with magnificent poplar and palm trees.

She turned slowly, every movement causing her more pain. She hugged herself as she was shivering feverishly. Then she saw it, the most oppressive building she had ever seen. It stood tall, around six floors. Surrounding the main building was a bleak grey concrete wall that stood taller than the height of four men - the twisted silver grey barbed wire on top of the wall catching the first of the morning sunlight as it rose above the trees. Searchlights beamed down on the area in front of the wall. The area between the wall and the main building was illuminated by the eerie light.

Alicia squinted in the strengthening sunlight. She moved towards the building, drawn irresistibly towards it. She needed to find some help and there was nothing else nearby, just endless trees and grass.

She walked forward slowly. Her mind was a complete blank, dulled by the pain. She was terrified and confused at her situation. Where was she and how did she get here? It was as if she was on autopilot, the body taking over from the helpless mind - independent of it. Vivid memories of her rape flashed through her mind, the smell of the dew on the grass, the sweet cloying air. The dried blood on her cuts and scratches reopened and bled again as she walked, causing her more pain. She winced with every faltering step that she took. Her arms were outstretched, trying to extend her body as far forward as she could - almost as though she would reach the building quicker by doing this. Suddenly from the trees to the left of her Alicia became aware of a dog barking, then another and another. From the shadows leapt three German Shepherd dogs, which ran towards her, their barking getting louder and louder until it was deafening. She fell to the ground and curled up in a ball with her hands over her head to protect her, screaming and crying.

Bright lights and men's voices followed them. One of the dogs grazed her back with its teeth and the others batted her with their large heavy paws. The police officers shouted commands to the dogs, which immediately ceased their attack and sat back on their haunches - eyeing their prey.

'My God!' exclaimed the first officer. 'I recognise this girl.' He bent down and carefully moved Alicia's hands away from her face. She was shaking uncontrollably.

'It's OK ma'am,' the officer said in a formal but kindly voice. 'You're safe now.'

Sirens wailed in the distance. The police officers had wrapped Alicia in a blanket supplied by one of the hospital staff. Within moments the ambulance pulled up and Alicia was carried in on a stretcher, accompanied by one of the police officers. She was automatically put on a drip to administer painkillers for her lacerated feet, as she lay on the stretcher. She looked over to her left where the police officer was sitting and she eyed him cautiously. She hadn't seen him before. He smiled at her broadly. He was olive skinned with a dark moustache and had a distinct curl in his hair. She felt warmer now as the fluids going into her veins took almost immediate effect. She could forget about the pain for a while. Now she had to deal with the other more pressing issues.

'You don't have to speak now ma'am,' the officer said reassuringly. 'Important that you get yourself better first.'

'I want to talk though,' she replied in a hoarse weak voice. 'I don't know where I was, or how I got there.'

'I'm afraid I can't help you with that one either,' he replied formally. 'We only know that we found you in the hospital grounds, and that's all.'

'The hospital grounds?' Alicia said confused. 'What hospital?'

'It's a psychiatric hospital,' he continued. 'We thought you were one of the patients escaped at first.'

Alicia's heart began to beat faster again. It was like she had just experienced déjà vu, and she began to panic.

'Hospital? Where's the hospital? Where am I?' she stammered.

The ambulance man turned to the officer, 'Please sir, if you don't mind leaving this for now.'

'No,' she said again, insistent, 'I need to know.'

The police officer hesitated first, then said slowly, 'We're in Orlando centre ma'am.'

'But I live in Kissimmee,' she replied mortified.

'We believe you must have walked up the interstate. Witnesses reported seeing you.'

She lay back and sighed, a shallow resigned sigh. 'Is she dead then?'

'Is who dead?' the officer said, shocked by her question.

'Jennifer of course,' she said still staring at the ceiling, not looking at the officer.

179

'I must caution you Miss Buchanan, that anything you say to me now may be given in evidence in a court of law.'

'Save it,' she replied brushing the air with an uninterested sweep of her hand.

'I'm glad she's dead if she is dead. I'm tired of living my life like this - it's a living hell and it was all caused by her. Maybe I'll get a bit of peace now.'

At the hospital Alicia was rushed into the Emergency Room where she was treated for exposure. Her wounds, which were mainly superficial, were cleaned and dressed and she was moved to a ward an hour later. When the police had called at 240 Bay View Grove they had found nobody at home; no car in the drive, and Ted Fraser their neighbour had not seen anyone since the day before.

They finally located Adam and Courtney at a motel near Leesburg where they had driven the previous night. They had had dinner at a local restaurant but when their car had broken down on the way back home they'd had to check into the motel for the night. They'd left a message for Alicia on the answering machine at home, but she hadn't listened to it.

Courtney's face turned deathly pale when the police officer told her the news. Her nerves had been at breaking point the last few weeks - she couldn't believe that something else could have happened so soon after Gabrielle's death. Nothing seemed to be going right for them anymore.

The garage had got the car going again and they were back on the road within half an hour of hearing the news.

'What on earth is going on?' Courtney said as they sped down the interstate. 'I don't know how much more I can take Adam. I haven't felt the baby move for days, the stress is killing it I swear.'

'I'm sure everything's gonna be fine honey,' he replied, remarkably calm.

'How can you say that?' she replied. 'I don't think the police have told us everything. They're hiding something I know it. They just said they found her in her pyjamas in this hospital's grounds.'

'She's very disturbed Courtney,' he continued seemingly unfazed. 'It's all over Gabrielle's death, - you know she's been acting strange. She was probably just sleep walking.'

'Adam, this hospital is in Orlando centre. She walked up the Goddamn interstate!' she hollered back at him.

The police were waiting for them when they arrived at the Florida Hospital. Courtney spotted Detective Owens in the throng, a grave look on his face - more formal than ever. Brad North was standing beside him. 'See I told you,' she said sarcastically, noticing this as they swept past the front and into Adam's private parking space next to the front building.

She slammed the door of the vehicle so hard that the windows rattled. With her bag slung over her shoulder she strode off towards the police officers, leaving Adam struggling to get something out of the glove compartment.

'Tell me something I don't already know,' she said with a desperate air to her voice as she approached Detective Owens.

'Mrs Buchanan, Alicia is in a stable condition.'

'I already know that,' she snapped back. 'I said tell me something I don't already know.'

'Jennifer Thorpe is dead,' he replied grimly. 'So what does that have to do with Alicia?' Courtney replied.

'She was found in the grounds of the hospital. Jennifer Thorpe died last night at that same hospital.'

'Oh God!' Courtney reached in her bag for her pack of cigarettes. 'Maybe that's just coincidence?' she continued as she fumbled for her lighter.

'She was suffocated Mrs Buchanan. She was found with a pillow covering her face. There are also distinct signs of a struggle having taken place.

Courtney stood, her left hand on her hip and the other in front of her mouth, puffing nervously on her cigarette.

She turned to Brad, 'C'mon Brad, you must know something about this! You were with her last night for God's sake!' she glared at him.

A look of utter bewilderment flashed across Owens' face, which he then tried to disguise. Brad didn't say anything; he just hung his head.

'Yes I thought as much,' Courtney was disgusted. 'Take advantage of a young girl, but you haven't got the guts to own up to it.'

'It wasn't like that,' Brad protested.

'Anyway,' Detective Owens cut across him, 'this is not the place to discuss these matters further. I just wanted you to know, so that you can help us with our enquiries. Alicia may open up to you. We're going to have to interview her when she's released, which should be by tomorrow.'

'Well I don't know about that,' she replied indignantly, tossing her cigarette butt down on the sidewalk.

At that point Adam walked up. 'I'll let your wife fill you in,' Owens said as he turned to speak to the other officers. Brad and Officer Colton had already started to walk back into the hospital with Adam and Courtney.

'Not you North!' Owens shouted after him. 'You're coming with me! Colton you stay, Brewer go with him.'

Brad and Officer Delgardo (who had been the officer who'd travelled with Alicia in the back of the ambulance) then climbed dutifully into the waiting patrol vehicle with Owens, and immediately drove off at speed.

'Give me one good reason why I shouldn't have you thrown off the force right now?' Owens bellowed at Brad as soon as they cleared the hospital front. 'You are an idiot! I mean were you gonna tell me about this, or do I just have to guess? You're supposed to be solving the crimes! Christ it's difficult enough without an officer who can't keep his dick in his pants when he's on a case - especially when he's after one of the Goddamn suspects.'

'It's not like that I swear,' Brad replied defeated.

'Oh it's not like that! Oh don't tell me you're in love,' Owens replied mockingly.

'Hey Goddamn it I resign! You can screw it, screw you!' Brad shouted at him, ripping at his badge on his uniform breast pocket.'

'Hey, Hey,' Owens said calmly now, pulling Brad's hand away from his chest. 'I need you now - I need your information. If you want to resign you can do it after this case is over. For the time being nothing has changed. Stay away from that girl and there just still may be a glimmer of hope for you.'

After passing through the heavy wrought iron hospital gates and various security checkpoints on route, the patrol vehicle finally pulled up outside. The forensic team were still at the scene. Detective Owens strode confidently towards the entrance of the hospital, his long coat trailing behind him as he went. Officers North and Delgardo followed. Two men stood in front of the main door. They were removing their white coveralls and talking seriously to one another. Detective Owens walked towards the two men; he stopped in front of them and flashed his ID Badge.

'Detective Carl Owens,' he announced, shaking one of the half-suited, half-white coverall clad forensic team by the hand confidently.

'Hi,' the fresh-faced man replied, with a smile, 'Ian Masters.'

'I understand you were talking by phone with one of my other colleagues earlier, Jamie Harrison,' he continued earnestly.

'Oh Detective Harrison - Yes,' Owens replied.

'So,' Owens continued, 'have you got anything for me?'

'Well,' Masters replied folding his arms defensively, 'we have surface prints that we're sending off to the lab for ID.'

'Good,' Owens responded confidently. 'We'll have to take prints from the staff here and question them all of course.'

He motioned to his two companions; Brad stepped forward first.

'I'm gonna go in and have another look at the crime scene. I take it we can do that and that you have everything you need?'

Ian Masters nodded, 'We do, it's clear now.'

'Right then, let's get moving. Thanks again for your hard work.'

'If you call the lab tomorrow we should have the results,' Masters said as he turned to leave with his colleague who had just finished making some last minute notes. 'We're gonna rush these results through so we can see if you can't wrap this one up real quick.'

'Great, I'll speak to you tomorrow.' With that Owens and his two accompanying officers moved towards the hospital entrance.

'We've got to try to contain this one,' Owens said as he stepped inside. He lowered his voice, 'We have to keep the press out of it - no details should be leaked. I don't want them connecting this death with the murders in Kissimmee. It will be all over the News like before. We have to wrap it up and then we'll issue a statement when we're ready.'

'What about the staff at the hospital. Have they been briefed?' Brad interjected.

'Yes that happened this morning,' Owens looked at his companions gravely. 'It would help us a lot if this could be put down to suicide or even natural causes, so far as the press are concerned anyway.'

The hospital security was tight as it housed dangerous mental patients and also prisoners who were sick and had been moved there for specialist care. After the police officers had passed through a metal detector they were then led through a series of heavy doors. The doors opened and closed automatically as the security guard punched in a series of codes on the panels by the doors. There were also short adjoining corridors with staff rooms either side between these doors. The security guard who had accompanied them then stopped at the next checkpoint. 'If you continue on to the end, turn left, and Geoff 'll let you in. The ward doors aren't locked,' he announced. 'I'll be here when you come back to see you out.'

'Thank you,' Owens answered appreciatively.

The three men then turned and continued up the corridor. There was an eerie silence as they went, which was only broken by the sound of their echoing footsteps. The walls looked as if at some stage they had been white but they were now dingy, suggesting that they hadn't been touched for years. When they reached the end they rounded the corner and found another checkpoint, as the security guard had said they would. His colleague nodded to them as they approached. 'My God,' he exclaimed. 'We've had people die here a lot lately. It seems to be becoming a regular thing.'

Owens looked back at him gravely, 'It's routine, I can assure you. If somebody dies suddenly anywhere we always have to investigate. We have to be sure that there's been no foul play,

184

and in this case we're sure that there wasn't.' He wanted to remain as discreet as possible.

'We had an old lady the other week strangle herself with her own bed sheets,' the security guard continued. 'The police were here then. I tell you, it's just as well this place has a private road and is like Fort Knox. If it wasn't, I can see it now, it would be swarming with people. Ya know those folk that just can't stay away when they've heard there's been an accident or somebody's died. It just seems to me that so many people have this morbid fascination with death. There's some real sickos about. I reckon half of them ought to do some time in here.'

Owens bristled and chose to ignore his remarks. Instead he changed the subject and pressed him further about the previous night.'

'Last night, were you on duty here?' he asked officially.

'No I wasn't. I'm on day shift all this week.'

'Right, so there isn't an awful lot of point continuing this conversation then,' Owens replied pointedly.

'I have officers checking all of the records right now, and we'll be interviewing everybody who was working here to try to establish the facts.'

The double doors ahead of them were all that separated them from the crime scene. Jennifer's had been the first room on the right. These doors would normally be kept locked, like all the other doors in the hospital, however they had been left unlocked for ease of access during the investigation. All the patients were secured in their rooms.

As they walked through the doors Brad immediately looked to his right and saw through the glass panelling the now empty hospital bed. The body had already been removed and taken for post mortem. The pillow and covers had also been taken by forensics for further testing. Brad took a deep breath and tried the handle. The door was locked. He immediately turned to Owens who was just behind him and shrugged his shoulders. A nurse was already on her way over to them. Two security guards stood talking quietly to one another at the adjacent checkpoint. Brad concluded that from there they should have had a clear view of everything that had gone on in and around that room.

'Hi,' the nurse beamed at them, almost as though nothing had happened.

'You need to go back in the room I guess,' she continued.

'I understand that you have already been briefed. We need statements from everybody who was on duty,' Owens said abruptly.

The nurse's expression suddenly changed, showing concern, 'Yes I know. I wasn't here last night but the nurse who was on duty is deeply shocked by all of this. She wants to go home but she's being detained in one of the rooms down there.' She turned and pointed down to the end of the ward. 'Last room on the left down there. She's very tired and emotionally drained. She's making a statement to one of your officers at the moment.'

'What's her name?' Owens asked.

'Judith Simmons,' the nurse responded willingly.

'Aahh yes,' Owens recalled. 'Yes I did request that a full statement be taken from her. Now if you could let us into the room, we will speak to Miss Simmons before we leave.'

Owens had not been to the crime scene himself until now. The nurse unlocked the door and they entered the room - she closed it quickly behind them.

'Right then, this is it.' Owens straightened and scanned the room, scrutinising every inch. He walked over to the side of the bed and immediately his eyes fell on the panic button, which was on the wall to the side of it.

'What do you make of this?' he said beckoning to the others. 'If she had been attacked then surely she could have reached out and hit this button and someone would have come running.'

He pressed the alarm to test it. Straight away the door flew open and the same nurse who had just let them in appeared, flustered.

'Just testing it,' Owens sang out. He didn't turn around but was still scratching his chin thoughtfully inspecting the alarm. 'It's all right, you can go now.'

The nurse left the room silently, closing the door slowly and deliberately behind her.

'What if that other nurse had suffocated her?' Brad piped up. 'She was confused anyway because of the drugs she was on.

She wouldn't have panicked when the nurse first leaned over her - she would be used to that - and then when she held the pillow down, she wouldn't have been able to locate the alarm. She would have been in a blind panic, and totally disorientated.'

'True,' Owens said thoughtfully. 'But it just doesn't explain why the security said they saw nothing at all unusual. They'd seen the nurse go in and administer Jennifer's nightly injection like always. If the nurse had put the pillow over her face, they would have noticed surely. The light was on. All they apparently saw that was any different was the nurse going over to the window to adjust it slightly, so we'll have her fingerprints on there.'

'Unless they're lying and trying to cover up what happened,' Brad replied.

'Well if the fingerprints are on the window, we'll know that they're telling the truth about that at least,' Owens said with a sigh.

Officer Delgardo was over at the window, 'This window's locked,' he said. 'It's only open an inch, the bolt is at the top, and these bars are wrought iron.' He checked each one to make sure they had not been tampered with, 'Solid as a rock, there's no way anybody could have got in here from outside, it would be impossible.'

Owens left the alarm and walked over to the window. He scratched his head, perplexed. 'It *has* to be somebody internal. All these doors are locked for Christ's sake, the security is so tight. How the hell can anybody have got past? It has to be an inside job if it really was a murder but we can't rule out suicide at this stage.'

Owens looked over at Brad and gave him a wry smile, 'Looks like your girl's in the clear then.'

He began pacing then, frustrated, and confused by the whole situation.

'But what the hell was she doing in the grounds? It doesn't make sense, and how the hell did she get in?' He leaned up against the wall and stared at the ceiling, 'She doesn't even know how she got there. What, was she beamed up or something? Christ alive, this is crazy! Anyway, we can't say anything for sure until forensics get back, and we haven't got the scene of crime photos yet or official time of death.'

'The other thing is,' Officer Delgardo interjected. 'If it was an inside job, why didn't they remove the pillow and put it back under her head? It wouldn't have looked so obviously like a suspicious death. They could have disguised the evidence and it could have even passed off as death by natural causes.'

'I know I know,' Owens said, an air of desperation in his voice. 'None of this makes any sense. We're gonna have to speak to these people down the station. I will interview them separately, to see if their stories tally. We'll take Judith Simmons and Peter Cross the security guard first. They have to be our prime suspects at this stage.'

'Right let's do it,' Owens clapped his hands together, and the three men left the room.

The nurse, who had let them in, was on hand quickly to lock the door again behind them. 'Do you know when you'll be finished with the room?' she asked nervously. 'You see we need to get it ready for a new patient.'

'Not just yet. We'll let you know when it can be released. I may need to come back again and would appreciate it if you left it as it is for now,' Owens replied.

'As you wish. It's just that it's distressing for us to have to see it as it was left, if you know what I mean,' the nurse added with a sigh.

'Needs must, I'm afraid,' Owens came back with an authoritative air to his voice. 'Now which room was Miss Simmons in again?'

'I'll take you down there if you like,' she replied politely.

As she led them down the corridor through the ward, Brad looked through the other patients' windows. It was a disturbing sight. Some of them were up out of their beds pacing up and down and others were just lying in bed staring vacantly at the ceiling, as though they were in some kind of waking coma.

They entered the small white square room; it too had bars on the windows and just a simple round plain table in the far corner with four chairs around it. Judith Simmons was sitting on the chair furthest from them. She was a middle-aged woman, in her early fifties; she had an untidy bleached blonde bob, sharp features and dull brown eyes. She sat facing a woman police officer, who had been with her since she had finished her shift early that morning. It was now early afternoon and the tiredness and strain was showing in her face. The two women had stopped talking when Detective Owens and the other officers entered the room. Judith Simmons seemed very jumpy and nervy.

'Miss Simmons?' Detective Owens smiled, approaching the table and stretching out his hand to shake hers. She returned the gesture awkwardly. Her hands now shaking.

'Please try to relax Miss Simmons,' he returned, noticing her anxiety.

'It's actually Mrs Simmons,' she said falteringly.

'My apologies,' Owens replied.

'Thank you Jane,' he turned to his colleague. 'You can go now if you want.'

The officer, who also looked very tired, then left the room.

'Now Mrs Simmons, I know this situation is very hard for you, but we need to know what happened to Jennifer. Can you help us at all?'

She sighed, as she had already been through all of this with the previous officer and was now going to have to say everything all over again.

'It's very hard for me. I did care about Jennifer. I know she murdered that girl, but she didn't deserve to die like that.' She lowered her head and dabbed at her eyes, which were now moist again with tears.

'What actually happened then? Did you see anything, anything that can give us a clue?' Owens leaned forward, willing her to reveal what she knew.

'Nothing,' she replied with an air of desperation in her voice. 'That's just it, I saw nothing. I gave her an injection at 10.15 p.m., which is recorded in the logbook. I then left the room and locked it behind me, switching off the light. I didn't enter the room again until morning. All our movements are recorded with security - I have nothing to hide.'

Owens sighed and leaned back in his chair again.

'Look please,' she begged, 'please can I go home? I'm so very tired and I am supposed to be starting work again here at eight o'clock this evening.'

'I'm afraid we will have to take you to make a formal statement,' Owens replied sternly.

'What about Peter?' she asked her voice breaking with emotion.

'Peter Cross?' Owens said quizzically.

'Yes,' she cried.

'We'll be taking him down too,' he replied. 'We'll go now. I just need to ask you one last question at this stage.'

'OK,' she replied shakily.

'Do you know if Jennifer had wanted to kill herself?' He leaned forward again, looking directly into her eyes.

'Well that's just the saddest thing,' she said becoming emotional again. 'Her father was due to visit her today - she told me.' Judith grabbed for another tissue and blew her nose loudly. 'She always looked forward to his visits. It just doesn't make any sense, but then what future did the poor girl have? If she'd got out of here she'd have gone to prison almost certainly. Maybe she realised that and couldn't face it. Maybe she thought more about that than we will ever know.'

There was silence in the room. 'Yes, it's possible she may have wanted to kill herself, of course it's possible,' Judith continued with a touch of bitterness in her voice. 'Now please can we go and make this statement now. I'm going to have to answer all these questions again aren't I?' she said with frustration in her voice.

'Officer North,' Owens turned to Brad who was standing just behind him. 'Can you go and find Peter Cross? I believe he is in the staff room behind the checkpoint with Officer Monroe.

'Sure,' Brad replied, and turned to leave the room.

'Let's go,' Detective Owens turned to Judith Simmons who was already picking up her bag.

Brad walked back along the corridor towards the checkpoint; there was a deathly, oppressive silence. He noticed that one of the patients was up on his feet and his mouth was moving as if he were shouting. His neck was stretched and all the tendons were standing out - he was looking right at him. It then struck Brad that when they had travelled past the last time they had been talking amongst themselves and he hadn't noticed the fact that he couldn't hear the other patients. It dawned on him then that if Jennifer had been screaming in the darkness that night nobody would have heard her.

As he entered the staff room he found a much more welcoming environment. There was a coffee percolator and a well-stocked snack machine to his right. Straight in front of him a large leafy plant stood in the window, obscuring the sinister iron bars behind it. He noticed that there was also a TV set, a VCR/DVD player and a small kitchenette off from the other side of the room. Officer Monroe and Peter Cross sat reclining on the comfortable looking beige couch in front of the television - both with a coffee in their hand.

'Hi,' Brad said confidently as he stood eyeing them both. 'Detective Owens is leaving now for the station with Judith Simmons. You will have to come with us too Mr Cross as we need a formal statement.'

'But I'm back on duty at 9 p.m.!' he protested.

'Well Mrs Simmons is due back on at 8 p.m. - we'll try not to take up too much more of your time.' It was obvious to Brad that Peter Cross hadn't been too badly affected by the death on the ward.

He sighed and struggled to his feet, 'I was comfortable there.'

'Well I'm sure Jennifer Thorpe was comfortable in her bed last night before she suffocated.' Brad replied.

'Good point, I can't argue with that one,' Peter Cross smiled, failing to grasp that Brad had been serious.

All three left the room and met back up with Owens and Delgardo. They were all then escorted off the premises. Brad was so glad to be back out in the sunshine. He could breathe the fresh air again. The air in the hospital had seemed stale to him and the whole building filled him with an irrational sense of dread and fear.

Back at the police station Detective Owens interviewed first Judith Simmons, who stuck rigidly to her story. Owens had nothing to go on at this stage and considered that he had to let her go. He knew that until forensics came back with the information that he needed, he had no concrete evidence to support the murder theory. It was all just circumstantial. She left the interview room. He then went back out into the waiting room to a disgruntled looking Peter Cross and summoned him into the room.

'Am I gonna need my brief?' Cross said arrogantly.

'Well,' Owens replied sharply, 'that all depends on whether you think you need one or not, doesn't it.'

'Look,' he continued, 'we are just making routine enquiries at the moment. You are not a suspect but you may have seen something and be able to help us.'

Brad North was stood over by the desk at the station reception. He signalled to Owens who went over to him.

'Can I come in on this one?' he asked in a low whisper, 'I've got a feeling about him. I just want to hear what he has to say.'

'Actually,' Owens said scratching his chin thoughtfully, 'that would be good, because I still haven't interviewed you yet.'

'What?' Brad replied shocked.

'Yes North, don't think I've forgotten about last night just because I haven't brought it up since we arrived at the hospital,' he glared at him. 'I want to know everything that went on between you and that girl.'

They walked into the interview room, which was empty but for a square plain looking table up against the side wall. The walls were bright orange in colour and the tape recorder stood on the table. A high window provided the light at the far end.

Peter Cross went round to the far side of the table and immediately lit a cigarette as he sat down.

'I'm going to need an ash tray,' he then said.

Brad found one and gave it to him.

Owens started the tape recorder. He then spoke. 'This is Detective Carl Owens conducting an informal interview with Mr Peter Cross regarding the death of Jennifer Thorpe at Ashbrook Hospital late last night. The date today is Thursday 7th of September 2006, also present is Officer Brad North.'

Peter Cross leaned back in his chair feigning a confident air, drawing on his cigarette, and blowing the smoke out directly in front of him.

'Right,' Owens began. 'Can you confirm that you were indeed on duty the night in question?'

'I was,' replied Cross.

'Was anybody else on duty with you last night between the hours of 9 p.m. and 6 a.m.?'

'Well, yes,' Cross replied, 'Ben Shore. How it works is that I work from 9 p.m. through 1 a.m., then I sleep for an hour. Ben then takes over. We both work together from 2 a.m. until 6 a.m.'

'So last night then,' Owens leaned back and folded his arms, 'you were working until midnight? You would have noticed what time Judith Simmons attended to Jennifer.'

'Yes I did. I have to record every nurse or doctor patient interaction in the logbook,' he answered. 'We have to record all visitations to every patient.'

'So no unrecorded entry could ever take place to a patient's room?' Owens pressed further.

'No, that's what I just said wasn't it?' Cross snapped back.

'Look here,' Owens said adopting a no nonsense stance, 'you obviously have a problem with me asking you these questions, so can I deduce from that that you have something to hide? If you or anybody else made an agreement not to write an entry in the logbook, who would ever know?'

Cross swallowed nervously and lit another cigarette.

'Look, it wouldn't be worth me falsifying the logbook! I could lose my job, OK.' He leaned back in his chair again.

'Right then, let's talk about your visibility of the room,' Owens changed the line of questioning.

'It was dark in her room, the lights were out. After Nurse Simmons had administered her injection, it was at what time again?'

'10.15,' Cross replied immediately.

'You have a good memory,' Owens said with an air of sarcasm in his voice.

'Well it was the last time anybody entered her room that night, the last entry on the page,' Cross replied defensively.

'And do you always have cause to memorise what time a nurse goes into each room?' Owens continued.

'Look,' Cross was getting annoyed, he sat up straight again. 'It's my job, I don't do anything else but stand and watch. I'm bound to remember aren't I? Anyway, the girl died that night - it kinda sticks in your mind!'

'OK Peter, I won't press you further on the timings,' Owens relented.

'Let's talk about what you saw then.'

'You know what I saw already,' Cross sighed frustrated. 'Absolutely nothing.'

'Think back to last night Peter. I tell you what, let's do an experiment.'

Cross looked troubled.

'Officer North, you stay in here and we'll go and stand in the corridor,' Owens said leaning over to pause the tape.

Brad had an inkling as to what he was going to do next.

Owens motioned to Cross, who followed behind him reluctantly. Owens stood with his back to the wall on the opposite side of the corridor. He signalled to Cross to stand beside him.

'Right,' he announced. 'I'm going to turn the corridor light off and, Officer North, if you could close the blinds and turn the interview light off? Now Peter, don't look to the side of you, just look straight ahead as you would have been doing last night.'

The lights were simultaneously turned off and they were plunged into darkness.

'Now you see Peter,' Owens said, 'you can't see a lot now can you? But if we wait a couple of minutes your night vision will kick in and you'll be able to see again.'

He waited a couple of minutes.

'I don't see how this is relevant,' Cross protested.

'Well the point of this is to show you,' Owens reached to his right side and snapped the light back on, 'that when the light is on in the corridor, you don't need your night vision. You can see into the dark room perfectly well, can't you? That was the case last night wasn't it.'

As he said this, another officer came walking towards them down the corridor clutching a brown file.

'Detective Owens can I have a word?'

He waved a dejected Peter Cross back into the interview room.

'What is it Giles?' Owens said to the elderly police officer.

'We have definite time of death from forensics,' he replied eagerly.

'Great!' Owens clapped his hands together. He took the file, and hurriedly read down the report.

'Time of death, da da da, ahhh, 12.30 a.m.' He snapped the file shut and thrust it back at the other officer. 'That's all for now, thank you.'

Owens walked back into the interview room, triumphantly.

'What time did you go for your mid shift break again?' Owens paced menacingly round the back of Cross, who had already lit another cigarette.

He went to speak but Owens cut back across him before he had the chance, 'Oh yes, it was 1 a.m. wasn't it? Well that is a coincidence, because Jennifer Thorpe died at 12.30 a.m.' He banged his hands down on the table next to Cross making him jump. 'Well that was a whole half an hour before your break started. That's plenty of time to put a pillow over somebody's face and suffocate them.'

'NO!' Cross bellowed. 'Nobody went into that room after 10.15 p.m. It's the truth I swear it.'

'That maybe so,' Owens replied, 'but you're hiding something, I know it, and I'm going to find out.'

'You'll never find out,' Cross said indignantly. He then stopped speaking instantly, realising what he had just said.

'All I know Cross, is that you must have seen Jennifer struggling. You must have, you were standing right in front of her room,' Owens continued defiantly.

'Look, I'm gonna tell you now,' Cross replied his head in his hands, 'I know I'm going to get in trouble for it, but I'm not gonna have you lot pin a murder on me that I didn't commit.'

His hands were shaking uncontrollably.

'Go on, go on,' Owens sat back down in the chair and leaned forward.

Cross took a deep breath. The room fell silent for a few moments.

Owens then quickly leaned across to the tape recorder to take it off pause again.

'I was very tired that night,' Cross began. 'The wife and I have a young baby and I don't get much rest. Come midnight, I was dog tired.' He took another drag on his cigarette.

'OK, I know it was wrong, I shouldn't have done it, but I just couldn't cope any longer.' He held his head in his hands.

'What did you do Peter?' Owens asked, fearing the worst.

'I left the post unattended. I took my break early didn't I!'

'Damn!' Owens exclaimed, banging the table again. 'So you went and slept from twelve until two. Well that's just great isn't it! Oh fuck, it could have been absolutely anybody now couldn't it? It could have been the cleaner, the person who fills the Goddamn snack machine, it could have been just about anybody. I suppose the keys for the doors were all left at the post?'

'That's just it,' Cross replied sheepishly. 'I took all the keys with me and I locked myself in the staff room. When Ben arrived I still had all the keys. I checked, nobody could have gotten to them.'

'Jesus! I don't believe this, do you?' Owens looked over at Brad, exasperated.

'What about Simmons?' Owens continued.

'She knew I was doing that. I'd told her to knock on the door loudly if she needed any keys. She didn't think she'd need them either as all the patients are almost always asleep at that time normally.'

'Oh Christ so she was in on it too,' Owens shook his head in disbelief.

'I can't believe my bad luck. Ben had done this before - we often did it if it was quiet. Before the other one arrived ya know, no management about.' He looked back up and ran his hand roughly through his hair, digging his fingertips into his scalp. It was plain that he was annoyed and frustrated with himself. 'Just my fucking luck! There has to be a fucking death the night I take my damn break early!'

He must be telling the truth, Owens knew it. He leaned towards the tape recorder, his face like thunder.

'Interview with Mr Cross terminated at…' he glanced at his watch, 'seventeen hundred hours.' He switched it off with a swift flick of his finger, silence. He turned his face slowly back towards Cross - his mouth had disappeared to a fine line.

'Get out,' he snarled. Cross went to speak; Owens raised his hand to silence him, 'Just get out.' Cross stood up to leave.

'I guess you're gonna blow the whistle on me now then,' he finally said as he was leaving the room.

'Haven't you gone yet?' Owens hollered back.

Owens sank back down in his chair, his head in his hands.

'What a waste of time,' he said defeated. 'What a complete fucking waste time!'

'Well,' Brad replied, 'we haven't had the forensics report through yet. He could still be lying.'

'I don't think so,' Owens came back with a sigh, 'you can just tell. Obviously I'll check it all out, but I'm not gonna hold out any hope.'

'Which leads me back to you,' he said leaning back across the table towards Brad who was pacing over the far side of the interview room.

'Look,' Brad said stopping dead in his tracks, and turning to face Owens, 'there's something I feel I ought to tell you. I've been mulling it over in my head, whether I should, whether I shouldn't.'

'Yes, yes,' Owens gesticulated impatiently with his hands.

'When I was out yesterday with Alicia,' he hung his head, and paused for a moment longer, 'she told me that she wanted to go to see Jennifer.'

'And?' Owens eyes widened slightly, but on the whole he didn't seem particularly excited or surprised by this new revelation.

'Of course I told her point blank that she shouldn't,' Brad insisted.

Owens sank back into his chair, looking incredulously at him.

'Brad, we know that she did because she was found in the damn grounds,' he shook his head, frustrated. 'The issue here is not the fact that she went to the hospital, but that you're stressed out because she went and did what you told her not to. Jeez!' He rolled his eyes heavenwards. 'Right, if you have nothing useful to say at this stage, then you won't mind if we head off to the hospital and speak to the Buchanan girl directly. When we get there though, you can wait outside,' he said, standing up to leave, 'because I don't think I could stomach a lovers' tiff right now!'

Chapter 10

As Courtney turned her car into Bay View Grove her entire body and her emotions were numb. It was late afternoon now; she hadn't been home since their trip had been interrupted by the news that Alicia was in hospital again. She felt as if she was on the edge, holding on to her own sanity by a thread. There was a distance between her husband and her that had never existed before. Their lives had been idyllic - their holidays abroad and their afternoons lazing in the Florida sunshine seemed a world away. She sighed as she pulled up outside the house; a feeling of trepidation filled her. She mulled over in her head the events of the day - her arrival at the hospital, the police standing outside. She had felt no surprise at their presence, it was as if their lives had taken a sinister twist and it was somehow inevitable. She had to see this through to the end now. Her honeymoon period was well and truly over but she would ride the storm. She wasn't sure if her life would ever be the same again. Things that had been long buried were surfacing, and they had to surface. She couldn't live a lie. She sat in the car just staring at the front of the house, not wanting to go in, not knowing what she would do when she got in there. Her daily routine no longer existed, chaos had taken hold. Nothing was certain and she hated and resented that. Alicia had been quite lucid in the hospital and was adamant that she did not want to return to the house, but why? What on earth had happened there last night? She fumbled with the car keys turning the engine off and sat back again in the seat. She looked down their leafy perfect street. Their neighbours were going about their daily routines. Cars were driving out of driveways and people busied themselves - laughing and joking. Their lives weren't tainted like hers. Their lives were the way that her life had been before all this had started. She looked back again at her house; she remembered that warm feeling she used to feel when arriving home, the feeling of excitement. Sparkey would always be there to greet her and she would have the whole night in her house before she had to go to work again the next day. She'd felt safe and secure there, as if she had a big blanket wrapped around her shoulders. Now, looking at the house she had a different feeling. The house loomed in front of her. Not even the bright sunshine could change the fact that it now looked cold and empty, it wasn't the same house anymore.

She reached for the handle on the car door and stepped out onto the sidewalk. Her nerves were jangling and every noise around her made her start. It was almost as though if she saw her own shadow she would feel her heart in her mouth. She grabbed her bag from the back seat and then slammed the door and locked it behind her. She set off up the path towards the front door. Ted Fraser was in his front garden. He shouted across to her and waved and she smiled back returning his wave. At least there was still a little piece of normality to hang on to.

She turned the key in the lock and opened the front door slowly. She stepped in. The house was freezing. She put her bag down in the hallway and as she set off towards the kitchen to make herself a coffee she suddenly froze. She happened to glance up the stairs on her way past and it was then that she noticed the broken vase and flowers for the first time. They were strewn down the staircase with all the jagged pieces scattered over the wooden steps. She put her hand up to her mouth to stifle a cry. *Oh God, what the hell has been going on in here?*

Adam was still at the hospital. Alicia had said nothing of this to her when she had been there earlier. Courtney stood staring in disbelief, her eyes darting nervously around the previously neat hallway. Possible scenarios raced through her troubled mind and irrational thoughts came to her. She felt that all too familiar feeling of panic racing through her body, through every fibre every sinew. Nothing moved in the house. The house no longer breathed like it had before. It felt lonely and desolate - it wasn't her house anymore. She backed along the wall towards the kitchen; too afraid to turn around, too afraid to take her eyes from the devastation for fear that something else would happen. She thought she should call Adam and then realised that his mobile phone would be switched off as he was at the hospital. She edged into the kitchen, all the time listening. She clutched at her belly as she felt the baby move, as if in response to the excess adrenaline that was flowing through her veins. It occurred to her how little notice she was taking of the child within her. All of her thoughts centred around Adam's daughters - one dead and one very much alive. She resented that. She had dreamed of becoming a mother for so long. Although the baby had been a big surprise to her she had been pleased once she had told Adam and witnessed his delight at the news. Nothing else had moved as she traversed across the hallway to the kitchen. She decided that maybe that coffee would in fact steady her nerves. *This is crazy! Whatever has happened in this house I'll be damned if I'm gonna let it affect me like this, or the baby. Alicia was probably drunk no doubt so she can damn well clean up this mess when she comes back from hospital.* She reassured herself with some rational thoughts, took a deep breath and stood upright again. *All this talk of ghosts! I mean, it's the trauma isn't it? After all I haven't seen anything.* She then remembered the door slamming in the hallway that night. *No, there has to be a rational explanation for it. A ghost wouldn't slam a door - it would just fucking walk straight through it!* She chuckled to herself, amused by her conclusion. She flicked the switch on the kettle and it began to hiss into life as the element heated up. She glanced around the kitchen; everything looked the same as the last time she had seen it. She then looked over at the back door and tried the handle - it swung open. *Damn, she left the door unlocked. What is this open house?* She opened it to let in the early evening air, the sounds of the world outside, the smell of the flowers and the newly cut grass that she loved so much. The longer grass at the end of the garden swayed gently from side to side, as the breeze stirred it. The kettle then began to boil, steam billowing from the top of it. She made her coffee and ventured into the lounge where she flopped down on the couch and flicked on the TV with the remote. She looked at her watch. She had to go and collect Adam and possibly Alicia in an hour. She sighed again. She never got the chance to sit down for long, well apart from at work, but that didn't really count as relaxation. She caught the last thirty minutes of a chat show as she sipped her coffee. When this finished she was reluctantly forced back to reality again as she realised she was going to have to change out of her summer top. The temperature was cooling and she would have to go back out in the car. She talked herself round, first into thinking normally again and then into going up the stairs. She had decided not to touch anything that had been knocked over in the hallway, including the vase on the stairs. She wanted to leave them for Adam to see so he could weigh it up for himself. She wondered how he would explain this one away! It seemed to be his favourite pastime of late, lying and trying to cover everything up.

She walked back into the kitchen leaving her empty mug on the draining board. She then took one last deep breath to calm herself and ventured into the hallway. She paused again but couldn't hear any strange noises. The house was quite still and she was sure that it was empty. She gripped the bannister to steady herself as she negotiated her way carefully past the broken pieces of china and bedraggled flowers which were perched precariously on the wooden steps (the rest had fallen through to the carpeted hallway below). She reached the top of the staircase and rounded the corner, past the spare bedroom and then past the bathroom. The door of the bathroom was open and everything in there looked the same. The adjoining door to Gabrielle's old bedroom was closed. She trod carefully, almost on tiptoe, along the beige carpeted hallway as if she didn't want the house to be alerted to the fact that she was now upstairs. She reached the bedroom and then exhaled, relieved that she had made it and that everything in their room was as she had left it. She stripped off her clothes, throwing them haphazardly onto their bed; she inspected herself in the mirror and admired her developing bulge from a sideways angle, stroking her stomach protectively. She looked at her face and then at her stomach, marvelling at the fact that it was really her who was pregnant. She smiled at herself in the mirror and resolved that when this was over she was going to take some serious time out, some time for herself. She walked across their room and into their own adjoining bathroom. It was only small unlike the master bathroom, with a toilet, wash basin and corner shower unit, but it was big enough for the two of them.

After dressing she walked back over to the mirror and inspected herself again. Her thick wavy hair was now two inches below her shoulders and desperately in need of a cut and re-style. That would be the next little pampering treat that she would give herself. She blow-dried and styled her hair and put on a little fresh makeup. She felt better. She looked at her watch again and realising the time she quickly set off back down the corridor. Something made her stop halfway down. Standing there in the long passageway she stared straight ahead of her, wondering why she had stopped, wondering what it was that had instinctively prevented her from proceeding any further. Her senses heightened as she listened intently. The bare corridor walls loomed either side of her - all doors were closed apart from the main bathroom. Her left hand reached out to her side and found the handle to Alicia's door without her having to look at it. It made a squeaking noise as the handle turned, sounding like a metal spring slowly being compressed. The door opened. Her breath came fast and shallow. She turned her head and looked into the room. She didn't know what she had expected to find but the sight of the broken remains of the TV was the last thing she had imagined. She furtively gazed around the room, her heart now beating faster and faster. Instead of a feeling of fear she felt a tangible rage well up inside her. That TV had been her own. She had given it to Alicia on the understanding that it was hers to borrow until such a time as the girls moved out of the house. She pulled the door closed with a bang that echoed down the corridor. The sound seemed to wake the house - it seemed to come alive again.

She walked quickly to the top of the stairs, her anger growing by the second. As she neared the top and ventured onto the top step, she suddenly became aware of somebody following her. The hairs on the back of her neck prickled. She grabbed hold of the bannister again to steady herself. This thing was there, breathing down her neck, close enough to touch if she had reached behind her. But she didn't, she couldn't. She stumbled down the staircase, accidentally dislodging a couple more pieces of china that fell down through the steps to the hallway below. She quickly grabbed her handbag, not daring to look back. This presence was still there. It was breathing and it was real. She didn't want to look at it, her fear was too great. She ran to the back door and out into the garden, slamming it behind her. She was alone again.

She didn't stop running until she reached her car, and there she quickly found her keys and jumped in. The engine immediately purred into life. Without hesitation she drove forward at speed. It was then that she realised that she was facing the wrong direction for the hospital. She reversed the car almost hitting a neighbours gate post, drove it round and accelerated back up the road, her tyres screeching on the tarmac. She glanced in her rear view mirror at the house and felt a lump in her throat like pure bile. She felt nauseous from the shock and her anger and fear were explosive. She couldn't believe she had been run out of her own house. She didn't understand what was happening to her. *It must be in my mind. It has to be. Please God let all this be in my sick twisted imagination.*

Courtney burst through the door to the private room of the hospital where Alicia was sat up in bed, her father at her side. 'You broke my TV Alicia! Why the fuck did you break my TV?' she yelled angrily from the doorway.

'Hey hey!' Adam stood up and restrained his wife whose face was twisted with rage.

'What the hell is wrong with you? Don't come in here swearing! Who do you think you are?'

'Damn it Adam, I wasn't talking to you!' She walked over to the other side of Alicia's bed, her eyes were red from crying and her hand was shaking as she lifted it up to point accusingly at Alicia who just sat there seemingly unaffected by her stepmother's outburst.

'So little Miss I'm so perfect, I'm gonna have the whole Goddamn family running round after me forever.' Alicia turned to face her, still unmoved.

'What made you think it would be all right for you to come home drunk and go on a smashing spree?' Alicia didn't reply. Adam leaned across the bed and glared angrily at his wife, his fist clenched by his side.

'Now either you calm down or I'll make you calm down, do you hear me?' he said in a menacing tone, his expression changing from one of utter amazement to one of fury.

Courtney didn't stop; she carried on, in a mocking tone, impersonating Alicia. 'I know what I'll do tonight.' She walked to the back of the room skipping like a little school girl, 'I'll go back home drunk and I'll smash up my whole fucking bedroom. Oh and then I'll go down the stairs and break the expensive vase that's been sitting on the window sill undisturbed for far too long.' She turned back the tears now streaming down her face, feeling as if she had lost her mind. 'That's how it was Alicia wasn't it, tell me that's what happened.'

Adam leapt up from his chair and grabbed his wife, shaking her violently, 'Shut up Courtney! Pull yourself together for God's sake, what are you talking about?'

'Stop it, both of you!' Alicia cried out suddenly. Adam let go of his wife who stood shaking beside him, surprised and shocked by her own rage. Adam's anger then changed to bewilderment, 'What on earth is going on here?' his voice cracked with emotion.

'Well,' Alicia looked at them intently, 'you really want to know, then I'll tell you *exactly* what happened. First the TV lifted up off the ground floated around in thin air and then dropped on the ground and broke into pieces.' She counted the events calmly on her fingers, an almost sarcastic air to her voice. 'Not sure what else happened after that in the room, cos I got the hell out. Oh and then on my way down the stairs the vase lifted up, by itself, yes, that's right completely by itself, and smashed against the wall almost killing me.'

There was silence in the room. Courtney broke down again, 'Alicia please stop telling us lies. You were drunk and you broke them, *didn't you?*' she hollered. 'Please Alicia, tell me that's what happened and I won't be angry with you anymore.' Tears streaked Courtney's pale cheeks, her eyes pleaded with her stepdaughter's to say what she so desperately wanted to hear. For that split second the two women had connected and what Courtney saw in those doleful blue eyes was her worst fear realised. But still she would not believe it - she could not believe it.

'I'm not going home,' Alicia sat with her arms folded defiantly. 'You can forget it.'

Courtney had already left the room in tears; Adam had followed her but had been rebuffed again by his wife who'd told him to leave her alone. He had returned to his daughter's bedside alone.

'The nurses may say you can be released tonight and you can come back with us. Alicia I promise that from now on we'll take better care of you. We won't leave you on your own again.' Adam gazed at her intently.

'Dad,' Alicia became agitated again. 'I'm nineteen years old. I don't have to come home if I don't want to.'

'Well where are you planning on going then?' Adam leaned back in the stark hospital chair, his arms folded defensively. 'Listen to me. This morning you were found in the grounds of that hospital, in your night clothes. You can't tell me that you don't need us to look after you. That doesn't seem like the actions of someone who's in control. Oh and where was Brad when you were sprawled on the grass? He wasn't taking good care of you then was he!'

Tears welled again in Alicia's forlorn eyes, her frustration now spilling over. 'I'm going out with Brad and that's the end of it. I don't have to explain my actions to you.'

Adam leaned closer to his daughter in one last-ditch attempt to make her see sense. 'Alicia, your actions *need* to be explained, otherwise, how am I ever going to understand what happened to you last night?'

'I don't know OK,' she cried. 'You don't believe what I told you, which is the truth, so there's no point in even discussing it is there?' Her face had reddened, her eyes smarting from the tears. 'Dad, what's the point in talking about this anymore? You don't believe me. I'm not coming home and that's the end of it.'

'So what did the police say when they visited you earlier?' Adam continued, his dark eyes searching his daughter's for the truth.

'They asked me what I was doing there - what do you think?' she said sarcastically.

'Yes, yes,' Adam gesticulated with his hands.

'Well I told them I didn't know and that I had been drunk. Brad dropped me off, I got out the house and the alcohol had blanked my memory. That's all.'

Adam sighed as one of the nurses walked back into the room, a broad smile across her rounded oriental face.

'Hello Alicia, how are you feeling?' she said in a sing song upbeat tone.

'I'm feeling much better thanks,' Alicia tried to compose herself.

'I'm not sure that you're ready to go home yet,' she said, her face looked concerned.

'Let me check that blood pressure of yours, and your feet and back. They're only scratches but we need to make sure they don't become infected.'

Alicia began to cry again. 'But I have to get out of here! I've arranged to meet Brad and I'm moving into his house tonight.'

'What!' Adam half shouted. 'This is all a bit sudden Alicia. Do you honestly know what you are doing?'

She reached down and tried to open her bedside locker wincing with pain.

'Get my mobile out of my bag!' she demanded as her father shook his head in disbelief.

'No mobiles in the hospital Alicia. You can't make a call I'm afraid,' the nurse replied moving quickly to the other side of the bed to tend to her patient.

Alicia grabbed at her father's hand. 'Dad, you have to call Brad for me! He's going to meet me tonight. You have to tell him that I can't come, please!' she pleaded desperately. Her father reluctantly agreed and took the mobile out of her bag, slipping it into his pocket.

He stood up to leave. He was weary and the stress of the whole situation was beginning to show on his face.

He leaned over and kissed his daughter on the cheek.

'Now, we'll be in tomorrow to visit and I don't want another scene like there was today with Courtney. I admit she was harsh, but she wants to get to the bottom of all this just as much as I do. She cares about you too you know.'

Alicia didn't answer. A sullen expression settled on her face as she extended her arm reluctantly to the nurse to have her blood pressure checked.

As Adam turned to leave, Alicia called after him. 'Don't forget to call Brad.'

He left the room and found Courtney leaning against the corridor wall.

'Baby,' he said quietly. It was as if all the energy had been drained from him.

'Let's go home.'

Courtney walked over to him slowly, her long hair falling untidily around her face. She looked up at him through teary eyes.

'Come here,' he said protectively, holding his arms out to his distressed wife. The fight had gone out of her too. She relented and allowed him to embrace her, realising that deep down, she did still love him. He stroked her hair tenderly. 'Everything's gonna be OK,' he said. 'Let's go clean up this mess.'

When Brad walked back into the police station at the end of his shift he saw a familiar figure standing in the reception area. It was Jack Thorpe; his hairline seemed to have receded further since the last time that Brad had seen him at Gabrielle's funeral. His face was still as red as ever, but his eyes were hollow, lifeless, as though he was just existing.

Brad walked towards him. As he was so heavily involved in the case himself, and with the people in it, he felt it his duty to speak to him.

'Mr Thorpe?' he said cautiously as he approached.

Jack Thorpe's eyes seemed to come back into focus then as he returned from his tortured dream world. 'Are you waiting to talk to Detective Owens?'

He cleared his throat nervously, 'Yes, yes I am.'

'Can I help at all?'

As the words left Brad's lips, Detective Owens strode into the reception, cutting straight across Brad, and shaking Jack Thorpe's hand.

208

'Officer North,' Detective Owens addressed his subordinate.
'You've finished your shift for today. Tomorrow I need you back here to go over the forensic reports with me.'
'Sir,' Brad replied. His chest and shoulders ached from the stress he was under. He felt as though any respect that Owens may have had for him before had gone. He was sure he was only keeping him on side to prevent a leak from occurring in the ranks. He had definitely put his job on the line for Alicia and couldn't really be sure in his mind that he had made the right decision. *Perhaps Owens was right when he said that I was weak willed and unprofessional.* Brad looked at his watch as he left the police station; he had to meet Alicia in a couple of hours. He would have to keep it quiet. At least they had picked a bar that was out of town and that was never frequented by any of his contemporaries.

'Would you like a coffee Mr Thorpe?' Owens asked.
'Oh please call me Jack,' he replied earnestly, 'and no, I'm fine thank you.'
They walked into one of the bleak interview rooms together, Owens closing the door behind them.
'Now Jack how can I help you?' Owens sat down opposite Jack Thorpe and gazed at him intently.
He sighed. 'I just want to know when my daughter's body is going to be released. I want to put her to rest.' His voice cracked with emotion.
'In the next couple of days I promise,' Owens replied. 'We are just waiting for the final forensic reports. As soon as we have clarified the situation with you, and you are happy that you do not want any further tests carried out, then we will be speaking directly to the coroner who will issue the official report on the cause of death.'
Jack Thorpe nodded, his eyes cast down. His eyes were heavy and dark, the pain and grief was etched across his face.
'You know her mother doesn't want anything to do with the funeral,' he said suddenly. 'We never got on but I didn't think that she could ever turn her back on her own daughter. I don't want anything to do with her mother now either. I'm filing for

divorce; I'm sure she'll try and sting me for as much money as she can, but that's what she's all about. I realise that now.'

He looked up at Owens, the sorrow in his eyes was palpable.

'Jennifer was right about her all along,' he sniffed as he reached for his handkerchief and blew his nose hard. 'I should have taken more time with her. I got sucked into the way her mother thought and acted. In the end you start to believe that it's normal. Now it's too late. I can't tell her how sorry I am. I was going to tell Jennifer the morning that I was due to visit and you told me that she was…'

He broke down; Owens caught hold of his arm.

'Jack, Jack,' he soothed, 'you could never have known that would happen. I'm sure Jennifer knew how much you loved her.'

He blew his nose again and tried to regain his composure.

'Yes,' he tried to force a smile. 'I told her every time I saw her in that hospital but she wasn't the same anymore - it was as if her spirit, her very essence had already gone. But I told her anyway, because I still felt it, as I do now. It's hard for me because of what she did, but I can't stop loving her. I always will.'

'And so you should,' Owens affirmed.

'I have children of my own Jack,' he continued. 'It's unconditional love. When they reach adulthood you hope that you've brought them up the right way, but you cannot ultimately control the path they decide to take. You may not agree with it and even think it's wrong, but you still love them despite everything.'

'That's very true,' Jack Thorpe nodded his head. 'I'm glad that you understand me, because some people cannot see past what she did, which was a terrible thing I know. They could not understand why I stuck by her. It was suicide wasn't it?'

He looked questioningly at Owens, who had been taken aback by the suddenness of his question?

'Well, as you know, the information we have so far would suggest that that is the case. The time of death has been set at 12.30 a.m. She was securely locked in her room and records show that nobody entered the room after 10.15 p.m. This has been confirmed by the logbook records and witnesses. We will be able to rule out any foul play for definite tomorrow when the forensic reports come in. I will keep you well informed I promise.'

Jack Thorpe stiffened in his chair and sighed.

'I think it must have been suicide. In my heart I don't believe she wanted to live anymore. What kind of a life did she have ahead of her? At least she's free of it all now.'

He lowered his eyes again.

Owens patted Jack Thorpe's arm.

'Now Jack if there's anything we can do for you, just let us know. I will call you tomorrow anyway.'

Jack Thorpe's metal chair scraped loudly across the floor as he stood up which seemed to bring him back to reality again.

'Thank you for your kindness,' he said extending his hand again to Detective Owens, who responded by shaking his hand warmly.

'We will do all that we can I promise,' Owens replied.

Adam was the first to enter their house at Bay View Grove; Courtney still shaken by her experience remained on the doorstep even after he had gone in. She reached around the doorframe and tentatively placed her handbag in the corner of the hallway. She watched it for a few moments, waiting to see if it would move. It didn't. Adam called out from the kitchen.

'Do you wanna coffee Courtney?'

She took a deep breath and told herself she was just being stupid again. She stepped inside, her eyes flitting rapidly from object to object taking in her surroundings, making sure that nothing else had moved since she had last been in the house. Nothing else had moved as far as she could see. The pieces of broken china were still lying on the stairs, along with the dead flowers. They had been yellow roses and their thorns were still protruding sharply, even though the petals had now wilted and become brown at the edges. She walked into the kitchen reassured a little, but still feeling on edge. She didn't, however, feel that anyone else was there anymore, as she had done before. She was sure then that it must have all been in her mind, an imagined horror caused by her stressed state. She decided to take it easy that night and try to relax. She still wasn't about to

211

let Adam out of her sight, not this soon, as there was still that element of doubt in her mind.

They cleared up the mess on and around the stairs quite quickly and then Adam ordered a take-out Chinese from a local restaurant. They sat together on the couch watching TV. It was the closest that Courtney had felt to Adam in a long time.

Brad looked at his watch. Alicia wasn't due for another twenty minutes. He had purposely arrived slightly early at the out of town bar. He'd wanted to have a couple of drinks before he saw her as he didn't think he'd be able to break the news to her otherwise. He had been to this bar a couple of times before; it was more of a local's bar than a tourist haunt, which was why he preferred it. It was mostly men who went there and they would all sit round the large bar on stools, trying to chat up whichever barmaid was on duty, or barman for that matter.

As Brad walked in he checked around quickly to ensure that he didn't recognise anybody. It was a very large bar, almost old fashioned in appearance. It had wood panelled walls and a large open bar area. The bar itself was made of a much darker wood than the rest of the furniture. The seating arrangement was not dissimilar to that of a train, with rows of large high backed heavy bench seats covered in dark red vinyl which were spaced in pairs facing one another. A square plain wooden table stood in between. Over each table hung a large ornate light with a heavy brass fitting that many a customer would strike their head on as they stood up to leave!

At the far end of the bar were the billiard tables - around ten in total. The whole area was penned by a low, dark wooden divide; at the top of each panel was a pane of smoked glass with the name of the bar etched into it.

Satisfied that there were none of his colleagues present, he walked almost unnoticed over to the bar where he found a free barstool and sat down. He decided that when she arrived he would move to one of the tables, but until then he would stay here and open his tab.

Brad had an empty stool to his right and a man on his left, unshaven, wearing a baseball cap, a chequered shirt and blue jeans. He was conversing with another man who sat on his left, who was wearing almost identical clothing to him but who was clean shaven and considerably thinner than his drinking buddy.

'What can I get you sir?' the barman said as he approached Brad.

'Double scotch,' Brad replied nervously.

'Sure, do you wanna open a tab?' the barman asked.

Brad nodded.

He looked at his watch again - ten minutes to go until she arrived. The barman placed his drink down in front of him; he knocked it straight back and asked for another.

'Gee partner,' the man next to him piped up, 'the bar doesn't close for at least another five hours!' He laughed and pushed his tankard forward for a refill.

'Yeah I know, I'm waiting for someone,' Brad replied reluctantly.

'We're on our way to Miami,' the man continued. 'Gotta take a truck load of stuff down there. We're stoppin overnight - long day tomorrow.'

'Oh,' Brad replied uninterested.

'We just sleep in our cabs. That's the beauty of it - can go for some beers then have a ready made bed waitin. Don't have to pay no motel bills.'

'Right,' Brad answered, glancing down at the menu.

'Food's good in here, you should try it,' the other man then said. 'Nachos is huge, enough for a family of six, and that's just the starter.'

The men both laughed, 'Yeah, I think we're gonna order some food later. I might try the dolphin steak this time, supposed to be mighty fine,' the man next to him affirmed taking another swig of beer.

Brad screwed his face up in distaste, 'Now that is one thing I couldn't bring myself to eat.'

He looked at his watch again. She would be arriving any minute.

The men talked on and Brad listened, occasionally joining in. He ordered another drink and then, realising Alicia was running late, he relaxed a little as the alcohol began to take effect. After the initial conversation with the two men, they began to talk amongst themselves again and Brad was left in peace to mull over the thoughts that were going through his head. He checked his watch again. She was now half an hour late. He checked his mobile, there were no messages. Perhaps she hadn't gone home after all - he would go and see her tomorrow. He did think it a little strange that she hadn't contacted him but shrugged his shoulders resigned to the fact that she may not show. He ordered another drink. He wasn't in any particular hurry. He had to be at work the following day but it was still early evening.

Two hours passed and Brad was becoming increasingly drunk. He decided that he might just call it a day, get some food and go home. He settled his tab and made his way towards the door, having said goodbye to the truckers.

He was feeling very unsteady and didn't think that he would be able to walk home - it was a long way and he was too tired. He pushed open the bar door and walked out into the car park, swaying a little he looked around. The light from the bar illuminated the car park a couple of metres in front of him. Beyond that he couldn't make out anything; it had become so dark. He checked his watch and tried to focus on the time. It was around half ten, but he wasn't sure. There was quite a chill in the air and he shivered. He was only wearing a T-shirt and chinos - it had been sunny when he'd left his home.

He tried to work out what he would do, as he hadn't planned to spend the evening alone. He'd just assumed that now he would be with Alicia and they would head off up the road together. He could hear the cars and trucks rushing past about a hundred yards from him. There was a busy main road just in front of the bar - maybe he could hail a cab from there. He set off into the darkness at the front of the car park, still waiting for his night vision to kick in properly. He decided that if he couldn't hail a cab from the sidewalk he would go back in the bar and call one.

He stood at the edge of the road, his eyes now fully accustomed to the dark. There were no street lamps but the frequent swoop of car headlights as they rushed by illuminated his surroundings. He was only a mile from home, maybe he should walk after all. He couldn't face going back into the bar again.

The road sign ahead indicated that he should go left for Lake Buena Vista. He had gone to the bar in a cab but hadn't really paid much attention to how it got there. He headed along the sidewalk. The fresh air combined with the alcohol made it increasingly difficult to walk. He concentrated hard and tried to focus on the street ahead of him. He had only been walking for about five minutes when, without warning, a figure walking quickly appeared ahead of him. He thought at first that they were coming towards him, but he soon realised that in fact they were hurrying away. He seemed to be gaining on them but as he got closer they speeded up. He had realised by this time that it was a woman up ahead. He couldn't make out her clothes as it was so dark, but the hair was distinctive. He was sure that it was Alicia. He quickened his pace and broke into a slow jog, not wanting to alarm the person, if in fact he was mistaken. As he got within a couple of metres of her he recognised her outfit; she was wearing her black trouser suit. Strange he thought; she only usually wore that on formal occasions. The last time had been at her sister's funeral. 'Alicia!' he shouted.

She was within reach now. He could smell her perfume.

The woman continued to walk quickly but didn't seem to register the fact that she was being followed.

'Alicia!' Brad said again, frustrated now and angry. Not only had she stood him up but she was ignoring him too. 'It's me Brad! Where were you tonight? I waited for ages.'

Still the woman didn't reply.

He reached forward to grab her arm. The figure suddenly spun around. He stopped dead in his tracks, staring in disbelief. It *was* her. 'What?' she hollered so loud that it made him jump. He composed himself.

'Where the hell were you tonight?' he replied angrily.

She just stood there and began to laugh, which angered him further.

The moonlight caught her eyes and he noticed the mischievous glint in them.

'What are you playing at?' he retorted.

'Come on Brad, I'm only kidding. Let's go home.'

He shook his head in frustration, 'You'll be the death of me, I swear it!' He looked at her, beginning to melt again as he always did. His drunken state accentuated his feelings for her.

'So they let you out of hospital then? Why didn't you call me?' he pressed her further.

'I wanted it to be a surprise,' she answered, her voice returning to normal. 'I thought I was gonna have to stay in another night, but luckily they changed their mind.'

'Right, but that still doesn't explain why you didn't bother to go into the bar. Oh well, it's done now, I'm not gonna go on about it. Just don't do it again!' he mockingly scolded her, waving his finger.

She laughed again.

He caught hold of her arm and they walked together down the sidewalk, laughing and joking.

'You sure have been drinking tonight,' she remarked. 'Better not light a cigarette next to you, the explosion would kill us both.'

He laughed and hugged her tighter. 'Aren't you cold? Do you want me to warm you up?'

'How are you gonna warm me up then?' she replied flirtatiously.

'Wait and see,' he smiled.

As they walked the time just seemed to fly by. He noticed that she seemed particularly happy tonight. He was surprised as the last time he'd seen her, even though they'd had a good time together, he had been worried about her state of mind. Tonight it was as if all her troubles had gone and she was a much nicer person to be around. He looked sideways at her, warily, almost disbelieving that he had finally met up with his date in such bizarre circumstances. He was glad all the same.

Brad's place was in a small suburb, not far from Kissimmee where Alicia herself lived. The area where she lived was a lot more exclusive than his. He had a steady job that paid reasonably well, but he had never managed his money properly. He'd bought his small one bedroom apartment two years ago. He was hoping to move but as yet he hadn't got the finances - too many debts on his credit cards to consider applying for an extended mortgage.

There was a definite chill in the air as they walked. He felt freezing, colder than when he had first left the bar. He put his arm around her waist; she seemed to flinch at first but then embraced him back.

'This is really strange. I never thought I'd be needing a jacket tonight. Look at me, I've got goose bumps all over!'

'How far is it to your house?' she asked.

'Just round the corner,' he said pointing ahead to the next bend. They turned off the main road and headed into his estate. It was a hive of activity with people still coming and going. A beaten up saloon was parked up in the street - the bass of its ghetto blaster pounding the still night air.

'Damn!' he said under his breath. 'Those assholes don't care what time it is.'

He surveyed his estate with a look of displeasure - there was nothing scenic about it. He felt a little embarrassed about bringing Alicia back here and had put it off for some while. The apartments, lit up by the street lights, now stood in front of them. They all looked the same. There was no character to them - each with its dull beige facade and uniform dark panels around the evenly spaced balconies. He took her hand protectively as they walked past a couple of the residents who were shouting at each other in the street. He could hear a baby crying and a dog barking; it suddenly struck him how hellish his existence there really was.

He paused then on the sidewalk. It was almost as if his doubt had returned. A police siren wailed in the distance as he looked down at her. She had a contented look on her angelic face. In the half-light her eyes shone expectantly as they took in her surroundings. He swallowed nervously, suddenly feeling uneasy. He had gone this far now, he couldn't back out. *Where would she go at this time of night?*

He remembered Courtney's disapproval outside the hospital, sarcastically mocking his authority. He banished the thought from his head.

'This is it,' he said falteringly.

It was on the ground floor, indistinguishable from the others but for the number on the door. As they approached it a bright security light snapped on revealing a small patch of grass scorched yellow by the sun. *Not like the lush green grass in Bay View Grove* he thought. Brad's hands were shaking. He was developing a headache and felt nauseous. He was certainly not

217

in any fit state to give her what he believed she had come here for, but there was no turning back.

The door opened and he stepped in. She followed, her eyes taking in every detail. She noted the dark brown carpet contrasting with the pale walls and the fact that there was no hallway; she had stepped straight into his lounge. On a side unit stood his family photos; she noticed a photograph of him standing in his police uniform with an older man and woman. She assumed they must be his parents as they were both smiling proudly.

The room was extremely tidy, not a thing out of place. Even his magazines and papers sat snugly in a matching wooden rack by the side of his glass topped coffee table.

'It's awesome,' she said genuinely.

'You think so?' he replied, surprised.

'I love the couch! It's leather isn't it - matches the walls,' she continued. She closed the front door and walked straight over to the couch where she flopped down exhausted from the walk. She removed her shoes and swung her feet up onto the armrest reclining her head backwards and closing her eyes, enjoying the comfort of the large soft cushions.

Brad was in the kitchen fumbling in the units looking for painkillers. He found them and haphazardly poured three into his hand, tossing them into his mouth and gulping them down with a full pint of water. He suddenly felt starving hungry.

'Do you fancy something to eat Alicia?' he called out from the kitchen.

'No thanks,' she replied. 'I'm not hungry.'

'Well I hope you don't mind if I do. I always get like this when I've had too much to drink.'

She laughed, 'You'll get fat! Hey,' she continued, 'and don't burn the kitchen down!'

He made himself some sandwiches and returned to the lounge where he found her still lying on the couch staring up at the ceiling. He wolfed down his food in no time as though he hadn't eaten for weeks. She studied him as he ate. He kept glancing over at her, neither of them spoke but the tension in the room was building. He wanted to take her there and then on the couch but resolved to try to control himself. He didn't want to frighten her - he wanted it to be special. He put his plate down on the table and gently lowered himself down next to her, resting on his elbow as he studied her face. She looked up at him and his deep brown eyes gazed into hers, reaching into her soul, smiling at her. She felt her body come alive with excitement, every nerve ending responding, her body yearning for him. She reached up gingerly and touched his lips with her finger. He kissed it and then tried to take her hand in his but she snatched it back drawing it back into her sleeve.

'Hey hey,' he said protectively. 'It's me Brad,' he kissed her forehead.

'It's going to be different this time I promise. I love you remember?' He decided to take it slowly after what she had been through - he couldn't expect anything else. He sat back up and perched on the edge of the couch.

There was silence again for a few moments.

'I do worry about you,' he said.

'Why?' she responded.

'Well, I mean when you went off last night to the hospital.'

'Oh I was drunk, bit like you are now,' she interjected, her voice sounding slightly annoyed at the inference that she might be losing her mind.

'And now, you're wearing that suit. I mean why?' he said with a look of confusion on his face. 'You wore it to the funeral for Christ's sake.'

She didn't answer at first. 'I like it,' she finally said. 'That's all.'

He sighed, realising his argument was futile and put his hand down on her thigh.

'I'm sorry,' he said, 'it's just, I'm finding it hard you know. I don't know what to say half the time. I'm scared of putting my foot in it. It's just that I've never lost anyone that close to me and so I can't imagine what you're going through.'

'Hey,' she said with a smile. 'Do I look sad? C'mon lighten up, you're depressing me now.'

He began to laugh; her sense of humour always got the better of him. They both laughed, and then they kissed. Breaking from each other to draw breath Brad took her hand and led her towards the bedroom.

'Oh and by the way,' he said, an impish grin spreading across his face. 'You're sleeves are too long; either that or your arms have shrunk.'

'You cheeky...' she said running after him into his room, trying to take a swipe at him but missing. He darted around his room dodging her and laughing excitedly, jumping from side to side to avoid her flailing arms. He jumped onto the bed panting and collapsed onto his back in a star shape, his legs apart. She leapt on top of him and began to undress him feverishly.

'Easy!' he said still breathless, surprised at how forward she was being.

His shirt now off, she ran her hands across his smooth muscular chest, half massaging half caressing. She reached down then to undo his slacks. He readily accepted her advances and assisted her by lifting himself to aid their removal. Once naked he lay back. She seemed to stop then, realising suddenly that she was still fully clothed.

'Now it's your turn,' he said sitting back up and reaching over to take off her jacket. She reeled backwards at his touch, her eyes suddenly wild with fear.

'I can't,' she exclaimed, fighting back the tears. 'It's just that I don't think I'm ready. I can't go through with it.'

'Oh baby,' he breathed, frustration in his voice. 'Don't do this to me! You know how I feel about you - I promise you everything will be just fine.'

She looked back at him without answering, her head lowered in shame.

He reached out and touched her arm tenderly, 'Sweetheart, it's OK.'

She looked up at him - their eyes met again.

'OK I'll do it,' she suddenly said stepping off the bed, 'but you'll have to turn off the light.'

'OK,' he said eagerly, 'I promise I won't look.'

He reached over to his bedside lamp and snapped it off. The room was plunged into an eerie darkness. Brad could feel his heart thumping in his chest. Slowly he saw the shadowy figure before him cast off each item of her clothing. His anticipation was great and his excitement at fever pitch. She didn't speak; he could just hear her breathing rapidly, nervously. He looked and could now see in the dark the outline of a perfect female body. He could see the curve of her ample breasts as his eyes moved down to her tapered waist and rounded hips. Down further he could make out her toned slender legs. He now knew she truly was perfect. Lust took hold of him. He couldn't think as she moved towards him slowly. He longed to see her; he had to see her. At that precise moment his hand shot out, almost as if he had no control over it, fumbling for the light switch.

'What are you doing?' she asked her voice trembling.

It was too late, the light was on, and he saw her.

Her eyes wide, fearful, like an animal caught in a trap. Her entire torso and arms had been slashed to pieces, with huge gaping wounds that had bled and then dried.

He recoiled in horror, backing away from her across the bed, falling onto the floor.

Stumbling to his feet, he ran into the lounge and sat shivering on the couch. The room was now icy cold.

'Brad!' she cried, walking towards him.

'Get away from me!' he screamed in terror.

'Brad I thought you loved me,' she whined pitifully, mocking him.

'Get out!' he bellowed, not wanting to believe what he saw before his eyes. This was like something out of a horror movie. Surely he couldn't be experiencing this - how could it possibly be happening. At that moment the reality of everything suddenly hit him. It was *her! But she is…,* 'No,' he cried, battering the side of his head with his hands. He had nowhere to run to - there was silence again. He shook with fear as he sat there, too afraid to look up. Thoughts raced through his mind. He wished that he had never met Alicia in the first place, as everything in his life had turned upside down since the day he had answered that emergency call to Jennifer's café. This was more than he had ever had to face before; it was beyond the realms of reality as he understood it. His survival mechanism should have kicked in by now. He should have run or forced her out of his house and slammed the door behind him. Instead he felt an overwhelming grief come over him, as though he had just lost everything. He crumpled like a small child, vulnerable, naked. He fell forward and landed on his knees on the floor, not feeling anything - his mind numb. He began to sob uncontrollably, his hands clasped in front of him as if in prayer. Still not daring to look at his tormentor, who stood silently before him, it was as if instinctively he now knew everything.

'Brad,' she said quietly. 'I'm sorry if I frightened you. I didn't mean to. If you had left the light off as I asked.'

'Get away from me! Get away from me!' he rambled in terror.

'Our father who art in heaven, hallowed be thy name,' he continued rocking backwards and forwards on his bare knees. From his head sprang beads of sweat, which ran like drizzling rain down his forehead. His eyes were shut tight so as not to let in even a chink of light. Tears were escaping from the corners, running down past his nose to his lips.

'Brad listen to me. I'm not going to hurt you. I just wanted you to believe I was her - just for one night.'

She moved nearer to him and put her arms under his to lift him off the floor. He froze, rigid with terror. Still mumbling he tried to stand as she lifted him back onto the couch.

'Brad, if you would just listen to me. Maybe I could explain to you.'

'Though I walk through the valley of the shadow of death, I will fear no evil, for my God is with me,' he continued. It was then that she struck him so hard around the head that he was knocked backwards onto the couch.

'I'm *not* evil!' she bellowed. 'If you had listened to me, then I wouldn't have had to do that now would I?'

Brad was sinking into unconsciousness, the darkness behind his eyes was getting blacker.

She walked over to his drinks cabinet and pulled out a glass and an unopened bottle of whiskey.

She then walked to the kitchen and found the cupboard where he stored his medication. From there she walked to the drainer and from the drawer she pulled a large carving knife. She noticed a chopping board on the side and brought it over to the worktop. She found two more full packets of Paracetamol, and proceeded to crush every tablet to powder. She scraped the contents into the glass and filled it to the brim with neat whiskey.

When she had finished, she carefully placed everything back where she had found it, apart from the empty pill packet. She left this on the worktop, strewn haphazardly, as if left in desperation, a last cry for help. She walked calmly back to the lounge. She found Brad still sprawled across the couch. He wasn't injured - she had just knocked him out cold.

'Brad,' she whispered in his ear. 'Are you asleep?' He didn't answer her.

'Brad, I'm not going anywhere, so you'd better wake up.' There was still no reply so she slapped him again across his face. He groaned in pain and his eyes sprang open. Her face was only a short distance from his; he gasped again and began to choke. What used to have been to him the face of an angel now represented that of the devil. Yet still he was uncontrollably drawn to it, like a delicious temptation that couldn't be ignored or denied. In his confusion his hand automatically reached out to touch her. She knocked his hand away and slammed it back down beside him on the couch. He lay staring up at her like a baby at its mother, completely at her mercy, all control of the situation now lost.

'Brad,' she said softening her tone again. 'I brought you a little something to take the edge off. You've had a shock. If you drink this maybe we can talk about it.'

She raised his head so that his chin was resting on his chest.

'Now drink this. It'll make you feel better.'

She poured half the tumbler down his throat; he began to gasp and gag as the strong whiskey burned his tongue and throat. He tried to struggle then for the first time, but she was down on him fast. She yanked his head back, pinched his nose and poured the rest down his throat.

'Now swallow it!' she shouted. 'I'm trying to help you, you stupid man!' She saw his throat move as the whiskey went down. She let go of his nose then and his body immediately went into spasms of coughing and retching.

'If you bring it all back up, I'll just have to give you another glass. Do you want that?' she said. He shook his head violently.

'Well lay still then,' she retorted.

His eyes began to feel heavy - his whole body felt as if it was on fire.

She leaned forward and stroked his head as he slipped back into unconsciousness.

'I'm sorry Brad,' she said with a heavy sigh, 'but it has to be this way. I know maybe in time you could have accepted me the way I am. But then there would have been the problem of my sister, and who knows, we could have ended up on the Springer Show fighting over you.' She laughed to herself, 'Wouldn't that have been funny?' She looked down at him and felt his pulse, which was getting weaker. She picked up the glass, wiped it, and forced it into his hand until it had transferred his prints. She then let it drop to the floor beside the couch.

She looked back at him. 'I'm not a bad person,' she said her lip starting to tremble. She felt his pulse again and could feel nothing; his mouth gaped open, his face was waxy pale. She looked down at her own injured body. She comforted herself with the thought that any second she would see him get up from the couch and he would be standing next to her. It had to happen - she wanted it so badly. She wouldn't be alone any longer. She waited and waited for what seemed like forever, but he didn't move. She was sure then that he must have gone. Although she tried to deny it, deep down she knew that this was what happened when people died. This was what was supposed to happen. She threw her head back and screamed in frustration and terror.

Chapter 11

It was at that moment that Courtney opened her eyes. She had been sleeping peacefully, and suddenly she was back there in her bed with Adam fast asleep next to her. She felt feverish and had broken out into a sweat. Shadows danced before her eyes and she glanced anxiously around the room. Every sound was magnified as she tried to see into the darkness that surrounded her. She looked at her clock, the brightness of its display made the room seem even darker - it was 2.13 a.m. The curtain to her right suddenly billowed as a gust of wind blew into the room; she could feel her heart pounding. It was as if it had jumped up and was now somewhere just below her throat. It was then that thoughts of the day before came back to haunt her - her mind feeding the terror, which was growing by the second.

She turned onto her side to face Adam who had his back to her. Although he was there, it was as if she was alone - he slept on. She felt isolated in her misery; she contemplated whether she would feel any different if he was awake. Maybe it would distract her mind but they couldn't agree about anything. He had brushed off her experience saying she was imagining it - it was all in her mind. She was becoming paranoid. *This is crazy* she told herself over and over as she lay with her eyes fixed on Adam's back. She tried to direct her thoughts away from the things that frightened her. She was perfectly safe wasn't she? Nothing could possibly happen that wouldn't wake him up too. She closed her eyes again, rolled over onto her back and began to drift back to sleep, the covers pulled up around her ears. It was then that she heard it. She realised that she had heard this same sound before, only this time she was conscious - she couldn't ignore it any longer. A chill came over her then. It travelled down the entire length of her spine and left her rigid, paralysed. She lay as if in her own coffin, her gaze fixed on the ceiling. It wasn't in the room, she was sure. It was coming from outside, in the hallway. She didn't move a muscle and hardly dared to breathe, listening intently, trying to make sense of what was happening. She reached out and snapped on the bedroom light - nothing was there, nothing had moved.

'Adam, wake up!' Courtney said, as she jabbed her husband in the back. He began to stir and rolled onto his front. She jabbed him again more earnestly - this time in the ribs.

'Ouch!' he exclaimed. 'What?' his voice sounded dreamy and slightly aggravated.

'Adam,' she said again in a hoarse stage whisper. 'Listen!' His eyes opened and his forehead furrowed into a frown.

'Listen to what? Why's the light on?' he said perplexed.

'The crying,' she said frustrated. 'Can't you hear it?'

'I can hear something, but it doesn't sound like someone crying.' He turned to her, a look of confusion on his face.

'Well what does it sound like then?' she replied agitated. 'Can't you go and look out in the hallway? I can't sleep - it's been going on for about twenty minutes now.'

He sighed and hauled himself out from under the duvet.

He sat hunched on the side of the bed, yawned and then struggled to his feet.

'Where's my dressing gown gone now?' he said his hands on his hips, shaking his head in annoyance.

'Behind you on the back of the chair,' she answered; she, unlike her husband, was now wide awake and fully alert.

Courtney could feel her heart starting to pound again. She felt sick with nerves as Adam turned the handle on the bedroom door. 'Remember to check in the girls' rooms too,' she said, as he disappeared through the doorway, leaving it wide open. She lay expectantly, her eyes fixed on the dark entrance to their room. She felt her baby moving then, responding to her body's anxiety.

It was then that she noticed something was different. She was now hearing other sounds outside in the street. She hadn't been able to hear any of those when she had first woken, and the window had been open the whole time. Now she could hear the distant rushing of cars travelling down the interstate, the chirping of crickets, the faint sound of people walking and laughing. She lay in disbelief as the realisation suddenly dawned - she could no longer hear anyone crying; the sound had stopped the moment that Adam had opened the bedroom door. She thumped the duvet with her fist, knowing what would happen next. She heard a second door close in the hallway outside the bedroom and the soft padding sound of bare feet on carpet. Adam was returning having completed his search. She rolled onto her side facing the window. She heard him close the door and his dressing gown fall to the floor as he slipped back under the covers, moving over to her side of the bed. He put his arm around her but she stiffened, feeling so alone, unable to return his embrace. *Why did it stop? He thinks I'm going mad now. Maybe I am.*

A tear rolled down her cheek but she didn't wipe it away. She just stared vacantly ahead.

'Courtney,' he said softly.

'Don't even say it! I know already,' she snapped back at him. 'I'm hearing things and seeing things again.'

'Well I just think that maybe you're tired. We've had a lot on our plates lately - a lot of worry,' he replied, stroking her arm tenderly.

She pulled it away from him and moved to the very edge of the bed until she was almost falling out. She couldn't bear for him to touch her. All she wanted was to be believed. It was hard enough having to deal with everything that was happening but now she couldn't even rely on the one man she used to trust more than anybody else in the world.

Silence fell on the room again as Adam flicked the light switch off from his side of the bed.

Courtney lay still in the darkness; she felt empty and hollow inside. She felt a wave of unhappiness sweep back over her as though a black cloud had descended and engulfed her totally.

Twenty or so more minutes passed. She concentrated on the sounds outside as she tried desperately to get back to sleep. She just wasn't tired. The clock came into focus and she watched as the seconds passed - it was now 2.48 a.m. *Just as well I don't have work tomorrow.* The recollection that she had the day off lifted her spirits slightly. Perhaps she could read, but then if she turned the light on again Adam would wake up and get annoyed. She decided the only thing she could do would be to go down

227

stairs and maybe watch a video. If she fell asleep down there it wouldn't matter; she didn't have to get up particularly early in the morning. She pulled on her dressing gown and headed over to the door. Her heart began to pound in her chest again; she took a deep breath. She glanced back over her shoulder. The room was in darkness apart from the faint light from the street casting a ghostly patch of light over the foot of the bed. She could just make out the sleeping form of Adam under the duvet. Her mind began to play tricks on her again as she struggled to summon up the courage to open the door. She squeezed her eyes tightly shut, took another deep breath, and with one swift movement pulled open the door. She regained her composure and stepped forward, pausing whilst her ears strained to hear the faintest sound. She couldn't hear anything and set off quickly down the hallway. The walls seemed to tower on either side of her. She passed both of the twins' doors and headed for the top of the stairs - still she heard nothing. She rounded the top of the stairs and there she paused again. The moonlight flooded through the upstairs window illuminating the staircase.

She stepped carefully down the bare wooden steps, each stair creaking slightly as she went. Downstairs it was pitch black, and when she reached the bottom of the staircase she quickly found the hall light and flicked the switch. She stopped, out of breath but feeling safe again. She looked around her. The lounge was still in darkness as was the kitchen. As she walked across the hallway thoughts came back to her from the previous day and she was reminded that she was walking towards what had been her escape route. She took another deep breath. She must try to remain calm and rational. Maybe Adam was right - perhaps it was her hormones or the stress, which was causing her to imagine all sorts of strange things. It could be that she was isolating herself and excluding Adam.

She paused in the kitchen doorway and flicked on the light switch, waiting for the fluorescent tube to buzz and whirr into life. She put the kettle on and sat at the breakfast bar, where she started to flick through yesterday's paper. She still felt alert - not at all tired. Perhaps a coffee was not the best idea after all she thought, as she glanced through the pages. Still the house remained silent and nothing stirred. The only noise that broke the silence was the faint roaring sound of the kettle as the element heated, gradually building to a crescendo as it boiled. With a mug of coffee in one hand and the newspaper under her arm, she walked out of the kitchen turning off the light and stepped through the doorway to the lounge.

She discovered to her relief that everything was where it should be with nothing out of place. She walked to the television and turned it on, flicking through the channels, trying to find something worth watching but there was nothing. She placed her mug gingerly on the coffee table and sat down slowly and deliberately on the edge of the couch - not intending to stay there long. She had decided that she would try to get some sleep when she had finished her coffee. Her body was starting to give in to her tiredness now.

Courtney took a last gulp of coffee and stood up, stretching and yawning, as she walked back out of the room. She turned off all of the lights, plunging the house into darkness again. Her night vision then took over and everything began to come back into focus. She saw the steep winding staircase before her and moved towards it, beginning to climb. She shivered as she neared the top and paused to wrap her arms around herself - rubbing her upper arms to warm them. Why hadn't she felt cold earlier? She had been warm enough downstairs and wasn't heat supposed to rise?

When she reached the top of the staircase the long, dark hallway stretched ahead of her. She could see her bedroom door at the end. If she could just make it back to her room, she could close the door and be warm and safe again under the duvet. It was then that she heard it again. A shiver ran down the entire length of her spine, the hairs on the back of her neck prickled. She stood rooted to the spot.

'Who is it?' she said. She instinctively knew that whatever or whoever this was knew she was there, and knew that she could hear every sound.

It was a pitiful sound - a young child; a girl she was sure. The sound didn't seem to be coming from one specific place; it was all around her, echoing, becoming louder and louder, then fading again.

'Courtney!' she heard her name. The sound was like nothing she had ever heard before - it sounded as though it was coming through on an old radio. There was interference causing the voice to fade, but suddenly it came through clearly again.

'Find Brad!' She distinctly heard these two words come through. *Brad?* Her mind began to race again, her adrenaline beginning to surge. She felt overwhelmed by thoughts and questions; she started to feel faint from the sudden onslaught of emotion. *Brad? Alicia, Adam. Adam forgot to call him, but Why? Who?*

'Brad!' the voice came through again.

'OK!' she screamed. 'Who are you? What's happening to me? The voice faded again and she squeezed the side of head with her hands, both exasperated and terrified.

Although she was afraid, she knew that this time she couldn't ignore it. This was not her imagination, this was very real. She moved quickly down the corridor and the crying seemed to follow her.

She paused in the doorway and turned back to look, having reached the safety of her bedroom. She could see nothing; the crying had stopped again. She closed the door and slid down the back of it, now in a crouching position on the floor. She put her head between her knees and began to sob, rocking backwards and forwards, her head in her hands. Adam stirred again and raised himself up from the pillow, squinting in the half-light, trying to locate his wife. He sprang from the bed when he saw her and ventured over to her cautiously, a little afraid of what her reaction to him might be. He crouched down beside her and gently touched her arm; she jumped, her head flying back hitting the wooden door hard.

'My God Courtney! Honey?' he said, grabbing hold of her and pulling her to him. 'You're shaking like a leaf.' He held her, rubbing the back of her head with the palm of his hand.

'I'm not going mad!' she cried, 'I swear it.' She gripped hold of him hard, her face buried in his shoulder.

'What on earth happened?' he said concerned, his voice breaking.

'I heard it again,' she said, 'the crying. It was all around me - it's a girl, a young girl.'

'I was asleep. I didn't hear anything,' he answered monotone, annoyed that again his wife was talking nonsensically.

'I heard it OK Adam, and I'm not going crazy. I don't need to see the mad doctor. I'm *perfectly* sane.' She pulled away from him again feeling that he didn't believe her.

'OK OK,' he said holding his hands up defensively. 'Courtney let's get some sleep and talk about this in the morning.' He stood up helping his wife to her feet. Neither of them spoke again that night.

Courtney lay her aching head on the pillow and in the few seconds that it took her to get to sleep she had already planned what she would do the moment her eyes were open again.

At 6 a.m. Courtney woke, after only a few hours of restless sleep. She still felt exhausted, but her mind was now focused. Her sleep had been interrupted by disturbing and persistent dreams. There was a dark figure just out of sight in every scene - she knew they were there, but they didn't reveal themselves. Still the same message came through clear, 'Find Brad.'

Daylight had returned although not fully. There was enough light to dispel her anxiety and enable her to concentrate on getting herself dressed and out of the house.

She turned as she climbed from the bed to look at her husband. He slept soundly, oblivious to everything that was going on around him and seemingly unaffected by it all. She felt a sudden overwhelming hatred for him that moved her to tears, because it conflicted so strongly with her previous undying devotion. She knew she was alone now. Their close bond was getting weaker by the day as she became more emotionally detached from him. Although depressed about the situation between Adam and herself, she also felt empowered. She had to find out what was going on and she was determined to prove that what was happening to her was not a figment of her imagination.

She showered quickly and dressed, pausing to look at herself long and hard in the mirror as she combed her hair through. Her face was not the same anymore. It was hollowed at the cheeks and pallid. Her eyes were dark and heavy looking and the gleam had gone from them. She snapped out of her self-analysis and quickly pulled on her clothes, stepping up a gear. It was now quarter past six. She reached over the side of the bed for her handbag, accidentally nudging Adam as she did so. He only stirred a little and continued to sleep on. She took one last look at herself, now improved by a little make-up, and headed for the door.

Everything was as it had been - she could feel no presence or chill in the air as she walked back down the stairs. All seemed to have returned to normal. As she left, the breeze caught her hair and she looked back up at the house. It was as if she was looking for something but she wasn't quite sure exactly what that was. She got in the car and started the engine. She wound down the window, as the car was quite stuffy and hot, and wiped haphazardly at the smeared windscreen.

She backed slowly out of the driveway. She noticed Ted Fraser up at his window, watching her through a gap in his drapes. He had a concerned look on his face. She ignored him and continued on down the road.

Thoughts besieged her troubled mind again. She had been so determined that this would never happen to her and her husband. This marriage was going to be perfect and she could never have imagined waking up and looking at him the way she had that morning, with such disdain. The feeling that she couldn't ignore was that there was something that her mind had suddenly revealed, as if a door of awareness had been thrown open. The cloak of security and blind trust that had covered her before as she coasted through their early years of marriage in imagined bliss now lay in tatters around her. She still loved him but she was nobody's fool, and everything that she had ignored before and believed came back into her mind and she looked at it again afresh as if she had been given new eyes. She didn't like what she saw. The man at the funeral, the phone call that Adam had made, the lies that he had pacified her with.

She drove along the interstate confident, but sad. She had fought so hard to maintain the strong family unit, trying not to let his daughters destroy their perfect life, but she was going to have to risk losing everything to find the truth. She knew that the one person she had never wanted to drop her guard with or let into her private thoughts was the only person who was going to understand - and it was Alicia.

As she drove into the hospital car park, she felt that finally she was strong enough to hear what Alicia had to tell her. She held vital information about the past that she had never wanted to concern herself with before, for fear of her own jealousy, but she knew that the time had come to confront her fears and face them head on.

She found a parking space relatively easily and walked in through the hospital entrance in the early morning sunshine. She passed the reception barely recognising her friend Nicky who was on duty that day. She looked up from the desk and smiled at her, realising she must be visiting. She half waved at Courtney and went to speak but Courtney didn't stop. She just stared straight through her as she walked down the corridor and headed towards Alicia's private room.

She paused outside the door for a second, butterflies returning to her stomach as she turned the handle. Alicia lay asleep on her side; one of the nurses saw Courtney entering the room out of the corner of her eye. She quickened her pace having looked at her watch. She opened the door and leaned in, whispering so as not to wake her patient.

'Courtney, visiting hours don't start until nine.'

'I know,' Courtney smiled nervously back at her. 'It's OK, I just want to sit with her.'

'Well,' the nurse sighed. 'I guess, she is leaving this morning. I'm sure that'll be all right.'

With that the nurse left the room, closing the door carefully behind her. There was silence then. No machines beeped, there were no lines connected to Alicia's arms. It was just a clinical white room, like a budget motel room, with a small bedside table. She sat herself down slowly at the side of the bed, on the side that Alicia was facing. She sat gazing at her for the first few minutes, mesmerised by her beauty, perplexed by her colouring. Her hair, that was the biggest mystery of all.

She wondered to herself what she would say when she woke. She had to wake her, she had this inexplicable sense of urgency.

She reached out tentatively with her right arm and gently placed her hand on top of Alicia's head and stroked her hair; it was as though she had suddenly been taken over by an overwhelming impulse to take care of her. As she looked at her stepdaughter she felt as if she were her age again - so young and vulnerable. There was a light dusting of freckles across her nose and her face twitched slightly as she dreamed, her eyelids flickering imperceptibly.

As she stroked Alicia's hair she became preoccupied again with the events of the previous night and without realising, her hand was pressing harder causing Alicia to stir.

'Mom?' she said still asleep. She opened her eyes and tried to focus.

Courtney smiled.

'Oh it's you,' Alicia exclaimed downcast.

'Pleased to see me then?' she mocked.

'What time is it?' she said, stretching and yawning.

'It's early,' Courtney replied in a matter of fact tone. 'Listen, try to wake up, I need to talk to you. It's really important.' She spoke in a stage whisper, not wanting to be heard by anyone else.

'I'm sorry OK,' she continued.

'Sorry for what?' Alicia said, looking slightly puzzled.

'Yesterday,' Courtney replied, 'Oh I freaked out at you about the TV, and you see, well, the thing is..........'

'What?' Alicia interjected.

'The thing is, I know what you've been going through,' tears welled in her eyes as she spoke, as if she was finally able to rid herself of her burden.

Alicia sat up in bed and stared at her unmoved.

'You mean with my sister dying? Yeah I know that,' she said monotone.

'That's not what I mean,' Courtney replied. Their eyes met and connected again as they had the previous day.

Alicia's eyes widened with the sudden realisation. 'You've heard things, in the house?' she continued hesitantly.

'Yes,' Courtney answered, the relief flooding over her.

Alicia's bright blue eyes blurred with tears. She reached forward in a sudden impulsive movement and embraced her stepmother. The two cried together almost with joy at the powerful bond they had suddenly felt.

Courtney then pulled back abruptly, wiped her eyes and sat up straight, remembering the words she had heard the previous night.

'Alicia,' she said, her voice still hoarse with emotion. 'I think that Brad may be in trouble.'

'What?' she replied, her expression grave.

'I heard crying last night, a girl.'

'I know, I've heard it too,' Alicia said, panic now taking hold.

'This voice, well it said to find Brad. Do you know where he lives?' Courtney spoke rapidly, there was so much to ask and very little time.

'Yes, I have his address.' She leaned over the bed to her cabinet; Courtney helped her to get her bag. She gasped then. 'You mean Dad forgot to call him, to tell him that I...'

'Yes,' came her reply.

'Oh no!' Alicia said clutching her forehead with her free hand, 'No, No!'

'Quickly, we have to get out of here. Hang the consequences, they were gonna discharge you this morning anyway.' Courtney leapt to her feet and began to look around the room, 'Where are your clean clothes?'

Alicia was already out of the bed and on her feet. She pulled them out of her overnight bag and hurriedly dropped her night gown, pulling on a pair of beige slacks and a pink T-shirt.

'Have you got everything?' Courtney said looking out into the corridor furtively. 'Right then, wait here a minute - I'll check the coast is clear.'

She opened the door and peered outside. She could see a couple of nurses but they were walking away from the room towards the other end of the corridor. She looked left - nobody was walking towards them. 'Quick,' she motioned to Alicia.

The two women darted out into the corridor and walked briskly, not running, so as not to attract too much attention, past the reception again. 'Courtney!' Nicky called out, but she didn't stop. They made it outside to the car without a hitch. It was a hive of activity around the entrance but nobody stared at them - they were just part of the crowd.

They ran to the car and Courtney quickly found the keys.

'Where's that address?' She said glancing over at Alicia as they drove out of the car park.

'It's here,' she had it gripped tightly in her hand. She unfolded the piece of paper to read it.

'Jubilee Court,' she said, '3112.'

'Oh I know that, Nicky used to live near there,' Courtney recalled, and began indicating left to take a sudden detour.

'Courtney,' Alicia spoke up. 'I don't know what to do, I'm too scared to stay in the house.'

'You and me both,' she agreed. 'Let's go see Brad and then we need to sit down and have a talk. It's difficult for me you see, I didn't want to say anything. Well it's your father, he thinks I'm going crazy. He won't talk about it, just says I'm imagining things. But there's more to it than that, something I can't put my finger on, and I was hoping you might be able to help me.'

'Do you believe in ghosts?' Alicia suddenly said.

'Well, I guess I must do now. I know there are things that nobody can explain, like that,' Courtney concluded.

'I just don't know why all this has happened,' Alicia then said. 'Since Gaby died, the night she died even, I got woken up. It was awful it was as if she was trying to tell me what had happened to her. The picture got broken. I'm angry, I'm really angry, and I think she is too.'

'What about Jennifer?' Courtney asked. 'She's dead now too, and the crying, but it's a child. I just don't understand what's happening to us.' Her eyes filled with tears again as she reached down with her free arm and touched her swollen belly. 'My poor baby,' she said. 'What is he or she going through in there? Pregnancy is supposed to be a quiet time, a peaceful time. How can my baby possibly be growing normally with all the anxiety and stress that I feel constantly? What if the baby can hear me crying? Maybe he or she will think I don't want them.'

Alicia looked at her stepmother and seemed genuinely upset. She reached out and touched her knee protectively.

'I'm sure everything will be OK,' she said quietly. 'I'm so sorry. If we hadn't come to live with you, you would have been peaceful and quiet.'

As Courtney pulled into Brad's estate, she realised that although her life had been turned upside down, maybe she had been spared from living a lie the rest of her days.

'No,' she replied, 'I'm glad I've met you. I can't deny what's really true can I? I couldn't have buried my head in the sand the rest of my days, trying to pretend you didn't really exist.' The words were out before she had time to stop them. 'I mean…...'

'It's OK,' Alicia replied unshaken, 'I'd rather you were honest. I always hated you when I was younger because I thought you were the one who was keeping my dad away from me. I didn't even know you then but to be honest, now that I do, I think you're a much better person than my dad. I didn't know him either really - I just had this picture of him in my head.'

'Over there,' Alicia pointed to the row of apartments in front of them. 'That must be it - there's 3110.'

'Yes,' she replied, 'but he's 3112 - must be next door.'

Courtney pulled the car up and turned off the engine. As she sat there she began to feel anxious again. She took a long deep breath. 'Right, lets do it.'

Alicia opened her door slamming it behind her; she walked round to the sidewalk. They looked around the estate.

'It's still early,' Courtney remarked, glancing at her watch. 'People will be heading off to work soon.'

'Are you scared Courtney?' Alicia said her voice a little shaky. She looked at her stepmother, her eyes full of fear.'

'I don't think I need to answer that do you,' she said trying to force a smile. 'We're here - it's that one.' The number was not as easy to distinguish as that on the neighbour's door and was slightly obscured. They approached the door with trepidation.

'The curtain's open slightly,' Alicia motioned to Courtney, who was walking towards her across the untidy patch of grass in front of his window. She was quickly by her side. The two looked around again - nobody was about. They leaned against the windowpane, taking a few seconds to focus. They could just make him out in the half-light of the room, motionless, naked, his head lolling over the armrest of the couch.

'Oh my God!' Alicia clapped her hand over her mouth to stifle a scream. Courtney grabbed her arm.

'Right, now don't lets panic. He may just be asleep. You stand there, I'll go ring the bell. We should really have done that in the first place.'

Alicia stood rooted to the spot as her stepmother walked to the front door; her eyes fixed on her boyfriend. She felt numb inside, hoping still that Courtney would be right, and as soon as that bell was depressed he would stir and make a move to answer it.

Alicia heard the bell as it rang. She stared at him intently, willing him to move, but he didn't.

'He's not moving!' she cried hysterically. 'Press it again!'

Courtney rang the bell again. 'Anything?' she called out.

'No nothing,' Alicia replied, her emotions spilling over. 'He looks like he's dead.

'Oh no!' she cried, unable to contain her distress any longer, as the scenario she had feared the most played out before her eyes.

Courtney rushed over to her side, 'Alicia, please, we don't know that for sure. We have to think fast.' She ran her trembling hand through her hair. 'Try not to panic, we have to help him. You call 911 and I'm gonna try and get in somehow.'

She sprinted round to the side of the apartment her heart thumping. There was a narrow passageway between his apartment and his neighbours. She searched desperately for some way of getting in. There was a small window, but this was tightly shut. 'Damn!' she exclaimed. She ran round the back and finding a tall fence she grabbed on to the top and tried to pull herself up. She peered over into a small box garden and the door leading out to it was closed, 'It's locked,' she called out, 'I can't get in there.' She jumped back down into the passageway and ran back round the front of the apartment. Alicia had just finished calling the emergency services. Courtney ran back out into the street and, seeing a man shutting his car door, she called out to him, waving her arms frantically. He didn't see her and the car sped away. She thought quickly. She would try to force the front door whilst they waited for the ambulance. At least then she would feel as if she was doing something.

'Alicia, how long are they gonna be?'

'As quick as they can - about five minutes - I don't know,' Alicia replied her voice breaking with emotion.

Courtney thought about the night before, the grim realisation hitting her again, that she had been right, *and look at the consequences*. Where was Adam when she needed him? He was almost certainly at work by now tending to his patients, blissfully unaware of everything that was happening to them, existing in his own little world. Anger took hold of her as she listened to the sound of his daughter sobbing. She had to get in there and get in fast. She ran back up to the front door and rammed her body against it. To her surprise it came open easily in one swift movement and she was inside, with Alicia just behind her. Silence. The house was dark and there was a heady almost musty smell in there - a cocktail of stale air, mixed with stale alcohol. Courtney approached Brad's still form, fear gripping her again. Alicia cried out when she saw him, making Courtney jump. 'Quiet!' she bellowed - the sudden noise having jangled her nerves. She immediately reached out to catch hold of her hand, not meaning to have hollered at her like that. Seeing anyone like this was more than she could bear. 'What on earth has happened to him? This whole place reeks of alcohol,' she said with an air of disbelief.

She reached out cautiously to touch his arm, to see if she could feel a pulse. Eventually she did but it was very weak. She looked at his face, his mouth was open, encrusted with vomit and his eyes were just staring vacantly up at the ceiling. She put her face as close to his mouth as she could without making contact and could feel an occasional faint breath against her cheek.

'He's alive, thank God!' she proclaimed, her eyes filling with tears.

She looked round suddenly, aware that she was alone again. 'Alicia!' she called out. 'Didn't you hear me?'

Just then Alicia walked back into the lounge carrying a blanket.

'I brought him this,' she said her voice faltering as she approached her stepmother. 'I can't let the paramedics see him like this.'

They spread the blanket out over him and tucked it in either side.

'Brad,' Courtney said softly, 'it's OK, you're safe now - the ambulance is on its way.'

As the words were out of her mouth, two paramedics walked into the room. Just their presence was enough to send a feeling of calm rushing back through Courtney. She stood up shakily to greet them. The larger of the two, an African American, smiled warmly at her and she thought then that he had a serene, almost angelic face.

'He's my daughter's boyfriend. We just found him like this,' Courtney blurted out to him. 'His name's Brad, he's a police officer.'

'It looks like he could have severe alcohol poisoning or he could even have taken an overdose,' he said, as he bent down beside his patient. 'Has anyone found any empty packets of pills or anything like that?'

'No,' Courtney replied helplessly. 'I mean, there's nothing around the couch, apart from the empty glass. We only just found him.'

'Do you know if he's taking any prescribed medication?' he then asked.

Alicia shrugged her shoulders, 'I don't think so - he never told me he was, but I haven't really known him that long to be honest.'

'Have a look in the kitchen for me,' he replied with a reassuring smile, 'see if there's anything lying around.'

Alicia hurried away and within a matter of seconds came back clutching the empty packets in her hand. 'I found these on the side,' she said, her voice trembling. She leaned forward and handed them to him. He studied them briefly and nodded, satisfied that they had found the cause. The full horror of the situation was now unfolding. She caught hold of Courtney's hand and gripped it tightly. None of it made any sense and she felt anger towards Brad that he could have done this to her.

The two men worked quickly and efficiently. 'So you were just visiting then when you found him?' the other paramedic then asked.

'Yes,' Courtney replied trying to compose herself. 'We saw him through the drapes and when he didn't get up when I rang the doorbell, I forced the door open. We just knew something was wrong. He is going to be OK isn't he?'

Alicia still didn't speak. Tears were coursing down her cheeks as she watched the paramedic frantically working on Brad.

'He has a pulse,' the paramedic finally replied, 'but it's very weak. We'll stabilise him first and then get him off to the hospital.'

Minutes seemed like hours. They continued to work on him. The silence was broken this time by Alicia. 'He will be OK though won't he?' she said, an air of desperation in her voice. Courtney put her arm around her and pulled her protectively to her side. The larger paramedic didn't look at her but motioned to his colleague as they prepared to move Brad onto the stretcher.

'It's hard to say Miss,' he said gravely. 'He's very sick right now, but he stands every chance in hospital. They will take good care of him, I promise.'

Courtney felt desolate as they followed the stretcher out to the ambulance. She noticed straight away that all of Brad's neighbours had appeared, now that they were no longer required, and were standing on the sidewalk watching ghoulishly as his lifeless form was eased into the back of the ambulance. She knew that she could no longer look forward to the future. Every day from here on was going to be a struggle. Alicia may have to face losing somebody else who she had just allowed herself to get close to. Guilt consumed her. She should have reminded Adam to call Brad and maybe this situation could have been avoided. Suddenly one of the paramedics called out to her, bringing her back to reality with a jolt.

'This your car ma'am?'

'Yes,' she replied automatically.

'Are you going to be OK to drive it? Your daughter wants to go with Brad in the back of the ambulance. Do you want to follow on behind?'

'Yes, yes that'll be fine,' she replied fumbling for her keys. Her adrenaline still up, she hurried round to the side of her car and jumped in. As the engine started, she barely noticed the fact that her stereo had switched itself on - she didn't bother to switch it off; she couldn't think straight at that moment. Everything was so chaotic and confused; right now she was going to concentrate on getting to the hospital and once there she would look for

Adam. She had to try to talk to him again. They needed to fight this thing together - if only he would believe her. He was so pig headed and dismissive all the time. She followed the ambulance out of Brad's estate, its siren wailing and blue light flashing. She tried to keep up with it but tears were now streaking her face again, blurring her vision.

As she neared the hospital she heard a different sound that distracted her momentarily from the sound of the wailing siren up ahead. It took her a few moments to realise that it was her mobile phone ringing. She panicked and groped inside her handbag. 'Hello!' she snapped.

'Hi honey it's me,' Adam's warm silky voice replied.

'Adam,' she replied startled. 'What do you want? I'm driving?'

'I just called to let you know I've swapped shifts with Peter. I'm working nights tonight - is that OK?'

Courtney's mind was a blur; she wasn't really concentrating on what her husband was saying to her.

'But you're working days again tomorrow,' she recalled.

'I know babe, but Peter asked me. It was urgent - he's got problems.'

'Oh and we haven't I suppose,' she bit back sarcastically.

'C'mon,' he tried to soothe his wife.

'Are you going to the hospital now?' she continued earnestly.

'Yeah, I'm just waiting for my lift,' he answered.

'Good cos that's where I'm headed. I need to speak to you there - bye.' She wanted to end the conversation; she didn't have time for it right then.

'Hang on,' he said his voice becoming flustered. 'It's only one night shift, I…'

'Never mind that, I'm following an ambulance right now. Brad's in the back of it - Alicia too. I'll explain everything when I see you.'

'What?' Adam exclaimed.

'I'll talk to you in a minute - bye.' She cut him off just as the ambulance swung into the emergency arrivals bay. She drove to the car park and hunted for a space. There was a car in front of her backing slowly out of a space, seeming to take forever.

'C'mon!' she bellowed; she had no patience at the best of times when she was driving. Once parked she headed for main reception.

The first person she saw was Nicky again. She remembered a time when she used to be pleased to see her friend - now she heard herself inwardly groan. It made her feel guilty, but she just couldn't cope with anyone else at the moment. She didn't want to have to deal with the inevitable questions she would get or her own annoyance with herself for being so defensive and hostile. She was due back at work the next day and she couldn't face the thought of that either. Just a couple of hours ago she had completely blanked her friend and now Nicky's eyes were fixed on Courtney, tracking her progress from the other side of the waiting room. She looked concerned, and a little upset but not angry she thought. She couldn't bring herself to ignore her for a second time that day and so made a detour across the room, trying to make it look deliberate and not just an afterthought.

'Hi Nicky! Sorry about earlier. How are you, OK?' she said in an almost hysterically high pitched tone. Nicky saw straight through it immediately.

'I wasn't born yesterday Courtney. Look at you, you're a mess,' she said leaning forward and touching her arm lightly.

'Gee thanks,' she replied, with a waspish smile.

Courtney was agitated, she didn't have time for this.

'Nicky, I'm really sorry, I can't stop. I'll give you a call when things are a little less, well you know...'

As she said this she was distracted by the sound of the automatic doors sliding open. She turned instinctively and saw Adam striding through them, his white coat trailing behind him. He looked around, visibly shaken, his gaze resting on his wife. She acknowledged him with a slight nod of her head, and then turned her back on him again, reaching out to squeeze her friend's hand as a goodbye, but saying nothing. Turning towards Adam she sighed, feeling as though this was her last chance to try to mend the broken bond between them. She remembered how he used to make her heart skip a beat every time she saw him and how she had never before had cause to question him. She had adored him so completely with every inch of herself. Now she felt detached from him and empty inside.

'What's happened now?' he said as she approached.

'I don't want to talk here, isn't there somewhere private?' she said quietly.

'But I want to know - is it serious for God's sake!' he said trying to stay composed but obviously angered by his wife's calm manner.

'Like I said, let's go somewhere private so we can talk,' she said her voice beginning to break.

He didn't speak again, glancing around he thought better of it. He caught hold of his wife's arm momentarily and then let go, sweeping ahead of her down the corridor as though she were one of his patients, not bothering to check behind him even once to see if she was still there. She didn't want to be there, but something deep inside of her was willing her on, wanting her to believe that she shouldn't give up. It was as if her life was flashing before her, and although she could feel anger and bitterness corroding the inside of her, she was involuntarily remembering their happier times together, how it used to be, how it maybe could be again.

Adam took an abrupt left turn into his consulting office. Dismissing his secretary he closed the door and sat down facing Courtney. He leaned back in his chair and for a moment seemed lost in thought. Suddenly he leaned forward his eyes gazing deep into hers.

'Talk to me,' he said catching hold of his wife's hand.

'Now before you start panicking, Alicia is fine. It's Brad,' she said.

He sighed with relief and leaned back again in his chair.

'So what's happened to him?'

'Well it looks like he's taken an overdose,' she said and proceeded to fill him in on the details of how she and Alicia had found him. 'I haven't seen them yet, I only just arrived myself.' She sighed again, so far her husband had not picked up on the significance of it having been Brad who was in trouble. She had doubted that he would but a part of her had been hoping that he may have seen the connection.

'Why do I get the impression that you haven't told me everything?' he said looking questioningly at her.

'Oh it doesn't matter,' she said standing to leave.

'Of course it matters,' he said grabbing hold of her arm and squeezing it too hard. She pulled away from his grasp and sat down.

'Adam, you just don't seem the same person anymore. It's like I don't know you.'

'I don't know how you can say that!' he said exasperated. 'How have I changed?'

'You're secretive and you're stubborn. You won't believe a word I tell you - it's your whole attitude.' As she blurted out the words her emotions spilled over and she slammed her fist down on his desk.

Remaining calm he looked searchingly at her, almost trying to diagnose her.

'And I'm not fucking mad!' she yelled.

Tears began to course down her cheeks.

'I told you last night that I'd heard a voice speak to me in the hallway, talking to me about Brad. Now why do you think that would be hey? Do you think I'm making that up? Isn't it just a strange coincidence that today your daughter and I found him slumped naked on his couch, half dead.'

He didn't reply.

'I don't know Courtney, I really don't know. I'm sorry. How can I understand? It didn't happen to me. I'm not saying you're telling lies, just that maybe you're a little confused. The whole family is under a lot of strain at the moment.'

'Family!' she scoffed. 'Don't make me laugh.'

'I'm only trying to help that's all,' he said pleadingly.

'But that's just it isn't it Adam, you really are helpful *to other people*, but not to your own so-called family. Take tonight for example. You know damn well Alicia's just been released from hospital. You know her fears about staying in the house alone and you know mine. It didn't stop you helping out your old buddy did it?'

'Look, I didn't know you felt so strongly. I didn't know things were that bad,' he said apologetically.

'Adam, look at us. It's like there's a huge yawning gap between us. We used to be a unit - almost thinking and feeling the same. We're like strangers now.' Her voice was breaking again with emotion.

His calm and reasoned mood suddenly changed to one of anger. He leapt up from his chair and leaned accusingly across the table.

'Stop talking like this - there is no problem with us! You're poisoning our marriage with your ridiculous thoughts about us and everything that's going on. Why do you always have to complicate everything and create problems where there aren't any?' he yelled.

'There's nothing wrong with us - we're fine. We have a baby on the way and it's supposed to be one of the most exciting times of our lives.' He turned towards her, his eyes wild with fury, but they softened as they met with hers.

'Yes - supposed to be,' she continued.

'It's a good job you're still in the earlier stage of pregnancy. If you were rampaging around like you have been at the end of the second or worse still during the third trimester, well - I mean, all the stress...' He stopped pacing and sat back down in his chair.

'Courtney, I don't want to go through another marriage break-up. When I married you it was for life. From the moment we first met I have never stopped loving you. Why are you doing this? We have enough to deal with as it is.'

He leaned across his desk, reached out and lightly touched the side of her face.

'Please Courtney, can we just walk out of this room and start over - pretend we never had this conversation?'

She felt guilty then. He always had that knack of turning everything around, making her think that perhaps she was wrong, making her doubt her own sanity. Usually she would have been happy with his explanation but it was different this time. Deep within herself she knew that she was right. As she looked back at him she decided that maybe in time things would change. Maybe when she had discovered the truth she would be able to trust him again. Perhaps once she was satisfied and at peace within herself she would get back her old feelings. She could still be proved wrong after all. He was right about the baby too and she wasn't a quitter. She wouldn't give up on something that she had dedicated her life to. She would fight on and see it through to the end. With those thoughts in mind she realised that she would have to give up on one thing. She would have to give up trying to make her husband see the things that she could see. She was truly alone in that and she would have to accept it and try not to hate him for it.

She smiled back at him.

'OK, let's start again shall we?' she said squeezing his hand. 'I'm sorry.'

'Don't worry babe,' he said a faint smile appearing on his face. 'We'll be all right.'

She had a plan. She couldn't tell him what it was but she just hoped that when everything was over they would be all right again.

They saw Alicia through the window, still sitting at Brad's bedside, her head bowed as if in prayer. She had been with him since he was first admitted, staying with him during his initial treatment in the Emergency Room and then on into the private ward where he now was. A middle-aged couple were standing on the far side of the bed, comforting one another. Courtney opened the door slowly and they went in. The woman, who she believed to be Brad's mother, seeing Adam immediately assumed he was the doctor treating her son.

'Doctor,' she said her voice quivering and hoarse with emotion. 'My son - they say he's in a coma. Will he recover?'

'I'm terribly sorry Mrs…' He didn't know how to address her.

'Mrs North.'

'I'm not the doctor in charge here. I can find out who you need to be speaking to,' he added.

'I just can't understand it,' she said clutching hold of her husband's hand. 'We don't know what could have driven him to do this. He seemed so happy - he had everything to live for.'

'Sometimes even the people who appear to be perfectly happy can be hiding deep worries and fears,' Adam said with a frown.

'But he would have told us,' Mrs North continued with desperation in her voice. 'We were very close - he told us everything. He told us about Alicia here. It's just a shame we had to meet her in such terrible circumstances.' She began to weep; her husband put his arm around her protectively. He didn't say anything; he just stared at his son, disbelief and utter devastation in his eyes.

247

Courtney walked over to Alicia and gently put her hands on her shoulders, to let her know she was there.

She raised her head and turned to look at her stepmother, her eyes red and puffy from crying. Courtney felt so helpless. She knew that she couldn't really ease her pain. Alicia had suffered so much in her short life. Courtney knew that her own life had been relatively trouble free up until now. Both of her parents were still alive and she owned her own home. She had never had a brother or sister, so would never have to feel the pain of losing them. She knew that one day she would have to lose her parents though and possibly Adam too, as Alicia was now losing Brad.

As she stood silent, she looked over at Brad. He appeared to be breathing by himself but his eyes were completely vacant, as though his spirit, his very essence had already flown.

She turned away, unable to look any longer. This wasn't helping - she had to do something. She needed to speak to Liza.

A sudden noise caused her to turn towards the door; Detective Owens stood in the doorway, his hand over his mouth to stifle a cough. His face looked weary, his eyes troubled.

'I do apologise - I don't mean to intrude,' he said nodding towards Brad's parents. 'I had to come and see him. Mr, Mrs Buchanan,' he turned to Courtney and Adam briefly but then quickly looked away from them again.

His gaze fell on Alicia, and his expression changed again to one of contempt.

'What is she doing in here?' he said, unable to control his rage. 'If it wasn't for her, messing with his mind! I warned him, but he wouldn't listen! He preferred to throw his career and now his life away for her, and for what? He could have had anyone.'

Mrs North began to weep again.

'Do you mind?' Mr North spoke for the first time. 'I don't care who you are! I don't want my son upset - he can still hear you know. He's not dead yet - now get out!'

Detective Owens, visibly shaken by the onslaught, immediately left the room, closely followed by Courtney. Adam was about to follow his wife but stopped short in the doorway when Mrs North called him back.

'Detective Owens,' Courtney called after him.

'Mr and Mrs North have made their feelings perfectly clear,' he called back, 'I don't need to hear it all again from you. I'm not involved in this case anyway, for obvious reasons.'

'You can't blame Alicia for what's happened to Brad.'

'Well it seems a bit bizarre doesn't it?' he retorted. 'There seems to be a suicide theme surrounding our sweet angelic Miss Buchanan! First Jennifer Thorpe and now Brad.'

'It's just a horrible coincidence. Alicia loved Brad, and he loved her. He couldn't help it, if that is the reason he did this. He knew he shouldn't get involved with her. You can't blame her for his inner turmoil.'

He stopped then and sighed, turning to face her.

'Look Mrs Buchanan, I appreciate you're defending your stepdaughter but it really isn't necessary. I'm just sad that's all. I've lost one of my colleagues.'

'You haven't lost him - he's not dead yet,' she said, trying to sound positive.

'As good as,' he replied sadly, as he began to walk back down the hospital corridor. Courtney watched him go and felt a great sense of relief. She didn't want the police involved with any of this, least of all him. She considered he was biased anyway against her and her family. He still may say something of course, as part of the enquiry, but hopefully by then she would have got to the bottom of all this herself. She didn't need him to complicate matters even further. That was the first hurdle over and now she had to tackle the second.

Alicia walked out of the room then, looking weary and tired. The stress had obviously taken its toll. Courtney reached out to her and they embraced warmly.

'Alicia,' she said after a few moments. 'You know what I was saying to you this morning.'

She nodded.

'Well, do you think you could bring yourself to leave Brad, for a while? I mean rather than stay here - I just don't think it's healthy for you. I don't want you to be admitted again, especially after your abrupt departure this morning.'

Alicia's expression changed to one of sudden realisation. In all the mayhem since she had left the hospital that morning, she had completely forgotten about herself and the fact that she was supposed to be recuperating. It seemed to her as if an entire lifetime of terrible events had all taken place in the space of a few days. She reluctantly agreed.

They said their goodbyes to Adam, who was still in Brad's room talking with his parents, Courtney leaned over and kissed him lightly on the cheek.

'I'll change the shift tonight if you really want me to,' he said, as they turned to leave.

'No, it's OK Adam,' she replied. 'We'll be fine, thanks anyway.'

Courtney and Alicia then continued down the corridor and out into the midday sun. Courtney felt as if she were about to embark on the biggest adventure of her life, and for once she wasn't afraid.

She called up Liza on her mobile the moment they were away from the hospital entrance. Alicia immediately lit a cigarette. She had offered one to Courtney but she had declined. For the sake of the baby she was determined to kick the habit once and for all.

Alicia waited nervously on the sidewalk, not really paying much attention to the conversation that was going on beside her. It was as though she was in a parallel universe, somewhere between life and death. Existing, she thought, that's all it was. The only time she had ever felt alive since Gabrielle's death was when she had been with Brad. Now he wasn't there either. Maybe she was cursed, she thought, as she drew hard on her cigarette. She was brought back to reality by a tap on her shoulder.

'C'mon we're going to Liza's house,' Courtney said, almost with an air of excitement in her voice. 'She's got a friend who she thinks *just* might be able to help us.'

Alicia stubbed out her cigarette on the sidewalk and followed dutifully behind as Courtney walked back towards their car.

Chapter 12

As they turned into Bay View Grove all Alicia's most recent memories came flooding back - the night when she had fled from the house and woken up in the hospital grounds. She thought back further and remembered how happy she had been in that house when she and Gabrielle had first moved in. It had been the idyllic family home - days lazing by the pool and nights in watching TV. Now she couldn't face the thought of ever setting foot in there again. Liza was waiting for them on the doorstep. The last time Alicia had seen her was at Gabrielle's funeral. Liza walked hesitantly up the drive to meet them, an anxious smile on her face. That wasn't really very long ago, Alicia remembered, only a few days, but it seemed like a lifetime.

Liza gave her friend a hug and greeted Alicia nervously. Courtney realised that it was because she hadn't really spoken to Alicia at any length since Gabrielle's death and she probably found it difficult to find the right words, as many people do, when there is a death in a family.

Alicia was intrigued to find out what Courtney had planned as she couldn't think of a solution herself and wondered how anyone could possibly help them.

Liza ushered them into her house. It was spotlessly tidy; exactly the same size as their house across the street but everything was round the opposite way. Instead of walking into the lounge on the right you walked into it on the left, and the stairs went up the right hand side of the hallway. There was a distinct ethnic theme, with a large dark wooden bust of an African tribal warrior on the sill of the hall window. The walls were painted a deep golden colour and there was a bare wooden floor throughout. Alicia instantly liked it. Liza went straight into the kitchen and put the kettle on.

'Make yourself at home,' she sang out. 'Put the TV on if you like Alicia.' Courtney followed her into the kitchen.

Alicia decided to go and wait for them in the lounge where she sank into one of the large comfortable couches and closed her eyes for a second. She felt peaceful here. There was a faint smell of incense in the house that was quite intoxicating. She opened her eyes again to look for the source and noticed the remnants of a burnt out joss stick in an ornate scent burner standing on the stone surround of the fireplace. She glanced around. More figurines and busts stood proudly in all four corners of the room. Her attention was then drawn to the French doors at the end of the lounge that led directly out into the garden. She had always loved gardens; she stood up from the couch and walked over to the doors.

'Can I go outside?' she called out.

'Yes Alicia, just lift the latch and the door should just slide open.'

As the door opened she felt the warmth of the sun on her arms and she basked in it with a wonderful feeling of wellbeing. The garden seemed slightly larger than theirs and was extremely well kept. There were palm trees shading the pool edge and between two of the trees stretched a hammock. She couldn't resist and walked down the pathway that led to the pool and stood beside it for a moment trying to work out how she was going to get on the thing. She didn't want to end up wrapped up in it and then emptied back out as the hammock turned upside down. She had seen this happen before but mostly in cartoons - she smiled to herself. She carefully positioned herself in the middle and with relative ease managed to lie down. The hammock swayed very slightly in the breeze and she felt as if she were being rocked to sleep. She truly felt relaxed and could have stayed there all day. She felt safe too. She hadn't felt safe in hospital and she hated the clinical smell of detergent - the whole atmosphere in fact had made her feel worse.

She breathed in the fresh air, which was filled with a sweet smell that was like honey. She listened to the birds too; this must be what heaven is like she thought to herself. Maybe this is what Gabrielle is doing right now. That thought made her happy. It wasn't long though before her thoughts turned back to the present. Something was niggling at the back of her mind. She couldn't work out the disturbances in the house and didn't understand why whatever it was had been trying to frighten her. She had to believe that it wasn't Gabrielle. They had loved each other - surely she wouldn't want to hurt her. Then there was Brad, *oh Brad!* She felt more tears coming but she couldn't cry again- it was draining away all of her energy. She couldn't ever imagine feeling completely normal again, being able to get through a day without being reminded that she shouldn't be happy because of all the terrible things that had happened. She climbed off the hammock, realising that staying in her own company for too long made her think too much. She wanted to be back in the house where the conversation would distract her and she could feel herself again, if only for a short time.

She walked back towards the house and could see through the French doors that Courtney and Liza were already sat on the couch in the lounge, deep in conversation. They looked up as she slid the door open and instantly stopped talking.

'I wasn't sure if you had sugar or not in coffee,' Liza said.

'No, I'm sweet enough, or so I've been told,' Alicia said trying to smile.

'Oh, that's OK then,' Liza said with a broad smile. 'Come and sit down, get comfy,' she said pointing to the couch that was facing them.

'OK, so what's this plan then?' Alicia said as she perched on the edge of the couch so that she could reach her coffee more easily.

'Who's gonna say, then?' Liza said turning to Courtney.

'I will, if that's OK,' Courtney replied somewhat nervously.

Alicia looked at Courtney searchingly. There was a tense atmosphere now in the room that all three women could sense but which none of them wanted to acknowledge.

'Well,' Courtney said taking a deep breath. 'Liza has a friend called Sally Harris.' She paused, Alicia looked back at her as if to say, so what, is that it?

'Sally is a medium,' she continued.

'Oh right,' Alicia said realising what was coming next.

'Sally has agreed to come over this afternoon and go with us into the house just to see if she can shed any light on what's going on.' Courtney looked back at Liza who nodded to confirm that this was true.

'I mean it does really go against everything I've been taught,' Courtney said taking a sip of her coffee, 'but I'm willing to give anything a try quite frankly. There is something going on in that house. Both of us are too afraid to go in it and I really feel that we have to do this on our own.'

'OK,' Alicia said shrugging her shoulders.

Both Courtney and Liza instantly relaxed. 'Wow! That was easy,' Liza said.

'The thing is,' Alicia continued. 'I want to find out myself what's happening. I was thinking just now that it can't be Gabrielle. I mean why would she try and frighten us? I know she suffered a terrible death, but she loved us, and she's in a better place now. She wouldn't do that to us.'

'Exactly,' Liza said nodding so hard that Alicia thought her head might drop off.

'We've been talking about that,' Courtney said, placing her cup down on the table. 'Liza was thinking that maybe it could be Jennifer, or even Matt searching for Gabrielle. All we know is that it's something, well someone, should I say, because our house isn't the same anymore.'

'I agree,' Liza said her big brown eyes smiling at Alicia. 'It's very hard for you. I've spoken to Courtney many times before about my friend Sally and her work. Courtney has been brought up a strict Catholic and has trouble coming to terms with it. The church teaches that any communication with the spirit world through a medium is evil. The truth of it is, that although it may be wrong in the eyes of the church, it often does do a lot of good.'

'The thing is,' Courtney replied, 'the churches do have specially trained exorcists and always have done. They recognise more than anyone that you can have spirits in houses or anywhere for that matter. Often they are people who have died but seem to be trapped on the earth, not knowing where to go. They often have grudges or have died before they believed they should have done, and some don't even know that they are dead.'

There was an eerie silence in the room then for a few moments as the women just looked at each other. Liza was the first to break the silence asking who wanted another cup of coffee.

They all did so she gathered the cups and went back into the kitchen leaving Courtney and Alicia alone together.

'What does Dad think about all this?' Alicia asked.

Courtney sighed, 'Well the thing is, he doesn't know. I desperately wanted him to understand, to be involved in what was happening to us, but I couldn't make him. He never heard the things I heard - he just humoured me when I was telling him. Like I told you before, he's convinced I've gone mad and insists that there isn't a problem, but you and I know different.'

'But couldn't you have made him understand, to believe? It doesn't seem right that's all. For all his faults I still love him,' Alicia said sadly.

'Oh believe me Alicia I love your father too! Don't doubt that for a second. It's just impossible to make someone believe in something they don't have the capacity to understand. It's like trying to force somebody to believe in God. They'll humour you and nod and smile in all the right places when you are evangelising to them, but unless they are touched or reached by God personally, there is no way that you are ever going to change their mind. Personal beliefs run too deep for that. We don't have the ability to change somebody in that way. It's like your father. He doesn't believe in ghosts, spirits anything like that and he won't believe in it. That doesn't mean he doesn't love us. Do you see now why we couldn't involve him?'

'I guess,' Alicia replied in monotone. 'It's just sad that's all. You and Dad were the first proper family I'd ever lived with, and to see that breaking up, well, it makes me sad that's all. I don't want things to change.'

'Neither do I,' Courtney said, 'and it won't, but there is a lot going on here. I've realised a lot of things, lets put it that way. The garden is no longer full of roses - there are a few weeds starting to choke those roses and I've got to find those weeds and pull them out. It might sound a bit corny but that's what's happening. If we want to get back to how things were before I have to face the truth and deal with it.'

Liza came back in at that moment with another tray of coffee, but this time with biscuits too. Alicia's eyes lit up - she was feeling hungry, as so far today she hadn't eaten.

'Here's a little treat for you both,' she said in a motherly tone. 'I'll get us all some proper lunch when Sally gets here.'

'I don't know if I'll be able to eat anything when she gets here,' Alicia said pulling a mock, frightened face.

'Oh, Sally doesn't bite,' Liza replied laughing heartily. 'You'll be surprised when you see her - she really is quite normal actually. Oh don't tell her I said that - sounds terrible doesn't it?'

Courtney found herself thinking sentimentally about Adam again. She had to be strong and go through with this if she had any hope of saving her marriage.

'Shall we adjourn to the garden?' Liza said putting on a fake English accent. Courtney and Alicia both cracked up.

'That was an awful English accent!' Alicia teased. 'Not all English people sound like the Queen you know.'

'All right, all right,' Liza laughed. 'C'mon let's get outside, get some sun on that pasty face of yours,' she said bringing her hand down hard on Courtney's thigh.

The next couple of hours sped by. It seemed like no time at all before the doorbell rang. Alicia quickly lit another cigarette. It would be her last one for now even though she was so nervous and craved one even more.

Liza scurried off down the garden. Courtney and Alicia didn't speak; both of them knew what the other was thinking.

In a few moments peals of laughter could be heard coming from the kitchen.

'Oh well that's a good sign,' Courtney said in a low whisper. 'She's obviously got a sense of humour.'

'Wonder where she parked her broomstick?' Alicia joked.

'Stop it,' Courtney said feeling herself start to laugh. 'This is serious.'

'Well try telling that to them,' Alicia replied sarcastically, pointing to the house where the laughter had built to another crescendo. Courtney gave into it then and began to laugh herself.

'I'm glad you're here,' she said when she had finally calmed down. 'You always make me laugh. I'm too serious sometimes - that's my problem I think.'

After about half an hour Liza emerged into the garden closely followed by Sally Harris. Both women carried large trays groaning with sandwiches and cake.

'Oh great!' Courtney called out. 'What a spread - you shouldn't have Liza.'

'No you're right I shouldn't have,' she said bursting into laughter again. Sally Harris giggled behind her - they were just like a couple of schoolgirls. 'That's ten dollars each for the finger buffet,' Liza said as she placed one of the trays down on a free chair.

'Oh darn I forgot the table,' she exclaimed.

'Oh I'll get that,' Sally said.

The mood was very jovial. It seemed hard for Courtney to grasp that soon they would be going across the street to her house, trying to communicate with the spirit world.

Lunch was soon over; Courtney liked Sally Harris. She was a small elfin woman with short blonde hair. She had very petite features and was one of the slimmest women Courtney had ever seen. There was a genuine warmth about her. Like everybody else she had heard about the tragic death of Gabrielle and Matt and offered her condolences. Courtney was confident that she would be able to help them. Her easy going nature and lack of fear made them feel much calmer as the afternoon drew on. It was obvious to Courtney that they were getting close to the moment when she would say that they should go to the house and she wondered then if she'd feel quite so at ease once she'd opened the front door and stepped in.

'Now, I just want to tell you about what I'm going to do today,' Sally Harris said. 'Liza has explained to me about the problems that you've been experiencing in the house. I have dealt with this sort of situation before.'

'It's good to know that,' Courtney replied. 'You start to feel as if you are going mad after a while.'

'I know,' Sally replied. 'It's no easy thing for anybody who has experienced these manifestations. I'll see what I can feel in the house and then try to see if I can get whoever it is to come through.'

'They won't show themselves will they?' Alicia said, still a little worried.

'I must say to you that I never know quite what's going to happen. The thing is, whoever it is has already been showing themselves to you by means of the poltergeist activity that you've been experiencing. I can't promise you that that won't happen.' She paused for a moment and there was a nervous silence.

'Do you have anything that belonged to Gabrielle that was special to her that I could maybe hold when I'm there? It sometimes helps to direct my thoughts?' she said.

'Well her room is still exactly how it was left. Nobody has been in and touched anything apart from Alicia who borrowed one of her suits to wear to her funeral,' Courtney replied.

'Clothes are not good really,' Sally continued. 'Ideally we need an item of jewellery or an object of some kind that was quite special to her.'

'I don't want to go upstairs though,' Alicia said. 'I'm too afraid.'

'We'll wait and see when we get there. Your husband's at work today isn't he?' Sally said, turning to Courtney.

'Yes,' she confirmed. 'He's working all night and tomorrow too - I think he's finishing about one or two o'clock tomorrow.'

'Right, OK then.'

For the next few moments neither of them spoke. Liza then stood up and began to clear all the plates and cups. 'Let me help you with that,' Courtney said. Alicia took out her cigarettes.

'Did your sister smoke?' Sally asked her as she was lighting up.

'Yes she did,' Alicia replied.

'It must be so hard for you,' Sally then said.

'It is, and I'm very nervous,' she replied.

'You'll be fine,' Sally said putting her hand on Alicia's shoulder and giving it a reassuring squeeze. 'I think that we have to try to get to the bottom of this so you can get on with the rest of your life.'

Alicia knew that she was right but she wished that she could just skip all the hard times ahead and move straight into the distant future. The future where she hoped Brad maybe had recovered, where she had her own house and her own family. It seemed like an impossible dream at that moment.

'Shall we go then?' Sally suddenly said, catching Alicia by surprise. She had butterflies fluttering in her stomach. They were the kind she used to have when she'd been on her way to the dentist with her mother when she was small. She had been afraid of the drill and the dentist and scared that she'd never come out of there alive.

Sally took her hand and the two women walked together back towards the house.

Courtney and Liza were waiting for them in the hall; it was as if they had anticipated the exact time that they would be leaving.

Nobody spoke as Liza opened her front door. They ventured out onto the sidewalk and they all stood together staring across at the house, looking for signs of life. Courtney had been there that morning, but even to her that seemed like an age away. So much had happened between then and now.

'Right let's do it,' Sally said confidently.

Courtney tried to calm herself and then led the way across the road. There wasn't anybody else about, which was just as well, because she didn't want anybody to see her or her companions. She didn't want to sow seeds of suspicion in her neighbours' minds.

They walked along the empty driveway and up to the front door. Courtney already had the front door key in her hand and she noticed that both of her hands were sweating profusely.

The door swung open without a sound. She half expected it to creak as with all haunted houses she had ever seen before in films.

She stepped gingerly into the hallway. Everything was silent.

'Right, shall we start in the lounge? Sally said.

'I guess so. Strangely enough I always feel safe in there,' Courtney said quietly, not wanting whatever it was to be alerted to their presence.

They walked past the staircase and into the lounge where Liza sat straight down on the couch. It was obvious that she didn't intend to move and would remain there while they were in the house.

'What about the keepsake I mentioned?' Sally asked.

'Everything's upstairs,' Alicia said standing awkwardly in the lounge doorway, her shoulders hunched.

'Do you feel able to go upstairs with me?' Sally then said.

Courtney looked over at her with a winning smile. 'OK,' Alicia said reluctantly, 'but if anything happens I'm out of here.'

'Sure,' Sally said.

Alicia pointed up at the staircase, 'See that window ledge?' Sally nodded. 'That was where the vase was. It literally lifted up as I passed it and smashed against the wall behind me as I was running down the stairs. It's all cleared away now - I guess you must have sorted that,' she said looking over at Courtney, 'that was the most frightening thing that happened - that and the TV.'

'That's the poltergeist activity that I was telling you about,' Sally answered. 'They use this energy to let you know that they are there, to draw attention to themselves.'

'Well it certainly did that,' Alicia replied gravely.

Sally then moved towards the staircase and began to ascend. She turned to Alicia; 'You coming or what?' she said cheekily, which served to put her more at ease. 'I think we ought to start in your sister's old room.' Alicia shuddered as Sally said this, but she had been in there once since her sister's death and nothing had happened to her then.

The daylight that flooded through the window also helped to comfort Alicia as they neared the top of the stairs. She could see everything that was in front of her and behind her - there were no dark corners that something could leap out from.

They turned into the upstairs corridor; all the doors were firmly shut. As they neared Gabrielle's room she started to get the butterflies back again. Her hand automatically shot out and grasped hold of Sally's.

'It's this one isn't it?' she said pointing to the second door on the left.

'How did you know?' Alicia asked incredulously.

'Well I wouldn't be much of a medium if I couldn't tell you basic things like that now would I?' Alicia was amazed that she could still joke, especially at a time like this. It did help her though, making her feel more at ease and calming her nerves.

Sally caught hold of the door handle with her free hand and turned it. Slowly the door opened. Alicia lowered her eyes, unable to look. She heard Sally speak again, her voice sounding normal. She dared to peer over her shoulder.

'Oh it's so sad to see it like this,' she said visibly moved. 'It's as if someone has only just left the room - it still looks lived in, if you know what I mean.' They ventured inside; Alicia welled up seeing all of Gabrielle's things just as Sally had said, as if she'd been there that very morning. Her bed looked freshly made; her photographs still on the side. It was the same as the time when Alicia had gone in to find Gabrielle's black suit, but she had put it back in the wardrobe afterwards because she still felt it wasn't hers to keep.

Alicia walked over to the wardrobe. She felt more confident now - this had been her worst fear and she had conquered it already. She pulled open the wardrobe door with a swift movement, and then gasped in horror.

'What is it?' Sally said.

'The suit - it's gone!' She reeled backwards falling onto the bed. Sally was quickly at her side.

'Now are you sure that you put it back, really sure? I mean you may have put it in the wash since then.'

'I'm sure I did,' Alicia said her voice distant. She was confused, her mind desperately trying to find a rational explanation. It was then that she noticed that other things in the room had been moved around. The clock was on the opposite side of the room, her photographs had moved, and beside the bed was a necklace and her christening bracelet.

'Believe me Alicia, I am sure that your sister is not here. I cannot sense her at all, she has definitely passed over.' She stroked her hair tenderly. 'Really I'm sure it's not her who is causing this disturbance.' Alicia was not convinced, but maybe she could just be imagining that the things had moved around.

'Out of interest,' Sally then said a curious look on her face. 'Your parents haven't undertaken any building work on the house recently have they?'

'No - well apart from some routine maintenance on the swimming pool before it was opened a couple of months ago,' she replied standing up to leave.

'No I thought not,' Sally replied still perplexed. 'It's just that I can sense somebody in the house who isn't of the house, if you see what I mean. It could have been somebody who had lived here before. Often when building work takes place in a house, hauntings start; usually where previous residents are not happy with the changes that are taking place and are awakened shall we say. Often a spirit will consider it is still their house and not want anyone else to live there.'

'No nothing like that, no building. I'm sure.'

'Right,' Sally said stroking her chin thoughtfully. 'Anyway, shall we move on from here? I'm being drawn back downstairs. Whatever it was isn't up here at the moment. I think they are now downstairs.'

Alicia was relieved that she didn't have to stay up there a moment longer. Although Sally was not perturbed by anything, Alicia still did not feel safe there.

They walked carefully back down the staircase; Courtney was now back in the lounge with Liza.

They both started as the others walked in.

'Did you find anything?' Courtney asked anxiously.

'Not as such,' Sally replied, 'but I don't think this activity is being caused by Gabrielle. Even in her bedroom I can't sense her spirit at all - I'm sure she has passed.'

'Oh that's a relief,' Courtney said. It seemed to be such a surreal conversation to be having.

'I'm just going to take a look round the other rooms downstairs. I'm drawn to the kitchen right now.' Sally then disappeared back into the hallway. The couches in their lounge were currently positioned in an L shape, with the coffee table in between and the TV in the far left-hand corner. Courtney and Liza were sat on one and Alicia on the other - her body turned to face her stepmother. They didn't move or speak, just sat expectantly as if waiting for something to happen. After they had been waiting a while, they became aware of the fact that the temperature in the room was dropping quite rapidly, and then without warning it was suddenly icy cold.

'Sally,' Liza called out almost hysterically.

She came running and as she entered the doorway there was a strange noise coming from the ceiling and from nowhere, it seemed, a metal band dropped. It fell through the air at great speed landing on the coffee table. It bumped four times and then rolled around before it finally came to rest and lay still. They looked up expecting to see a hole in the ceiling but there was nothing; it was exactly as it had been before.

'Did you throw that?' Liza asked Sally angrily.

'No, you saw the same as I did. It dropped straight down from the ceiling.'

Alicia just sat and stared at it, her mouth dry. She swallowed hard.

'Oh my God,' she exclaimed. 'It's Gabrielle's christening bracelet.'

'Someone's coming through,' Sally suddenly said. Her eyes didn't roll up into her head and she didn't foam at the mouth as Alicia had expected she would. She just looked as if she were listening to a conversation in her head, nodding and waiting for a point at which to interrupt whoever it was that was speaking to her so she could relay the information.

'Has your mother passed over?' Sally suddenly said.

'Yes,' Alicia said hoarsely her eyes filling with tears. 'Your mothers name was Sandra, no Sarah,' Sally said correcting herself.

'How can it be my mom? She wouldn't have frightened me like that,' Alicia cried. As she did the christening bracelet leapt up off the table and fell back down again, zinging and spiralling as it came to rest.

Sally continued to converse with what appeared to be an invisible force.

'Your mother's here, but she doesn't want to frighten you. She's frustrated because she can't find her daughter.'

'Mom?' Alicia called out, her voice trembling.

'Sally, I don't understand. Why is Sarah here?' Courtney said incredulously.

'I told you,' Sally replied, 'she can't find her daughter. She's looking for Gabrielle.'

'Why isn't Gabrielle with her?' Courtney asked. Sally listened for a few moments, as if Sarah was replying directly to Courtney's question.

'She says she doesn't know. She keeps looking but she can't find her?' Sally seemed different, although she was still herself. It was as if she had entered another realm. Her voice was the

263

same, if a little deeper, but the quality of language she used was totally different.

'Ask my mom if she smashed the vase or my TV!' Alicia said tears streaming down her face.

All three women watched intently as Sally continued to converse with the spirit of Alicia's mother.

'No, she says she knows nothing of that. She says she has been looking but she has not moved anything or made her presence known in any way prior to today when she moved the christening bracelet. She wanted to prove that this is really her.'

'So that must mean that it wasn't her last night either. Oh great, so we're getting nowhere then,' Courtney said frustrated.

Sally didn't answer straight away. She was listening intently to what the spirit had to say.

'As I said before she has not made her presence known before today,' Sally answered in her own voice this time.

'I've just asked Sarah if she would mind giving me a break for a moment. It makes me very tired conversing with a spirit like this.'

'Has she gone?' Alicia asked.

Just as she said that Alicia began to giggle uncontrollably, and her tears which were still flowing, glistened in her eyes as she smiled.

'No she hasn't gone,' she laughed, 'she just blew on the back of my neck and tickled it, just like she used to do when I was young.'

Courtney began to feel emotional then. For the first time she saw Sarah as a real human being, even though she had passed away. Before she had always just been Adam's ex-wife, someone she was always jealous of. Now she saw her for the loving mother that she had been.

The situation had taken a complete turn around and was no longer a fearful experience.

'There is more to this than meets the eye,' Sally then said, a serious look on her face. 'She has told me to ask you if you will help her?' Sally turned directly to look at Courtney.

'Who me?' she replied in disbelief.

'Yes,' Sally nodded. 'She believes there is a reason why she cannot find her daughter, but because of where Sarah is in the spirit world it would be impossible for her to intervene and resolve the situation. She believes you have the strength and the determination to see it through. She says she will be able to be at peace then.'

Sally then began to converse again. It was obvious that the spirit had more to say and couldn't rest until she had said everything that needed to be said.

Sally nodded and went to speak again to the others but it was apparent that she couldn't find a point at which to interrupt the spirit.

'Mom always had plenty to say,' Alicia said laughing, as she flicked back her hair. Courtney shot her a look. She had always been brought up to respect the dead and Alicia's easygoing, cheeky remark seemed out of place somehow. She resolved however that it was Alicia's much loved mother, so it was bound to be slightly different for her and although this was such a totally alien situation to be in, Courtney was absolutely sure that she wanted to help Sarah.

Sally finally spoke. 'Sarah says that when Courtney and Alicia go on their journey, they should look for the key to everything. She says again that she cannot rest in peace until the truth is known. Yes, yes…' she continued out loud, as if the spirit was becoming impatient. She seemed to then stare intently first at Courtney and then at Alicia.

'She says you must ask Ruben. She then says I love you Alicia. She's gone now.'

Sally breathed in and out slowly. As she did the room returned to its normal temperature and everything went back to how it had been before. The christening bracelet was the only thing that was left. Alicia immediately grasped it in her hand and held it against her chest.

'My mom was awesome,' she said through her tears. 'I wish you could have met her.'

'Well I have kind of,' Courtney said moving over to sit by her.

'No I haven't kind of, I have.' She and Alicia then hugged each other.

'Hey you two, I'm feeling left out over here. Don't I get a hug too?' Liza said.

'I'll give you a hug, soppy,' Sally said.

265

'Ask Ruben,' Courtney said the words out loud as she mulled them over in her head. 'Who and where is he?'

'I tell you what,' Sally said, having now completely returned to normal. 'She was one of the most determined and precise spirits I've ever come across, I can tell you.'

'That's my mom,' Alicia added.

'Seriously though,' Courtney said. 'This potentially has the power to change everything. She's confirmed what I was feeling that something definitely isn't right, but it seems far more serious than that. She said she cannot rest in peace until the truth is known - was that what she truly said Sally? I'm not saying I disbelieve you, but...'

'Yes,' Sally said seriously. 'I give you my word that it's not in anybody's interest for me to fabricate or embellish what I hear from a spirit. Anybody who does that is not a true medium. Our mission in life is to help people like yourselves. I promise you that those were her exact words.'

Courtney accepted the explanation. Her mind was preoccupied going over the words again, struggling to find a meaning. 'The truth, the truth about what or who?' Courtney continued out loud. 'Find the key to everything, the key to Gabrielle, to Adam; Adam,' she said his name again. 'No we can't tell him,' she then said almost arguing with herself, 'Sarah said we have to go alone. But go where?'

'Ask Ruben,' Alicia suddenly said. 'Ruben - that name seems familiar to me but I don't know why. He was probably one of the waiters I used to work with in the Jamaican restaurant.'

'Oh this is too complicated now,' Courtney said slapping her hand against her forehead in frustration. 'We don't know who Ruben is and we don't know where to go on the journey. I'm getting involved in something that probably isn't any of my business anyway; I mean my marriage could definitely be on the rocks if I go ahead with this - frankly the list of potential problems is endless.'

'Of course it's your business,' Alicia chastised her. 'You're married to my dad, you're part of the family. Anyway, think of it like this, we could have even more problems if we just ignore it.'

Courtney knew she was right, but deep down she wished she could just be transported back in time to her old life, before all of the problems started, before Gabrielle and Alicia ever moved in.

'Listen,' Liza said reassuringly. 'Why don't we all go back to my house. While we're here you two pack a bag and stay at mine the night, then we'll have another think about it all tomorrow.'

'OK,' Alicia said confidently. 'I'm not actually as afraid anymore, but it would be good to have a sleep over.' She sprang up from the couch and darted out of the room and up the stairs.

'Can you grab me some clean underwear while you're up there,' Courtney called after her. She pulled a face at Liza who had just given her another one of her knowing looks. 'All right, so I don't think I've got the courage just yet! Well you can always go up if you're so confident,' she retorted.

'I don't need to though do I?' Liza teased back.

'Ahh you're just as scared as me,' she laughed. Courtney then got up, walked to the foot of the staircase and bellowed up the stairs for Alicia to bring down her toothbrush.

'Yeah all right,' came her muffled reply from somewhere in her bedroom.

Alicia returned within five minutes with a bag packed. 'I got you a new T-shirt and some clean socks too, cos I've heard about your feet!'

'Hey cheeky!' Courtney scolded. 'I'll have you know my feet always smell divine!'

Back out in the driveway with the door firmly shut behind them, they almost felt like new people. The nerves had gone and there was a feeling of relief that it was over.

Courtney spotted Ted Fraser out of the corner of her eye; he was walking up the road towards them with a bag of groceries. He nodded at Courtney in acknowledgement as he got closer, and then took a detour across the grass to get to his driveway.

'Hey Courtney how's it goin?' he called out. 'Been a hive of activity lately your house. I've hardly had any sleep.'

Courtney frowned. 'Really?'

'Only kidding ya,' he replied with a wink. 'Alicia is that you?' he then said peering at her through the group. 'How ya doin?'

'Yes it's me Ted. I'm getting better now thanks - got released from hospital this morning and got back just before lunch.'

He scratched his head puzzled. 'I must be needing my eyes tested, cos I was sure I saw you leaving the house this morning.'

'No, can't have been me,' Alicia smiled back.

'Don't worry darlin it's my eyes, better make that appointment! Well I must get this little lot packed away - great seein ya.' With that he turned and walked towards his front door.

They finally made it up to bed around 1 a.m., having spent the entire evening talking avidly about the afternoon's events. Sally had left at seven o'clock, but the others had continued unabated until Alicia had finally taken herself off to bed and uncontrollable yawning had taken hold of Liza and Courtney.

Courtney and Alicia were in Liza's guestroom at the front of the house; Courtney had seen it briefly when she had deposited their overnight bag earlier on. It was a large room, about the same size as Gabrielle's Courtney thought. She remembered that the staircase was on the right, opposite to hers, and they were in the first room on the right, facing out into the street. The room was a little cold and although the weather was still fine during the day, the temperature dropped at night. Liza wouldn't put her heating on, unless there was a snow blizzard, and that never happened anyway. Courtney stood over by the window. Alicia was already tucked up in bed, her long blonde hair spread out across her pillow and halfway across Courtney's too. She left the light off whilst she got undressed for bed - she didn't want to wake her. The light from the street lamp outside flooded in through a gap in the drapes. Instead of closing them she moved to the shadows to get changed. She was dwarfed by the dark wood wardrobe that towered behind her. As she stepped into her night clothes, she noticed that her trousers were beginning to get a little tight round the middle; it wouldn't be long she thought before she would have to start looking for proper maternity clothes. She was dreading that and she had already vowed that she would never be seen dead in a pair of dungarees; they were so unflattering in her opinion. She was not totally at ease about the prospect of developing a big bump for a stomach - not because of vanity but because she didn't like to draw attention to herself. She worried that total strangers would start coming up to her in the street asking her when the baby was due. She didn't like all the fuss that went with being pregnant. Some people thrived on it but she just wasn't like that.

She lifted the heavy duvet and slid carefully underneath, trying to prize her pillow carefully out from underneath Alicia's marauding tresses. She wasn't as tired now as she had been when she'd been downstairs in the cosy lounge. The walk upstairs and the drop in temperature had revived her.

She sighed. *What am I doing here? I should be over the road, not here.* The day's activities were still playing on her mind. She had spoken with Adam earlier that evening - he'd called her from work. They had chatted normally and she'd told him about their day at Liza's - she just omitted to mention what they'd been doing! She felt as if she was betraying him. Courtney had made Liza promise not to say anything to Grant as he and Adam were such good friends and she couldn't risk it. Courtney trusted Liza completely. She recalled the day that she and Adam had moved in and Liza and Grant had helped them unload their removal van. She'd thought then what a good neighbour she would make, so helpful and friendly with an unmistakable warmth about her.

Courtney was distracted temporarily from her thoughts as she heard Liza making her way down the corridor to her bedroom. The inch of light that had shone through the gap under the door was suddenly extinguished as she snapped off the hall light. The house was still. She felt alone again. Alicia was fast asleep beside her. How she missed the feeling of Adam's warm body against hers - the feeling of closeness and safety; she was still cold.

Images flashed across her mind - a replay of the christening bracelet as it fell from the ceiling. She had never seen anything move like that before - it had opened her eyes to another dimension. She was still desperately trying to draw any kind of conclusion from what she had seen and heard. They had spoken at length about it all evening without arriving at any conclusions. She still didn't really understand what was happening in the house. Sally hadn't been able to establish who was causing the disturbance and the only thing that was clear was that Adam's ex-wife was haunting them. She shuddered for the first time and began to feel resentment again. Although she had improved remarkably on the jealousy front, she began to think of it from a different standpoint. Adam's ex-wife was watching them? *But for how long?* 'Damn cheek!' she said under her breath. How ridiculous it sounded. *She's dead, what's the point in worrying about someone's who's dead?* She felt guilty then and hoped that Sarah wasn't able to hear her thoughts as well. *She's put her trust in me - why would she have said those things if they hadn't been true?* She wondered how many people have a problem with their husband's ex-wife haunting them - *most couples like us just have the problem of the ex-wife taking them to court and bleeding them dry over child support, but not this.* She turned on her side trying to get to sleep. Her head hurt but still the thoughts came and she wished she could flick a switch and just turn them off so that she could get some rest. She was uncomfortable on her side and rolled onto her back again with another sigh. *Who is Ruben? Oh who gives a shit?* She chastised herself because she just couldn't let go of it all and clear her head. *He was someone Sarah knew, so it's quite likely that Adam would know him too. Of course. Then it's also possible that he doesn't know him, because he left her ten years ago, three years before she died.* She suddenly realised another thing; she had no idea why he'd left Sarah - such a basic and obvious question! It had never occurred to her to ask him. Courtney had totally blocked his previous life from her mind, as if he had just been beamed down from the heavens at the age of thirty-nine and placed in the hospital where she worked, ready for him to fall in love with her and marry her. She couldn't believe she had been so naïve. She'd had such blind trust in him. *God I was a complete fool. He'd already lived half his life and I didn't bother to ask him why he'd left her. All I knew about was the car crash and the kids and that was it - the sum total of my knowledge. I didn't like to ask. Crap! I should have damn well asked - silly bitch! Look what's happening now - not at all surprising really, considering.*

She could feel an overwhelming sense of grief rising up from her chest. She stifled it as that feeling made her weak; she had to stay strong; she had to go on.

She sat up and angled her watch face so that she could make out the time in the half-light. It was already one thirty; she was going to be fit for nothing in the morning if she didn't get some sleep. She lay back down again and closed her eyes.

She was still too troubled and decided she had to call Adam. If she found out who Ruben was she could finally get some sleep and deal with it in the morning - hang the consequences! If he got angry, so what? It wouldn't be the first time. At least she would find out what she wanted to know. She knew she shouldn't call him unless it was an emergency but she would anyway. Still lying down she reached sideways and slid her phone towards her until it was in grasping distance. It beeped loudly as the display screen lit up and the network details appeared on the screen. It startled her as she'd forgotten she had the volume turned up so high! Adam had adjusted it because she could never hear it when it rang in her bag. She turned and checked on Alicia to make sure she hadn't woken up but she slept on oblivious.

She played with the settings for a while, still trying to pluck up the courage to call. If she asked him about Ruben she would have to explain how she came to know of him - unless she lied. Maybe it would cause more problems at this stage as Sarah had said that she and Alicia had to go on this journey alone. Her heart was racing as she decided she would call despite her misgivings. She couldn't cope with her thoughts any longer. Maybe just the sound of his voice would pacify her. She scrolled through her address book and quickly found his work number. She paused again, her finger hovering above the call button. Just as she was about to press it, the phone suddenly became red hot, scorching her hand. She shrieked in pain as the phone shot out of her hand skidding and spinning across the floor with such force it was as though she had reached back with her arm and hurled it with all her might. Alicia sat bolt upright, woken by her stepmother's cry.

'It was there, just resting in my hand,' she stammered.

The mobile had clattered against the wall, finally coming to rest at the foot of the door.

'What on earth happened?' Alicia said bewildered.

Courtney explained everything; her hands were now shaking uncontrollably from the shock.

'Oh God,' Alicia replied. She was now wide awake herself. 'I'll put the light on.'

'I haven't had any sleep - I just can't,' Courtney said, 'I've got too much going on in my head. I can't stop thinking about today, trying to make sense of it all.'

Courtney winced and screwed her eyes up as the light came on; she had been awake in the dark for so long.

'Someone obviously didn't want you to call Dad,' Alicia said as she climbed back into bed.

'That's for sure,' Courtney replied half laughing, half crying. 'I can't deal with this. Do you think your mom is trying to break us up? I mean, perhaps she's still in love with your dad, who knows.'

Alicia thought for a minute and then looked directly at her.

'No, I don't think Mom wants that. I just think that if that was her she probably thinks it's best if Dad doesn't know.'

'Well she seems to know him better than I do,' Courtney said sarcastically.

'She's bound to be able to see more than we can - she's dead isn't she,' Alicia replied slightly annoyed at her stepmother's obvious jealousy.

'Oh I'm sorry,' she breathed, realising that she shouldn't speak to Alicia about her mother like that, it wasn't fair. 'It's just so hard. All this is right in my face now. I've got to deal head on with everything that I'd pushed to the back of my mind and ignored for so long.'

'You're glad you know me now though aren't you?' Alicia said, her eyes wide and sad looking.

'I don't mean you. You know how I feel about you, and it gets stronger every day.' Courtney touched her arm lightly to show her that she meant it. She wasn't a particularly demonstrative person by nature - at least she had always thought she wasn't. Just lately though, she had often felt the urge to embrace Alicia.

The two women sat up in bed, their pillows bunched up behind them. They looked straight ahead deep in thought, neither of them had touched the mobile for fear that it would still be hot. It remained on the floor where it had landed.

Courtney was trying to think what to do next. Her arms were folded almost indignantly at the latest invasion of her privacy. She looked at her watch again; it was now two forty-five.

'I give up,' she said out loud then. 'I'm not going to try anymore to sleep. It's only one night, no big deal when you think about it.' She paused for a moment.

'What do you think could be the key?' she then said, turning towards Alicia.

'Well I don't know really,' she answered honestly. 'I was actually thinking about this journey that we have to take. My mom and dad both came from Philadelphia. When she says the key to everything, it's obviously something connecting us as a family. That's the only place I can think of because that's where we all were before.'

'That's it,' Courtney said. 'You're right! God it seems so obvious. If it isn't the family, then maybe they would know. What about Thelma and John?' Courtney tried to disguise the excitement in her voice.

'What Nanny and Grandpa?' Alicia replied.

'Yes, I mean do you think they'd know who Ruben is?' Courtney felt everything was beginning to take shape. She felt calm inside and no tell-tale doubts entered her head to make her think otherwise.

'Well it's possible I guess,' she replied.

'Why don't we go tomorrow? I can pay for some flights for us on my credit card?'

'What about your work?' Alicia answered.

'Oh never mind that, I'll call in sick. I can't work with everything up in the air like this - I wouldn't be able to concentrate anyway.'

'What about the baby?' Alicia then said. 'You can't fly can you?'

'That'll be OK,' she replied after a moment. 'I thought about that already and checked it out, it's only from about six months that you can't - I'm pretty sure about that.'

'Well that's OK then,' Alicia said nodding.

'Great, so we'll go then?' Courtney said her eyes wide with anticipation.

Alicia nodded and smiled back.

'Should we call Thelma and John to warn them?' Courtney added.

'Not now, I don't think they'd appreciate that,' Alicia said laughing, imagining her grandparents' reaction to a phone call at this unearthly hour.

Courtney climbed out of bed and walked towards the door.

'Don't worry, I'm not going to call them - just gonna put it on the side for the morning. I wanna see if it's still working.'

She reached down to pick the phone up and lightly touched it - it was cold. As she lifted it up she noticed that the display light was still on. Weird she thought. She walked back to the bed before looking at it and climbed under the covers pulling them up to chin level. She placed the phone in front of her and focused on the display.

'My God!' she said, utter disbelief in her voice.

'What now?' Alicia replied, craning her neck over to see the display.

As she looked she saw what it was that Courtney was so surprised about.

'And I swear I didn't touch it - you'd have heard it beep,' Courtney said.

The display read: *Thelma and John*, with their telephone number underneath.

'That's amazing!' Alicia said aghast.

Courtney looked at her with a wry smile. 'I reckon we're definitely going to the right place.'

Alicia smiled back and then turned and lay down on her pillow, curling up on her side. 'I'm gonna try and get some sleep now,' she said wearily.

Courtney got back out of bed and having cancelled the display on the mobile and locked the screen, she placed it down carefully on the bedside cabinet.

As she switched off the light she paused for a moment to listen - nothing. Even her own mind had cleared. She yawned, lay back down in bed and almost immediately drifted off into a deep sleep.

Chapter 13

There was a loud knock on the bedroom door. Courtney opened her eyes, the sun was streaming through the chink in the drapes; she was disorientated at first, not sure where she was. Someone knocked again.

'Come in,' she called out hoarsely. The door swung open and in walked Liza, beaming from ear to ear, with a tray of hot drinks and what looked like slices of toast on a couple of plates.

'Morning sleepy heads, got you some breakfast!'

Courtney rubbed her eyes, 'What time is it?' She sat up and tried to focus, 'Urgghh, I feel half asleep still.' She looked at Alicia who was just stirring.

'Oh it's only eight thirty,' Liza said. 'Hope this isn't too early. Did you sleep OK?'

Courtney proceeded to tell Liza everything that had happened the previous night, and what they had planned for that day.

Liza looked astounded, 'So you're off to Philadelphia then? Wow!'

'I'm gonna call my mom today to get her to cover for me,' Courtney replied. 'I'll get her to say we've gone to her house in Leesburg for a few days - I don't want Adam to get suspicious.'

'But what if he calls you there?' Liza said, looking worried.

'Don't worry, I'll ask him to call my mobile. If he calls Mom's house phone, she'll have to say that I've nipped out and to try me on the mobile.'

Liza looked thoughtful, 'Yeah, I guess that could work, it's just awkward. I couldn't imagine lying like that to Grant - it would tear me apart.'

'Well you're lucky then aren't you,' Courtney snapped back. 'Unfortunately for me, my relationship right now isn't as strong as yours, I don't really know what's the truth and what isn't at the moment, so one extra lie won't make much difference.'

Courtney could feel herself getting annoyed with her friend; she often gloated, without really realising it. Then she thought about where she was and how kind Liza had been and decided to change the subject.

'I'll give you a lift to the airport if you like,' Liza then said.

'Could you? That would be great,' Courtney said taking a sip of her coffee. 'I have to leave the car for Adam - he had to get a lift in yesterday. Gone are the days when we used to go to work together. I *never* go now and he goes more often than he has to - says a lot for us doesn't it?'

'Cheer up,' Liza said her smile returning. 'You're off to Philadelphia today. Think of it as a vacation - you two need one.'

Alicia had finally managed to prop herself up on her elbow and was already tucking into her breakfast.

Courtney began to feel a bit brighter. 'I must book those tickets,' she said swinging her legs out from under the covers. She stood up and turning to look at Alicia she clapped her hands together. 'Right c'mon, got to get moving!' Alicia pulled a face, complaining that it was too early.

'We have to pack and everything,' Courtney continued. 'Listen, I'll go over the road and book the tickets. Then I'll come back for you and we'll both go pack - how's that?'

She nodded finally in agreement.

Liza had already left the room; Courtney grabbed her clean clothes, took a shower and got dressed.

It was already nine o'clock. She looked at her watch again as she crossed the road and walked towards her house. She felt differently about it today, not really nervous about going in - she almost didn't have time to feel afraid. She opened the front door and headed straight for the lounge. She called a travel agent who managed to reserve her two seats on the one o'clock flight to Philadelphia International for that same day. After she had put down the phone she felt a sense of relief that she had managed to acquire some tickets at such short notice. However, her apprehension was now beginning to grow as it was no longer an idea - they were actually going. She walked back towards the lounge door, but she stopped before she reached it. A thought had suddenly occurred to her; she looked back over at the phone and at the bureau on which it stood. *I wonder...* She walked towards it and lowered the front. Inside tucked towards the back she found Adam's black leather bound address book. She placed it on the top by the phone and paused for a moment, her heart pounding in her chest as she opened the cover. She ran her finger down the letter dividers and stopped when she got to R. The address book fell open almost by itself and her eyes feverishly scanned the pages. Nothing. She couldn't find any reference to a Ruben at all. She snapped the address book shut, frustrated. She was about to put it away when she stopped, opening it again; *stupid, Ruben's his first name!* She looked at her watch - only *nine twenty-five, good.* She started at A and spent the next twenty minutes searching every page in the address book. She had passed J, K, L nothing. She was beginning to give up hope when halfway down the second page of M's there was a solitary letter 'R' with an address and telephone number written underneath. 'It's in Philadelphia,' she breathed. Her heart was beating even faster. She was sure that this R must be Ruben, unless it was an old girlfriend of Adam's. She grabbed a piece of paper and scribbled down the information, placing the address book back where she had found it in the bureau. She couldn't believe it, everything seemed to be happening so fast. Sarah's words echoed in her mind, it was all coming true. For a moment she wondered if she was imagining all this and then she remembered the phone display last night; there was no explaining that one away.

Perhaps this R *was* someone else - she would take the number anyway. She folded the sheet of paper and placed it in the back of her purse. Satisfied that she had everything she needed she headed for the front door. 'Oh God, Mom!' she exclaimed out loud as she opened the door. She slammed it again in annoyance and returned to the phone - this time to call her mother. She explained that she and Adam were going through a bit of a bad patch and that Alicia had wanted to go see her grandparents. She knew that Adam wouldn't approve, so thought it best that she said she was staying at her house. Mary wasn't happy about it at all. She hated lies, always had done. She could tell though how upset her daughter was and decided that on this occasion she must make an exception and so reluctantly agreed. She made it clear, however, that this was on the understanding that when Courtney returned, she made an effort to sort everything out with Adam. Courtney agreed to this, 'That's what I want to do too Mom,' she said, 'I have to find out a few things first for my own piece of mind, that's all.'

'I'm not happy about this Courtney, but you are my daughter.' There was a sadness in her voice.

Courtney felt on edge again as she left the house. She paused briefly in the driveway to make sure she hadn't forgotten anything else. It didn't matter just now she thought, as she would be going back there to pack once she'd managed to get Alicia out of bed. Liza opened the front door as she walked up the path.

'Everything OK in the house?' she asked.

Courtney confirmed that everything had seemed normal and told her that she'd managed to get the flights booked for that afternoon.

'Where's that stepdaughter of mine?' she said as she began to climb the stairs.

'She's in the shower,' Liza called back.

'Miracles do happen then,' she replied sarcastically.

Courtney collected her things and returned to the lounge to sit with Liza.

'I feel really strange,' she said.

Liza smiled at her and gave her knee a squeeze. 'You'll be fine - you're stronger than you think, you know.'

As she did this Alicia appeared in the lounge doorway, with their overnight bag packed and ready.

'You got the flights?'

'Yep,' Courtney replied making a move to leave. 'We've got to be quick - we've got less than an hour to pack,' she said glancing at her watch.

'We'll need to leave at eleven I reckon to make it to the airport for check in,' Liza added.

Back at their house Courtney paused at the foot of the staircase; she remembered again all the reasons why she should remain downstairs. She banished the thoughts from her head and proceeded up the stairs, mentally listing everything she had to take. It had been a year since she'd had to pack to go anywhere.

Walking hesitantly down the corridor she passed Gabrielle's room and paused briefly to listen - she heard nothing, just the muffled sound of Alicia downstairs talking on the phone. She didn't feel the same as she had done the other night - there had been a definite presence in the hallway then. It was such a strong feeling that she felt as if she could have reached out and touched it. She saw the welcoming sight of her bedroom. Warm bright colours with the sun shining into every corner banished the darkness. She felt a fluttering of contentment in her chest. It was as if she had had a glimpse of how things had been. Every inch of her house used to give her that same feeling of happiness and she wanted to keep hold of it and never let go. She couldn't imagine her house ever being the same again, but in that brief moment she had felt as if there might be hope. They were about to embark on their journey. She was breaking free from her former self, the self that bound her and gave her a false sense of security. Finally she was allowing herself to grow and mature and be the person she had always shied away from and ignored.

She began pulling clothes out of her drawers. She was only going for a few days so she wouldn't need that many clothes. Pulling the largest overnight bag from the closet she stopped to look at her holiday photo that sat proudly in its frame on the shelf. The smiles said it all - the perfect couple, the happiest couple that had ever lived. Nobody had ever been or ever would be as happy as they had been, she thought, her eyes filling with tears. That's what she had thought and believed with all her heart. She had to get that back - she wanted it back so badly. This time there would be no lies, no secrets and they would be honest smiles. *Adam*, she thought about the fact that he would have no idea where she was when he got home. She wasn't sure what to do - call him or write a note? She checked her watch, there wasn't time to write a note. She would call him when they arrived at Thelma and John's, when she was safe.

Alicia appeared in the doorway, making her jump.

'God, don't creep up on me like that - I almost had heart failure!'

'Sorry,' she replied with a mischievous smile. 'Just to let you know, Nanny and Grandpa say it's fine to stay at theirs - they can't wait, especially Nanny. She's going shopping now to get in loads of food for us!'

'She doesn't have to do that, we could eat out,' Courtney said, as she crammed the last of the clothes she had selected into her bag.

'No, she'd rather cook for us. Nanny's like that, she loves cooking; she always does massive portions.'

'Great!' Courtney smiled, 'Cos if I put on weight, I have an excuse!' She zipped her bag shut. 'Right are you ready?'

'Just about,' Alicia replied, 'I've just got to sort out my wash stuff and make-up.'

'Yeah me too,' Courtney said dashing into her bathroom to gather her various beauty products. 'Meet you downstairs in a minute.'

As Courtney opened the front door, Liza was stood there about to press the bell. They both jumped.

'We're still a bunch of nervous wrecks, aren't we?' Courtney said.

Liza had already backed her car out of the drive and the engine was running. She seemed more excited about the trip than they were, chatting away as she placed their bags in the back. Within minutes of leaving they were on the interstate heading for the airport. The windows of the car were down and the breeze ruffled Alicia's hair. She didn't seem to mind but just stared out of the window, with a faint look of satisfaction on her face. Liza kept double-checking, making sure they had everything they needed.

'I have everything Liza. Stop worrying - you're making me nervous!' Courtney finally said.

As they approached the airport Courtney felt her butterflies return. She swallowed nervously as Liza's car swept round to the drop off bay.

They hugged outside the car and Courtney felt as if she didn't want to leave her friend's warm embrace. Then she looked at Alicia smiling back at her, her eyes brimming with excitement, and she felt safe again. Courtney smiled and waved as Liza drove away.

'We're here!' she said eagerly. Alicia caught hold of Courtney's arm and they walked through the automatic doors into a hive of activity. The silence of the car had been replaced by a multitude of voices. Announcements were coming through over the PA and people were struggling past them with heavy bags. Everywhere they looked there were holidaymakers sporting their Disney memorabilia. Jaded parents tried to control their excitable children who didn't seemed to notice their holiday was coming to an end. Courtney and Alicia's was just beginning.

They looked around for the check-in desk and after a short while their two bags were tagged and sent off down the conveyer belt. Courtney had never before checked in a bag for herself, previously it had always been done for her. She was surprised at how easy it was and how organised she seemed to be. Pleased to have been relieved of their luggage they went through to the departure lounge.

Courtney really craved a cigarette then! She had always smoked before getting onto a plane as she was always a bag of nerves at the prospect of flying. Her mind invented every possible disaster scenario and catastrophe that could arise. She decided that she had to try to forget her fears and insecurities and concentrate on Alicia. They stopped at a coffee shop; the smell of fresh coffee beans was overpowering.

'I don't think I'll be needing to drink any,' Courtney said, 'just smelling it is enough! Shall we get a cake too?' she said, a naughty expression on her face, as if eating a cake would be a dreadful indulgence.

Alicia readily agreed and the two sat sipping their coffee and breaking off small pieces of Danish so that it would last twice as long.

'We'll get a meal on the plane too you know,' Courtney joked, 'and then when we arrive at Thelma and John's, if what you say is true, we'll be stuffed full with even more food.'

'I know,' Alicia said with a wicked grin, 'isn't it great!'

'Do you get nervous of flying?' Courtney enquired.

'A little, but it's the safest form of transport, so they say.'

'Who are they?' Courtney replied. 'People always say *they* said and I've always wondered who *they* are. Maybe there's a board of people somewhere called *they* who know everything about everything.'

'What?' Alicia said with a confused look on her face. 'Are you mad or something?' she laughed.

'Quite possibly!' Courtney replied. 'Not long to go now.'

They sat for the remainder of the time just people watching. People always fascinated Courtney. She began thinking as she glanced at them that all of the people were important to somebody. Most of them she would never see again, and if they glanced at her they would probably not even give her a second thought; she was just a stranger. It made her feel insignificant, a nobody. No-one was interested in her life apart from her close family. If she died, none of these people would care or even notice she wasn't there anymore. Unless there is a God, she thought. He would notice everyone. She always felt closer to God when she got on a plane. She hadn't given God much thought in her every day life, until recently that is, when all the trouble had started. She knew it was because she was nervous of flying. As a child she had been brought up to believe in heaven and that it was somewhere in the sky. Being in a plane she was somehow closer to it, should she not reach her final destination. She needed to think about these things - almost as an insurance policy.

She was snapped out of her trance by the announcement over the PA.

'That's us,' Alicia said gleefully. 'Look it's boarding on the screen now, let's go.'

'What gate is it?' Courtney said calmly, trying to keep her anxiety to herself. 'Ought to find a restroom first, I can't stand the ones you get on planes. When you flush them, it sounds like the bottom just fell out the plane and you're gonna get sucked out.'

Alicia laughed and they hurried to the nearest one.

'We have to go on that electric monorail thing as well, so better be quick,' Courtney remembered.

When they reached the monorail there was a queue of people waiting to get on. Courtney felt her anxiety growing by the second but she took deep breaths and within five minutes they were standing inside one of the trains, gripping the handrails tightly.

A computerised voice spoke as the doors closed, Alicia laughed, 'That always gets me every time.'

Courtney looked out of the window as the train made its way to the next terminal. She looked down on the rows of aircraft attached to tunnels, and those taxiing back into their bays. They looked so formidable. She was more nervous now and her hands began to sweat so much with the tension that she could barely hold on to the rail. She told herself *'calm, you are very, very calm'* in an effort to quell the panic.

Once off the monorail they only had a short distance to walk before finding their boarding gate. They were greeted by a beaming stewardess who checked their tickets again. 'Philadelphia International,' she trilled. 'Straight ahead please, just follow the tunnel down to the aircraft.'

There was no going back now. Courtney thought of Adam then. She was leaving him behind. He had no idea that she was going anywhere and he would be all alone in the house. She felt sad again. They reached the doorway and were greeted by a steward who winked appreciatively at Alicia as he ushered them in. Adam always maintained that all air stewards were gay - well this one obviously wasn't.

Classical music filled their ears as they made their way through the aircraft. She presumed this was being played to drown out the sound of the plane's engine. It did have the desired effect and Courtney felt calmer as she opened the overhead locker and crammed in her handbag. Alicia had asked if she could sit by the window. Courtney didn't mind - she wasn't keen on the window seat anyway.

As the plane taxied to the runway Courtney smiled to herself. She could almost have been on a bus as it bumped and bounced along.

Finally, after a long wait the plane turned into a different animal altogether as it accelerated down the runway. The force of it was awe inspiring. Courtney always felt emotional whenever she took off in a plane - she didn't like the feeling of losing control over her own destiny. The plane continued to climb, dropping in the air currents, bumping, then rising again, higher and higher. Alicia had her nose buried in a book but Courtney couldn't read - she wouldn't be able to concentrate. She turned her head and looked out the window. Through the white clouds beneath she could just make out tiny cars rushing along on the interstate, no bigger than ants; she had no clue which road it was she was looking at, it was impossible to determine exactly where they were above Orlando. She saw the tiny houses with bright blue spots behind them - most of the houses in Orlando must have swimming pools, she thought. The plane started to bank right, the ground disappeared and there was just blue and white sky. They passed through a large bank of cloud and as they emerged bright sunlight streamed in through the window, causing her to have to shield her eyes. She was in a different world, above a vast terrain of white and silver, like a land from a fairytale. The soft white clouds looked so inviting and she wondered if it would be like landing on a large feather duvet should she jump out. She knew this was all fantasy but she liked to dream. The sun glimmered and shone on the clouds. *It's absolutely beautiful.* She was amazed by what she saw; she had never paid much attention to the view out of a plane before. When she had flown with Adam his broad sheet newspaper usually obscured the window and she would spend her time flicking through the uninteresting in-flight magazines, waiting for the meal to arrive.

She turned back and closed her eyes, still thinking about the view and feeling peaceful at that moment. The stewardesses were on their way down the aisle with the drinks trolley. She wasn't really thirsty but she could never turn down anything that was offered to her, be it food or drink. Her mind wandered again and suddenly she was back there on her wedding day. She remembered everything that happened but this time as an outsider looking in. She was watching the day like a home video playing in her mind. She had been so excited. Very little planning had gone into the wedding - everything had happened so quickly. She hadn't wanted a lot of fuss, she just wanted to get married, without anybody noticing. She'd have been happy not to have had any guests at all. At the time she had still been in denial about Adam's past. She barely acknowledged the fact that he had been married before - the thought of it made her physically sick. The only way she could cope with the situation was by pretending that it had never happened. Not being able to face the truth she just ignored it. All she knew was that she was madly in love with Adam and nothing was going to change that. Whatever happened she had to marry him.

The trolley came level with their seat.

'Would you like a drink from the trolley ma'am?' the stewardess smiled winningly.

Courtney asked for an orange juice and Alicia a glass of white wine.

'Where were you a moment ago?' Alicia asked candidly. 'You weren't here that's for sure!'

Courtney sipped her orange juice. 'I was just remembering my wedding day, strangely enough. I don't know why, it just all came back to me.'

'Tell me about it,' Alicia said, taking her by surprise. 'You've never told me about it before.'

'I didn't think you'd be interested,' Courtney replied.

'Well you're wrong then,' Alicia said as she struggled to open her bag of airline peanuts.

'Give me those,' Courtney laughed snatching them from her. 'Why they seal these bags so tightly I'll never know!'

'I don't know where to start really. We got married March fifth, two days after my birthday actually. I can't really remember why it was that date.'

'It was only four years ago!' Alicia said incredulously.

'I know, but you can't remember everything. It was a Saturday, very traditional and boring I know. It's always easier for people to make it on a Saturday. I didn't really plan much in advance. I bought my dress in a department store.'

'Did you? You look awesome in the photo in the lounge.' Alicia looked surprised.

'Why thank you,' Courtney smiled back. 'It was a silky material, quite a luxurious feel to it considering the price! I liked how the flowery pattern broke up the white - quite subtle. I think it was supposed to be an evening dress, not really meant for weddings, but it did the job.'

'It was in a church wasn't it?' Alicia said. 'It looks like one in the background.'

'No that was taken outside the reception hall, we just had a civil ceremony.' Courtney took another sip of her drink.

'Who was the groom's man?' Alicia then asked. 'There's a picture of him too.'

'Oh that was Ian,' Courtney said, a smile of recognition returning to her face. 'He's great, one of your dad's best friends. He was another medic in Leesburg - they shared an apartment before we got married.' Her smile gradually faded then as her mind wandered - her happy memories were suddenly blighted.

'I felt really weird on my wedding day,' she said leaning back in the seat again, a far away look on her face. 'It was like it wasn't happening to me. I was a different person then. I was happy but I was so darn desperate to get married. Now I look back and I think why? I'm happy, don't get me wrong, but maybe I did it for the wrong reasons. I used to be so jealous of your mom. I can't believe that now. I didn't like the fact that she was still Mrs Buchanan when I was the one with your dad. She had died and I was jealous - it seems so selfish now when I look back. I just wanted to be Mrs Buchanan, not Miss Walsh. I felt inferior, probably because of the way I'd been brought up. I don't know why I let it rule my life. It became almost an obsession. Now I feel guilty that I misled your dad - he had no idea how I felt. I just kept it all locked up inside. Oh I'd rant on at him and have a go about most things he did. I'd blame it on my time of the month or make something up, but all that time it had been eating away at me like a cancer. I don't know why he stayed with me to be honest.'

'Maybe he really loves you,' Alicia answered.

'I never met Adam's parents,' Courtney suddenly said disregarding Alicia's reply. 'I was jealous of your mom for that too. She did meet them and they would have been at her wedding.'

'I don't remember them either,' Alicia replied. 'I think they were quite old when they had Dad. I know Grandpa Fred was in his mid forties when Dad was born.'

Courtney was silent then. She felt as if she had exorcised another of her ghosts and felt happy that Adam's story tallied with Alicia's. Her mind was turning over rapidly now, throwing up various arguments supporting her inner conflicts - her contentment was short lived.

'Sometimes I think the only thing your dad and I have in common is the fact that we're both only children - no brothers or sisters,' she mused. Alicia fell silent. Courtney thought about what she had just said and then apologised, realising how insensitive she had just been. She hurriedly changed the subject and commented on the distinctive smell of the in flight meal being prepared in the galley. She always looked forward to the meal, although she considered the portions were criminally small. She felt almost excited at the prospect of opening the lid on the anonymous tin carton to find out what was inside! Alicia rubbed her hands with glee as she discovered the contents of her carton, chicken and vegetables.

'You can't really go wrong with chicken can you,' Courtney remarked already tucking in to her dinner, 'unless you're a vegetarian.' She looked at her watch. 'We must be halfway by now,' she said, picking up her bread roll and beginning to unwrap it.

'We're due to land at three eighteen,' she continued, 'it's after two already. Your dad will be back by now. I should have called before we left just to get it over with, but having said that I don't think he'll get suspicious until late this evening when I would have been due back from work. Damn! Work - I forgot to call.' She struck her hand against her forehead in frustration, and then they both looked at each other and burst into laughter.

'That's typical,' Alicia said. 'That was the first thing you should have done.'

'Oh well, my shift isn't due to start until three. I'll call as soon as we reach the terminal.'

They had just finished their meals, when the 'fasten seat belt' light flashed on above their heads. A feeling of dread came over Courtney who up until now had felt quite at ease on the aircraft. After about five minutes the plane began to bump and drop suddenly. She clutched at Alicia's arm.

'It's only a bit of turbulence,' Alicia said incredulously.

The hostesses continued up the aisle swaying slightly, but still managing to collect with relative ease the passengers' untidy meal trays as they went. Courtney closed her eyes again; she tried to concentrate on something else until it passed. She thought about her baby then, resting her hand protectively on her stomach as the plane continued to pitch and roll. She felt very alone at that moment. She had always felt safe with Adam when they had flown together. Even though she still worried about her safety, the thought that they would at least be together if they died consoled her. Now it was just her and Alicia, and because she felt responsible for her it was different. She was the one who was supposed to be strong. She released her grip on Alicia's arm and opened her eyes again, realising that she had to quell her panic. Just then the movement stopped and to her relief the warning light went off and she could relax again.

There was less than an hour of the flight to go. The Captain made a sudden announcement, his smooth authoritative voice eradicating any last trace of fear that remained within her. He apologised for the turbulence saying that they had had to climb to avoid bad weather over Virginia and had caught the tail end of it. He assured them that there would be no repeat of the incident for the remainder of the flight and informed them that they would be starting their descent in around twenty minutes' time. Courtney bristled with excitement, catching hold of Alicia's hand and smiling at her broadly.

'We'll be flying over Washington soon,' Alicia said her voice brimming with anticipation. She craned her neck to look out of the window. 'I don't think we'll see much though, there's thick cloud below us at the moment. Oh, I forgot to tell you that the weather's usually crap here.'

'I didn't think it was going to be bright sunshine somehow,' Courtney replied with a smile, 'Not in Pennsylvania. I did learn something in geography at school you know, but thanks for the reminder.'

Courtney felt the pressure change in her ears as the aircraft began to descend. She checked her watch again - it was three o'clock.

'Not long to go now. I make it eighteen minutes,' she said turning to Alicia, who was too busy looking out of the window to take much notice of what she was saying.

'We're not going to tell your nan about Sally Harris are we? We agreed on that,' she said. It was important that they get their story straight.

289

'And we're not going to mention Ruben straight away either - we need to tread carefully.'

Alicia grunted an agreement, still distracted. 'Wow look at that! I can't believe I'm back here again.'

Courtney asked Alicia to move so that she could see out. She saw the dense city almost all around them; she could see skyscrapers, much more vast than those in Orlando. The cityscape reminded her a little of New York, but on a slightly smaller scale. She felt her butterflies come back now they were almost there, and she was very much aware now that she had a job to do.

'I expect Nanny will be wearing her red duffel coat. I've never seen her in anything else.' Alicia remarked as the plane touched down. Courtney braced herself but the landing was fairly soft as the wheels thumped against the tarmac and the engines roared as the brakes came on.

'Your nan wears a duffel coat?' Courtney finally said as they were standing in the aisle waiting for the doors to open. 'Do you think they'll be waiting for us in arrivals?'

'Oh definitely,' Alicia replied nodding her head and smiling. 'They'll both be there, beaming from ear to ear, I can assure you of that.'

Chapter 14

The airport was bustling with activity, much the same as the airport had been in Orlando, only there was one noticeable difference - none of the children were wearing Goofy hats or Disney T-shirts. There were far more businessmen than casually dressed passengers on this weekday flight. Courtney sent Alicia to collect the baggage from the carousel whilst she went off to find somewhere relatively quiet where she could call work and Adam, before meeting up with Thelma and John.

Work was the easy part - she just told them she would not be back that week because of problems at home and stress, which was not far from the truth.

She was relieved that she had got through to them before they had tried to call her. She had a reputation for being the most unpunctual person at work anyway, which in this particular instance had proved to be an advantage. She dialled Adam's number and had an overwhelming feeling of nausea as she counted the rings; she was just about to leave a message when he answered, taking her by surprise.

'Adam,' she said her voice sounding a little shaky.

'Hi babe!' he replied. 'You at work?'

'Not exactly,' she answered, 'Alicia and I…well we needed to get away, not from you - don't get me wrong.' She stumbled somewhat, desperate to find the right words and when she paused for a second it gave him the chance to jump in.

'Gone away, what do you mean?' he sounded almost desolate at the news. 'Where?'

She explained that they had gone to stay with her mother for a while, just for a few days, for a rest, to get away from all the stress.

'I need a vacation too!' he ranted. 'You didn't think to ask me - I don't believe this!'

'Adam,' she tried desperately to soothe him, 'I didn't mean to upset you - I didn't think you'd mind, honestly.'

Adam was gone. The line was dead. She felt an emptiness - her emotions had been battered so many times; it was as if she couldn't feel anything anymore, nothing could touch her. She tried to call him back and she left him a message, telling him she loved him, begging him to understand. Deep down she was glad that he wasn't with her. She was angry - she didn't need him, she could survive quite easily on her own. *All he ever does is undermine me, make me feel like a brainless idiot.*

She walked back to baggage reclaim and looked around for Alicia. There was a tightening in her chest, tension. She wanted to cry but no sound would come out. She still loved him, regardless, despite everything. She blamed herself to a certain degree for internalising all of her thoughts; she had probably exaggerated some of her feelings and allowed her imagination to run away with her. At least now she had the chance to find out for definite, at least that was what she was hoping.

'There you are.' Courtney found Alicia, their bags at her feet, smoking over the far side of baggage reclaim. She was crying. Courtney didn't need to ask what was wrong with her - she had been remarkable so far and had not yet mentioned Brad. Courtney put her arms around her and gave her a hug. 'It'll be all right,' she tried to reassure her.

'Will it?' Alicia said through her tears. 'I'm not so sure.'

'We must stay positive,' Courtney said earnestly. 'Come on, we're in Philadelphia, we're going to see your nan and grandad, maybe get a cheesesteak.' She tried to gee her along.

Alicia laughed through her tears, 'You heard about cheesesteak?'

'Why sure,' she replied. 'Best food in town I heard, well next to your nan's home cooking anyway.'

She rested her arm on Alicia's shoulder and they walked side by side through to the arrivals lounge. Within seconds of the doors opening, there was Thelma in her bright red duffel coat. She was waving frantically from behind the barriers and beaming with the warmest, most welcoming smile that Courtney had ever seen. Her doting husband John stood beside her, upright and almost military in his bearing. He was a little more reserved but his faint smile was genuine.

'Told you,' Alicia whispered, indicating her nan's red coat as they approached.

'I think it looks great,' Courtney countered. She jabbed Alicia playfully in the ribs and tickled her, making her hoot with laughter.

'Nanny!' Alicia called running on ahead. Thelma stood, legs astride, her robust arms outstretched, waiting to embrace her precious granddaughter. Tears sprang into her eyes.

'How are you sweetheart?' she cried. 'You get more beautiful every time I see you.'

'You OK Alicia?' John interjected. He seemed very frail now and staggered a little as he waited for his hug. Courtney stood by feeling a little awkward, waiting for Thelma and John to acknowledge her. She didn't have to wait long. Within moments Thelma was on her like a steam train, her ample body almost bowling her over, completely smothering her. Courtney eventually came up for air with Thelma smoothing her hair back as her own mother did and gazing into her eyes. Thelma looked elegant, her pale blonde hair cut in a short tidy crop with her round face barely lined. Her bright blue eyes smiled back at her with total acceptance.

'Welcome to Philly,' she said. 'It's your first time isn't it?'

'Yes,' Courtney said still trying to draw breath, surprised to have been given such a warm welcome. Thelma took her hand; John had caught hold of both of their bags, his bony arms obviously struggling with the weight.

'Let me carry those John,' Courtney said rushing to his side, 'I can manage, honestly.'

He handed over the bags reluctantly and led them through the arrivals lounge, his pace quickening as they neared the doors leading out into the fresh afternoon air. Courtney looked around her as they stepped onto the sidewalk. The crisp air nipped at her face and she wrapped her arms around herself instinctively. She could now see why Thelma had been wearing that duffel coat. As she looked around taking in this unfamiliar place, she felt as if she was ten feet tall. Reflecting on the journey they had taken so far she felt proud of herself for the first time in her life and felt a real rapport with this place, even though she hadn't seen very much of it yet. John located his car and before

293

long they were on the road again. Courtney was transfixed by
the view as they drove along the interstate and she barely spoke.
Thelma was talking relentlessly in the front passenger seat; John
answered her occasionally when she paused for breath.

'Oh there are so many places we can visit,' she sang out, turning
her head to speak to Courtney and Alicia. 'How long are you
staying again? I can't remember.'

'Well we have four full days here - we're due to fly back
Thursday,' Courtney replied.

'That's plenty of time,' Thelma said, delighted, we can go to
City Hall. You like history?' Courtney nodded, but she didn't
pause long enough for her to reply. 'There's Fairmount Park, oh
it's wonderful there - so big! You can completely lose yourself!
You should come back in July when they have the most
spectacular firework displays for Independence day, not to
mention the open air concerts, and there's Hoagie Day...' she
tittered, pausing to draw breath again briefly; 'Oh and of course
we have to go for a cheesesteak - that's an absolute must.' She
looked at Alicia waiting for her agreement.

'Cheesesteaks are absolutely the best - you can't beat a good
cheesesteak! I've had a few in my time,' Thelma said patting
her generous stomach. 'You can probably tell.' She laughed
heartily. Courtney hadn't heard a laugh quite like it before. It
was shrill but rose right up from the pit of her stomach - almost
two toned. John then laughed automatically, as if just the sound
of his wife guffawing was enough to set him off regardless of
whether anything funny had been said or not.

'Oh and there's Independence Park,' Thelma continued, 'Great
place. That was where the Declaration of Independence was
read for the first time. There are tons of museums and did you
know that there were a couple of very big Hollywood movies
filmed here a few years back?' She looked at Alicia again.

'The Sixth Sense and Twelve Monkeys wasn't it?' Alicia
confirmed. Courtney was impressed, 'Hey I think I'm gonna
like this place.' She turned and looked back out of the window,
'Wow just look at that skyline! It's awesome,' she breathed.

'Oh that's downtown, the main city, business centre. We live in
South Philly so will be heading off that way,' Thelma said
pointing haphazardly to her right, just missing John's head with

her outstretched hand. He tutted and scolded her. Thelma just laughed again.

Alicia was amused by her nan's enthusiasm - she hadn't seen her this happy in a long time. Her laugh had always delighted Alicia since she was quite young. She remembered that their mother used to say that it sounded like a cross between a hyena and a bullfrog and she giggled at the recollection.

'What's so funny missy?' her nan said, totally oblivious to the fact that she was the source of amusement.

Alicia said it was nothing but continued to chuckle to herself in the back. Courtney had an idea what it was and gave her a knowing smile.

They had been driving now some time. Courtney was fascinated by the architecture of the buildings; everything was totally different to what she was used to in Florida. The buildings there were flatter with less character, and even the colours and trees in Florida were different.

As they neared their destination the buildings were grandiose - all town houses in streets somewhat regimented, but each still somehow unique.

'It's the next street; we're going to park up wherever we can,' Thelma chirped. 'We don't have garages up here.'

John pulled in by the sidewalk and they climbed out. Courtney took a moment to take in her surroundings. The street was wide and the sidewalk made up of pale grey paving slabs. She gazed in awe at the red brick buildings rising up majestically before them. As she turned to look down the street, she noticed that the pattern of trees continued as far as she could see; one paving slab was missing at regular intervals and a large green leafy tree jutted up from each strategically placed space. The road was a darker grey than the sidewalk, and made a stark contrast that was pleasing to the eye.

The street was full of activity, cars pulling in and out of spaces, people walking; a lady with her dog crossed the road.

'We're lucky with the weather today,' Thelma announced as John lifted the bags from the car's trunk. 'There's a chill in the air, but the sun's still shining. It wasn't like this yesterday - horrible! Grey it was.'

Courtney smiled back. She was nervous about asking Thelma and John anything right then, and wasn't sure that she wanted to at all. Everyone seemed so happy and she thought that it would be a shame to cast a shadow over a perfect day. She felt she had left her troubles far behind as she reached down and picked up her bag off the sidewalk.

'It's that one, 4240 - they're divided up 'a' to 'c' inside. You'll see on the buzzer that they're all separate apartments. Ours is 4240a on the ground floor,' Thelma said proudly.

They walked up the white stone steps to the heavy wooden door, holding on to the ornate wrought iron railing. Courtney looked up and noticed the black carved archway above the door. The dark brown door was edged in white, and set against the red brick of the building it looked very grand. She had never been up close to a house like this before in her life. 'It's amazing,' she said half out loud, half under her breath.

John smiled. 'That's just the outside, you haven't seen inside yet!' he said managing to sound grateful rather than boastful.

He turned the heavy key in the lock and carefully pushed open the door. 'We've got a smaller key for our front door,' he remarked. 'Sometimes I feel like a jailer with all these keys.'

Courtney's footsteps echoed on the wood panelled floor, a staircase stretched up in front of her. She looked around in amazement at the hand carved bannister and the paintings on the wall. The hall had a musty aroma about it, which far from being unpleasant evoked thoughts about the history of the house.

She followed the others a short distance until they reached the apartment, which was adjacent to the staircase on the right.

'Are these houses *very* old?' she asked, as they stood huddled together, waiting for John to open the door.

'Oh yes,' Thelma replied with gusto, 'turn of the century these.'

The door swung open and John led them in. Courtney stepped eagerly onto the doormat, wiping her feet vigorously so as not to dirty the plush cream carpet that lay before her. They walked into the hallway and Thelma took their jackets from them, hanging them on the coat stand by the door. The doors off the hallway were all matching and were made of a rich dark heavy grained wood, each one with a gold handle. Thelma showed them to their rooms, which were directly opposite each other.

Once inside Courtney found that she had an ensuite shower - it was just like a home from home, comfortable and cosy. She felt no atmosphere here and didn't feel the need to constantly look over her shoulder as she had in her own house. She wondered about Adam and what he was doing. She had to stay focused. She couldn't afford to let herself become melancholy again, not now. There were things she had come to do and she must not allow herself to consider the consequences.

She showered and changed. Feeling refreshed, she ventured back out into the corridor in search of the others.

In the kitchen Thelma was busying herself chopping vegetables and there was something else bubbling on the stove.

'Roast chicken OK for you?' she said without lifting her gaze from the worktop. Courtney didn't have the heart to tell her that they had already had chicken on the plane, and besides, whatever else was on the boil smelt divine.

'I've heard all about your cooking,' she said leaning up against the wall.

'Oh you have, have you?' Thelma laughed.

'Yes I've heard you are one of the best - Alicia really rates you!'

'Well that's good to know,' she said beaming from ear to ear.

'I always dreamed of having a nan like you,' she added.

Thelma blushed, 'Oh stop it!'

Courtney asked her if she needed any help, but Thelma told her to go and sit down and relax as she was on vacation.

Courtney smiled and as she turned to leave the kitchen she noticed that the door by the coat stand was now ajar. She pushed it open cautiously and made her way in. John was sat in the far corner reading the paper; he looked up and nodded to acknowledge her, then continued to read his paper. The room was spotless, almost regal in appearance, with antique furniture in almost every corner. There was a grandfather clock, and above the fireplace on a dark wood shelf stood a number of photographs in matching gold frames. She had forgotten that there would be photographs and immediately felt herself start to panic. She had never seen what Sarah looked like before, and from where she was standing she was sure that she could make out one which just had to be of her.

She had to have a closer look, and walked purposefully towards them, hoping that John would not think her odd or notice her anxiety. She reached the fireplace with part of her not wanting to look, but her curiosity had got the better of her.

She was drawn immediately to the photograph she had spotted from the doorway; she picked it up and stared intently at it. This woman wasn't dissimilar to Thelma Courtney thought; she had the same rounded face, the same intense blue eyes. Her hair was long, blonde - she had a faraway but contented look on her face and her lips were slightly parted, as if she had been in the middle of speaking when the picture was taken. *It has to be her.* She couldn't believe that she was looking at Adam's ex-wife, the face she had dreaded most of all was now staring back at her. She remembered what had happened in the house, *she* had been in *her* house, but she was *dead.* Her mind raced. She tried to work out if she would have liked her had they met. Could they have been friends? She thought about Adam kissing her and felt a churning inside as she put the photo back down on the side.

She looked at the other photos - calmer now. There was Alicia and Gabrielle's graduation photo that she had seen before, and beside it a picture of the girls with their mother. She gazed at the girls' faces, fascinated; she had never seen a picture of them when they were young before. She looked at their mother and looked back at them and although they had similar colouring, their face shapes even at that young age were completely different. Neither Alicia or Gabrielle had a round face, theirs were more oval. Their features were different from hers too. She thought it strange that they didn't really resemble their mother at all. Somewhere she had always imagined Sarah as a stunning beauty, the image of the girls, but the truth was that apart from her hair and eyes, she was actually quite ordinary.

The next photograph that caught her eye was of a young boy - she could tell straight away that he had to be a relative of Sarah's, his face was the same as hers. Her curiosity aroused but she decided not to ask John right at that moment and anyway she could hear Alicia talking in the hallway. She quickly scanned the rest of the photographs, which were of Thelma and John at varying ages up to the present day, including their wedding photograph. She was pleased there wasn't a photograph of Adam and Sarah's wedding. She wouldn't have wanted to see him looking young, radiant, and happy with another woman by his side. She turned and sat herself down on the edge of the couch. John had put down his paper and appeared to be having an afternoon nap - his head had lolled to one side and his eyes were closed.

She got up and walked towards the door, Alicia was cackling in the hallway. Courtney raised her finger to her lips as she approached, to signal to her to be quiet.

'Your grandad's asleep,' she said. The aroma of roast chicken filled the apartment. Courtney stood in the hallway, her hands tucked awkwardly into her jeans' pockets. She didn't really know what to do with herself at that moment.

'Are you sure you don't want any help?' she asked again. Thelma again declined saying that it was almost ready and they would be sat down within half an hour. Courtney was redundant; she was so used to doing everything in her own house - it was an alien feeling.

She decided to go and have a rest before dinner and maybe read for a while to distract her mind.

Within no time at all they were all sat around the dining room table at the far end of the lounge, with a vast spread of food in front of them and a jug of gravy steaming in the middle. John was more animated now, his nap had obviously done the trick. Courtney's plate groaned with meat! She had a healthy appetite and loved her food but she knew instinctively she was going to struggle with it - there was just too much chicken, at least half a bird it seemed.

'Wow, this all looks delicious,' she said as she began to negotiate her way around the vegetable dishes. Alicia's face told a similar story, she didn't hide it as well as Courtney.

Thelma asked Alicia how she was getting on and she began to explain about Brad. Without including too much detail she gave an overview of what had happened and how it looked as if he had tried to take his own life. Thelma was clearly shocked, 'Oh no not that young police officer who was at Gaby's funeral?' she said.

John reached forward and stroked his wife's hand protectively.

'That *girl* did too, didn't she?' she continued. 'I'm not surprised though,' she said her expression having changed to one of contempt - she couldn't even bear to utter Jennifer's name.

'It's a terrible thing, terrible thing,' John said shaking his head. Thelma dabbed at her eyes with her napkin; 'She's constantly reminded,' he then said lowering his head in sadness. 'We were just beginning to come to terms with it and then...' he cut his words short, unable to carry on.

'Oh I'm sorry, Nan. I didn't think, I didn't mean to upset you - it's been so hard for you.'

Courtney felt a surge of adrenaline and a feeling of panic welling up inside her again. She had no idea what they were talking about. She placed her knife and fork down as her appetite had gone - she had to say something; she couldn't leave it.

'What do you mean?' she blurted out. There was silence then - it was as if time had stopped.

'You mean you don't know?' Thelma finally said incredulously. 'Adam didn't tell you.'

Alicia looked equally as surprised as the others. 'I just assumed that you knew,' she said, looking slightly nervous. 'That's why I didn't mention it.'

'Know what? Mention what?' Courtney said, her frustration now getting the better of her.

'Sarah, our Sarah, she took her own life,' John said his voice cracking with emotion. Courtney gasped, tears springing into her eyes, as her worst fears were confirmed.

'Oh I'm so sorry,' she cried, 'so sorry.' The previously pleasant atmosphere at the dining table now seemed irretrievable.

'Do excuse me,' she said desperately trying to stifle her emotion.

Courtney felt Alicia's hand touch her arm in an attempt to comfort her, but she couldn't speak at that moment. She felt guilty now - she was crying for herself, not for Sarah or for them. Thoughts flooded her mind; she didn't understand why Adam had told her what he had. What was the big secret?

'I'm so sorry,' she finally stammered again. 'I didn't know, I thought she'd been killed in a car accident.'

'Adam told you that?' Thelma said shocked. 'But why?'

'That's what I want to know. Listen I'm really sorry; it's just come as an awful shock, I really don't want to upset you.' She stared down at her plate; not knowing whether to stay or to go. Nobody spoke, it might make matters worse if she left the table now.

'I was going to ask you Courtney,' Thelma finally broke the embarrassing silence. 'How's the pregnancy going?'

'Oh fine, almost halfway now,' she replied falteringly, 'I'm not having any problems really, although I haven't been taking much notice of it to be honest - there's been too much else going on.'

'You must take care of yourself dear,' Thelma responded. Courtney forced a weak smile.

'I just feel so tired today - it's probably the travelling.' She attempted to clear a bit more of her plate.

Part of her now wished that she hadn't found out about Sarah at all - ignorance is bliss she thought. The problem was that now she needed to know more but she couldn't press them further at the table. She had created an awkward situation already by getting so upset so she would have to wait. The trouble was that her imagination was already going into overdrive.

'I think we all need to have an early night tonight,' Thelma said. She too seemed to be struggling with her food. It was such a shame Courtney thought, she'd gone to all that trouble and now nobody felt much like eating. You could have cut the atmosphere with a knife; it had so suddenly gone from being jovial to melancholy, with each of them now afraid of saying the wrong thing.

John was the first to break the silence this time. 'Maybe we can talk about everything tomorrow,' he said, realising that there was unfinished business that could be put on hold until the morning. Courtney felt heartened. She was going to be able to find out more and they weren't just going to clam up and pretend nothing had ever happened.

Courtney and Alicia helped John load the dishwasher, whilst Thelma had a lie down. He then went to join his wife in their bedroom, leaving the two women alone together. They sat on the couch in the lounge, both feeling emotionally drained. It was getting late and Courtney still felt confused and saddened, remembering how excited she had been when they had first set off on their journey and how grateful she was for the warm reception they had received. She just wished that her new found happiness could have lasted at least one day.

'I really put my foot in it today,' Alicia said with a big sigh. 'I managed to upset Nan, Grandpa and you.' She took a sip of the coffee that Courtney had just made her, 'Damn, why couldn't I have kept my big fat mouth shut?'

'Don't worry about it,' Courtney said resigned. 'We're here to find out the truth - it wasn't meant to be a vacation. I just can't believe it never came up before in conversation between the two of us.' She raised her hands in despair, 'I mean first Jennifer, then Brad - they've done the same thing, and you never thought to say anything to me about your mom.'

'I didn't associate them with Mom. People kill themselves every day. It happened a long time ago and a lot of it I've just blocked out - it's too hard to deal with.' Alicia's pain showed in her eyes as she looked back at Courtney. 'Well you know now, so that's all that matters,' she then said looking down at her coffee cup.

'I just can't believe it,' Courtney continued her eyes filling with tears again. 'How could your father have lied to me? I just don't understand.'

'I don't know,' Alicia answered frankly. 'It's a mystery to me - I mean it happened three years after he'd left anyway.'

'Do you know why she did it?' Courtney asked tentatively.

'Not really. Perhaps she'd just had enough - she didn't leave a note. It would have been easier for us to know that it wasn't our fault instead of having to spend our whole lives wondering why. It used to upset Gabrielle so much.'

'I'm sorry,' Courtney said, putting her arm around Alicia. Alicia clung to her as if she didn't ever want to let go.

'It will be all right,' Courtney said gently. 'We'll be strong for each other. I've got a feeling that we're going to need to be. We have to go through with what we came here to do, however painful it is. I mean look at everything we've had to deal with at home. If we can cope with that we can cope with anything, right?' She smiled warmly at Alicia.

Courtney knew that Alicia was the one who gave her inner strength and she hoped that they could support each other. Both of them had very positive characters and if one felt down the other would always try to be cheerful. She got up and walked towards the TV.

'You tired?' she said to Alicia who was now lying stretched out across the couch. 'You can't stay there,' she laughed, 'I'm coming back in a minute.'

'Oh can't you go sit on the chair over there - I'm comfortable,' Alicia pleaded.

Courtney promptly picked up a cushion from the chair and hurled it at Alicia who just managed to dodge out of the way. 'No I won't,' she replied indignantly. 'You haven't answered my question!'

'What about being tired? Well I was - still am really, but I want to wait until I'm too tired to keep my eyes open, if you know what I mean,' Alicia said, reluctantly hauling herself back up again.

'Right then, let's watch a movie or something, take our minds off everything. Tomorrow's a new day. I wonder if your nan has got any microwave popcorn?'

'I doubt it,' Alicia laughed. Courtney switched on the TV and began flicking through the channels trying to find something for them to watch.

Adam looked at the clock, 'God!' he exclaimed out loud. He ran his hand nervously through his grey flecked hair, cursing as he paced up and down the lounge, his mobile pressed firmly against his ear. 'Answer the damn phone Courtney!' he hollered. The bright light of the lounge contrasted with the darkness beyond, casting his reflection on the patio doors as he paced back and forth.

'Courtney! It's Adam,' he said, his voice tinged with anxiety. 'This is the third message I've left for you now. Please babe, call me back, I don't know what's happening. I just want to make sure you're coming back to me.' He flipped his mobile shut and slumped dejectedly onto the couch. He checked his watch again; it was after eleven. It was his first night alone in the house and already he was finding it impossible to cope. He put his head in his hands and wept. He thought about Courtney and how much he missed her. What if she had left him? The thought of losing her was unbearable. He lifted his head again, his eyes bleak, his face care worn. He didn't know what to do - he hadn't eaten, he'd forgotten how to cook anything; he couldn't be bothered even to try; he felt useless. He stared vacantly at his reflection, at the dark hollows of his eyes staring back at him, and shuddered.

He thought back to the summer - the days by the pool, the house had been full of laughter. He swiped at his eyes with the back of his hand to brush away the falling tears. His life with Courtney had been absolute bliss before the girls had arrived. It's true that life had become difficult then, but they'd got through it. Everything had changed when Gabrielle died. Thinking back, he realised that it was then that Courtney had begun to slip away from him. He had to get her back. It was clear-cut, he simply couldn't exist without her.

He checked his mobile, still no messages, nothing. He slammed it down on the coffee table, angry and frustrated.

He switched on the TV and rapidly flicked through the channels, pausing every so often for a couple of seconds, then moving on again. He remembered how much Courtney hated him doing that. She could never see the point of channel hopping, even during the ads. Suddenly, without warning, the TV switched itself off. He stopped and stared at the screen, a bewildered look on his face. He pressed the button on the remote, nothing; he stabbed at it again and again, still nothing.

'Great! Goddamn power cut now!' he said out loud, but the lights were still on. He looked around warily and then walked over to the TV set, jabbing at the button on the front of it, but it was completely dead. He kicked it and walked back to the couch, slumping down and hurling the remote onto the table as he went. He sighed, grabbing for his mobile; he would give it one last shot and try Courtney again. He raised the phone to his ear and as he did, he glanced down at the remote, just in time to see the infrared light on the end of it flash once, switching the TV back on. He dropped the phone in fright, staring in disbelief as the TV began to flick channels by itself. 'Give me that!' he shouted, making a grab for the remote. His heart was beating faster and faster. *Crap TV, it's not been working properly for ages. You pay cheap you get cheap - that's what Pop always used to say, and boy was he right.* Adam satisfied himself that this was all due to some faulty wiring. He sat back having finally rested on a movie channel, and with his arms folded defiantly, he began to watch.

That was when he heard the first bang. It had come from upstairs. He turned the volume up on the TV and tried to ignore it but his heart was beating so loudly in his chest that he could barely hear himself think. He tried to concentrate on the film and ten minutes passed. Suddenly, closer this time, there was another bang. He leapt off the couch and strode to the door. Once out in the hallway his glance flicked from corner to corner. He looked up the staircase but couldn't see anything in the gloom. It was then that he noticed a pair of shoes right in front of the door. They weren't Courtney's he thought; he hadn't noticed them earlier. They must be Alicia's, but he would have had to step over them when he'd arrived home. He put his hands up to his head again, feeling a headache coming on. He left the shoes where they were and went into the kitchen for a couple of aspirin. Returning to the lounge, he was relieved to find that the TV was still on the same channel. He had worked solidly for the past two days and was exhausted but couldn't bring himself to go to bed - not without Courtney. Checking his mobile again he swung his legs up on the couch and tried to relax. Before long fatigue began to get the better of him and his eyes grew heavy. He tried desperately to stay focused on the TV, but something else had caught his attention, something had flickered in the far corner of his vision. He turned his head and looked at the patio doors, but could only see his reflection - the rest of the room was empty. He got up to go and pull the drapes when suddenly, as he neared the doors, he felt the hairs on the back of his neck rise. He exhaled shakily, his breath hanging in the air in front of him as if it were a cold winter's day. He stared in horror at his reflection, terrified by the realisation that his was now not the only figure standing staring back at him from the window; just behind him, less than a metre back, he could see his nemesis.

'Alicia?' he stammered, still in denial. He saw her reach out and he felt her hand on his shoulder. She didn't speak - she just stared, wide-eyed and scared. He spun around to find - nothing - just the coffee table and the couch. He ran out into the hallway. 'Alicia is that you?' he called again.

His breathing was quick and erratic, his heart drumming faster than ever. He felt faint and perspiration sprang from his forehead. As he turned back towards the lounge however, he instinctively knew that the house was empty again - he couldn't sense anything or anyone. The cold feeling had left him. He was alone again.

He walked distractedly back to the lounge and closed the door behind him. The drapes still open he hurried over and pulled them shut with such force that they almost came off the rails. He returned to the couch and tried to settle down. He didn't want to believe what had just happened - he couldn't believe it. It was his imagination, it must be. He was overwrought, tired and anxious - that's what it was. That's what it always had been. He began to drift off to sleep again when he was suddenly awakened by what he was sure was the sound of knocking on the patio doors - and it was coming from outside. He froze, suddenly realising that the TV must have switched itself off again. He swallowed nervously. 'This has gone beyond a joke,' he said under his breath. He walked hesitantly towards the drapes and slowly pulled them apart - fearful of what he would find, still hoping for a plausible explanation. He closed his eyes, reassured himself again and then opened them. He felt a scream rising from the base of his throat as he realised he was seeing the same image he had seen before. It was her again, standing in the middle of the lawn, moving towards him with her arms outstretched. He jumped back in abject terror and as he did she vanished into thin air. He closed the drapes and leaned against the window, his eyes wide and heart pounding. Slowly he released his grip; he couldn't stay by the window all night. As he turned cautiously, his body racked with fear, he saw another flash out of the corner of his eye as the figure ran past the lounge door. Anger suddenly gripped him. Anger that he had been reduced to this quivering wreck. He ran to the door, determined not to be trifled with. He didn't like mind games and something was playing a cruel one with his. He slammed it shut, and as he did, so all of the doors upstairs spontaneously slammed one after the other, again and again; the noise was so deafening that it seemed to shake the very foundations of the house. He sank to the ground with his back against the door and his fingers jammed in his ears, like a small child who was being bellowed at by its parents.

'I can't hear anything - I'm imagining all this!' he shouted. 'It's all that crap that Courtney and Alicia have been talking - they've infected my brain.' But he knew that this wasn't true. He'd been fooling himself all along. He sat blinking slowly in the silence and darkness that followed.

Dad… an automatic thought came into his head, so clear that he couldn't ignore it, and yet still he was surrounded by silence - utter impenetrable silence.

I'm not hearing this.

Dad… the thought came clearer this time, and more forceful.

He cried out and clutched at his head in frustration. 'I can't hear you! I don't want to hear you! Leave me alone!'

As he said this, the silence was abruptly shattered as the kitchen door slammed. He jumped and clutched at his chest as fear gripped his upper body in a vice.

Oh but you can, you liar! You know who I am. The voice in his head retorted, *You've known all along - you're not going to ignore me any longer.*

'Leave me alone,' he whimpered.

Afraid and freezing cold he wanted to die right there and then. Where was the perfect life he had known, the carefree days, the laughter? It was all gone and now all he was left with was a nightmare and nobody to help him.

I'm not mad. I'm completely sane. I won't allow this to happen to me. He struggled to take control of his mind.

I'm still here… came the voice, stronger than ever.

He squeezed his eyes tightly shut, straining to banish the intruder from his head.

As he sat still, back straight against the door, he suddenly felt it being pushed from the outside. The handle pumped up and down frantically, the glass pane rattled in its wooden frame. There came two dull thuds as the door was kicked from the hallway.

He leapt up and jumped clear of it as it flew open. Spinning around and crouching low in a primitive battle stance, in a vain attempt to defend himself, he felt an icy blast pass straight through him. He stood rooted to the spot, letting out a desolate cry for help - desperately searching the shadows, trying to see something, anything - but there was nothing. He turned expecting to see something behind him, but there was just an empty black space. He had had enough; he was giving up. He held his hands up as if in surrender.

'What are you doing? Why are you doing this to me?' he cried, defeated.

He waited for the voice in his mind to tell him the reason - this time he was ready for it; he wanted to know, to put an end to his torture. He waited for what seemed like an age, but only moments had passed. He could see his breath in front of him again, like a ghostly white mist; he was not alone, the presence was all around him, but all he could hear was the sound of his heart beating in his chest. Maybe this was the end. He would spend eternity in nothingness, dead inside.

'Damn it!' he yelled, summoning up what seemed like the last of his strength, 'Tell me why? Please! I can't take this anymore.'

No sooner had the words left his lips when the atmosphere changed again and he was squinting in the bright artificial light of the lounge, where the TV was still blaring. His senses had awakened and he was standing beside the coffee table, his vision slowly coming back into focus. His limbs began to tingle as the blood surged back through them and he struggled to come to terms with what had just happened to him. He felt a sudden impulse to turn and look towards the patio doors. The drapes were open again and in the condensation that had formed on the glass he read the words that had appeared there. He was filled with the utmost dread.

Because I'm not Dead…

The words echoed in his head as he read them again, and as he stared in horror, the letters began to contort and slide down the windowpane, twisted and ghastly. His reaction was swift. He had to get out; he couldn't stay another moment. He ran to the table and grabbed his mobile. Within seconds he had found his coat and pulled open the front door only to find Ted Fraser standing on his doorstep. Adam jumped sky high at the shock of seeing him there.

'You OK Adam?'

'Just fine thanks Ted. Can't stop - got to get to work.' He hurried past him, his hands still shaking as he struggled to get the car key in the lock.

'It's just I heard banging and shouting,' Ted continued, his face etched with worry.

'Look Ted, got a few problems at the moment - nothing to concern yourself with,' Adam replied brusquely. 'Now if you don't mind, I'm in a hurry.'

He yanked open the car door and jumped in. Within seconds he was reversing down the drive at speed. Ted stood there perplexed, watching as the car disappeared round the corner; he turned then and walked gloomily back to his house.

Adam fumbled for his mobile as he drove erratically down the interstate, steering with one hand as he desperately searched through his phone book. Finally finding the number he was looking for, he called it. A hoarse irritated voice answered.

'It's me,' Adam said.

The voice on the other end fell silent.

Adam's emotions then spilled over, 'What in God's name have you done?' he bellowed.

Chapter 15

Courtney opened her eyes, bewildered at first. Then she remembered where she was, and turned to look at the clock on the bedside table. She could hear sounds of movement outside accompanied by Alicia's dulcet tones and then she heard the most welcome noise of all - Thelma's infectious laugh coming from the other end of the hallway. There was a knock on her door. 'Come in,' she sang out. Alicia walked in and immediately sat down on the edge of her bed.

'Nan's making fried breakfast - do you want one?'

Courtney smiled and nodded, throwing back the duvet and climbing out of bed. Alicia pulled open the drapes. 'Look, it's sunny again. Nan can't believe it,' she said excitedly.

'What are we doing today then?' Courtney said wandering off into the bathroom and splashing her face with water.

'Well Grandpa's gone off to get some shopping. I think we might be going out somewhere when he gets back.'

'Just give me a minute then and I'll just get showered and changed,' Courtney answered.

After breakfast the three women sat in the lounge sipping their second cup of coffee. The conversation was flowing freely between them now and the atmosphere was no longer tense. It was as if the upset from the previous night had been completely erased.

'I learned a long time ago,' Thelma said, 'that you have to think of tomorrow as a new day.'

'That's what I always think,' Courtney answered, sinking back into the chair. 'You can't live in the past, you have to constantly move on. I always live in hope that things will get better, that things will go back to how they were.'

'That's a positive approach - I like it,' Thelma nodded her approval.

'I don't know what to do,' Courtney then said. 'I've had about six missed calls from Adam. He's left a couple of frantic messages as well. I don't think anything's happened, he's just convinced I've left him.'

'You ought to call him,' Thelma said. 'You need to talk about everything - get it all straightened out and try and give him the benefit of the doubt.'

'But how can I after he's lied to me? It's not the first time. What he's told me all along about Sarah's death was a barefaced lie. I really don't feel like talking to him at all, I've seen him in a different light.'

'Oh come on,' Thelma replied with a wry smile, 'you don't strike me as a shrinking violet Courtney. You should confront him about it, make him squirm. It's not the end of the world - it's just details. I'm not saying he was right to do it though, don't get me wrong.'

Courtney sighed, 'I will call him, but not now, later. He's at work anyway.'

Alicia hadn't spoken yet; she was sat watching the TV, not really taking any notice of their conversation.

'Thelma,' Courtney said, feeling braver, 'I couldn't help but notice your photographs on top of the fireplace. I hope you'll forgive me for asking, but that young boy - who is he?'

'John said you'd been looking at the photographs,' she replied still smiling, 'I'm surprised you didn't ask me yesterday actually. He looks just like Sarah and me doesn't he.'

'Well I didn't like to say anything yesterday,' Courtney said. 'You know what with...'

'I know,' Thelma interjected. She paused then momentarily. 'He was my son...Benjamin died when he was only eleven. He fell from a climbing frame at school. The internal bleeding was so bad and he suffered extensive blood loss from his broken leg.'

'Thelma, that's awful!' Courtney felt emotion flooding over her again, but kept hold of it, tight in her chest.

'We couldn't wrap him in cotton wool,' Thelma then said her voice tinged with sadness. 'He was a haemophiliac. You always run that risk with a son with haemophilia.'

Courtney took another sip of her coffee. 'It's inherited isn't it?' she said.

'Yes,' Thelma replied, a far away look in her eyes. 'That's why I feel so desperately guilty sometimes. Ben inherited it from me. I'm a carrier - my father was a haemophiliac and I blame myself entirely. I knew the risk when we decided to try for a family. Some would say I was selfish, let my desire for children outweigh the importance of their quality of life. Yes, I suppose I was selfish,' she concluded.

Courtney didn't answer; she didn't know what to say.

'Look at me now,' Thelma said with a defeated look on her face, 'I have nothing. Both of my children are dead, even one of my granddaughters. Perhaps that's the punishment I deserve for wanting them so badly - it's not like I didn't know the risks. John and I discussed it on many occasions.' Her lip quivered as her emotions got the better of her again.

'Thelma, if this is upsetting you, shouldn't we talk about something else?' Courtney leaned forward and put her hands around hers, giving them a sympathetic squeeze.

'No no,' she reassured, 'I don't mind talking about it - that's as long as you don't mind a silly old woman blubbering.'

Courtney had heard about haemophilia, but she didn't really know an awful lot about it. Thelma explained about the clotting factors in the body, and how if one of those is missing it can cause prolonged bleeding to occur.

'Usually it's not a life-threatening problem,' she said, 'but if a sufferer with severe haemophilia has an accident, it can prove a lot more serious and difficult to treat than for a person without it. My father lived to a ripe old age. I suppose that's why I never thought of it as a serious problem back then - seeing him so healthy. But then he never suffered a serious injury. I mean he had bumps and bruises growing up, don't get me wrong, and injections. My goodness, his arm used to look like he'd been beaten up after his annual flu jab, even though they always used to do it just beneath the skin for safety's sake.'

Thelma got up from the couch and stretched. She wandered back into the kitchen and filled up the percolator again.

'Seems a shame to be stuck indoors, in this weather,' she called out. 'We'll go to Fairmount Park once John gets back.'

'That would be great,' Courtney said from the doorway, 'I thought you might need these,' she said with a smile handing

Thelma the cups. 'It is only males that have haemophilia isn't it?' she then said.

'Yes that's right,' Thelma replied, pouring the coffee. 'Females are just carriers, that's what makes you feel the most guilt. The fact that you never have to suffer from the effects of the illness, but your child does. I remember I used to pray every night that I'd have another girl when I was pregnant with Ben, but it wasn't to be. I often think that Sarah was so fortunate having twin girls, I mean what are the chances of that happening?'

'Well fifty fifty for a girl,' Courtney replied, 'but I wouldn't like to say for twins, especially identical, so she was a carrier too?'

'Oh yes,' Thelma said passing Courtney her coffee. 'It terrified her. She was beside herself when she first met Adam,' she paused suddenly, as if something else had just occurred to her, 'but it was strange really, when she actually came to getting pregnant, she never mentioned it. She must have blocked it from her mind.'

'God it must have been a terrible worry for her,' Courtney answered, as they walked back through to the lounge together. Courtney looked at Alicia still slumped on the end of the couch and it suddenly dawned on her that she must be a carrier too.

Her thoughts were distracted then as the front door opened and in walked John carrying bags groaning with food. 'Oh good,' Thelma said happily, 'You're back, we can go out now.'

'Well give us a chance to put this lot away first, I can only do a hundred and one things at once,' he answered sarcastically with a grin.

As they drove through the leafy tree-lined streets, Courtney was preoccupied. She had checked her mobile again to find another missed call from Adam. She had placed it quickly back in her handbag before Alicia or Thelma had a chance to get on at her to return his call. She couldn't right at that moment - she had too much else on her mind and she instinctively knew that she shouldn't bring up that morning's topic of conversation again that day, especially in front of Alicia. Adam had known this too. Something else he had deliberately kept from her. She wondered how many other secrets there must be. How could he have lived with himself? How could he have gazed into her eyes all of those times? How could she have not noticed? All she had seen was his seeming honesty, passion and devotion; there was no hint of the shadows that lurked in his past, no sense of guilt or wanting. She had believed she had known him completely, inside and out, now she thought that she could never really have known him at all.

They had already passed the Liberty Bell and Independence Hall. Thelma gesticulated animatedly in the front of the car. She spoke proudly about her hometown and Courtney wished that she could have been in a better frame of mind to properly appreciate the depth of her and John's knowledge. As they passed City Hall she saw its mighty towering pillars, the grandeur of its classically styled architecture, drawing people from all corners of the city to see it. She gazed at the impressive building as the car waited at a set of traffic lights. She looked at the people gathered on its steps, dwarfed by its size, some taking photographs, others just talking, huddled in small groups. She saw a couple kissing on the sidewalk, just yards from the car, their bodies entwined in an intimate embrace - they seemed so happy. She felt a lump in her throat as she recognised a feeling of jealousy rising within her that she could never have imagined experiencing before. This was wrong, *she* had always been the one envied by others, 'one of the lucky ones' her friends had always said, as they reinforced her feelings of self-satisfaction. Unlike her, her friends had never found their perfect partners, their soul mates. Instead they would move from one man to another, with monotonous regularity, the trend being to discard each along the way like a worn out pair of shoes; always wanting a better pair than they had previously had, a more fashionable pair. She had felt secure and safe in the knowledge that she would never have to find anybody new. She would never be the one crying on a friend's shoulder. Oh no, that was her job, she was supposed to be that shoulder.

Thelma continued to point out the sites as they passed them. Alicia had protested at first about the enthusiasm of their two tour guides, as she said that she had heard the same stories a thousand times, but she was silenced by her grandmother, who pointed out to her that Courtney hadn't been to Philly before. It was true that they had a wealth of knowledge between them.

314

Thelma had talked endlessly about the signing of the declaration of independence as they passed Independence Hall. John had told of how at one time Philadelphia had been the capital of the United States. Courtney had always been interested in history - she found she could completely immerse herself in it. She liked to imagine what life would have been like at the time, especially enjoying the individual stories of the people back then. She often pitied them for the hardships that they had to endure and it made her appreciate everything that she had. Both she and Adam liked to watch any history documentaries that came on the TV; it had been something else they'd had in common, along with their love of books. Adam would have enjoyed this tour she thought to herself, even though he'd lived there before. Perhaps that was why she couldn't concentrate on what was being said or properly appreciate anything she saw, he wasn't there to enjoy it with her. Maybe they weren't as incompatible as she had thought. She was so confused, one minute she hated him, when she remembered the lies and the deceit, the next minute her chest ached from the pain of missing him. Courtney looked at Alicia and smiled, trying to disguise the sadness in her eyes. Thelma suddenly announced that the Philadelphia Museum of Art was fast approaching on Courtney's side of the car, so she looked dutifully out of the window. Thelma was shifting from side to side craning her neck round looking for the next point of interest as they went. They were now driving along Ben Franklin Parkway and according to Alicia they were nearing their destination. They had decided first to stop somewhere along Kelly Drive to have the picnic lunch that Thelma had prepared for them. There had been some dispute between Thelma and John as to which beauty spot they ought to stop at, apparently there were so many of them in that area. John had wanted to go to his favourite spot down at Boathouse Row, but this idea had been rejected out of hand by the overbearing Thelma. It had become apparent to Courtney that John would not protest once overruled, as all he seemed interested in was a relatively quiet life.

They parked up in an area surrounded by towering leafy trees, which shaded the picnic tables on this unusually sunny day in Philadelphia. The area was practically empty and as far as

Courtney could see there was only one other family tucking into their lunch.

Thelma said that it was the perfect day to come here, as it was midweek, and the children were still at school. Courtney felt warm in the back of the car and was so comfortable that she was reluctant to move. She stretched as she got out of the car, fastening her coat against the biting wind. The fresh air cleared her head and she looked around her, immediately noticing a large ornate water fountain right in the centre of the expanse of lush green grass in front of them.

'What a beautiful spot!' she exclaimed.

They discussed where they should sit. John spotted a table right down by the river's edge, some way off from the other picnickers.

'We used to come here all the time, this exact same place,' Alicia said thoughtfully. 'Nan used to bring us all the time when we were younger. There's another bigger picnic area that's easier to get to further back along Kelly Drive, with a covered grandstand, but Nan only took us there once - said it was too crowded and we never came again.'

Thelma shot her a frosty look. 'And what are you doing still smoking?' she said, scolding her granddaughter who had just lit up. 'I thought you were going to try and give up.'

'Well my life *has* been a bit stressful lately,' Alicia replied. 'You can't blame me.' Thelma didn't say anything further; she just muttered something under her breath.

The picnic bag was on the table within seconds as Thelma quickly forgot their quarrel. She had everything in that bag - paper plates, cutlery, cups, and a whole host of different foods. There was chicken, savoury rice, potato salad, Courtney was amazed. She hadn't been for a picnic herself since she had been young, when her mother and father used to take her out to Silver Springs near her childhood home in Leesburg. As they ate, John talked about the river, apparently called the Schuylkill; it was one of the two main rivers in Philadelphia, the other being the Delaware. It was an intensely relaxing and peaceful place despite the fact that the towpath along the snaking riverbank was a hive of activity. People on rollerblades and push bikes whizzed by along the winding paved path that seemed to stretch as far as the eye could see. It was four miles long and ended at the Falls Bridge, John had confirmed as he gnawed on a chicken leg. Courtney looked ahead as she ate. She felt a warm feeling inside as she looked at the tranquil scene before her. Although John had told them it wasn't the cleanest river, it still reflected the blue sky as the turbulent water flowed rapidly, towards its unknown destination. She had been told that this was the perfect place for people watching, and it was true. Just along from where they were sat, was a fisherman. She watched him casting his line, waiting patiently for what seemed like an age, and then there was a sudden flurry of activity that caught all of their attention. He was up out of his seat, his rod back, reeling in frantically. From his effort it looked as if he'd caught some sort of monster, but when she saw it, it was no bigger than a small sprat!

'It's hard to believe we're in the middle of a huge city - all this open space, the trees, the river, it's amazing,' she said.

Thelma nodded vigorously and beamed, delighted that her choice of venue had met with Courtney's approval.

Thelma then asked everyone what they wanted to do next.

Alicia said that she wanted to go somewhere she hadn't been before, just to make it a bit more exciting for her.

'Well we're off for a cheesesteak tonight,' Thelma said, busily packing the empty plates and cups back into the picnic bag.

'Yes well that's hardly different is it!' Alicia scoffed. 'Only this time I guess I can drink.'

'Well no you can't actually young lady,' Thelma replied, 'you're still under the age limit.'

Courtney blushed as Thelma looked over at her for back up. 'You haven't!' she then said horrified. 'You've been letting her drink?' Courtney tried to respond but was interrupted by Alicia.

'You saw me drinking at the funeral Nan,' she said tossing her hair back in annoyance. 'Get off my case, I'm trying to enjoy myself here!'

'Well Courtney can't drink,' Thelma reprimanded. 'You should be supporting her right now!'

Courtney held her hands up, 'Honestly,' she said, 'I don't mind as long as she doesn't get blind drunk.'

'Well quite,' Thelma said zipping up the bag.

'Do you know what,' she then said her eyes suddenly brightening, 'I've just thought, why don't we drive into Fairmount Park and visit the Japanese House and Garden.' John shrugged his shoulders.

Alicia smiled; she had just realised why Thelma had suggested it.

'I was supposed to go on a trip there when I was in ninth grade wasn't I, when we were at Philly High?'

Thelma nodded 'Yes and you were sick and had to be sent home. Gaby went and you didn't.'

'That was it,' Alicia laughed. 'It's not that I particularly wanted to go - it was just that she did and I didn't.'

They all got up and trudged across the grassland back to the parking lot, and before too long were driving along Kelly Drive again. As John turned into Fairmount Park, just moments later, Courtney was amazed by the sight that lay before her. There was a great expanse of trees and the greenest grass she had ever seen. Flowers of every colour imaginable bloomed along the expansive paved pathway that wound through the centre of the park - it was like entering a different world, with the sunlight making it seem even more picturesque. It was totally different in Florida, she thought. There wasn't anything like this - the only parks they had on this scale were the theme parks, where the pace was fast, money flowed freely and tensions ran high. Here it was completely peaceful with people from every walk of life enjoying themselves the old fashioned way, appreciating the simple things in life, strolling with their dog, jogging or just sitting and relaxing on one of the park's many benches.

Courtney glanced over at Alicia as John drove on through the park, passing under the trees which were leaning over from either side of the road. Their heavy branches met in the centre, beckoning them, celebrating their arrival as though they were a bride and bride groom and the trees the wedding guests - their arms linked as they cheered the happy couple on their way to their honeymoon.

She noticed that Alicia's expression had suddenly become troubled along with the sunshine's departure. Her mood had darkened - she had been reminded of the reality of her apparent isolation. She was a long way away from the idyllic setting that the rest of them now felt part of.

'What is it?' Courtney asked.

Thelma bristled in the front of the car and turned to look at her granddaughter - her head jolting like a startled animal, as if her own enjoyment rested entirely on the shoulders of her companions.

Instead of offering some quickly thought up, flippant explanation, Alicia was unable to hide her true feelings.

'You don't understand how awful my life is now!' she blurted out. 'It's been unbearable since the day she died - but then my life was unbearable when she was alive!'

'What do you mean?' Courtney asked cautiously, afraid of what her stepdaughter was about to divulge.

'You know Gabrielle always had boyfriends,' Alicia continued bitterly, 'she used to go here with them sometimes. She had sex with one of them by that fountain over there. I remember her telling me now - she always used to brag all the time. She just didn't understand what I was going through - how could she?'

Silence hung awkwardly in the air. Thelma had obviously decided to block out the conversation by beginning to make small talk with John, keen that he too didn't hear his granddaughter's words. Then it was just Courtney and Alicia.

'Do you mean the rape?' Courtney said, having guessed straight away what all this was about.

'Yeah,' Alicia answered bleakly. 'She didn't even stop to consider my feelings - she just considered me to be emotionally deficient and liked to rub it in that she wasn't. *Look at what I can do. Look at all the men I can get!* I hated her for it. I wished her dead once - no not once, many times. Guess my wish came true,' she said, a stray tear rolling down her cheek.

It was not the first time Courtney had heard Alicia speak like this about Gabrielle, only now it seemed somehow more poignant.

'She was so beautiful and she knew it - and how she loved it!' Alicia's mouth contorted with hatred and her voice broke with emotion.

'But that's the part that I don't understand,' Courtney interjected. 'You were just as beautiful as she was - you looked identical. I would have killed, probably still would, to look as good as you do.'

'But what's the good of it when you don't have anything to back it up,' she replied, her voice hollow. 'You say I look beautiful, but I don't feel it, I never have done. I've always felt ugly and disgusting - rotten to the core since that night. It shows in my face, in the way that I carry myself, in my mind. I'm the most hideous creature that ever lived and breathed, so it makes no difference to me what anybody else says.'

'But didn't you realise when you looked at her that you were looking at a carbon copy of yourself?' Courtney answered. 'I've often thought that if I had had an identical twin it would have solved a lot of my own insecurities about my appearance. I would have been able to see myself as others saw me.'

'It doesn't work like that though,' Alicia replied in a frustrated tone. 'When I looked at her, I just saw Gabrielle. That's all. No-one else.'

There was silence between them again as Alicia wiped her eyes. Thelma's voice was still droning relentlessly from the front of the car.

'And you know what is the worst thing of all?' Alicia said, gazing sorrowfully back at Courtney. 'It's Brad. He told me I was beautiful all the time. I'd finally found a man who I could trust, who I could imagine spending the rest of my life with. I'd even started to believe what he said about me, because he made me feel beautiful, you see? Now he's dying and he was my one chance - my only chance.'

'Oh don't say that Alicia,' Courtney said forcefully, 'Brad may pull through. Please don't give up hope - I'm not going to.' She pulled her stepdaughter to her. 'Just hold on to his words. He was telling you the truth and you should try to let what he said filter through and replace your negative thoughts. It's what he would want. He loves you remember. It's going to be all right, I promise.'

Courtney decided then that she would call the hospital when they got back for another update. They had already called before they arrived to find that there had been no change in his condition, and that he was still in a deep coma. Maybe Adam would be able to tell them more if she could bring herself to call

320

him later. She knew she had to, she hadn't had any more missed calls since the morning, but she knew that it was almost certainly because he was at work. Thelma suddenly spoke up from the front of the car, having caught the tail end of the conversation, wanting to reiterate Courtney's point that everything would be all right in the end. Courtney hoped with all her heart that it would be all right but this time she really wasn't sure. It was difficult to know what to say for the best; she was tired of lying. She had always believed before in some kind of God, one who looked down on everyone from on high, helping people who were in need, directing people to each other and intervening to prevent accidents and injury. She had realised lately that the reality was often quite the total opposite. Everyone was on their own and she feared that she had lost the strong faith that she had once had. It wasn't even just shaky now, it had gone completely. It made her feel cold and empty inside.

As they came back into sunlight, Alicia suddenly noticed the 'tree house' - as she called it. It distracted her from herself for a moment and seemed to snap her back into a more positive mood. 'That must be it! It's unreal isn't it? Gabrielle used to tell me about a house with a tree growing through the middle of it - I never believed her though.'

'Oh the Tree House, yeah, didn't you know?' John said, cheered by his granddaughter's sudden lift in spirits. 'That was built back in the 1840's.'

'Perhaps she wasn't as big a liar as I thought she was then! I remember the time when she said she found a kitten in a trash can and took it to her friend's house. That wasn't true, and she used to always tell our friends stuff about Mom, making up stories of what she did when she was drunk - always exaggerating.' Alicia turned to Courtney with a smirk on her face.

'She used to tell our friends that Mom was always drunk, running around naked in the garden and all sorts.'

Courtney half laughed, embarrassed, 'Where did that come from?'

.

'Stop talking ill of the dead,' Thelma suddenly said, visibly disturbed again by the turn in conversation. 'They're not here to defend themselves.'

'But I know a lot of what she said wasn't true, cos I was there remember,' Alicia said indignantly.

'Yes well, that's enough now, thank you.' Thelma's tone was now distinctly agitated. Alicia looked over at Courtney with a mock guilty look on her face, obviously now in a mischievous mood. They didn't speak again after that, until they reached the Japanese House and Garden. John had remained silent the whole time, just staring straight ahead, concentrating on where he was going in.

He only spoke once and that was to ask Thelma where they ought to park. Neither of them were big fans of walking as they were both in their early seventies and couldn't cope with long distances. John had told them yesterday that his sciatica was playing up.

They arrived, parked up and walked into the garden, which was surrounded by imposing dark green poplar trees. It was cooler in the shade. In the centre of the clearing there was a large ornamental lake almost entirely covered in red and green lily pads, and around the banks of the lake, green moss grew in abundance, covering the surrounding grass land. A fine mist swirled above the water, giving the whole place a mysterious atmosphere. They began their slow walk along the towpath that led round to the Japanese house that was nestling against the far bank of the lake. The house, with its earthy brown sloping roof, complimented its surroundings perfectly. A number of people had gathered there, and it was then that Courtney noticed that the house was actually built on a wooden platform over part of the lake. They walked towards the gathering and at the centre of the group they saw a small man dressed in traditional Japanese costume standing by the water's edge. He was holding a wooden dish containing what looked like some sort of fish food.

'Oh I've heard about this!' Thelma exclaimed excitedly. 'Look at the water.'

They found a free spot on the stage. Leaning out as far as they dared they saw, swimming towards the man, a dozen or so large golden fish.

'Koi carp,' Thelma announced.

Courtney was amazed as she listened to the man explain how the fish had been trained to swim to the house for feeding. He gave everyone the opportunity to throw some food in for the fish, whose frantic mouths were opening and closing just above the surface of the water.

Courtney said how she wished she'd brought her camera, but then she hadn't intended this trip to be a sightseeing one.

She still hadn't found out nearly as much information as she needed; she'd found out about the haemophilia, but didn't see how that was particularly relevant. All it had done was confirm that Adam hadn't told her the whole truth. She was floundering, a bit like the fish in the water. It was proving very difficult. She wondered again about Sarah and remembered what had happened round at Liza's house. She reminded herself that she was here for a purpose and she just had to bide her time.

Their tour guide then led them into the house, explaining that at one time on that site there had been a three hundred year old Japanese temple called Nioman. John stroked his chin, absorbing all of the facts and figures like a sponge. Courtney thought it was amazing how they were so interested - always keen to find out more about their beloved hometown. This in spite of the fact that they didn't enjoy the best of health and had experienced so much heartache in their lives. She wondered how they had managed to cope. That was the way it should be, she thought. Life was for living. You should make the most of every moment - after all you never know when it could be your last. She shuddered at that thought, and turned her attention back to the tour.

'Does this house have a name?' Alicia piped up after he had finished speaking.

'Yes Miss, it's called Shofuso, which means Pine Breeze Villa,' he replied.

Alicia grinned at her nan.

The tour was almost at an end. As he led them back out onto the wooden platform a keen breeze blew across the lake. Courtney shuddered as the clouds started to roll in - it appeared that the weather was about to turn. Thelma and John thanked the guide and they all walked back along the towpath to the car. Alicia

323

began chatting excitedly as she lit another cigarette and she talked about that evening - she was looking forward to going out for the cheesesteak. She said that she would take Courtney down South Street, which apparently was where all the good nightlife could be found, and where she and Gabrielle had often gone clubbing.

'I don't know about that,' Thelma said. 'I think your grandpa and I are a little old for clubbing.'

'Well that's OK, you two can go home and we'll get a cab back later,' Alicia said with a cheeky grin.

Courtney gave Alicia a disapproving look, which was meant to remind her of the reason that they had gone to Philadelphia in the first place.

As they rounded the corner that led out of the clearing, Courtney noticed a young couple walking towards them. She didn't think anything of it until Thelma let out a cry - she had stopped dead in her tracks, staring straight ahead.

'It's not her Thelma,' John said harshly, catching hold of his wife's arm to steady her, but she didn't seem to hear him, and rushed forward. As Courtney took a closer look she could see the striking resemblance.

'Sarah?' Thelma said desperately - the likeness truly was uncanny.

Alicia's lip began to tremble and John went over to the young woman, apologising profusely. He explained to her that it was an unfortunate case of mistaken identity. The woman herself was visibly shaken and her partner quite rattled - clearly annoyed by the incident.

Courtney walked forward and apologised again on their behalf - her tone was authoritative and firm. She felt anger towards this man and looked at him with distaste. She didn't see that John should have to grovel any further on his wife's behalf. Quite clearly this man had not lost a loved one or he would have been more understanding. Maybe one day she thought he'd remember this incident and remember how unsympathetic he'd been.

'C'mon John, let's go. You've said enough,' she said taking his arm. Courtney felt a deep affection for Thelma and John at that moment as though they were her own family and in a roundabout way she supposed that they were. 'Will you be OK to drive John, or would you like me to? I'm insured for any vehicle,' she added as they neared the car. Thelma wasn't crying now. She was just extremely quiet as if she had internalised everything that had just happened and was trying to deal with yet another setback. John assured Courtney that he would be all right, but thanked her anyway for her kindness. Alicia was upset by the incident, more so for seeing her nan in such a state. Her grandparents were like her bedrock; they were the one constant, the only people that had always been there. As long as they were happy she was happy.

'I'm so sorry,' Thelma said as they were driving out of Fairmount Park. 'I'd been having such a great time too, and wasn't the house wonderful?' she tried to make light of the incident.

Courtney spoke hesitantly, 'It must be so hard for you both.'

'I don't care what anyone says,' Thelma replied. 'When you survive your children you have to live with so much guilt. If only I could turn the clock back...'

'You can't think like that love,' John said putting a supportive hand on her knee. 'We made the decisions that we made at the time. We could never have predicted everything that has happened since - least of all Sarah.'

'I know,' she replied sorrowfully. 'She's with me all the time Courtney. She was with us today. A parent's bond with a child is never broken - it transcends even death. You'll find that when your baby's born.'

'You feel her presence then?' Courtney pressed her further. Alicia looked at her quizzically wondering where her line of questioning would lead, but Courtney had no intention of mentioning what had happened in their house with Sally Harris.

'Oh yes,' Thelma said with conviction, 'I talk to her too sometimes. It was so strong today I think that's why I reacted like that when I saw the girl. I was convinced in that split second, utterly convinced.'

'I often wonder about what the church preaches, you know about people that take their own life,' John suddenly said. 'I'd always respected the church and the teachings of the bible, but since Sarah died a lot of it didn't make any sense to me anymore. The way we were treated at her funeral. I mean the pastor was respectful to us but you could see it in his eyes that he didn't think she had gone to heaven. People didn't know what to say to us and would cross the street rather than have to speak to us. It's such a taboo really I suppose, something people would rather not have to face. Believe me we didn't want to face it either, but we had to.'

'Adam went to the funeral didn't he?' Courtney then said, suddenly realising that this was something else that she had never thought to ask her husband. Something else she hadn't wanted to know.

'Yes he came back for the funeral. He was in a terrible state, terrible,' John said.

Courtney felt as if a knife had just been thrust into her chest. Tears welled up in her eyes; she felt helpless, as if all her power had just been taken from her and she felt anger towards Adam. *He was never supposed to have loved her! I was the first and only one he's ever truly loved.*

'He was still in love with her then?' She managed to force the words out. Silence. The light was failing now; the streetlights were coming on.

'Do you really want me to answer that question?' Thelma said sensing the awkwardness of the moment.

'I can't hide from the truth for ever, can I,' she replied, trying to disguise her feelings. She turned to look at Alicia who was gazing out of the window, trying to avoid eye contact with her. She felt totally alone at that moment.

'He was,' Thelma finally said frankly, 'but he hadn't met you then. That's all history and we have to concentrate on what's happening now. That's why you and Adam need to sort everything out, you have to look to the future.'

Courtney didn't answer her; she couldn't right then. Everything she had believed was slowly being overturned in her mind. She needed time to think.

'I think we have a lot of talking to do,' Thelma then said. 'John, I'm tired of all the secrets, all the lies. It's time we were honest about everything.'

Courtney heard her but it was a voice in the distance. She didn't feel she was strong enough to cope with any more of the truth. She could feel her soul drifting into a dark pit of despair.

'That goes for you too Alicia,' John added. 'There's a lot you don't know either and I think you're old enough now.'

Hearing this Courtney felt a glimmer of hope and realised that she was no longer alone. Alicia wasn't a conspirator, she was on her side. She didn't know any of this either - how could she? She was only eleven when her mother died. Courtney felt a warm hand reach out then and take hold of hers. She looked round suddenly feeling herself back in the here and now and strong enough to fight on. Her eyes met Alicia's. Their mutual understanding and strong bond of unity had returned.

'Not now Thelma,' John said softly. 'Tonight, if everyone's agreeable, when we go out for dinner we'll try and find a quiet table. You're family too now Courtney and you both deserve to know the truth.'

Chapter 16

Nobody spoke for the rest of the journey; nobody needed to - they were waiting. The darkness that had enveloped the city was now scattered by the sudden brightness of the streetlights. Coloured lasers pulsed into the night sky like an irregular heartbeat, illuminating the crowded streets below, now bustling with people. Courtney saw the tall office buildings in the distance, their windows beads of light in uniform rows. Music drifted in through Alicia's window. There was a confused mixture of scents in the night air, different types of food blending together. Courtney looked at her watch. It was only six o'clock, and yet it seemed like the middle of the night. They still had to get showered and changed and she still had to call Adam.

The car came to an abrupt halt; Courtney realised that she must have drifted off.

'What time is it?' she said wearily, straining to see out of the window into the gloom outside. She recognised her surroundings then, although the darkness had at first made them seem unfamiliar. They were home.

'You've only been asleep about ten minutes,' Alicia said, as she stepped out of the car onto the sidewalk.

'I think a shower will wake me up,' Courtney said, gathering her handbag and throwing the strap haphazardly over her shoulder as she slid across the cold leather seats to the open door.

Thelma looked at her watch; she had a faraway look on her face, as if her bubbly robust facade had finally begun to show cracks. John seemed less troubled. In a moment they were back inside in the warm and light flooded through the hallway as John flicked the switch. They stood a little uneasily, gathered together by the lounge doorway.

'I think we should leave in about an hour if we can,' Thelma said taking charge of the situation. John nodded and turned into the kitchen to put the picnic bag on the side. He opened it and began to unload it.

'Don't worry about that now John, I'll see to that,' Thelma said brushing past Courtney in an attempt to get into the kitchen to shoo her husband back out again.

'Right then, let's go,' Courtney said with a sigh. She had a strong craving at that moment for a cigarette; it was overwhelming. Alicia walked wearily down the hallway towards her room with barely enough energy to pick her feet up as she went, scuffing them aimlessly across the carpet.

'Alicia,' Courtney called after her. She ran and stood beside her. 'I'm gonna call your dad now. Did you want to speak to him to ask him about Brad?'

'You can,' she answered in monotone. She stopped and turned to Courtney, her expression grave. Checking that her grandparents were out of earshot she spoke in a low whisper, 'What do you think they're gonna tell us tonight? I'm so worried.'

'I don't know,' Courtney replied with another sigh, 'but whatever they do tell us, remember I'm always here for you.' She took Alicia's hand in hers. Courtney could feel the tears beginning to well in her eyes again. It was the emotion of everything that had happened over the last few weeks, the unnerving anticipation of what still might happen, and the fact that her brain was telling her that if she just had one cigarette, everything would be fine again. She couldn't speak. She released Alicia's hand, which fell limply as she did so. Her mind too was so preoccupied that her every movement was an effort.

'Give me a knock when you're ready,' Alicia said with what almost seemed to be her last breath.

Courtney nodded and turned away quickly, knowing that she was about to be engulfed by another tide of emotion.

She walked into her room and as she closed the door she sank to the floor, unable to hold herself up anymore and no longer needing to. She felt the relief of finally being alone, of finally being able to cry. She thought about what Thelma had told her about Sarah and how her fantasy about the circumstances of their entire marriage had been destroyed in just one sentence. She had existed in a protective cocoon, a web of lies that she had created for herself. She had lived and breathed it every day, never wondering, never thinking for one moment that she was wrong. She wept, her head resting on her knees. She felt a pain in her chest so intense that she could barely breathe, then came the nausea. She gripped hold of the edge of her bed and managed to pull herself up to her feet, turning blindly, her vision blurred by her tears. She rushed into the bathroom, her head hanging over the basin and began to retch. As she cried she was suddenly interrupted by the sound of her mobile ringing again. *Adam.* She managed to compose herself and splashed her face with cold water, blotting it dry on the hand towel. She rushed into the bedroom and as she picked up the mobile and saw his name on the display, a missed call. Her anger had been replaced by different feelings. She felt guilty and wanted him again. She pressed the button, her heart beginning to beat faster, 'Adam,' she stammered as he answered.

There was momentary silence at the other end of the line.

'Why haven't you returned my calls?' he finally said, enraged, but his wavering tone revealing his vulnerability.

'I'm sorry,' she said hesitantly, 'we've been on a day trip today.'

'How are your parents?' he asked, 'Alicia having fun is she?' His sarcastic tone rang in her ears. The lies, all the lies and *I'm lying to him now.* She covered the receiver with her hand so that she could regain her composure and stifle the tears that threatened to overflow.

'We're OK. Listen Adam,' she said beginning to move the phone away from her lips, 'I'm going to have to go - I'll be back soon.'

He didn't reply. As she slowly lowered the phone all she could hear was the sound of him crying. She dropped the phone on the bed, almost out of fright, shocked. She could still hear him; she retrieved it.

'Courtney, you have to come back! I'm dying without you. I'm at work - I can't sleep, I can't eat.' She heard him but the lies had made her cynical. Now, instead of feeling pity or love, she just imagined him saying the same to Sarah, the same words replaying at a different point in time, like an old record. He had probably said it to her countless times, probably even after their divorce. *He was so in love with her, so devastated when she died. Bitch.*

'Adam,' she said, her tone more forceful, 'we're coming back in a couple of days. What on earth's the matter with you?'

'Problems, big problems,' he mumbled beginning to regain his composure, 'you don't want to know. I just can't cope that's all, I need you back here with me.'

Courtney was stunned, and in her confused state struggled to make sense of the situation. 'I've only gone away for a few days. You've left me on my own in the house before - what's the big deal? I was afraid and you still left me alone.'

'This isn't about me being afraid,' he snapped back, 'and it's not about something you and Alicia *thought* you heard in the house. It's about me and you, it's about your defiance. I don't know what's happening anymore.'

She was angry now. How could she ever agree with him or have any hope of their partnership ever getting back to what it was, when he flatly denied everything she had ever told him. He wasn't even open to suggestion - he wasn't even attempting to humour her anymore.

'Look, I'll come back when I'm good and ready, and not before. There's a lot you don't know about me and I'm sure as hell there's a lot I don't know about you!' She paused then, on the brink of saying something that she knew she shouldn't. He went to answer but began to cough violently; she cut across him before he had a chance to recover.

'Have you heard how Brad is?' she asked instead.

'No change,' he finally said in a matter of fact tone. 'He's stable, but still in a progressive vegetative state.'

'Oh God,' she exclaimed, thinking then about Alicia and how she would break the bad news.

'Anyway,' he jumped in, interrupting her train of thought, his tone sounding agitated again, as if he had suddenly remembered the conversation that had gone before. 'We've had an argument, a difference of opinion, but we can sort it out. We just need to talk about it. So much has gone on, it's enough to put a strain on any relationship. I don't care about anyone else, I only care about you.'

'Oh so much so that you've made me out to be completely mad!' she replied sarcastically.

'That's not the case. I don't think you're mad, I just think you've been under a lot of stress.' He leaned forward in his office chair his hand clawing through his hair in desperation, 'We're the same you and me; we're soul mates remember. That's what you always told me before - we belong together. Oh please honey, can't you come back sooner? I've made mistakes recently, I realise that now. Maybe I'd started to take you for granted, I can see that now. Please give me another chance.'

'Adam,' she said shaking her head in disbelief, 'we haven't split up, why can't you get that through your thick skull? Why do you keeping talking all this crap? I've only gone away for a few days.'

He was dumfounded, staring straight ahead, his eyes wild with anxiety as he watched shadows from passing vehicles dance across the far wall of his clinical office. He reached forward and picked up the gilt framed photograph of his wife and stroked her hair, his eyes filling with tears again as the previous night's events replayed through his mind like a waking nightmare.

He blew his nose vigorously.

'Courtney?' he implored, gazing into her joyful, blissful eyes as he put the photograph back. 'Are you still there?'

'You getting a cold or crying again?' she asked, her tone softening slightly.

'Bit of both I think,' he answered dejected. 'We have so much to talk about.'

'You have so much to tell me?' she replied. 'I'm not stupid Adam - I know there's something going on. I just don't know what.'

'I don't know either honey,' he answered, his words filling the empty room. He wanted to talk to her for longer but she cut him short after that, saying that she had to go and take a shower. At least he had got to speak to her; at least they hadn't parted on bad terms. He blew his nose again and started to cough. Walking over to the water dispenser that stood next to the one rather sick looking pot plant that he had in the room, he noticed how everything seemed sparse and neglected - lacking in character.

He took a sip of water and looked down at his watch. Time seemed to have stopped; every minute seemed like an hour. Waiting. He wondered if it was like that for Courtney. Probably not, he concluded - she was going on day trips and no doubt would be going somewhere tonight. He wished he could be with her. He felt so alone. He couldn't bring himself to tell her about the previous night - his pride wouldn't let him and he had an overriding sense of shame. She was right. She had always been right but the stakes were too high. He walked aimlessly back to his desk, back in the chair where he sat to consult with his patients, to give them the news they either wanted to hear or that they had been dreading. He felt powerful there, their notes in front of him. He would stroke his chin, considering his verdict, after often just a cursory glance down a page. Death to some, life to others, a budget to balance, age to consider. He had always prided himself on being fair. His mind free of worry before, he would devote his full attention to his work, knowing that his personal life was rock solid, dependable, loving. He no longer felt he could give his work his full attention. He wasn't even on duty and yet he was sat there mulling over everything in his mind. It felt as if he was on a downward spiral and he was afraid that he would never get out of it, that nothing could ever be normal again. His eyes were heavy, his body drained, sickness was beginning to creep in. His head lolled forward as his exhausted mind still fought to stay awake. He couldn't let his guard down. He tried desperately to focus on his watch. It was then that there was a loud knock on his office door.

Courtney stood on the sidewalk, waiting whilst John parked up. Thelma rubbed her hands together vigorously, blowing on them and stamping her feet, trying to stay warm. Courtney couldn't understand how she could possibly be cold; she had a thick scarf around her neck, her big red coat on, and some heavy-duty gloves. *Perhaps the blood gets thinner as you get older - although she's got enough insulation round her stomach to keep the both of us warm.* She reprimanded herself for the unkind thought she'd just had; she got a lot of those. They would just pop automatically into her head, without any warning. Alicia stood slightly apart from them, looking up the street, drawing rapidly on a cigarette. She seemed anxious. Courtney was too, but she was also hungry. They were in a side street, a very ordinary street, and the building they were stood outside was like any typical shop front, with flats built above it. The restaurant, for all the fuss Thelma and John had made about it, was nothing like Courtney had expected. However they had assured her that Gerry's Steaks and Hoagies did by far the best cheesesteak in town. John appeared before too much longer, his brown suede coat buttoned up to his neck and his nose and cheeks red from the cold. He smiled at them uncertainly.

'Right lets go get our cheesesteaks,' he said enthusiastically, holding the door open for the others, who were all eager to get back into the warm. The restaurant was busy; there was a tumult of voices and the sound of a fruit machine churning out somebody's winnings. Courtney looked around at the food customers were eating and noticed that they all appeared to be eating the same - what she guessed must be a cheesesteak in a roll, accompanied by a side of fries. She dug Alicia in the ribs. 'Doesn't look like there's much to choose from!' she said in feigned surprise.

Alicia shook her head and laughed, 'You can get *different* cheesesteaks here, and besides, this is Philadelphia - what else could you possibly want?'

John was already speaking with the manager who then proceeded to show them to a table in the corner. Courtney and Alicia sat next to each other with John and Thelma opposite.

A beer advertisement hung on the wall by the table and the off white chipped wallpaper was peeling off in places, revealing the plaster just above the table line where the chairs had apparently been scraped continuously against the wall.

The manager was poised to take their order. Courtney had only glanced at the menu but given that the choice was a little limited for those who didn't want the cheesesteak, it was more a case of whether you wanted fries or onion rings to go with it.

'You just want to try the plain cheesesteak don't you?' Alicia said taking charge. 'So you don't want the hoagie, the grinder or the stromboli then?'

'The what?' Courtney replied a confused look on her face. The others, including the manager all laughed. It was obviously one of those Philly 'in' jokes, Courtney thought, looking embarrassed. 'Yeah I'll try the cheesesteak, with a side of fries,' she said. The others all followed suit, ordering the plain cheesesteak and a round of drinks, all alcoholic apart from Courtney's (despite her desire for a glass of wine.)

'You're not going for the belly filler tonight then Nan?' Alicia said cheekily to Thelma who was sat rather awkwardly opposite her.

'No,' Thelma said, a faraway look on her face, 'I'm not feeling all that hungry to be honest. Did you manage to get through to Adam in the end Courtney?'

Courtney explained how she had spoken to him and that he had begged her to come back early.

'But why?' Thelma said a little surprised. 'You've only gone away for a short break, just to get away from it all. Wasn't he interested in what we'd all been up to?'

Alicia and Courtney exchanged glances and Alicia's eyes were sending silent signals that they ought to come clean. Courtney thought for a moment and decided that if Thelma and John were prepared to reveal this big family secret tonight, the least she could do was tell them the truth also. 'The thing is,' she began hesitantly, looking first at John and then at Thelma, 'he doesn't actually know that we're here.' She paused, waiting for a reaction. John's brow furrowed with concern.

'Why ever not? I don't understand,' Thelma said, a baffled look on her face.

'I told him that we were going to stay with my parents. I didn't want him to become suspicious,' she replied.

John shook his head, his eyes narrowing. 'But what could he possibly be suspicious of? I don't understand.'

Courtney took another sip of her drink and at that moment a waiter arrived at their table with steaming plates piled high with cheesesteaks and fries. 'Wow that looks great!' she exclaimed, turning her attention to the meal in front of her. She turned to John not wanting to appear as if she was avoiding the issue. 'John, shall we discuss this after we've eaten? I might get indigestion otherwise.' He nodded, already loading his fork with fries.

She saw Alicia then pick up her cheesesteak and take a big satisfying bite. Following her lead she carefully lifted hers to her mouth and bit first through the roll and then on to the juicy pieces of beef inside. The others were all staring at her, waiting to see her reaction, she savoured the flavour, it was slightly salty for her taste, but extremely tender all the same, and it virtually melted in her mouth.

'I love it,' she declared. The others, relieved, were then able to get back to eating theirs. 'I like the cheese too, unusual flavour.'

They ordered more drinks, Alicia asking for another large glass of white wine. Soon after the drinks arrived, Courtney sank back into her seat, unable to eat another bite. There was an awkward silence. It was as if her stay of execution was now over. The plates were cleared away promptly by the waiter and Alicia lit a cigarette, much to the disapproval of Thelma, who was powerless to stop her.

'So why would Adam have been suspicious?' John finally asked.

Courtney sighed and looked uneasily at him.

'The thing is,' she began slowly, 'we actually came here because we wanted to find out if you knew of somebody,' she paused again. 'Adam's been acting so suspiciously lately to be honest. A lot has happened as you know, probably a lot of it's the stress of losing Gabrielle, but there's something I just can't put my finger on.'

John's expression was still one of abject confusion. 'But I still don't understand why you couldn't have told him you were coming here,' he said.

Thelma looked searchingly at Courtney and Alicia, shifting her gaze from one to the other.

'Because the person we're looking for lives here,' Courtney said. She waited, butterflies rising in her stomach; they were on the brink of discovering if their entire trip had been worthwhile. 'We're looking for someone called Ruben.'

No sooner were the words out of her mouth, when she realised that Thelma and John knew exactly who he was. Their expressions told the story. Thelma looked shocked and John's lower lip began to tremble.

'I don't believe this,' he exclaimed, his eyes showing relief rather than concern. 'That's exactly who we were going to tell you about tonight.'

Thelma caught hold of his hand. Alicia stared at them, her eyes wide, fumbling for her cigarettes, lighting another one automatically. 'Wait!' she suddenly cried, signalling to the waiter, 'I'm going to need another drink first.'

Courtney's heart raced with anticipation as she gazed searchingly at Thelma and John ...*we were right to come here all along*. The wine arrived. Alicia took a swig, slamming the glass back down on the table. 'Right Nan, Grandpa, we're ready. You can tell us,' she said.

Thelma reached forward and took Alicia's free hand in hers. She breathed out slowly as though she was psyching herself up to be able to reveal what had obviously been such a heavy burden for so many years.

'Alicia and Courtney,' she said glancing across at Courtney, making sure that she felt included in the conversation. She then rested her gaze on Alicia and there it stayed.

'I know why your mother took her own life,' she said her voice hoarse and quiet. Courtney's eyes were fixed on Thelma, noting every change in her expression; she glanced over at John whose face mirrored that of his wife's.

'Your mother had an affair,' Thelma said in a business like fashion. Alicia's brow furrowed and she pulled her hand free from her grandmother's tight grip.

'An affair?' she said incredulously. 'But why?'

'I don't know for sure,' Thelma replied, she paused then, taking a moment to reflect before continuing. 'I was angry with her of course - both of us were. I mean how could she have ruined an otherwise happy marriage, ruining any chance you girls had of growing up in a stable family. It broke our heart. *Ruben!*' Her voice spat his name and her face twisted with disgust. 'He was supposed to be your father's friend; a doctor he was. Huh!' She scoffed at the idea, shaking her head. 'It went on for years, even after your father had found out and left her because of it. I suppose in the end she realised what a terrible mistake she'd made. She had obviously fallen head over heels for this man, but the excitement wasn't there for him anymore. There was no longer the danger of sleeping with his friend's wife. Now that she was available he didn't want her. He'd probably found himself some other bed partner by then.' She paused again.

'We don't know for sure that he found someone else,' John added.

'Well who cares!' Thelma cried. 'It's irrelevant now, but he still ruined our daughter's life. I often think how things could have been different, if only she hadn't fallen for that man.' Tears of frustration rolled down her cheeks, leaving a streak in her heavy make-up.

Alicia looked puzzled. 'I can't believe it. I never thought Mom was the type. She didn't leave a note though did she.'

'Are you OK?' Courtney reached over and lightly touched Alicia's shaking hand, just to remind her that she was there.

'Yes I'm all right. I'm just amazed really, utterly amazed. I was always led to believe it was Dad's fault that they'd split up and all along it was hers. How could she have lied to us like that? She filled our minds with poison about him, and all to cover her dirty little secret. Gabrielle never got over finding her like that, with the empty whisky bottle and empty packets of pills strewn across the floor by her bed. I even used to feel sorry for her. I hated her for leaving us like that, but I thought that her heart was so broken over Dad that she just couldn't live without him. I even forgave her.'

'She made a big mistake that's true,' Thelma replied sorrowfully. 'That's why we thought you ought to know the truth. Not that we wanted you to hate your mother, far from it. We don't hate her - we hate what she did, but we still love her. She's still our daughter.'

'That's why we didn't want to tell you until you were older sweetheart,' John said. 'Everyone when they're young thinks of their mother as being perfect, almost superhuman. She can cope with anything or do anything. It's only when you get older that you realise the truth - all humans are prone to weakness. Nobody's perfect and often we give in to temptation, and that's usually when the trouble starts. In your mother's case she was lucky to get away with it for as long as she did. She only admitted it to us about a year before she died.'

'So when did the affair start?' Courtney asked.

'She said it was when you girls were one year old,' Thelma replied.

Alicia shook her head. 'I'm disgusted frankly,' she said bitterly. 'So that's the secret then - that Mom was a whore?'

'No no,' John's face was etched with anxiety. 'Please don't think that way.'

'But it's true isn't it?' she cried, getting up from her seat and flinging her coat over her arm. 'I need some air,' she said angrily, fighting back the tears.

John patted Thelma's arm protectively. By now they had attracted the attention of the other diners.

'Do you think we should all go?' John said.

'No, give her a minute - I'll go and check on her in a second,' Courtney replied. Her mind was in utter confusion. This was not what she had been expecting to find out about Ruben. Although the news was devastating for Alicia, it didn't answer the questions that she still had. All that it had done was to confirm what she had already suspected since earlier on that day, that it had obviously been Sarah who had ended the marriage. If it hadn't been for her going astray and her killing herself, then she and Adam would still be together now.

'Can I just ask you something?' Courtney said, looking at Thelma.

'When Sarah died, why didn't Adam take the girls with him?'

Thelma didn't answer straight away, as if searching for the right words to say.

'It was me, all me,' she said breathing slowly and deliberately. 'Adam truly was a good father, utterly devoted to those two girls. He had wanted to take them with him.'

'So why didn't he?' Courtney added.

Thelma sighed. 'When I lost my Sarah, I couldn't bear to lose the girls as well. I managed to persuade him shall we say.'

'It wasn't just that,' her husband interrupted. 'The girls were settled at their schools. They'd just started at Chestnut Grove when their mother died - all their friends were there. It was a good school, the girls were extremely academic. You might not realise it now but they were straight A students through middle school.'

'I thought they boarded?' Courtney said, confused again.

'They did board for a time at Philly High,' Thelma replied. 'They were in 9th grade when they started there and getting to be a bit of a handful if the truth be known. John and I couldn't cope with them. All the loud music and boys turning up twenty-four seven at the house. Gabrielle told me her best friend was boarding there and the idea grew from that. I lived to regret it though, after what happened to Alicia. That poor girl has been through so much. I wouldn't be surprised if she never wants to look me in the eye again after today. I had to tell her - you do believe that?' she implored, her eyes moistening again.

'Of course,' Courtney agreed. 'If there's something I've learned over the last few weeks, it's that you can't hide from the truth, as much as you'd like to.' She paused momentarily, 'It must have been a heavy burden for you to carry all these years.'

Thelma nodded. There was an awkward silence; John was craning his neck trying to see where Alicia had gone. Courtney thought that she ought to go outside to see how she was. She didn't really know what to say - she felt utterly desolate, empty inside. She hadn't found out anything too damning or scandalous. All she had established was what hadn't been said - he hadn't lied about the boarding school. She had always thought of him as a cad who had dumped his wife for a better life, moved off down South looking for the single life where he wouldn't have to stay making love to the same woman. She had always comforted herself with the thought that their love life must have gone stale, that Sarah obviously hadn't been any good in bed. It used to ease the pain of knowing that he had produced two daughters with her. She had told herself on many occasions that he must have been drunk when they'd made love and that he probably couldn't remember it. Now everything had been turned on its head and she was suddenly faced with the fact that he obviously wasn't the villain that she had previously made him out to be. *Sarah was! What a bitch! And she wasn't even anything to look at.* Courtney felt they were no closer to finding any answers and she felt now as if the whole trip had just caused them all more pain. Why were there strange things happening in

340

her house? Why was she still afraid to set foot in there? She realised that her mind had drifted off and noticed that Thelma was waving a hand in front of her face. She snapped back to the restaurant, dazed, her head aching.

'One other thing I wanted to ask you both, if you don't mind,' Courtney said slowly. 'Did you ever meet this Ruben?'

An expression of disparagement returned to Thelma's face. 'No,' she announced, almost theatrically. 'I'd never have wanted to set eyes on him either. Sarah was very sneaky with her affair; she kept him away from her family. When I did find out, she assured me that the children had never been introduced to him. Good job too!' she added her tone now aggressive. 'I don't think I could have ever forgiven her if she'd dragged those poor girls into it. They'd suffered enough.'

Courtney nodded and smiled faintly, content that she had exhausted all the possibilities.

She tried to give them some money towards the food, which had left a rather sour taste in her mouth, but they waved it away, happy to pay the entire bill. She made her way outside, buttoning up her coat as she went, preparing for the cold autumn night and the freezing gust of wind that came as she opened the door. She found Alicia kicking stones into the road, as a child would do. Her hands were shaking from the cold as she took a long drag from her cigarette.

'You OK?' Courtney asked. She could tell that Alicia had been crying.

'I just can't believe that they didn't tell me before!' she began in earnest. 'I mean, all that time I wasted caring about the fact that Mom had killed herself and I needn't have bothered. She deserved to die for what she did - she just couldn't keep her legs closed. It makes me sick and I should know - it's not worth it. Look at my experience of sex, that was definitely not worth losing my family over. It almost ruined my life - that kind of depravity makes me sick!' She spat out the words like venom from a cobra.

'Alicia, not all sexual relationships are like that. Some are very loving.'

'Yeah but Mom wasn't happy with just one was she? She had to go and put it about like a prostitute! She made Dad leave - it was *her fault!*' The tears rolled down her face.

Courtney sighed, at a loss really to know what to say. She was hurting too, but for different reasons.

'It takes two,' she urged, trying to pacify her. 'This Ruben was as much to blame as she was. He knew she was married - he was your dad's friend! I mean you can't get much lower than that.'

Alicia's face twisted with revulsion and hatred as she lit another cigarette.

'You didn't know any of this before did you?' she then said accusingly. 'It must have come as a bit of a shock to you too.'

Courtney tried to play down her feelings. 'Yes it did really. It was more a case of what your father left out rather than not telling the truth. But it's true he didn't tell me, which is still not being completely honest. I never asked him much about your mom, so really I guess I'm partly to blame. But how do I know that if I had asked he would have told me the truth? He lied to me about how your mom died.' She paused, looking far off into the distance, almost for inspiration. 'There has to be something else.'

'What do you mean?' Alicia replied vacantly.

'Well think about it. Everything that's happened to us in the house. You were so scared that you ran out into the night and were found in the hospital grounds where Jennifer ended up dead the same night. I was driven out of the house and that night Brad tried to kill himself.' She paused as if her mind, moving like the arm in a jukebox, had finally rested on the record it wanted to select.

'Yes that's the irony,' Alicia said through her tears. 'I can't believe the one man I thought I could love ended up trying to do himself over - exactly the same way as Mom. I never told him about it either.' She sniffed and wiped her hand across her face.

Courtney's heart began to race; this was too much of a coincidence. 'My God, so the only people who knew about this at the time…'

Alicia interrupted her. 'Yeah, were me, Nanny, Grandpa, Gabrielle and Dad.'

'We have to go home!' Courtney suddenly announced. 'Tomorrow.'

'No, not until I've confronted that asshole who ruined Mom and Dad's marriage,' Alicia replied, resolute.

'What good would it do?' Courtney rebuked. 'You're only going to torture yourself more than you have already.'

Alicia shook her head, 'I'm sorry, but I have to see him. I have to make sure he knows what a mess he made of everything.'

'I suspect he knows that already,' Courtney replied. 'I mean, he must know your mom's dead.'

Alicia wouldn't be swayed.

'All right, tomorrow morning we'll pay him a visit,' Courtney relented, reaching inside the fold of her coat and pulling out the piece of paper where she had written his address and phone number. 'If we go and have a look, then will you be happy?' Alicia nodded hesitantly. 'But we must tell your grandparents we're leaving tomorrow afternoon,' Courtney continued. 'We need to try and get on a flight too - it's such short notice. Oh God!' she exclaimed stamping her foot in frustration.

That night back in her Philadelphia bed, Courtney lay awake deep in thought. She stared up at the ceiling, blinking slowly in the half-light. They had managed to get a couple of seats on an outbound flight for one o'clock the following day. She hadn't called Adam again that evening, as she would see him the next day. Something at the back of her mind was telling her not to - let him suffer a little bit more, catch him unawares and not give him the opportunity to hide anything else from her. She was sure that he would do if he was given any advance warning.

She couldn't get Brad out of her mind - the coincidence of his suicide attempt. She thought about Sarah. How could Ruben have been the key? He was just her 'bit on the side', a home-wrecker. It certainly didn't account for all the strange goings on in the house. The thought occurred to her that perhaps Sarah's spirit had just sent her on a wild goose chase, so that Alicia would find out the truth about her affair. Maybe in the afterlife she had to come clean about her sins before she could be forgiven. Courtney was angry now; she had started to think of Sarah as the poor trampled on housewife, dowdy, and a martyr to her cause…whatever that was. Now she had returned from the grave to trample her down. That was it. She had been duped all along; Sarah just wanted her to find out how much Adam had loved her, to find out how wrong she had been for believing that she was the one and only true love in his life. *All that crap about Ruben and finding the key. The key to my unhappiness maybe.*

Her mind then switched back, lifted momentarily from its downward spiral of bitterness and self-pity, as Alicia's voice played in her mind, as clear as if she was standing beside her.
'Yes that is a sad irony….the one man I thought that I could love ended up trying to do himself over, exactly the same way as Mom…..'
She was supposed to meet him that night. Her eyes darted fervently around the room as everything began to fall into place. *What if? No.* She shook her head wanting instantly to disregard the thought. *But it makes sense, the house…everything.*
But why didn't Sally Harris detect her spirit in the house?
She swallowed nervously, and sat bolt upright in bed as the sudden awful realisation hit her. She blurted the words out, immediately clamping her hand over her mouth; *no-one must hear.*

Chapter 17

Courtney had barely slept that night, drifting in and out of a light and troubled sleep. She was rudely awakened by the piercing tone of her mobile's built in alarm, exacerbating the pounding headache she had developed during the night. Her mind got caught in a loop again, trying to make sense of everything, trying to arrive at a tangible conclusion and not succeeding. She swallowed some painkillers that she found at the bottom of her chaotic handbag. Having dressed and splashed her face with water in an attempt to revive herself, she managed to struggle out for breakfast. There was a sombre atmosphere at the table and conversation was strained. Alicia was giving 'yes' and 'no' answers to her grandmother's enquiries about her state of health and mind. Courtney was preoccupied. She didn't feel hungry but she dutifully ate the waffles and scrambled eggs Thelma had prepared. As she wiped at the corners of her mouth with her serviette she made eye contact with Thelma. They were troubled eyes looking back at her, empty and full of regret. She wished then that their trip hadn't had to end so abruptly and on such a bitter note - as there had been good moments. She excused herself from the table; conscious of the time and aware that Alicia had already gone back to her room to finish packing her things. She reassured Thelma that Alicia would come round eventually, given time, and that she would speak to her again when they got home.

With only two hours before they were due to leave for the airport, Courtney and Alicia finally left Thelma and John's house, in search of Ruben. All Courtney had was the scrappy piece of paper with an address on it, but Alicia had said that she knew where it was. Ironically it was only about three blocks from Thelma and John's house and within walking distance. Courtney hadn't told them where they were going - she didn't want to twist the knife in any deeper than it already had been.

They turned the corner out of John and Thelma's road. Courtney still didn't see what their going to his house would achieve. She was only doing it to appease Alicia who was still visibly shaken by the news she had received the night before. Her whole countenance seemed different today. Her shoulders were hunched and her expression grave. She had seen glimpses of the real Alicia throughout their trip but this wasn't her - she hated seeing her like this. An oppressive atmosphere hung in the air between them as they walked. She felt that Alicia had finally retreated within herself, and that the rage must now be seething deep down inside of her. She was like a time bomb ready to go off at any moment, given the right trigger. She feared that going to see Ruben would do just that and serve no positive purpose whatsoever. She had resigned herself to it though and knew that Alicia wouldn't back down - all her efforts to dissuade her had been fruitless. As they walked along the road in silence, they passed a public garden, which was set on an island in the middle of the road, surrounded by a low wrought iron fence. Courtney noticed a young mother sitting inside on a bench, cooing over her newborn baby. Seemingly she didn't have a care in the world. Shaded by tall leafy trees, the morning sunlight filtered through a gap in the leaves' protective canopy creating a perfect picture. Courtney looked longingly at them. They were blissfully unaware of her and Alicia, alone in their own magical world - the mother tickling the baby's tummy and laughing as he kicked his legs and waved his hands excitedly in response. Courtney looked away, the sight too painful for her. Somehow she felt as if she had abandoned her baby.

'If we do get in there, I swear I'm just going to smack him or something,' Alicia suddenly said.

'Don't be stupid,' Courtney rebuked. 'You want to get a criminal record now to add to our problems? This whole idea is stupid if you ask me! I mean, what are the chances of him being home on a week day morning, had you thought about that?'

Alicia made a grunting noise and then continued as if Courtney had said nothing.

'It's just the thought, you know, of what Mom did. I can't get it out of my head, ever since last night, and I've got enough to worry about already.'

'If we do see him,' Courtney sighed. 'I just think this is going to make you feel worse, especially if he's the way that Thelma has described him - a charmer with absolutely no remorse. I can imagine him being all smarmy, all smiles, or making some quip about your mom that's going to upset you even more.'

'I'll cross that bridge. It's just something I feel I have to do - I'm sorry OK! You can wait outside if you want.' Alicia looked at her for the first time since they'd left the house.

'No way!' Courtney said, 'I'm not letting you go in there on your own. You can forget that.'

They had been walking for some time now and Courtney's mind was still a blur. She had been torturing herself all morning and all night, wondering if maybe, just maybe she was right about what she had thought the previous night. She couldn't bring herself to say Sarah's name, not even in her mind, so overwhelming was her fear that if she even uttered it, it would confirm everything and make it seem like reality. She knew that she had to suppress her suspicions until she had some concrete proof. Maybe when they got back Adam would come clean, maybe she would walk in to find him a gibbering wreck - at least then they would finally have some common ground she thought. She couldn't mention anything to Alicia - not now. It would send her over the edge. It was important, but her evidence was wholly circumstantial. She couldn't throw a theory like that into the arena when it was just a gut feeling. Besides, she didn't want to risk someone else thinking she was mad.

'It's round the next corner I think - yeah, cos this road is Belmont Street. My friend Gemma used to live here,' Alicia said, pausing as they reached the crossroads and looking to her right. 'This is it - Hartford Street. I was sure it was.'

Courtney looked at her, a worried expression on her face. Now that they were actually in the road, now that they were on his doorstep, she started to feel a dreadful anxiety welling up inside her, 'This is a mistake,' she said. 'I seriously think we should go back.'

Alicia refused and they argued on the sidewalk for a couple more minutes; Courtney finally admitted defeat. 'OK you win, but you dare do or say anything that gets us both in trouble and I'll…' she exhaled heavily. 'Where is it then? I can't see the numbers on the doors.'

'Here,' Alicia replied, pointing up at the black door - just up the steps from where they were standing.

'Are you sure?' Courtney checked back on the piece of paper.

'2114, yeah look!' Alicia confirmed triumphantly. 'See, we didn't have to worry about not catching him at home! It's not his home is it? It looks like his surgery.'

Courtney noticed the brass plaques by the side of the door and swallowed nervously. They ventured up the stone steps, trying to make out the lettering as they neared the door. It was already apparent that he was not the only doctor in the building - there were four plaques in total. Their glance came to rest on the second one down, 'Ruben Moya,' Courtney said, she paused, 'Moya,' she then repeated, realising they had just discovered his surname. 'My God!' she exclaimed, 'Look at all the letters after his name.' She paused again. 'What do we do now? There's a buzzer for each doctor but we can't exactly ring his and say that we've got an appointment. We'll have to find some other way of getting in. We'll have to wait.'

They retreated back down to the sidewalk and after only a couple of minutes (although it seemed like an eternity) someone opened the door and came out. They hurried back up the steps and slipped in behind them, before the door closed again.

A palatial hallway stretched before them and there was a steep staircase ahead. They saw an empty reception area to the immediate left and what looked like one of the doctor's offices to the left of the staircase. They stood rooted to the spot for a moment, not knowing what to do next. It was then that Alicia noticed the floor plan on the wall and they saw the names of the doctors and their corresponding floor numbers. Ruben Moya was on the third floor. They began a cautious ascent of the staircase, speaking in a low whisper as they ventured further up; they passed the first floor and then the second. They had decided between them that Courtney would do the talking, or rather Courtney had told Alicia that she would be the one who spoke, and that Alicia was to keep quiet.

They finally arrived at the third floor. Courtney paused to catch her breath, taking a moment to admire the expensive looking paintings on the wall and the highly polished antique dresser on which stood a vase of fresh flowers. Ahead of them there was only one door on which "Waiting Room" was written in ornate lettering. They hadn't seen anybody since they had entered the building and as they neared the door Courtney could hear a woman's authoritative voice coming from somewhere within the room. They paused by the door. Courtney checked one last time that Alicia wanted to go ahead with this; she nodded vehemently. She took a deep breath and turned the handle. The door scraped slightly against the carpet as it opened. It was a light airy room with a row of pink soft back chairs and a table in the centre on which was a neat pile of magazines. As they turned to their right they saw the reception desk. The woman glared at them like a pointy-faced guard dog.

'Can I help you?' the receptionist asked - annoyed but slightly curious. 'It's just that you didn't buzz up.'

'Oh sorry about that,' Courtney replied. 'I pressed the wrong button on the door.'

She waved them over and asked them to take a seat.

'Can I take your name?' Her face up close revealed her age. It was heavily lined and her bleached blonde hair, darker at the roots, was scraped into an immaculate bun, which was piled high on top of her head. She peered at them, waiting for a reply, heavy eyelids partially obscuring her watery green eyes.

'Courtney Buchanan,' she replied, clearing her throat nervously. The receptionist jotted it down and smiled politely, suspicion hovering in her eyes.

'Now how can I help you?'

'Well, I've just moved into the area you see,' Courtney began. 'Dr Moya was recommended to me by a friend who's been treated by him before.'

The receptionist nodded and smiled bleakly. 'You do realise that this is a private clinic?' she then added. 'A consultation with him doesn't come cheap.'

'What are you saying?' Courtney replied, offended by her implication.

'I'm sorry but I have to make that clear to all potential new patients. It's standard procedure,' she replied, with condescension in her voice.

'Well if money had been a problem I wouldn't have come here in the first place,' Courtney replied indignantly.

'Quite, quite,' the receptionist relented. 'So you'd like to make an appointment with Dr Moya? How soon would you like that to be?'

'I really would like to see him today if possible. I'm pregnant you see and I'm a bit worried because I think I may have a clot in one of my legs - it's become very swollen.'

The receptionist looked at her incredulously, a faint look of amusement on her face.

'Madam, I don't mean to be rude, but I don't think that you'll be needing Dr Moya's services.' She raised her hand to stifle a laugh.

Courtney glared back at her, 'And why would that be?'

'This is a fertility clinic. Dr Moya is a leading expert in the field.'

Courtney could feel herself becoming hot with embarrassment. Panic set in - she had to think quickly. Alicia had her heart set on this. *How the hell are we gonna get to him now*?

Alicia began to rise from her seat; Courtney put her arm out instinctively to stop her, whatever she was planning to do. In the moments that followed it seemed as though everything was happening in slow motion. Alicia began to lean over the desk.

'What are you doing?' Courtney heard herself say. The telephone was ringing. The receptionist raised her hand to forestall any further enquiries whilst she answered the call.

'Yes, this is Dr Moya's office,' the receptionist sang out.

'Hi Susan, how are you?... No I'm afraid he isn't - didn't he tell you? Obviously not... yes, he had to go to Florida yesterday - urgent business he said...'

Courtney was up and out of her seat before the receptionist could say another word. She didn't need to.

'Yes I've had to call all his patients and rearrange their appointments...'

They heard the receptionist's voice grow fainter as they hurriedly closed the door behind them.

Courtney had called Thelma from the cab when they had first left the airport, just to let her know that they had arrived back safely. Her voice had sounded strained and distant - perhaps she was still upset about the way their trip had ended. She watched the old familiar landscape as their cab sped down the interstate. She had mentioned to the driver that she was pregnant and he was driving as if she was about to give birth! She wanted to tell the cab driver to slow down as she wasn't in a hurry, and now that they were back the urgency had gone. She needed to snatch every moment she could, every second seemed important. She needed time to plan ahead, time to plan everything she was going to say and how she was going to say it. She saw a sign for Kissimmee; they were almost there. It was too soon. They were too close to the house - the house she used to call home. She had to face her fears again, face her suspicions. It was time for the truth. Her feeling of anticipation was intense. Overwhelming. The cab swung into Bay View Grove. Alicia hadn't said much since they got off the plane. Courtney had tried to make conversation in the cab at first but then she stopped, realising that she didn't really feel like talking either. She felt comfortable with the silence between them, and for once didn't feel that she had to fill it by speaking for the sake of speaking. The cab pulled up outside the house with a sudden screech of brakes; she winced at the noise as she had wanted their arrival to be as discreet as possible. Ted Fraser was walking down his drive. *Oh no!* He was the last person she wanted to see right now. He always seemed to appear whenever they were coming or going - almost as if he waited for some activity before deciding to go out himself. On this occasion he just smiled faintly and waved, heading off up the road. He didn't wait on the sidewalk for them to get out of the cab; he just walked on. Perhaps she had offended him in some way. Their bags now out of the cab, they stood side by side at the foot of the driveway, eyeing the car in the driveway, neither wanting to be the first to cross the threshold.

Courtney was the first to approach the front door. The house hadn't changed since the last time she saw it. It still seemed imposing and gloomy in the waning daylight, radiating an unearthly chill - discouraging people from entering. It was now nothing like the sunny, incandescent, white picket fence residence it had always been in Courtney's minds eye. She felt an overwhelming wave of sadness as she put her key in the lock, as though the key's penetration had awakened the house. Its very essence seeping through the walls, enveloping them. Warning them. Stay away.

She opened the door slowly and stepped into the hallway - Alicia followed closely behind. She knew that any moment she would be face to face with Adam. Alicia made a move to the foot of the staircase but Courtney signalled to her to come back. 'Hello!' she called out at the top of her voice. She listened intently but she could hear nothing. There was silence.

Courtney grabbed hold of Alicia's arm; she immediately pulled free and whipped her head round in annoyance. 'What are you doing?' she said, 'I just want to go put my bag in my room, - what's the big deal?'

'I just thought we could go and sit in the lounge for a minute. You can make us both a coffee,' Courtney replied.

Alicia rolled her eyes. 'I've been sat down for hours! I quite fancy standing up for a bit actually, if that's all right with you.'

'Well after you've made the coffee you can go and stand out the back and smoke then,' Courtney said. 'You haven't had a chance to do that for a while either.'

Alicia didn't answer and wandered into the kitchen. Courtney approached the lounge door, expecting a reprieve, a stay of execution. She would just sit down for a moment, gather her thoughts and prepare for Adam to walk in. She would try to talk to him rationally about everything, without arguing again. She still had a headache and she was tired. Evening was already drawing in. She pushed open the door and immediately jumped, putting her hand up to her chest in fright. Adam was sat facing the door, not uttering a word, staring straight ahead - his arms folded.

'Adam, why didn't you say anything; didn't you hear us in the hallway? You had to go and make me jump - my nerves are shot now!' She stood in the doorway, not wanting to move any closer. He looked back at her suspiciously, his legs crossed, still wearing his white doctor's coat. But he can't be on the way to work, she thought. His hair was dishevelled and he was unshaven. He coughed then, breaking the silence, a dry, painful sounding cough. He looked old she thought.

'Had a good time at your parents' house then?' he finally said.

'We didn't go there,' she answered.

'I know you didn't. I'm glad you've admitted to it - I thought you were gonna stand there and lie to me again.'

'You're a fine one to talk about lying!' she replied, her anger bubbling over as she remembered everything she had gone through in Philadelphia and all the things she had discovered about her husband from other people.

'Why did you tell me that Sarah had died in a car crash? Why didn't you tell me she'd killed herself? What was the point in that? I can't believe that you looked me in the eyes all those times when we said we'd have no secrets! You promised me and all the time you'd been lying. God what a sucker I must have been!'

'That's not the issue here,' he retorted. 'The fact is that you went flying off to Philadelphia, behind my back, sneaking around, checking up on me, trying to dig up as many old skeletons as you could.'

'Well it's just as well I did,' she replied hands on hips. 'I'd never have found out anything from you that's for sure! You've been acting weird for ages Adam. I mean look at the state of you now! Have you looked in the mirror lately? And why on earth are you wearing your doctor's coat when you've finished work? You always go straight upstairs and change when you get in, unless you're just about to go that is?'

'I only just got back,' he said angrily. 'Don't you want to know why I lied about Sarah? Well that's what you asked me.'

'You were the one who changed the subject!' she yelled.

'Listen,' he leaned back exhausted. 'If you want the honest truth - this is the honest truth.' She rolled her eyes and regarded him sceptically.

'I was embarrassed.' He made eye contact with her. 'It was too horrible - I didn't want anything to taint our marriage. I didn't want you to think that she'd killed herself because I left her.'

'No, don't worry. I already know that she killed herself because she felt guilty and because Ruben dumped her - wanted nothing more to do with her,' Courtney said sarcastically.

Adam bristled.

'Thelma and John's words, not mine,' she added.

'So what else do you know then?' he said.

'I know that Sarah was a carrier...'

'Of haemophilia?' he interrupted, 'I'm impressed with your detective work. So you know about Ruben then? Well I already knew that. You see, when you went to his offices this morning, you made a big mistake - you left your name. His secretary called him and he called me. When I called Thelma and John it put them in an awkward situation and I managed to find out eventually that you were flying home today. I mean, what if something had happened to you both Courtney? What if you'd been in a crash? How the hell would I have ever found you? You never told me where you were going; I didn't have a clue. How selfish is that? I've been worried sick about you.'

'Worried what I'd find out more like,' she snapped back. 'Listen, Alicia's in the kitchen so keep your voice down. I want her to be tested to find out if she's a carrier or not. I think it's only fair that she knows - nobody's ever told her.'

Adam didn't answer her. A figure had stepped out of the shadows behind her, by the window; she sensed a movement coming nearer to her. She spun round to see a man standing there but she couldn't make out his face properly in the half-light. As he drew closer she saw him - his hollow face, prominent cheekbones, feminine jaw line. She knew instinctively that it was Ruben but still she couldn't believe that it could be. With his thin face and dark eyes he was nothing like she'd imagined.

'You've been here the whole time? What the fuck's going on?' she said, her nerves now at fever pitch. 'Adam?' She turned and looked back at him. He was up and out of his chair moving towards her.

'This is Ruben, but I reckon you've already guessed that,' he said apologetically.

'Get away from me! I knew he would be here, I just knew it,' she said. 'You'd better keep him away from Alicia. She wants to kill him for what he's done and I'm not surprised. This weekend she's discovered that everything she has ever been told has been a lie and she blames you for all of it.' She turned to Ruben, who had retreated back into the shadows.

Alicia was out in the garden now; Courtney could just make her out, wandering around aimlessly; a cigarette in her hand.

'You've gotta get him out of here,' she said. 'And I mean now. She mustn't see him, I'm serious. She'll go mad.'

'You don't understand Courtney. God knows Ruben and I will never see eye to eye, and certainly we'll never be friends, but I asked him to come. I thought that he might be able to help with everything that's been happening in the house, everything you've told me about.' Adam sat down on the couch.

'Don't get comfortable,' she continued angrily. 'I told you just now, I want him out. We need to talk about all this somewhere else.'

'Listen,' Ruben said. 'It's best if I go Adam. I'll get a room for the night and meet you at the hospital tomorrow. We can discuss it further then.'

'Excuse me for being flippant,' she said with an incredulous laugh, 'but why have you hired a fertility expert to exorcise our house? Surely the local pastor would have been a far better bet.'

As Courtney said this, she saw Alicia heading back up the garden, 'Right, get him out now,' she said.

Adam sprang to his feet, 'I'll drive him somewhere.'

'What about his bags?' she called after him.

'They're in the trunk,' he replied as he closed the front door behind him.

The kitchen door slammed and a moment later Alicia walked into the lounge.

'Where's Dad gone? I could see the back of his head through the glass. I couldn't even see you though. I heard you both arguing again, that's why I went out - I've got a headache now.'

Courtney thought quickly. 'Oh he's just been called to an emergency, not sure how long he'll be.'

She had promised herself no more lies, but the truth was that she was just too tired and couldn't cope with the thought of another emotional outburst. Now was not the right time. She needed to find out as much as she could from Adam first.

'I'm gonna go and sort my stuff out then,' Alicia replied heading for the staircase.

Courtney smiled and nodded. 'I'll give you a shout when your dad gets back and then I'll fix us something to eat.'

'OK,' she answered dolefully. 'I'm gonna go and see Brad in the morning by the way.'

By the time Adam got home Courtney and Alicia had already eaten. Courtney had left some food for her husband on the breakfast bar but it was two hours before she finally heard the front door slam and his footsteps on the staircase. The floorboards along the hallway creaked as he ventured along it - the house was in darkness. She lay in their bed apprehensive, her body tired but her mind refusing to shut down. Alicia had gone to bed an hour before her and although she no longer seemed afraid of being in the house, Courtney feared that her feelings towards her mother had now been irretrievably damaged. Their bedroom door swung open, the handle ricocheting off the wall as it always did when Adam opened it, but she was too preoccupied to criticise him for it. She no longer felt comfortable in his presence. Now she felt like he was a stranger. He snapped on the light and she pulled the duvet up over her head to shield her eyes from the light.

'Courtney,' he said, sounding out of breath and distinctly agitated and ill at ease. He had closed the door as if he wanted to separate himself as quickly as possible from the rest of the house.

'Are you too tired to talk?' he asked.

Now feeling able to emerge from under the covers, she looked over at him. Still in his doctor's coat, he had already started to undress. As she lay in her pyjamas she watched him slip off his underclothes, surprised that he still felt able to do this in front of her without embarrassment. He hesitated then. He was visibly shaking. He pulled open his middle drawer, hauling out an old T-shirt, and then she saw him take his jeans from the closet.

'You can't sleep in jeans,' she said.

'I don't think I'm gonna sleep anyway,' he replied, 'there's too much going on in my head. Anyway if something happens to Alicia - if she runs off again - I can't go after her naked.'

He sat down on the bed beside her, his back resting against the wall. 'I mean, remember last time. She went off in the night and ended up in those hospital grounds.'

'We were away,' she recalled, 'we had no way of knowing.'

'I just feel as though I've been such a crap father, totally useless,' he said bleakly. 'I've even started losing it at work now - I just can't concentrate.'

So where did you drop him off?' she then said, changing the subject.

'Oh this motel,' he answered sombrely, turning to look at her.

'Stayed for a beer then?' she added, noticing that his breath reeked of alcohol. 'Were you ever going to tell me about him? If I hadn't found out all this by myself we would have grown old together and I would have died without ever knowing the truth. It's like I never really knew you at all!'

His forehead had furrowed into a frown, which was the only indication that he didn't agree with what she'd just said. His eyes were devoid of all emotion.

'Is there any point in us talking now?' she said with a sigh of resignation. 'Do you want to wait until you've sobered up?'

'What's the point?' he said, leaning backwards, his head against the wall. 'I'm not going to sleep. We have to talk now - I don't think we've got time to waste.'

'Well if you'd got back earlier…'

'Look,' he cut across her, 'how could we talk with Alicia here? I needed to talk with you first. She must suspect something - she was there with you today at his clinic. She's not stupid.'

'She hasn't said anything to me,' she replied sitting up in bed so that they were beside each other.

'I just feel so desperately empty Courtney. I feel as if someone's taken my heart, ripped it out of my chest and just left me with a gaping wound. There's nothing but a dull pain - no emotion. I've felt this way for a long time; I just couldn't bring myself to admit it to you. I just want everything back the way it was before, just you and me, our hopes for the future - a bright future, no problems. You were right when you said everything has changed.'

She felt a sudden panic inside of her as she interpreted his words. *He's realised he never loved me. He's still in love with her.* As though he had read her mind he then spoke again.

'But one thing I do know is that I love you now the same as I always have. What we have is worth fighting for and I'm not

357

going to give up. I know that I'd be lost without you - I'd have no reason to carry on.'

'But you felt the same way about Sarah and I never knew it,' she said.

'You did know it. You must have known it,' he answered flatly, 'I have a past. What kind of a man did you imagine I was? Someone who would have two children with someone I didn't feel anything for? Did you think I walked out on my family because I was bored with them, because I wanted to reclaim my lost youth?'

'That's what I wanted to believe,' she said, overwhelmed with feelings of jealousy and self-pity as she realised that he was telling the truth.

'Well I did love her,' he continued. 'I'm sorry if that isn't what you wanted to hear. I'm sorry for having loved someone other than just you, but it happened and I can't change it. Why should I have to change it?'

Bitter tears flowed from her eyes as she could feel herself being pulled further and further away from him.

'How do you think that makes me feel?' she cried. 'Knowing that you would still be together if she hadn't done what she did - to think that I was just a make do, a less than perfect replacement for her. I'll never match up to her will I? Let's face it, although I've seen her picture and she's not exactly a great beauty.'

'Well that's where you couldn't be more wrong,' he replied.

'Oh thanks a lot! Stick the knife in a bit further, give it a twist too, why don't you! I forgot, don't tell me love is blind isn't it? OK, so she was practically a model. Happy now?' she said with resentment in her voice.

'Shut up a minute! You're not listening to me.' He raised his voice in frustration. 'I'm not talking about what she looked like, I'm talking about you - when I met you. I never expected to be able to love anybody again and you showed me that it was possible. I couldn't believe my luck - you're stunning! A lot of the guys at work fancied you but I was the one who got you.'

'I find that hard to believe,' she said through her tears.

'Now, being with you, I can see how imperfect my relationship with Sarah really was - no way near as close as you and me. Let's face it, she was screwing around on me for years.' He paused then and sighed. 'What I'm trying to say, and obviously not managing to say very well is that had I known then what I know now, or if I had been able to see into the future, things would have been a lot different. If someone had told me back then that I was going to meet the love of my life in some place called Leesburg, at the age of thirty-seven, and that I could save myself an awful lot of heartache by just staying a bachelor until then, then I would have.'

Courtney, amazed at what she was hearing, began to feel her spirits lift as his words finally began to break through, challenging her anger and soothing her bitterness.

'You mean, if you'd known you were going to meet me, you wouldn't have married Sarah?' 'Most definitely not. Of course I love my children now, but if I had never known them I could have just concentrated on this little one.' He reached out, placing his warm hand tenderly on her stomach.

Sunshine, a hot summer's day, sitting in the garden, the pool water glistening in the sunlight, birds singing and memories of their perfect holidays together in Marbella, flooded back into her mind, banishing the depression and the gloom. She moved closer to him; the invisible barrier between them had lifted. He lay down on the bed and gathered her in his arms as she sobbed, this time with happiness. It was the warmest tightest embrace of their marriage. She felt strong again, loved and empowered.

'I'm ready now,' she said, 'ready to talk. I need you to tell me about Ruben.' She pulled back from him again and they lay facing each other like two dizzy teenagers. She needed to look into those deep brown eyes, and as she did, she felt that old familiar quiver in her stomach as he gazed happily back at her.

He began cautiously. 'You want to know everything?'

Courtney nodded.

'Well it all started back at university in Philadelphia. That's where Sarah and I first met.'

'Sarah was training to be a doctor?' she interrupted.

'Not exactly. Ruben, Sarah and I were all friends there to begin with, and after a while I got together with her. We married two years later and then kind of lost touch with Ruben. He used to annoy me anyway, when I was with Sarah. For a start he wasn't happy when we got together. He said it was because we never wanted him around anymore; he had other friends but I guess I was his best friend. I didn't want to go out to bars with him anymore, drinking and looking for women. So I guess he was sore about that. Anyway, I got my doctorate and he went on to bigger and better things. He and Sarah were both studying together; he was studying Eugenics whereas Sarah was majoring in the agricultural uses of the techniques. He wanted to specialise in IVF. His dream was always, so he said, ultimately to be able to eradicate disease in humans. He had all these big ideas about how he was going to practice PGD, and be the first man to carry out the techniques of Germline Engineering on a human embryo.'

'What the hell is PGD?' Courtney asked bemused.

'If I can remember rightly, it stands for Preimplantation Genetic Diagnosis. It's where they take embryos in the developmental first stages called blastomeres and they basically use micromanipulation to perform a biopsy on each blastocyst. This then enables them to analyse individual cells by using a method called PCR. Don't say it, what does that stand for?' He paused and scratched his head, desperately trying to remember. 'Polymerase Chain Reaction,' he then said slowly, 'Impressed?' He smiled back at her.

'And then?' She hurried him along.

'Well this test can identify any gene defects that the embryo may have and then eradicate them before the egg is implanted back into the mother. We used to joke that Ruben was gonna be the next Hitler. Do you know about all the experimentation that went on in Nazi Germany?' Courtney nodded.

'That was all Eugenics - trying to create the perfect human race by improving both physical and mental characteristics. Did you know there was a law passed in America in the first half of the 20th Century that enforced the compulsory sterilisation of the insane?'

'Oh my God,' she answered, 'That's appalling! You can't do that to people, everyone should be able to choose surely - it's a basic human right.' She was shocked. 'I mean you could say that had I been born all those years ago, I could have been sterilised.'

360

Adam laughed. 'Don't be stupid. Taking a short course of Prozac for a bout of depression doesn't make you insane.'

'I don't know. Sometimes, especially lately, I've felt as though I was going insane,' she paused again and looked back at him.

'Carry on then.'

'The law as it stands in this country prevents geneticists such as Ruben from practising their techniques on human embryos.' Adam's expression was grave as he spoke. Courtney had already come to her own conclusions but she still found it impossible to believe.

'They are allowed to experiment on animals,' he continued. 'They've created cows with increased milk production and genetically modified mice. The mice were created with a deficiency that mimics human disease. The theory is that they will be able to learn from these mice new techniques for treating and eradicating diseases.'

'So how does Alicia fit into all this, because I know that she does somehow?' She was eager for him to get to the end of his explanation.

'You have to promise me that this stays between us - no-one must ever find out what I'm about to tell you. Promise me.' He caught hold of her hand, his eyes frightened, pleading with her.

'I promise - just tell me.'

He took a deep breath.

'When Sarah and I first started talking about having a family.' He paused again, looking at her for approval; she nodded and waved him on with her hand. 'Well, it came up about her being a carrier of haemophilia. I didn't know about it before I married her. She was paranoid that she would have a boy who would have the disease just like her brother. I remember it well, that day, the day I got home and she said to me that Ruben had called out of the blue. He had wanted to talk to me apparently and she'd told him about our plans. He and I hadn't spoken for a long time. I was really angry with her at first; I didn't want him back in our lives again. I guess with hindsight, that I never completely trusted him. Anyway, Sarah persuaded me to take a trip to his new clinic - that would be twenty years ago now. He convinced us that he would be able to help. It was such a stupid thing to do, looking back, but the lure of being able to have a disease-free healthy baby was too great. Before we knew it we'd signed up to take part in his top secret, illegal experiment. I mean what must I have been thinking of? My babies weren't even conceived naturally. They were created in a petri dish in a clinical laboratory, supervised by the man that I now hate more than words could ever express. He guaranteed us females, but he took it one stage further.'

'What do you mean?' She stared back at him.

'He completely eradicated the gene in the germline cells,' he replied. Courtney looked back at him still confused; she was agitated again now.

'The germline cells are the cells that contain the DNA that is passed on to the next generation. Effectively this meant that the buck had stopped there. The family's ever-present shadow had been removed forever.'

'So he eradicated the haemophilia gene then?' she said, frowning suddenly and shaking her head as bitterness welled up inside her again. 'I can't believe you put yourself through all that, giving him a test tube full of your sperm - the humiliation. God you must have been in love with her. How do I know you'd have put yourself through all that for me?'

'Of course I would.' He sighed again, dumbfounded that her emphasis seemed always to be on his relationship with Sarah. She didn't seem shocked or particularly surprised by what he was telling her about Ruben. He decided to let it go - he didn't want to argue again when everything seemed to be going so well between them.

'That was then. This is now Courtney. I'm trying to tell you what happened - no more lies remember - that's what you said.'

'I'm sorry,' she said.

'When he'd completed the modification, he implanted the fertilised egg into Sarah's uterus.' His expression changed then to one of disgust as he recalled the event in the light of what happened in the years that followed.

'So ours is your first naturally conceived baby?' she said with a cautious smile.

'Yep,' he answered. 'That's why I was so shocked when I found out you were pregnant. You see after Ruben had carried out his preliminary tests in the lab, he told me that I had an extremely low sperm count and that we'd have problems trying to conceive naturally. I always believed it. Now I see that it was his way of insuring that we went through with the IVF treatment. Manipulative bastard,' he added.

'Why couldn't you have told me all this before?' she said desperately. You knew I wanted a family of my own. I know I'm pregnant now, but you knew I might never be able to have a baby with you when we got married and yet you kept it from me.'

'I'm so sorry Courtney.' She could see the genuine remorse in his eyes. 'I just wanted to be with you so badly. I was selfish. I was just thinking of me and my needs. Can you ever forgive me?'

The truth was out now and nothing that had passed before seemed to matter to her anymore. At that moment she'd have forgiven him anything past, present or future. She nodded. He embraced her again but she pulled away quickly, as he hadn't finished the story and she wasn't satisfied yet.

'So did Sarah have a normal pregnancy after that?'

'Relatively. I mean there was a certain amount of anxiety on both our parts, not knowing whether the babies would be normal, guilt that maybe we had made the wrong decision. But when they were born, all that just seemed to melt away. They were just perfect and I couldn't have been happier.'

'So you didn't regret it after that, not until recently anyway?' She pressed him further.

No sooner were the words out of her mouth when a door suddenly slammed out in the hallway. Adam froze, his expression immediately changing to one of terror. His eyes widened and he gazed at the door, his lower lip trembling. Courtney was stunned by his reaction. Since the séance in the house she had been less nervous and hadn't felt anything untoward, apart from her initial anxiety about entering the house that afternoon. She couldn't believe that her husband, who had always been oblivious to everything they had experienced there, was suddenly a nervous wreck. She tried to reassure him.

'I'll go take a look,' she said.

She knocked on Alicia's door and established that it had been her slamming the door as she returned from the bathroom.

'It's all right, it was Alicia,' she affirmed as she walked back into their bedroom.

'But it's not all right is it?' He was sitting up again. 'This is the whole point of me telling you all this,' he paused and lowered his voice to a hoarse whisper, 'I think something went wrong.'

He turned to her, his whole body trembling. She could see tears rolling down the face of the man who had always before seemed invincible - a professional through and through.

'What do you mean something went wrong?' she said incredulously. 'I don't understand. What's happened to you? You were never like this before.'

'I'm sorry Courtney,' he said, pain and regret etched on his face.

'Everything you've ever told me, everything that's been happening in the house - I could have put a stop to your suffering weeks ago. I know what's going on here,' he lowered his voice to a whisper, afraid to utter the words any louder, his eyes still wide with fear. The perspiration glistened on his forehead. 'I've seen it with my own eyes. I've heard it.'

'How could you?' she answered angrily. 'You made me believe I was going crazy! You even said to me, 'You've been under a lot of stress lately.'' She mimicked his voice. 'Too right I damn well was!'

'I'm so sorry. What more can I say? What do you want me to do to prove it? I'll do anything.' There was desperation in his voice.

'Why did you do it? I don't understand,' she said, moving away from him to the edge of the bed. He reached out to her, trying to get her back, trying to make her understand.

'I was too proud,' he said running his hand nervously through his hair. 'I thought it was my imagination at first and I fought against it. I still don't want to believe it even now, but there's no other explanation.' He looked at her; the fear in his eyes was tangible. 'I never intended to let it go on this long. You have to believe me Courtney. After a while it just became easier to carry on pretending - I didn't want to lose face.'

'So what it comes down to is your pride was more important than your wife's sanity. Do you have any idea how alone I felt?' She was expecting him to say he was sorry again, but he didn't.

'Yes I do know how alone you felt, because I felt alone too. I was totally alone. You had Alicia and I had nobody.' She went to speak. 'I know, I know, it's all my fault. I accept that totally - I'm the guilty one here, not you,' he continued with resignation in his voice, 'I just thought if I ignored it, it would go away, and if it didn't go away, I could sort it out. That's what men are supposed to do isn't it? They're supposed to be the fixers and protect their family. I've failed. I can't fix this problem by myself, I don't even know where to begin.' He paused again, more tears coming into his eyes as he fought to maintain control of his emotions. 'I'm so frightened Courtney.'

She was angry with him, but he had backed down, taken responsibility and admitted his guilt. She felt that they had made progress as a couple. She would accept his apology and move forward in the strength that she'd gained from knowing the truth at last. They would move forward together.

'I should be so angry with you,' she said turning to look at him again.

'Are you?' he said his voice still shaking.

'Yes, but I know now that you're sorry. At least you know the truth now, we both do.'

The haunted, fearful look in his eyes seemed to melt away in that moment. He felt secure again; knowing that the one he loved more than anyone else in the world had forgiven him.

'That still leaves us with a problem though,' she said before he could say anything else.

'What's that?' he answered, wiping his eyes and frowning again.

'Well what the hell can Ruben possibly do about all this?'

Chapter 18

Alicia looked at the display on her alarm clock, it was 4 a.m. She felt tired, but she couldn't go back to sleep, she couldn't settle. Her heart was beating faster than ever; butterflies were fluttering furiously in her stomach. She had a strange feeling of anticipation - one she recognised as a mixture of excitement and dread. She compared it to the feeling she had when queuing for a roller coaster - overwhelming fear that was overcome by the desire for the heady feelings of exhilaration and personal satisfaction that she would get when she made it through to the end of the ride. She felt hot as though she had a fever. Something wasn't quite right. Her dreams had been vivid as usual. They were usually always dark and menacing and she very rarely had a pleasant sun filled dream anymore. She couldn't remember the last time she'd had one but last night had been the first time since Gabrielle's death.

She'd dreamt about Gabrielle, their recent lives together flashed through her mind as she watched from the outside. Instead of being herself in the dream she had been an unknown spectator, seeing herself as others saw her. The arguments, the laughter, the day they'd first moved to Florida, their friends and their first day at Jennifer's. Everything had been stored in her mind's eye, a perfect play back as if it was all happening in the present. The realisation had hit her for the first time upon waking from that dream, the stark reality. Her mind had fooled her into thinking that everything was as it appeared, with no mention of the horror that had followed these events. She blinked slowly in the murky half-light of the room, tears stinging her eyes. She remembered then how she had once dreamt when she was young that she'd been given a puppy for Christmas. In her dream she'd woken to find the puppy in the basket by the side of her bed, its bright eyes gazing up at her, tale wagging frantically from side to side. She remembered when she woke from that dream she had immediately looked down by the side of her bed to greet her new puppy, but there was no puppy. It wasn't even Christmas and she realised then that it had all been a dream. Tears had filled her young eyes and she had sobbed uncontrollably for an hour, so distressed at the loss of her imaginary puppy. She had never had one in the first place; it had only been wishful thinking; her child's mind able to get over the loss of something she'd never had by the time she'd finished eating her breakfast. She'd had a sister though, and at that moment the pain of losing her was too much to bear. She was suddenly faced with the prospect of having to accept her loss all over again, as she remembered that she was in fact dead. An all-consuming grief washed over her, a feeling of desolation; the panic as she came to terms once more with the knowledge that she would never see her sister again. She would have to go through the pain and fear of death herself before ever having the chance to see her, and even then she wasn't sure that she would. What if there was no God? What if there was no heaven?

She felt a scream rising up from the depths of her stomach, a cry of disbelief, of anger and utter devastation. She stifled it and pressed her face down into her duvet cover, crying, beating her fists in frustration against the bed.

'Gabrielle,' she sobbed, calling to her from the pit of despair and loneliness that she had fallen into. There was no reply. The room was silent but for the sound of her sobbing. She thought about Brad then. It was too early to visit him, visiting time didn't start for another five hours. She flopped back down onto the bed, emotionally numb, tears still coursing steadily down her cheeks. She stared vacantly up at the ceiling. If it wasn't for Brad, she would have nothing left, she thought; she might as well be dead herself. She wished that she was dead in that moment. She wanted freedom from her pain, she couldn't imagine ever being able to feel happy again. She'd seen glimpses of how life could be when she had been with Brad. He had helped her forget; not forever, but just for long enough to be able to feel temporarily normal again. She could lose herself in his eyes, his warm inviting eyes. She remembered the surge of electricity that passed through her body whenever they connected, drawing out the raw passion within her. She had felt alive, and every nerve in her body had tingled, but now she was just existing with no specific purpose, and nothing to look forward to. She couldn't stay in that room a moment longer. She wiped her eyes and switched into autopilot - the only way that she could function. She pulled her jeans from the back of a chair, the same ones she had worn for the last three days. She didn't have any inclination or desire to look for something else to wear, it just didn't interest her, or seem important anymore. She hauled a clean T-shirt over her head and sat staring at herself in the mirror for a few minutes, sinking into an almost trance-like state. She imagined that she was sat with her sister again and she reached out and touched the glass, running her hand over the reflection; it was cold. She snapped back to reality and dragged a brush through her knotted hair. She was ready. Within minutes she was out in the hallway, down the stairs and standing by the front door. The house was still, not a living thing moved. Silent shadows crept across the walls in front of her, cast by the street lights outside. She contemplated eating then and walked into the kitchen. She helped herself to a few slices of dry bread - it was food, it didn't have to be anything special. Eating was another essential function, it was only fuel to her and it may rid her of the dull ache that she had in the pit of her stomach. She opened her bag and stuffed the remaining bread inside. She made a move towards the front door, hesitating as she grasped the handle. She turned it and the door clicked open. She knew where she was going; she'd made up her mind - she was out, physically free, but in her mind she was still captive.

Out into the street she went, her footsteps reverberating on the sidewalk. She looked around nervously; the air was still stagnant and oppressive, and although the sun hadn't yet come up, the darkness seemed to be lightening slowly. Nothing moved, the street was still sleeping. She pressed her bag tighter against her side grasping the strap protectively on her shoulder, her hair hanging lifelessly. Once out of Bay View Grove she slowed her pace, afraid before that she could have been detected. She'd dared not look up at any of the windows for fear of seeing drapes twitching in the half-light. She had to be alone, she had to go there. Memories flooded her mind, thoughts of that night, the night she had been run out of the house. She hadn't known where she was going then but this time she was dressed in regular clothes and she had shoes on her feet. Utter confusion and loneliness still filled her, numbing any other feelings that she may have had. She felt self-pity as she had so many times before. *Why me?* A question she had asked herself so often before and for which there was no answer. She knew in her heart that she wasn't the only person alive who had ever suffered, but still it didn't seem fair. Her burden was too heavy for her to bear. Perhaps God had made a mistake; if he is up there she thought. Perhaps he had intended this immense load for someone else to carry. It should have been someone with broader, more robust shoulders. She had been walking for ten minutes, not really noticing where she was. She suddenly realised that she had almost reached her destination. Although she didn't know what purpose it would serve, something was driving her on, willing her to go, convincing her that not everything was how it seemed. She walked past the coffee shop where she and Brad had been together; she hadn't known then that they would spend the whole day together and not just a stolen moment. She had recognised the look in his eyes; her eyes had mirrored his. Both of them knew that they needed each other and craved the other's love so badly. But both were treading carefully, denying their true feelings, scared of rejection, afraid that it was all just a perfect dream and that any moment they would wake up to reality. Alicia had woken to hers that morning. Perhaps everything that had passed before had just been a dream, perhaps she was dreaming now. Her hair caught in the shoulder strap of her bag, tugging at the roots sending a sharp shooting pain down the side of her head. This was her reality; pain was her existence and her legacy.

As she walked she contemplated death, her own death. She had decided that it may be her only option, to be laid down beside her sister in the churchyard, take her chances in the next life. She thought about Courtney then and her dad. She wondered if they'd miss her. Perhaps Courtney would, she thought, but then she still wasn't sure if Courtney's feelings for her were genuine. She and her sister had been forced upon her, her life had been fine before they'd come along, causing havoc and destroying her marriage. *They'd be better off without me too. They'd be rid of their problems completely then and could start afresh, and as soon as the baby came along they'd be happy together again.*

The heavy iron gate of the churchyard creaked loudly as she pushed it open, the winding path leading up to the imposing church of St. Bartholomew's stretched before her. The sun had begun to struggle through, though still weak, the light not yet fully formed. Early morning mist hung eerily around her, the sweet, cloying air permeating her lungs. She stepped inside and closed the gate behind her with a sudden bang that jolted her nerves and sent her heart racing again. A chill was in the air; she walked to her right into the gloom, towards the area where she thought that the coffin had been lowered into the ground. She was the only living soul in that place. She imagined the decaying, disfigured corpses beneath her feet, envisaged them reaching up through the damp moist earth, grabbing hold of her legs and pulling her down, trapping her with them in their coffin, jealous of her life. She would trade places she thought - she wasn't afraid. There was only the sound of her footsteps on the ground and the occasional cracking of broken branches beneath her feet. She passed by some overgrown head stones, so old that their inscriptions were barely readable. She heard a rustling sound in the foliage surrounding the graves and she jumped again, putting her hand to her chest in fright. It was only a bird. It emerged from tangled grass, something she couldn't identify was hanging from its beak as it then took flight, flapping its wings only inches from her face. She looked further ahead of her and spotted what she thought must be Gabrielle's grave, still covered with the flowers that had been placed there on the day of her burial. She walked towards it her heart still pounding as she drew near to what she now thought of as her own destiny. As she approached her sister's grave she felt numb. She paused before it, glancing nervously around, making sure that she was still alone. Her moment at the graveside was her time. Her moment to grieve for the other half of her, her twin, her companion she had thought would be by her side for life. The flowers were beginning to wilt, revealing the stones that lay beneath them, marking the area where her body lay in a perfect rectangle. *Gabrielle Buchanan, beloved daughter and sister*, she read. *Beloved - one who is much loved* - she pondered the words in her mind. She waited for a moment. Surely something should happen, surely she should feel comforted by the fact that she was so close to the sister she had lost, but she felt further away than she had ever felt. She felt hollow inside, pain and nausea racking her entire body. She let out a cry, a desperate cry like a wounded animal caught in a trap, desperate to free itself. She sank to her knees, falling forward onto the grave, her face pressed into the faded blooms.

'Gabrielle!' she cried. 'Where are you? I just want to be with you. I can't live anymore - I just want to die.'

There was no answer.

The sun was beginning to burn the mist away that surrounded her but she saw nothing. She could feel the hard ground, cold beneath her. The smell of death pervaded her and she willed it to take her too and rid her of her unbearable existence. She heard a noise behind her, footsteps. Maybe it was the pastor come to pray with her she thought, or maybe another grief stricken relative come to seek solace by the grave of a loved one. She didn't move, hoping that she would not be noticed - hoping they would pass by and leave her to her grief and sadness. She felt sick to her stomach, her entire body was icy cold. She thought about Brad again at that moment. Another wave of nausea came over her and she struggled to her feet, not wanting to be ill on her sister's grave. She felt dazed and rubbed at her face with her hand, the familiar taste of salt now on her lips. She breathed a desperate, longing sigh, taking one last look at the grave, having decided that she would leave this place and go to the hospital. She hadn't felt close to Gabrielle here and it hadn't brought her any comfort after all. She hesitated then, listening, as she suddenly had an overwhelming sense that she was being watched. She looked to her right, but saw nobody. Feeling cold again she shuddered and as she turned to go, her heart missed a beat. There standing in front of her was a woman whom she recognised immediately; she took in a sudden gasp of air, filling her lungs. Her head still dizzy, she rubbed at her eyes again, blinking slowly then staring straight ahead of her in disbelief. What she was seeing couldn't possibly be real - it must be just her tortured mind playing tricks on her again. She was wearing a different T-shirt, one of Alicia's favourite ones with a black and white stripe across the middle, and her fur trimmed beige jacket. Her face looked the same, but not as it had done the last time she had seen her. It was no longer pale and her hair was now styled the way she had always worn it when she had still been alive. Alicia panicked then, and was too afraid to speak. She felt light headed as though she were about to faint. Gabrielle just stared back at her, expressionless. Alicia was confused and frightened and she ran back to the path as fast as she could, her gaze fixed on the iron gate.

'Alicia!' Gabrielle called after her sister.

She froze and turned back to see Gabrielle right behind her again.

'You can speak?' Alicia said in dismay.

'Of course I can speak,' she replied.

'But you're supposed to be dead,' Alicia said staring back at her sister in amazement. 'You don't look it anymore, you're not even pale now. You are dead aren't you?'

Gabrielle broke down in tears, real tears that flowed from her haunted eyes. 'I don't know!' she cried.

'What do you mean you don't know?' Alicia said aghast.

'You have to help me,' she sobbed, pulling up her sleeves and revealing the dried up grisly knife wounds on her hands and arms. 'I can't cover these with make up.'

Alicia recoiled from her in horror. 'Get away from me!' she cried. 'You're dead! I'm imagining all of this, you're just a ghost or something. You're not my sister, you can't be!'

'But I am,' Gabrielle implored, she reached out her cold hand making contact with her sister's arm. Alicia pulled her arm away from her, gasping for air. She swallowed nervously, still wanting to run but her feet were as heavy as one of the gravestones that surrounded her. She was rooted to the spot.

'But I saw you at the funeral home, I saw you in your coffin! You're not wearing the same clothes, you had a blue dress on. Dad saw you at the morgue, Courtney saw you there too.' There was silence for a moment as the two sisters eyed each other. Alicia heard the iron gate creak open.

'Quick,' she said signalling to Gabrielle to follow her. They walked back into the shadows of the trees, Gabrielle stepping over her own grave as they went. They found a bench in the corner of the churchyard. Alicia slumped down on it, exhausted by the whole bizarre experience. Her 'dead' sister sat beside her. 'So you mean to tell me you never really died? You've put us through all of this misery for some sort of sick practical joke?' Alicia said.

'You don't understand,' Gabrielle replied her breath hanging in the air in front of her. 'God how can I make you understand?'

'Don't speak to me about God,' Alicia retorted. 'What don't I understand?'

'Everything went black, pitch black,' Gabrielle said, her voice hoarse with emotion, 'I remember the pain, but even that has started to fade now.'

'The pain of being stabbed?' Alicia interjected.

'Yes it was like nothing on earth.'

'No worse than the pain I've felt at losing you,' Alicia replied indignantly.

'But all of a sudden I couldn't feel the pain anymore,' Gabrielle continued. 'I was just surrounded by darkness, and then I don't remember anything else.'

'But you weren't breathing, you were pronounced dead, you *were* dead,' Alicia said pulling her bag off her shoulder and placing it down on her lap, hugging it close to her.

'I woke up then Alicia, I woke up in my coffin. Have you any idea how frightened I was? I had all of my senses still, I could still feel and my body ached. I was trapped, the coffin lid was bearing down on me, suffocating me, I couldn't move.'

'So how did you get out?' Alicia cut in.

'I don't know exactly, all I knew was that I had to get out. I thought I must be dead, that I'd gone to hell. I thought that if I closed my eyes I could will it all away. I wanted to find Matt, I felt so alone. I didn't know what I'd find when I did get out, all I knew was that I had to. I couldn't stay in that coffin. I closed my eyes, I felt this surge of energy come from within me and then I was out.'

'So you just passed through a solid wooden coffin?' Alicia said, screwing her face up in disbelief. 'That doesn't make any sense, how can you have passed through a solid object when you're solid yourself?'

'I don't know I just did. I can appear and disappear now at will,' Gabrielle answered in monotone.

'All this is fucked up completely,' Alicia then said. 'None of it makes any sense, so where did you find yourself when you got out the coffin then?'

'Exactly where you were standing,' she pointed across the churchyard. 'Right in front of my own grave, imagine that, reading the inscription on your own headstone.'

An unearthly shiver passed down Alicia's spine. This girl sitting beside her on the bench couldn't possibly be from this world she thought, *she can't possibly be my sister.*

'I am your sister,' Gabrielle responded.

'You can hear my thoughts now too? Oh God,' Alicia exclaimed getting up from the bench and pacing in front of it. 'Well what do you expect me to do?' she then said as Gabrielle stared back at her wide-eyed.

'I need you to help me,' Gabrielle pleaded, 'I'm not dead but I'm not properly alive either. I don't know what the hell I am.'

'A freak of nature, that's what I reckon,' Alicia snapped back.

'Oh it's all right for you isn't it,' Gabrielle said angrily. 'You're still little Miss Perfect! You're not in the same hell as me, you have no idea what I've been through. I'm so alone Alicia, I've looked for Mom and I can't find her, I can't find Matt either.'

'Oh Mom's haunting our house currently,' Alicia said flippantly. 'That's where you'll find her.'

'But I've been in the house the whole time,' Gabrielle replied, her frustration spilling over, 'how do you think I got these clothes? And I've never seen her there.'

'You've been in the house the whole time?' The truth was beginning to dawn on Alicia. 'It was you,' she said turning angrily to her sister, a look of dismay on her face. 'You were the one all along, trying to frighten me, and it was you that ran us out of the house.'

'I was so angry Alicia, I was so frightened and confused. I didn't know what to do, you have no idea. I was so jealous of you that you were still alive and I was just the living dead. Sometimes a real person and at other times invisible, able to move objects with just the power of my mind. I could do whatever I wanted, I just wanted you to know that I was still there.'

'Great by scaring the crap out of me,' Alicia retorted, 'some loving sister you turned out to be! That night when I ended up in the hospital grounds, you ran me out of the house! That was all your doing, I could have died out there.'

'I know,' Gabrielle replied. 'All I could think of was to get revenge and the only way I could get justice for myself was to kill her.'

'You killed Jennifer?' Alicia said dismayed by what she was hearing. 'That makes you a murderer.'

'She murdered me first remember,' Gabrielle said beginning to cry again.

'And where was I in all this eh? You were hoping that they'd pin it on me weren't you?' Alicia's face contorted with anger. 'How could you do that you bitch? If you're a Goddamn ghost, they're hardly going to catch you now are they, but that wasn't enough for you, was it, just to kill her? You had to involve me too, make me suffer.'

'I know, and I truly am sorry. You have to believe me,' Gabrielle said, her voice full of regret. 'You're right - I did want you to suffer, I wanted you dead so I wouldn't have to be alone any longer. I thought, why should you still be alive? We're twins, we're supposed to be together, we're bonded from birth.'

'I don't believe I'm hearing all this,' Alicia said, sitting back down on the bench with a heavy sigh.

There was a long silence then between them, which was finally broken again by Alicia, 'So do you eat anything then?' she suddenly said.

'Sometimes, I'm not dead am I?' Gabrielle replied in a matter of fact tone. 'I couldn't deal with hunger pains too. If I get them and I can't get any food, I just make myself invisible again. Don't worry though, I won't be wanting any of that stale bread that's in your handbag.'

Alicia looked back at her in amazement.

'I saw you put it in there before we left the house.'

Alicia shuddered again, 'So why did you wait until now to show yourself? Wanted me to suffer a bit more did you?'

'You haven't suffered!' Gabrielle scoffed, changing her tone completely. 'How about your new romance with wonder cop? You didn't seem too bothered about me when you were with him!' Gabrielle paused. Alicia gasped as the sudden awful realisation hit her - her eyes now wide with abject horror and disbelief.

'No!' she exclaimed, putting her hand up to her mouth, a new scenario now playing in her mind of the events that had led up to them finding Brad as good as dead on the couch. Gabrielle didn't answer - she hung her head in shame.

'He's dying!' Alicia raged, her throat dry, the words scraping painfully across her vocal chords.

'Why should you have a boyfriend when I can't?' Gabrielle shouted back, her voice defiant. 'Why should you have all the love and adoration when we're the same person?'

'We're not the same person!' Alicia cried. 'We never have been and we never will be. You've obviously never been in love if that's how shallow your thoughts are.'

'Don't patronise me,' Gabrielle retorted, 'I was in love with Matt remember and it cost me my life.'

'No you weren't Gabrielle! You were in lust, couldn't resist someone else's man, just wanted a bit of sordid sex after hours at Jennifer's - a quick thrill.'

Gabrielle leapt up and struck her sister. Alicia had always thought before that she was the weaker of the two, but not anymore. She got straight back up and pushed her sister down hard onto the bench.

'Don't you dare touch me!' Alicia shrieked. 'Couldn't bear to see me happy could you? Just because you fucked up your own life, you thought you would do the same to mine. I could have been happy with him, I could have had a life, but not any more. You've taken all that away from me. How could you?'

'But you'd have forgotten me if you'd stayed with him. I'd have always had to be alone. I couldn't let that happen.'

'No because you're a selfish bitch, always have been and always will be,' Alicia screamed.

'He wasn't right for you anyway,' Gabrielle said.

'Liar! He was perfect for me and you knew it. How was he then? Cos I never got the chance to find out,' Alicia yelled, bitter tears stinging her face.

'I don't know,' she replied her eyes downcast. 'He freaked when he saw me naked.'

Alicia laughed incredulously. 'I bet you kissed him though didn't you,' she said leaning over her sister menacingly.

'Yeah, but he was drunk and he thought I was you anyway, so what the hell does it matter?'

Alicia smacked her sister hard across her face, her pain and anger too much to bear.

Gabrielle winced, putting her hand up too late to protect herself. 'That hurt,' she said pitifully.

'Good I'm glad it hurt,' Alicia screamed back. 'It was supposed to, bitch!'

She felt such an intense loathing for the sister who sat cowering before her; she hated her right then with a murderous passion.

'I never want to see you or speak to you again do you hear me?' Alicia spat the words through her tears. 'You are nothing to me! You no longer exist as far as I'm concerned and I will never grieve for you again, as long as I have breath left in my body.' She turned on her heels and began to run.

Her words struck Gabrielle like the knife that had slashed her body before. The pain almost splitting her in two. She stumbled after her.

'Alicia please,' she sobbed as her sister ran from her. 'I love you. You have to help me, you're my last hope.'

Alicia spun around defiantly. 'You have your punishment,' she said, 'and you will never get an ounce of pity from me again. Now leave me alone!'

She ran on blinded by tears, and didn't look back until she was halfway down the main road. When she finally did, Gabrielle was nowhere to be seen.

Chapter 19

Courtney woke to find herself in Adam's arms. He was still fast asleep and they were both lying partially clothed on top of the duvet. They had made love that night for the first time in what had seemed like ages. Courtney had felt so distant from him for a long time and she hadn't been able to bear for him to touch her. In recent times the question of sex between them was unmentionable. To her it would have felt like a violation, attempted rape. She was beginning to wonder how it was that she ever managed to conceive in the first place. Last night however was different; it was the same as it had been when they'd first met. She could never have imagined that she could ever feel as happy as she did right at that moment. Everything was out in the open now. She felt strong and had even begun to like herself, now feeling worthy of the best and confident that she deserved everything that she had and could ever have in the future. She had dared to face the truth and had found that it wasn't as devastating as she had first thought it would be. She felt closer to him now than she ever had done before. Lying there safe and secure again, she glanced around the room. The sun was already up, shafts of light venturing through a gap in the drapes, the dust floating in them. She appreciated her bedroom again for the first time since all the disturbances had begun. The sunlight reflected on their terracotta walls, brightening everything. She glanced over at their photographs on the side and felt part of them again. At that moment she imagined herself back there, on holiday in Marbella. She fancied that if she got up then and opened the shutters, she would see the bright blue sea stretching out before her, the golden sand and palm trees waving gently in the summer breeze. Even the slightly worn closet doors looked radiant in the sunlight. Adam stirred. As she turned to look at him, he opened his eyes. Courtney felt that surge of energy within her again as she smiled back at him. Leaning forward he kissed her tenderly.

'I've been remembering our vacations in Marbella,' she said wistfully.

He smiled and pulled himself up so he was resting on his elbow. He gazed down at her.

'We must go back one day,' he said. 'We can take the little one with us - they love children in Spain. We can get some more pictures then, with the whole family in it.'

'What Alicia too?' she said.

'I doubt she'd want to go. Do you?' he replied.

'I think it's likely, she doesn't really see her friends anymore, not since…' She paused then.

'Oh well, she can babysit for us then,' he said with a half laugh. 'What time is it?'

'Just after nine,' she replied glancing at her watch.

Adam suddenly sprang from the bed, a look of horror on his face, 'Oh God, I set my alarm for eight. I'm supposed to be picking Ruben up right now.'

'Well you obviously didn't set it,' she replied. 'Just give him a call - what's the big problem? He'll just have to wait.'

The tranquil, perfect moment was suddenly ruined at the mention of Ruben. Courtney was brought back down to earth again. Everything may have been all right between them, but there was still him. There was still the house outside their bedroom door, there was still Alicia, Sarah and Gabrielle. She went over all the pieces of the puzzle in her mind.

'What do you mean, you had to meet Ruben at nine? Don't you mean we?' she said, as she headed off for a shower.

Adam was already hauling his clothes back on. 'I would have told you everything that happened there,' he said, struggling to do up his belt. 'You'd better make that a quick shower then if you're coming too.'

'Well of course I am. No more secrets, that's what we decided.' She raised her voice to be heard over the sound of the rushing water.

'I wouldn't have kept anything from you,' he called back. 'I just didn't think you'd want to see him again that's all.'

'He's of no consequence to me,' she replied, 'I'm surprised you want to see him to be honest.'

Adam didn't answer. He could sense the drift of the conversation would revert back to Sarah and him; all the things they had already been over and cleared up. He didn't want to risk another argument; he was still afraid of that happening. Their new found happiness still seemed too good to be true right then.

'I'll go and put the coffee on,' he said instead, 'see you in a minute.'

Courtney dressed quickly. She could hear Adam downstairs, the muffled sound of his voice on the telephone. She strained to hear what he was saying but he was much too far away for her to make out his words. Although there was a certain amount of urgency about everything that they had to do that day, she had a strange feeling of calm, and the house definitely seemed at peace today. She glanced at the wicker basket in the corner of their room. There was housework to do and a big pile of washing from their trip to Philadelphia that she needed to get on with. Surely everything was fine now, surely all this fuss with Ruben was completely unnecessary. A thought then occurred to her, that the problem all along could have just been caused by the negative energy that was flowing between Adam and herself. Perhaps that had resulted in the oppressive atmosphere in the house; perhaps her internal fears about the state of her marriage had manifested themselves as eerie, unearthly voices and things going bump in the night. She had read and heard stories about disturbed teenagers who, it was believed, had invoked poltergeist activity in their houses. Perhaps the same principal applied here. It must have been all the arguing and the trauma since Gabrielle's death that had pervaded the walls of the house, filling it with the all consuming sadness and gloom that it seemed to posses in recent weeks. As she sat on the edge of the bed putting on her makeup, her curiosity got the better of her. She decided that she must go with Adam to meet Ruben again, she wanted to find out what he had to say for himself. She wanted to know how he would react once he found out that Adam had told her about his secret experimentation. She smiled to herself. She was no longer on the outside looking in, she was in the thick of it and she felt that she could cope with anything that life had to throw at her. She took a deep satisfying breath. She felt her baby move within her and she lay her hand on her stomach in response, now happy, excited and hopeful for the future.

Courtney walked down the stairs, her jacket on and bag over her shoulder.

She stood in the doorway to the kitchen. Adam was sat at the breakfast bar, drinking his coffee and eating some waffles. She walked over to him; he smiled as she approached.

'Do you want some coffee?' he asked. She nodded; he stood up and poured her a cup. She joined him, stealing a waffle from his plate as she sat down; she was feeling ravenous.

'I can make you some of your own if you like,' he said.

'No it's OK,' she laughed, 'I only want one.'

'Do you know what?' she suddenly said. 'Us being here like this, it reminds me…'

'Reminds you of what?' he replied swallowing his last mouthful of coffee.

'Well it's like we've gone back in time.' He looked at her, his expression one of complete confusion.

'It reminds me of the morning when you first went to pick up the girls from the airport. I've got the same feeling in my stomach, like you have when something big is about to happen.'

'I guess it is,' he answered, his voice serious. 'Is it exactly the same then, because you were dreading that day?'

'No it's not,' she said. 'We're together this time. It's the same, but this time I'm going with you. I've been thinking a lot and I realise I was so resentful about them coming here that I cut myself off from the whole situation. I cut myself off from you because I blamed you for all of it.'

'Well they were my daughters, so I guess it was my fault really,' he answered getting up to go and wash the breakfast things.

'Yes, but when I married you, I married you and everything that came with you. I shouldn't have behaved the way I did; I was selfish, I should have stuck by you. I should have gone with you to the airport when I had the chance and faced my fears head on. Instead of getting on with it I wanted to put it off just that little bit longer, drowning my self-pity in wine and then showing you up.'

'Come here,' he said putting the cups and plates down and walking back over to her, his arms outstretched. He hugged her tight. 'I don't blame you for that, it was a big change to our lives, and now I'm not sure if we even made the right decision. Your gut feeling was right about it, them coming here has caused us nothing but heartache and grief. We were fine before they arrived.'

She released her grip on him and pulled back, looking deep into his eyes.

'But you know what,' she said, 'for all that, I'm glad that I met them, I liked them both. I love Alicia now and I've learnt a lot about myself, and about us. God knows I regret what happened to Gabrielle, but I can't help believing in fate. People's destinies are not in our hands.'

His eyes showed his emotion, as the painful memories flooded back to him.

'We don't know that the same thing wouldn't still have happened to her had she stayed in Philadelphia,' Courtney continued.

What she had said seemed to make sense to him. Maybe all this wasn't his fault after all, perhaps it was nobody's fault.

'I promise never to go anywhere without you again,' he said. 'We're a team you and me. I'm never keeping a secret from you again and I'm really sorry that I did.'

'Well I hope you don't mean I have to go *everywhere* with you,' she laughed, 'I'm not going to the bathroom with you every time that's for sure.' He laughed too, wiping at the fresh tears that had appeared in his eyes.

'I'm so sorry for everything I've ever said to you, anything that has ever hurt you. I love you so much,' she said, stroking his arm tenderly.

'I love you too,' he answered with a radiant smile.

'Are you ready then?'

She nodded wholeheartedly, and this time she really was.

'Let's go,' she replied.

As Alicia sat gazing at Brad, she realised that she had already been by his bedside for an hour. She hadn't moved in that time and it occurred to her that she could stay looking at his face all day and never tire of it. His parents had been there when she'd first arrived; they had kept a permanent vigil by his bedside since he'd first been taken ill. They would take it in turns to have an hour's sleep in the relatives' accommodation, when they could, or just fall asleep through sheer exhaustion in one of the chairs by his bed. Brad's mother had said to Alicia that she didn't want him to be left alone, not even for one moment, so when she arrived, they took the opportunity to get their heads down for a while. Alicia was pleased as she had so wanted to spend some time with Brad on her own, and now she had the chance. She had so much she wanted to say to him that was private. She wanted to be able to cry, without anybody seeing her, trying to comfort her or spoiling the moment. As she sat by his bedside, she willed him to speak in her mind. She spoke to him softly, tears flowing from her tired eyes. The machinery around him clicked over sporadically; the electronic sound of his heartbeat rang in her ears. He was in the same room as he had been the last time she'd seen him, a private wing in intensive care. The room was clinical and bare. She recalled her own hospital room, the one she had been in the first time. It at least had been painted a pastel yellow, which was more pleasing to the eye and slightly more homely, but this was white, starch white, deathly white. The only break in the monotony was the fresh bouquet of purple and yellow flowers that nestled in a vase on a small table under the window. She had noticed that the rim of the vase was chipped, which annoyed her. He deserved a perfect vase, not one that was blemished like that, but then he couldn't see them anyway, so what did it matter? She sighed. Reaching for his hand, she took it in hers and squeezed it. The hand was lifeless in her grasp and if she'd let go of it, it would have just slipped back down limply onto the bed. There it would stay until the next person arrived in the room and held it once more. His eyes were closed, his eyelids flickering occasionally. Every time they did she thought that this was it, this was the moment when he was going to wake up, and everything would be back to normal again. In her heart though, she knew it couldn't be for the best. Sitting there she thought about Gabrielle and how she was the single cause of all of her distress. Everything had revolved around her in life, and now even in death, she still had that hold over everyone. She mulled over what had happened at the churchyard that morning. She was still in a state of complete and total shock and confusion, nothing seemed to make any sense to her anymore, and how could any of that possibly have been real? She wondered where Gabrielle was now, as far away as possible from her, she hoped.

Then the thought came to her that for all she knew, she could be in the room with them right at that very moment. Maybe there was a remote chance that she felt guilty and was waiting in the corridor outside, giving her at least a moment alone with the man she loved. More likely she concluded, she was sitting on the opposite side of the bed, invisible to the naked eye, kissing Brad on his other cheek, caressing his face and hair, whispering more terrifying words into his ear, trying to kill him all over again. She leaned forward to claim back her man; she pressed her face against his cheek and kissed it.

'I'm so sorry Brad,' she whispered, 'I should have met you that night. My dad didn't call you to let you know I was still in hospital, I'm still so angry with him.' She paused, 'I'm sorry, I should have just run out of there, done something, anything, so that I could have still met you, and none of this would have happened.' She sobbed gently into his pillow, her fingers nestling in his hair, rubbing at his scalp, desperate for him to respond, to say that everything was going be fine, and that he forgave her. She knew that he must have known that it was Gabrielle he had seen. She imagined his abject horror at the sudden realisation. She knew that the shock of it was what had made him ill, that and the alcohol and the pills that she was sure Gabrielle had forced down his throat, in an attempt to steal her boyfriend from her, and have him join her in death. It hadn't worked yet, he was still here. But she knew that his future looked bleak, the doctors had spoken before about possible brain damage. She loved him so much that part of her just wanted to set him free - free from his useless, lifeless body, so his spirit could fly again. Then she thought about her dreams, how she had imagined them together always, married, with a family of their own, and her desperation returned again, wanting to keep him with her, wanting to hold on to him forever, never letting go.

'Please Brad,' she whispered, 'I know you can hear me,' she swallowed nervously, 'I know what happened to you. I've seen her myself and I want you to know that I've told her that I *never* want to see her again as long as I live. Oh Brad.' She sobbed again. 'Please speak to me! I'm dying inside, I need you so badly, I'm lost without you. If only I'd been with you that night. God, why did you allow this to happen? I don't understand. Why are you doing this to me? Did I do something that was so terrible? Am I never meant to be happy?' Her voice cracked again as her frustration and anger began to brim over. Still he didn't move, even his eyelids had stopped flickering now; there was nothing; no sign that he could hear her, no sign that he was even there at all. All she heard was the monotonous beeping of his life support machine. She looked at the monitor as the green line rhythmically peaked and troughed. She kissed him again and tenderly placed his hand back down so that it was just above the sheets. It twitched once, a reflex movement. She watched intently but it didn't move again. She retreated back to the chair by his bedside, feeling defeated and hollow inside - there was nothing she could do for him; she had nowhere to go, nothing else to do. At that moment, everything just seemed to her to be so utterly hopeless. She stared vacantly out of the first floor window; not really registering anything she was seeing. Another beep from the heart monitor diverted her attention back to him and there her gaze rested again, watching, waiting.

Courtney sat in the passenger seat of the space wagon, Adam at the wheel; they had already picked up Ruben from the motel where he was staying and were now nearing the hospital. He sat silently behind her in the back of the car, she felt a little awkward in his presence; filled with uncertainty. Adam had assumed that Alicia was still in bed when they'd left the house, he hadn't wanted her to see Ruben at all. After Courtney's warning they both feared that it would only worsen the situation and cause her more pain. Adam's expression had been grave when Courtney had told him that Alicia would be visiting Brad at the hospital that same morning. Neither of them knew what to expect or really what they were going to do there. Courtney had assumed that they were going to the hospital to talk on neutral ground, but she was doubtful that Ruben would be able to do anything to ease the situation in the house. Now that she knew about the twins' genetic modification, prior to their birth, she failed to see how this had any relevance to the supernatural activity that had taken place at her home - that had been Sarah.

Courtney had greeted Ruben as he'd stepped into the car with a simple 'hello.' He seemed ill at ease and his movements seemed to her to be very nervy. He wore an expensive leather jacket, casual slacks and a crisp smooth crew-necked sweater. She noticed his eyes, they were hazel coloured, and as he smiled, heavy lines formed creases in the corners; they seemed safe eyes though she thought. She hadn't paid any attention to their colour when he'd been at the house the day before. All she had noticed was that they were well spaced apart. She'd always been suspicious of people whose eyes were too close together, although she knew it was irrational, an old wives tale that had been passed down through the generations. His expression now seemed to be more open and welcoming, and his face not unattractive, if a little gaunt. The smart modern cut of his hair and the smell of his cologne were two of the hallmarks of a wealthy man. Adam had reverted to his formal businesslike manner; the atmosphere in the car was tense as they pulled up outside the hospital. Adam was the first to break the uneasy silence.

'We're going to have to go in the back way,' he said. 'There's a security door round there - my pass should swipe us in.'

Courtney knew why they had to go in this way. They had discussed the fact that she was off sick from work and she certainly didn't want to have to explain herself to her friend Nicky, or to anyone else for that matter. She just wanted to get this meeting over with, have Ruben sent back to where he'd come from, and try and get back to some sort of normality before the baby arrived. She had already decided that she would extend her sick leave period so that it coincided with the start of her maternity leave. She wasn't altogether sure in her mind yet if she would ever return to work. There was no real reason for her to as they could live quite comfortably on Adam's salary alone. It was time, she thought, to finally surrender her financial independence. She had always liked to keep her own salary as a kind of safety net, in case she and Adam should ever split up. She realised now that their marriage, having been tested, had proved to be rock solid still. She didn't have to pretend anymore and she wanted to have the time to be the best mother she could possibly be to their child.

As the car came to a halt, she automatically gathered her bag over her shoulder and moved to open the door. Adam suddenly took hold of her arm, making her jump.

'Sorry Courtney,' he said, realising he'd given her a fright, 'but there's something else I need to tell you, something that I didn't want to say to you when we were in the house.' He glanced over at Ruben who still sat motionless in the back, not uttering a word.

'The reason I said to you that I think something went horribly wrong with his experiment,' he said again looking coldly at Ruben, is because I've seen her.'

'Seen who?' she replied agitated. 'Sarah?'

Adam looked back at her, a bemused look on his face, 'No, not Sarah, Gabrielle. I've seen Gabrielle.'

'My God!' she said, putting her hand to her mouth. 'What do you mean you've seen her?'

Adam ran his hand awkwardly through his hair, glancing nervously around the car. She looked searchingly at him.

'So it's true then?' she said, wistfully. He looked back at her with surprise. Until this moment she had all but disregarded her suspicions about what had happened to Brad. Now she wasn't so sure.

'How do you know, have you seen her too?' he asked.

'No, I can't explain it really, I just suddenly thought about Brad. I had this bizarre theory about what happened to him and then came to the conclusion that it may have had something to do with Gabrielle.'

'I know I'd thought the same thing myself,' he answered grimly. 'You see it's not just a straightforward ghost either, or whatever else you'd like to call it. She's solid, she's real, she touched me.' He paused, swallowing nervously. 'But at the same time, she can pass through a wall, a door anything.' His voice rose, almost disbelieving the apparently nonsensical words that were coming from his mouth. 'She told me that she wasn't dead, that she can still think, still feel, but she's not truly alive either. I don't know what the hell she is.'

'And you knew about all this I take it?' she said turning to Ruben.

'Yes,' he replied in a matter of fact tone. 'Adam called me when you were in Philly. He was beside himself, he blames me for all of this. But I still don't see how my elimination of one rogue gene from a DNA profile can possibly effect somebody's ability or inability to live or die.'

'Well it could have affected it, you were messing with nature,' Adam cut in. 'You were using procedures that had only ever before been tested on animals, and even then no-one knew what the long term effects would be. Well maybe now you have your proof. Let's face it Ruben, my daughters were your guinea pigs, and I was a fool to have ever agreed to any of it in the first place!'

'Don't be too harsh on yourself,' Ruben answered almost condescendingly. 'You were only doing what you thought was best for your children. Anyway it was Sarah who was the driving force behind it all, not really you. Her obsession with the disease had almost become paranoia.'

'Look, hang on a minute!' Courtney said angrily staring straight at Adam, 'Never mind all that, didn't it ever occur to you that you ought to have told me that you'd seen Gabrielle, before you went crying to him?'

Adam shook his head in frustration. 'I know, I was wrong. I thought like I said to you, that I was protecting you by keeping all this business with the twins a secret - it's all so sordid and messed up. I wanted to keep us separate from it, but it all got out of hand and that's why we're here, to try and resolve everything once and for all.'

'Do you honestly believe,' she snapped back, 'that if he has created some sort of a freak of nature, who can't die, that he'd have the faintest idea what to do about it? You said yourself that this area of science is considered completely unethical, not to mention dangerous, as not enough is known about it.'

Ruben put a hand up to prevent Adam from replying. 'No, she's right,' he said. 'If all this proves to be true and I find there's nothing I can do, then I've made a huge mistake - one I will no doubt regret for the rest of my life. Don't give up though, as I've said to Adam, I have a few ideas and theories that I've been working on, and that's why I wanted to meet at the hospital.'

'So that's why we're here then, so that you can carry out some more experimentation?' Courtney rebuked. 'It's a bit late for that by the sound of it.'

'No, don't say that,' Adam said. 'Gabrielle wants us to help her, that's why Ruben and I believe she will be here today. She moves about you see, and she knows that there's nothing we can do for her at home. I'm sure that she has been listening to our conversations.' Courtney rolled her eyes at how ridiculous all of this sounded.

'And how do you know that then?' she said.

'Ever since that night, I've sensed her presence. She wasn't at the house this morning for example. I can't feel her now either, so there's a chance she will be inside, maybe following Alicia around, although Alicia probably won't be aware of her.'

'Well I'm glad that you're so sure,' Courtney replied mockingly. 'What are you planning to do then, have her sent down for some emergency x-rays?' She laughed scornfully.

'This is not a laughing matter Courtney,' Adam said, glaring back at her, 'this is deadly serious.' He reached for the handle of the door and climbed out of the car, closely followed by Ruben.

'Oh don't you think I already know that,' she hollered after him. She was angry that she had been excluded again, but she knew that this was no time to be having an argument. She just couldn't believe everything she had heard Adam say that day. It was as if there was now a different dimension to him, that his eyes had suddenly been opened. Now it seemed to her that he had finally realised that not everything in the universe made sense, that some things couldn't be understood fully by the human mind, and yet still he was sure that science would provide all the answers. She sat in the car for a moment longer, still thinking.

'Are you staying in there then?' Adam said through the open window.

'Not on your life,' she replied indignantly, suddenly alert again.

'I'll go and find Alicia,' she said as she stepped out of the car, 'After all if your theory is correct, then we'll need her to be there too. She was made in the same mould as Gabrielle don't forget, so is just as much affected by all this.'

Adam stood by the side of the car; his jeans still creased from the previous day, his old sweatshirt hanging loosely from his shoulders. He sighed, defeated, and turned to walk on ahead of her. Courtney's defences were up again. The sun, still bright, should have cheered her spirits, but as she walked silently along she took no notice of anyone or anything around her. Not really knowing what lay in store for any of them once they were inside the hospital, she quickened her pace and drew level with the others.

'So where shall I meet you both then, once I've found Alicia?' she asked. 'I mean, I haven't got a clue what I'm going to tell her. Will you wait for us in your office?' Adam glanced over at her. It was obvious that he had got it all planned out in his mind. 'No, Ruben and I have discussed this. We need to be somewhere where nobody's going to see us. When you've found her, you need to go down the fire escape into the hospital basement, making sure you don't let anyone see you.'

'Well I'll try my best, but unfortunately I don't have the ability to make myself invisible,' she answered flippantly.

'Well you have to try not to get noticed, it's important,' Adam replied forcefully. 'Once you're down in the basement, you need to head for the third room on the right. It's a disused theatre, nobody ever goes in there. I have the key and I'll be locking the door after us, so you'll need to knock twice on the door so that I can let you both in.'

As they approached the security door, Adam began to look around again nervously. He swiped the card in the reader and Courtney heard the heavy lock click open. A second later he was in, she followed closely behind. The corridor was empty, apart from one of the catering staff who rattled her trolley noisily past them, but didn't seem to register their presence. They were next to the hospital kitchens; she got her bearings quickly, deciding on the best route to take. She said a hurried goodbye to Adam and turned and walked rapidly towards the fire exit. Pushing the handle down hard the door swung open, and she began to climb the staircase. She knew that Brad's room was located on the first floor, towards the end of the corridor, and had already worked out that she was at the right end, so should be able to find Alicia within moments of arriving on the first floor. She paused, taking a deep breath before opening the second door. She was more nervous right then about having to admit to Alicia that Ruben was with them than about the prospect of seeing Gabrielle. After a moment of deliberation, she opened the door a crack, and waited. She couldn't hear any voices nearby so proceeded to open it a little further. She saw a nurse walking away from her down the corridor and slipped through the door, taking care not to tread too heavily. She reached Brad's room within seconds, and, as she had expected, saw Alicia through the glass sitting at his bedside. His parents were on the other side of the bed, their eyes hollow with grief and lack of sleep. There was another girl sitting with them who she had never seen before, very striking with long dark hair and large dark eyes. She paused again before turning the handle. As she entered the room, they all looked up, eager to see who had broken the monotony of their vigil.

'Courtney,' Alicia said wearily.

'How is he?' she asked.

'No change,' Brad's father replied dejected.

'I'm so sorry to hear that,' she answered, 'it's so dreadfully sad.' Nobody answered her; she coughed nervously and turned to Alicia. 'Would it be OK if I had a word with you in private? You can come straight back afterwards.'

Alicia looked over at Brad's mother, who nodded.

'You go dear,' she said, 'We'll be fine.'

'I'll come straight back, I won't be long - I promise,' Alicia said, as she leaned over to kiss Brad tenderly on his cheek. 'I'll be back soon,' she whispered.

Out in the corridor Courtney directed her towards the fire escape. 'Who's that with Brad's parents,' she asked, wanting everything to appear as normal as possible.

'It's Brad's sister,' Alicia answered. 'Anyway, what's all this about? Why the urgency, what's going on?'

'Alicia,' Courtney said, 'Now don't freak out now, but your dad and Ruben are here.'

'What?' she frowned.

'Your dad called him, he'd seen Gabrielle. It's a very long story, but I promise when we get downstairs they'll explain everything to you.'

'What do you mean downstairs, what are they doing down there?' Alicia said confused.

'We have to go somewhere private that's all,' Courtney replied a little dismayed that Alicia didn't react to what she'd said about Gabrielle. 'Aren't you shocked about Gabrielle?' she said opening up the fire door.

'No,' Alicia answered nonchalantly, 'I've seen her too, this morning in fact. It scared the living crap out of me, I went to visit her grave, although now I wish I hadn't bothered.'

'You did?' Courtney interjected.

'See if Dad had told us that yesterday, then I wouldn't have bothered to go to her stupid grave. Apparently she followed me all the way from the fucking house?' Courtney's mind was in turmoil; Alicia had just confirmed everything that Adam had said.

'So where is she now then?' Courtney asked, moving quickly down the stairs.

'Don't know, and I don't care, probably not far away though. You know that she admitted to me that she'd killed Jennifer and that she'd as good as killed Brad. She was jealous of us you see.'

Courtney was stunned by what she was hearing, but also conscious that they had to remain undetected. 'Listen, we'll talk about it when we get in the room. We mustn't let anyone see us.'

They soon reached the basement. It was cold down there and unwelcoming, the dark empty corridor stretched ahead of them. Alicia shivered and rubbed her arms with her hands.

'I don't like it down here,' she said.

Courtney had already found the third door, and was knocking.

The door opened slowly. Courtney's eyes met Adam's as he peered through the gap warily, making sure that they hadn't been followed.

'Look I'm not completely stupid,' Courtney said, 'Do you think I'd have knocked if there'd been someone there?'

'All right, just get in quick,' he replied, opening the door for them.

'Alicia?' he said when he saw her, checking her identity, as he was no longer sure in his mind which one of his daughters was standing in front of him.

'Yes it's me, and before you ask, I don't know where the freak's gone, and I don't really care either.'

'Why are you calling her a freak?' he said, assuming at that moment that Courtney must have already told her everything.

'Well she must be a freak if she managed to survive being stabbed about forty times, and then wake up in her coffin and magically remove herself from it, only to find herself standing looking at her own headstone.'

'How does she know all this?' he said turning to Courtney.

'Because I've seen her too Dad,' Alicia said, tears springing into her eyes, 'OK, no hang on perhaps I just made it all up!'

'Just get in, and close the door,' Adam replied, angered by his daughter's sarcasm.

The theatre door swung shut and Adam double locked it, leaving the key in the door. There were no windows in the room; it was a large room, Courtney thought, but it still felt claustrophobic to her, as the air had an overpoweringly stagnant smell about it. She could see marks on the far wall where the paint had chipped off; there were patches of mould there. Disused equipment and instruments were still lying on trolleys rusting. There was even a set of surgical gloves hanging limply over the tap on the wash basin in the far corner. It was as if someone had left the room in the middle of something and forgotten to come back. In the centre of the room was the examination table, which had also begun to corrode.

'What did they do in here?' Courtney asked still eyeing the room.

'Autopsies,' Adam replied flatly. 'The morgue's just up the corridor, but they've done out another room now closer to it, so they don't need this one anymore.'

'I'm surprised they haven't cleared all this lot out. It's not very hygienic is it?' she continued.

'Where is he then?' Alicia suddenly said, tired of the inconsequential conversation that was currently going on between Courtney and her father.

Courtney had already guessed that he must be in the alcove at the far end of the room; it was a small add-on, with a square archway connecting the two areas. Ruben stepped out from the shadows, his eyes suddenly revealing his fear.

'It's you!' Alicia exclaimed, to their surprise.

His wild eyes stared back at her; he was unable to speak; unsure of what she would say next.

'I saw you, you were at her funeral, standing there like a spectre under the trees. You were staring right at me the whole time.'

Courtney realised then that it must have been him who Adam had seen, and she remembered again how he'd lied to her, and made secret phone calls, not wanting her to discover the truth. There was an uneasy silence and the atmosphere in the room became oppressive.

'You need to tell her the truth,' Courtney said.

Ruben approached the group who by now had moved away from the door towards the centre of the room.

'Alicia,' he said, his arms outstretched.

'Don't you come near me!' she cried, tears now coursing down her cheeks. 'You ruined my life, you broke my mom's heart. You broke up her marriage and now she's dead, and it's all because of you.'

You don't understand,' he pleaded, 'It wasn't the way you think it was. I helped you, I gave you and your sister hope for the future. You never had to worry about giving birth to a son.'

'What is he talking about?' Alicia said turning, bewildered, to her father.'

'Alicia listen to me,' Adam said catching hold of her hand, which she immediately withdrew. 'Your mother was a carrier of a disease called haemophilia,' he continued, 'It means that the blood takes much longer to clot, and…'

'I know what haemophilia is,' she cut in, 'I'm not stupid you know.'

Adam proceeded to tell her how he and her mother had gone to Ruben for help, and how he had told them that he could eradicate the gene from their genetic make up, preventing it from being passed on to the next generation. He then went on to tell her how he believed that the procedure may have gone wrong, in light of what appears to have happened to Gabrielle. 'We thought we were doing the best for you,' he said sorrowfully, as Alicia stood aghast, a look of abject horror and dismay on her face.

'My God!' she said through her tears, 'So you mean to tell me that I'm some sort of circus freak, like her! So when I come to die, the same will happen to me. Is that the legacy you've given to me?' Her eyes were wide with fear. 'So what you're saying is that the one thing I want to do more than anything else in the world, I can't do?'

'Oh don't say that please Alicia,' Courtney said her eyes filling with tears at the thought of losing a person that she had grown to love.

'I have nothing to live for!' she cried angrily. 'My boyfriend is dying, I've lost everything.'

'You have me, and your dad,' Courtney said earnestly, 'There's your new baby brother or sister.'

'I don't suppose your baby's been genetically modified too has it? My God, a family of freaks, who'd have believed it to look at us!' Alicia raged, bitterness in her voice. 'No, I'm sorry Courtney, but you, Dad and a baby I don't even know - that's not enough to convince me to want to live.' She turned towards the door; 'I'm going to be with Brad.'

'No!' Adam cried, 'You can't go, not now, nothing's been resolved. We have to speak with Gabrielle, you're her sister, don't you want to try to help her? We don't know where she is.'

'She's over there,' she replied pointing towards the alcove. 'And I sure as hell don't want to help that murdering bitch!' Courtney stared straight ahead of her, shocked by Alicia's sudden revelation, her heart pounding as her eyes strained to see her in the shadows. As they looked on, Gabrielle emerged from the corner of the room. Ruben reeled backwards in fright, and ran towards the door.

'No!' Adam hollered at him, 'You did this, now you face it.' He stopped dead in his tracks, and turned slowly. Courtney could see his hands trembling. There were beads of sweat on his forehead. He had a look of dread in his eyes.

'Alicia,' Gabrielle called from the corner of the room, 'I'm sorry, please forgive me.' She was crying. A look of dismay then washed over Ruben's face as he tried to understand what he was seeing.

'I've told you already,' Alicia replied, 'I never want to see or speak to you again.' She had turned her back on her; revolted by the sight of the sister she had grown to hate.

'But we're both the same!' Gabrielle cried. 'We both know that.'

'I may be on the outside,' Alicia said angrily, 'but I'm not selfish like you, and I don't judge people just by their looks alone.'

'Yes you do, you hypocrite,' Gabrielle yelled back.

Adam, still trying to come to terms with the sight of his dead daughter, realised that this conversation was getting them nowhere.

'Just shut up the pair of you!' he shouted. 'Now Gabrielle, putting aside any feelings you may have about this man standing here with us, just remember that he is here to try to help you, and make amends for the past.'

Adam then turned to Ruben. 'If you could run those ideas by us now.'

Ruben jerked his head nervously to face him, and then immediately averted his gaze, afraid now to take his eyes off Gabrielle, who was standing, moving and breathing before him.

'Gabrielle,' he began, his voice shaking, 'Can I ask you if you're fully aware of everything around you?'

'Yes of course I am,' she replied, moving a step closer to him.

'Can you feel your physical body? What I mean by that is do you feel completely yourself, can you still feel pain?'

'Yes I can,' she replied impatiently, 'Look how is this helping? I need you to do something,' she cried, desperation in her voice.

'Bear with me Gabrielle,' he continued, 'We'll come to how I'm going to help you. First I need to take you back to the moment of the attack - are you able to recall that? I know it must be hard for you, but I need you to tell me exactly what happened.'

'Well,' she said cautiously, 'the bitch was stabbing him. My hands and arms got caught in it first, I was trying to stop her. I'd fallen forwards on top of him and was trying to shield him. I remember then being stabbed in the back. At first it just felt as though I'd been punched until the pain kicked in.'

'So you remember all that clearly?' he confirmed.

'Well that's what I just said wasn't it,' she snapped back. Courtney was trying to see Gabrielle's eyes in the half-light, but from where she was standing it was impossible, as the shadow was obscuring them.

'I have a deep wound in my chest - I think that must have been the final blow,' Gabrielle then said, 'It's dried up though now like the others.'

'So what happened next?' Ruben said, his voice becoming a little clearer and more authoritative.

'Everything just went black, completely pitch black, and I don't remember anything else until I woke up, in there.' Her voice quivered as she recalled the fear that she had felt when she realised that she was trapped in her own coffin.

'So when you say everything went black,' he continued. 'Did you not see a tunnel with a bright light at the end of it, or feel yourself floating away from your body?'

'No, nothing like that. Like I just told you, everything just went black,' she answered, in frustration.

'But she was pronounced dead at the scene,' he said turning to Adam for confirmation. He nodded in response.

'No tunnel of light,' Ruben said, thinking out loud. 'But her brain would have been starved of oxygen.'

'Look I don't understand what you're getting at,' Adam interrupted his thought process.

'In almost all near death experiences, people have seen a tunnel of light,' he replied, 'I mean, obviously we don't know about the ones who have died and not come back, but the ones that have come back, in those cases, the stories they tell are almost always the same. Scientists put that down to the brain being starved of oxygen, just before death occurs, stating that it induces a hallucinogenic state within the patient.'

'Yes and...' Adam said impatiently.

'This theory has been proved countless times,' Ruben continued, 'Trainee fighter pilots taken to g-force speeds in special flight simulation chambers have been known to black out during these endurance tests. They too have reported seeing the same tunnels of light, exactly the same as with the near death experience, again caused by lack of oxygen to the brain.'

'But how is Gabrielle not having seen a tunnel of light relevant? What does that mean in terms of genetic modification?' Courtney said unsure of what he was getting at.

'Well, what if the lack of oxygen was just a trigger for a more complex mechanism within the brain?' he said, looking over at them eagerly, almost with excitement in his eyes, as his theory developed. 'What if this mechanism was built into all human beings at their creation, to aid the process of death, by pacifying the person in their moment of utmost fear, whilst at the same time setting their spirit free from their body?'

'So you're talking about a switch in the brain, a kind of ejector button that releases the soul at the moment the patient dies?' Adam said, trying to make sense of his logic.

'Yes, shall we say, like a death switch,' he replied, putting a name to his theory.

'Gabrielle didn't see a tunnel of light, and that has led me to believe that maybe it isn't all conjecture and people's expectation at the point of death. It must be a biological part of every human brain. That's what I believe she must be missing, that's why she can't pass on to the next life. This is amazing,' he continued enthusiastically. 'That has to be it, the only explanation there could possibly be. To think that I never believed in anything like that before, wow, my eyes have certainly been opened up today!'

'Well that's all very well,' Adam said angrily, 'but that still leaves you with the problem of what you are going to do about it.'

Ruben's expression suddenly changed again. It had already dawned on him that there was absolutely nothing he could do, he'd known that all along. He'd just wanted to see her with his own eyes. The damage he had done back then was permanent, irretrievable, he had no chance of reversing the consequences of his actions. There was no escaping from it now, locked in that room, with no possible solution. To fight or to flee, he had to decide, as his day of judgement had arrived. He backed away from the door, and slid along the back wall, his gaze fixed, not moving from them. It was then that Courtney noticed that the key was missing from the lock. She saw the flash of tarnished metal as he drew the gun from his inside pocket. His expression had changed again; he had a manic almost victorious grin on his face as they realised for the first time his true intention. He was laughing at them as though they should have known that this would happen, and how could they have been so stupid to have thought otherwise.

Chapter 20

'What the hell are you doing?' Adam bellowed making a sudden lunge towards him. Ruben cocked the gun and aimed it directly at him, his hand shaking. Courtney screamed at Adam to come back and Alicia ran towards the door.

'Where are you going?' Ruben mocked, 'You can't get out, the door's locked.'

'Give me the Goddamn gun,' Adam shouted. He had stopped just short of him, his hand thrust out.

'Did you honestly believe that I'd let you live once our little secret got out?' Ruben sneered. 'Or let anyone who you'd told for that matter?'

'Listen Ruben, we can talk about this can't we?' Adam said backing away, his arms raised above his head as Ruben aimed the gun towards his head. 'This is stupid! I mean it's not in any of our interests to reveal the secret, it affects all of us too much. We made a deal back then remember?'

'Yes,' Ruben replied, 'and the deal was that nobody was ever told. Well I'm sorry Adam, but everything's changed now. You can't blame me for something you've done.' He moved the gun away from Adam, aiming it directly at Courtney. 'Hey, Adam, I just figured that if I shoot her instead, I'll be getting two for the price of one - one bullet to kill two people, an economy killing!' He laughed menacingly at his own joke.

'You're sick,' Adam replied, his voice now shaking. Courtney stood paralysed with fear by his side. He then moved to stand in front of his wife, 'You'll have to shoot me first.'

'Dad no!' Gabrielle cried. As quick as lightening Ruben backed away from them again, and spun round, aiming the gun directly at Gabrielle.

'That's a point,' he said using his free hand to scratch his head, 'We haven't even helped poor Gabrielle yet. I almost forgot about her, hiding away in that corner. I was going to try my new experiment on her.' As the words were out of his mouth, he fired at her chest again and again. There was no explosion as the bullets were released, just a sterile clicking sound, like the sound of a slaughter man's gun in an abattoir. Gabrielle cried out in pain as the bullets struck her. 'Let's see if that doesn't do the trick,' he said. Adam watched in horror as his daughter died all over again, her body twitching and arching on the ground, reverberating with every fresh bullet that embedded itself in her flesh. Alicia suddenly ran at Ruben roaring like a creature possessed. Still firing at Gabrielle he was momentarily caught off guard; Courtney screamed out to her as she rammed into Ruben with such force that he was knocked off his feet. As she was coming down on top of him, his arms were flailing wildly and the butt of the gun struck her on the head. She too slumped to the floor. Courtney held Adam back. He was shouting at him to leave his daughter alone, powerless to help, with no weapon of his own, and his pregnant wife beside him. He fell backwards, weeping; this was all his fault.

'Silencer,' Ruben said getting quickly to his feet and brushing himself down with his free hand. 'Good idea huh? I didn't want to draw attention to myself when I was killing you all.'

'So that's it then,' Adam said pulling himself together, 'You're just going to kill us all one by one, and then just leave us here.'

'I don't see why not?' he said, reloading the gun, his wild eyes still staring back at them. 'That's what I'd planned to do. Why, do you have any particular preference who goes next out of you two?'

'Please, I beg you,' Adam pleaded, 'if you're going to kill anyone, then let it be me. I'm the one you hate, you don't even know my wife. You only met her for the first time yesterday and she's pregnant for God's sake.'

'No!' Courtney interrupted angrily, 'Neither of us deserves it and I'd rather die myself than have to live without you.'

'Oh how touching,' Ruben replied, 'Well I'll tell you what, you argue it out amongst yourselves, and whilst you're thinking about which one of you it's going to be, I'll tell you a little story.'

'Can't you just let me check on my daughters?' Adam said.

'Well I wouldn't bother,' he answered coldly, 'because one was dead already, so it doesn't make an awful lot of difference, and the other one, well we all heard her say that she wanted to die, so let her! That's what I say.'

'You really are a heartless, twisted bastard!' Adam cried.

Ruben slumped to the ground then, his hand caressing Alicia's hair, his eyes suddenly filling with tears of self-pity.

'I wanted these girls to be so perfect,' he said, his gaze still fixed on Courtney and Adam, the gun still aimed, ready to shoot either one of them. 'Well they're not are they!' he cried. 'My daughters, my perfect daughters.'

'Your daughters?' Adam said the life draining from his face.

'That's right, *my* daughters!' he hollered back. 'I had high hopes for these two. They were my little angels, physically perfect in every way.'

'They're not your daughters, they're mine,' Adam shouted back.

'Oh Adam,' he mused, 'You really are stupid, did you really think that I was going to use your jerk off to create my masterpiece, and let you be the father of Sarah's babies?'

Adam and Courtney stared in disbelief as again Ruben's hand reached out and caressed Alicia's lifeless body.

'Sarah was the love of my life, but she never wanted me did she Adam? She just wanted sex from me.' His voice twisted with bitterness. 'I bet these girls never knew that their mother was like that, I bet you never bothered to tell them that did you? It didn't really matter who it was. Oh there were others,' he said smiling wickedly back at Adam. 'She used to tell me that you were always tired, you would never give it up. She was sex mad you see, she couldn't get enough of it, and you just didn't deliver the goods did you Adam. That's where I used to come in, she used me to satisfy her constant physical needs. That was her only major fault really. I used to tell myself that if you weren't there, then she almost certainly would fall in love with me, eventually. I even considered killing you back then, but I knew how much Sarah loved you.' He spat the words, as tears flowed from his eyes. 'I'd never have got her to love me, if I'd taken you away from her. It doesn't matter now though because she's dead.' His finger moved shakily back to the trigger. 'So when I finally told you about our affair, and you left, I thought that now maybe things would be different, because you'd proved that you weren't the kind of man to stick around and take care of your responsibilities. I still held on to that hope that one day that hard exterior of hers would crack - that she'd realise that she couldn't cope with bringing up the children alone. I could have lived with being second best to you, so long as I had her - that was all that mattered to me.'

Courtney reached over and squeezed Adam's hand, just to let him know that it was all right, and that she was there with him. She still couldn't believe that she was stood staring down the barrel of a gun, she had never anticipated any of this.

'Don't you want to know what happened next then?' Ruben suddenly yelled. Courtney jumped, and released her grip on Adam's hand. 'Well,' he then continued, his voice returning to normal, 'when I was designing the twins, I had to eliminate almost all of my genes, the darker genes always predominate you see. I wanted them both to be fair haired like their mother. I've always preferred blondes. I couldn't just stop at their looks, oh no, I didn't want my daughters to be branded dumb blondes. They had to go on to do great things with their lives. Like their father.'

'I don't believe I'm hearing all this,' Adam said his voice breaking.

'Sarah broke my heart when you left her,' Ruben continued, disregarding Adam's words, as though he hadn't spoken. 'She blamed me for it, can you believe that? She blamed me. In the years that followed, I tried and I tried to get her to change her mind, to let me live with her, let us be a family together, but she wouldn't - the stubborn bitch! In the end she left me no choice. I had to play my trump card. I had to tell her that the twins were really mine. I called her up one day and I told her everything over the phone. I'd even organised a DNA test to be carried out for the very next day. I told her I had to see her that night and asked her if I could come round, but she said no. She said I had to wait until tomorrow, when the children were at school, like I always fucking did. I couldn't wait until the next day though,' emotion racked his body again as he began to sob, beating himself around his head with his free hand like a man possessed. 'I couldn't wait, just one fucking night could I. I waited until I knew that she would be asleep - this terrible panic had come over me you see. I had to be with her, I had to see her that night. We couldn't be separated, not now that she knew that I was the father. I'd had a key cut before - I hadn't intended to use it like this. She didn't know I'd got a key, she wouldn't have minded once I'd moved in though.' His speech was rambling and incoherent as the gun trembled in his hand. 'It must have been about twenty past one in the morning when I arrived at the house. Her bedroom light was off and I knew she was a deep sleeper. I crept in the house and up the stairs and pushed open the girls' bedroom door; I watched them sleeping for a moment. It was like I was their proper daddy, and I was on my way to bed to join their mom, having stayed up to drink some beer and watch the late night ball game on the TV. I tiptoed across the landing and into Sarah's room. I'd crushed up the tablets into the glass before I woke her; I'd already filled it with neat whiskey, which I knew was her favourite nightcap. She often liked a whiskey before bedtime. I even had gloves on, I'd got it all planned out. You see, it all came to this because when I'd told her everything on the phone, instead of acting rationally, she had to go and lose it on me, being the hot-headed, neurotic bitch that she sometimes could be.' He paused again, Adam and Courtney never moved from the spot. Adam was waiting for his opportunity to seize the gun, but so far Ruben had not averted his gaze from them for one second and his finger was permanently poised on the trigger. 'I loved her so much, you know, and that was the gratitude I got,' he then said. 'See I blame her for all that really. If she hadn't said to me that she was going to expose me, and blow the whistle on my genetic research, my life's work, my destiny, then I wouldn't have had to kill her.'

'You killed Sarah?' Courtney said in disbelief.

'She should never have said that to me, you see, should never have said it,' Ruben rambled on, 'I did give her one last chance though when I woke her. God, you'd have thought that I'd been a total stranger when she saw me; not one of her lovers. Boy did she scream. Well she did for a second anyway, until I forced a pillow over her face to stifle it. I couldn't have my girls frightened by all that noise. Once she'd calmed down, I took the pillow back off her and I asked her again if she would consider changing her mind, for the sake of our family. She swore at me and told me no, and that I would never be a part of her family.

But she'd made me part of it, don't you see? I loved her. That was when I drowned her in whiskey and pills. I remember I held her nose so tight that it bled. She had no choice but to open her mouth to try to breathe, so she choked to death.'

'You deserve to rot in hell for that!' Adam said through his tears.

'Well I guess you'll never know where I'm going Adam,' he replied with a faint smile. 'You ought to be more worried about where you're going first my friend.'

'I'm not your friend Ruben,' Adam replied scornfully, 'I've always hated you, and now I know the truth I always will. So she never loved you then, she only ever loved me, despite your best efforts and deception. And the fact still remains that you will *never* take my daughters away from me, because to them I have always and *will* always be their father.'

Courtney looked across at her husband and their eyes met. She saw his love for her shining through his tears, and all of a sudden she felt safe. She decided right there and then that if she never did make it out of that room that she wouldn't care, so long as she could die by his side.

'Yes she did love you, she always fucking loved you!' Ruben shouted back, with tears of loathing and hatred stinging his eyes. 'She just couldn't help herself, and that's why you're going to have to die, because I can't bear to live with that knowledge a moment longer.' The gun was pointing directly at Adam, and this time Courtney knew that he was going to pull the trigger. He was obviously insane. They knew too much, and his story had come to its end. Without thinking this time, she suddenly stumbled forward in front of him.

'So be it,' Ruben said, his voice hollow and empty. 'May God forgive me for what I have done, and for what I am about to do.'

It was too late; the gun had gone off, the final bullet had been fired. But it was still Adam who reeled backwards from the force of it, and almost instantaneously, as he did, he found himself shrouded in all encompassing darkness. He panicked momentarily, but then he noticed up ahead of him a small pinprick of incandescent white light, that appeared to be growing larger before his eyes. As he watched he concluded that either it was travelling towards him, or he was travelling towards it. He wasn't sure at that point which, but he had a feeling that it didn't really matter. The light came closer and closer, until it enveloped him, and he became part of it. He knew instinctively that he must be dying. He was shocked at how quick and how relatively painless it had been, he had just felt as though someone had struck him hard in the chest with a clenched fist. He reached out in his blindness and tried to feel his way, but he soon realised that the room he'd been locked in had now completely disappeared, the walls that had surrounded him, holding him captive, had just melted away. His eyes were not accustomed to this unearthly almost translucent luminescent light. He could barely bring himself to look at it, and yet when he finally did, he was in awe of what he saw before him. He was faced with a power and greatness that he had never imagined possible. He instinctively fell to his knees as the scene before him began to reveal its unimaginable beauty. He cried tears of unbearable sorrow as his life flashed before his eyes, and he found himself faced with all of his shortcomings, now realising for the first time that none of it had gone unnoticed, and that he was accountable for everything that he had ever said or done.

Coming to from his grief he became aware that he was surrounded by colours that he had never seen before, previously undiscovered by the human eye. Before him lay a garden, teaming with life, radiating laughter and joy, a fountain of crystal clear water stood in the centre, sparkling in the morning sunshine. At the end of the garden he saw an ornate archway, with flowers blooming from the low walls beside it and they were growing before his very eyes. Beyond the archway were green fields and rolling hillsides, the sun was glowing burnished red and gold as it began to set behind the hilltops. Further beyond these hills he could see a cornflower blue tranquil sea, with golden sands and magnificent palm trees swaying gently in the midday sunshine. High above birds of paradise swooped majestically in the clear blue sky. It was as though he could see for all eternity. His fear now gone, he felt immersed in pure peace and love, like nothing he had ever experienced before. All of a sudden he became aware of his body again, of his hand being squeezed tightly, he looked to his right and he saw his wife smiling back at him, she was there with him. He looked down and saw that he was still wearing the same old jumper and the same worn jeans. There was no blood oozing from any fresh open wound and as he felt his chest he could still feel his heart beating. They were not alone in this place. The intense light had now formed into glowing human shapes that were moving towards them. He couldn't see any of their faces, but for two of them he didn't need to, he recognised his parents' spirits without the need for any physical resemblance. The scene then retreated further backwards; the sweetest music filled his ears, filling his heart with excitement and joyfulness. He felt he wanted to dance, which was something he would never normally want to do. Still he couldn't move from his knees, and then to their right, he saw his tormentor, cowering on his knees, still clutching the gun in his trembling hand, his other hand shielding his eyes from the powerful light. It was then that Adam saw him, the greatest figure of them all, with beams of light, like showers of gold radiating from him. His heavenly company retreating respectfully as he moved towards Gabrielle's lifeless body. Adam rubbed at his eyes. He was crying in wonder as the towering embodiment of light reached down tenderly to her, touching her forehead. She immediately revived, stood up and then seeming automatically to realise where she was, and in whose presence she was in, fell to her knees, weeping tears of gratitude. No words were uttered that were audible to him - they were obviously not meant for his ears. His attention was then drawn to a sudden stirring to the right of them. He turned his head and watched in amazement as Alicia slowly rose to her feet behind Ruben, who was still shielding his eyes from the light. She walked past him undetected and also knelt at the feet of the being of light, who placed his hand on her head.

As Adam looked on, he saw Gabrielle suddenly look up as though somebody was calling her name, and she rose again to her feet. The scene before him was gradually moving further backwards so that he no longer felt part of it. He felt his heart ache with longing as it slowly began to slip away and he reached out his hand towards Gabrielle, realising suddenly that she no longer resembled herself as she had looked on earth - she had become one of them. She turned almost instinctively and gazed down at her sister, who raised her head to acknowledge her for the first time. Their eyes met, their anger and bitterness having melted away. Gabrielle smiled then and he knew that she would not be coming back. Tears of self-pity sprang into his eyes, because he realised that he was going to have to start missing her all over again. She walked forwards, slowly at first, towards a throng of celestial beings who had gathered in front of the archway, their magnificent forms gleaming in the bright sunshine. One had stepped out from amongst the crowd and was running to meet her, arms outstretched. She quickened her pace and the two met by the fountain, in a jubilant embrace.

'Look after her,' Adam said quietly, glad that she had finally found her mother. As he said this the scene then gradually retreated further, until it had vanished completely, almost as quickly as it had come.

The four walls had returned and nothing on the face of it appeared to have changed in the room. His heart felt as though it were about to burst from his chest, so real and so intense was the experience he had just had. He had never been so sure about anything in his life. As he sat with his wife, replaying it all in his mind, becoming awe struck all over again, he suddenly became aware of Ruben, as he appeared back in his peripheral vision. He was still racked with anguish, his body shaking with grief, crying pitifully. He seemed unaware of their presence in the room.

'Sarah, I'm sorry,' he sobbed, 'Don't leave me again, I can't live without you!' He let out another tortured cry. 'I won't live without you!' The gun was in his mouth before either Courtney or Adam could utter a word. Alicia was left kneeling in front of them, her head bowed; only now she was facing a dirty mould encrusted wall.

Adam pressed his wife's face to his body to shield her eyes as Ruben pulled the trigger. His body slumped to the ground twitching as death claimed him. Adam was now back in the here and now, thinking quickly. The horror of the grisly corpse that lay beside them had suddenly awakened him and he felt the desperate urgency of this new situation compel him to take action.

He took Courtney's hand in his, and finally found his voice. 'Let's get out of here,' he said. 'We have to move quickly. I'm going to need you to take Alicia with you - drive straight home and don't speak to anyone until you get there.'

Courtney nodded as her husband helped her to her feet, and then their eyes met again and she felt she had connected with his soul. She realised then that Adam too believed that they had both just witnessed a miracle, and in that moment she knew that whatever else happened that day, or in the near or distant future, none of it mattered because her life was now complete.

Florida State Police

Witness Testimony

With reference to case number: S67845
Concerning the suicide of Dr Ruben Moya on Tuesday,
12th September 2006

I confirm that my name is Adam Thomas Buchanan. My
address is 240 Bay View Grove, Kissimmee, Orlando, Florida. I
am 45 years old, born on the 26/02/1961 in the city of
Philadelphia, Pennsylvania. I confirm that I had known the
deceased, Mr Ruben Moya for 25 years. I first met him in
September 1981, when we were both students together at The
Pennsylvania School of Medicine. We were friends for
approximately 7 of those years.

Mr Moya contacted me five days ago, on the 9th September, after
many years of us having had no contact with each other. He
informed me that he needed to see me urgently, and asked if
sometime during the morning of the 12th September would be a
convenient time. I was of course surprised by his call, as we had
had nothing to do with each other since he had informed me in
January of 1996 that he had been having an affair with my then
wife Sarah Buchanan, for the past two years. This revelation
caused the break-up of my marriage at that time and I was
compelled to move out of state to Florida that same year, where I
started a new life in Leesburg, and eventually met my current
wife Courtney Buchanan in March 2000.

Mr Moya told me during his phone call that his intention was for
us to meet at my place of work, as he wanted to be able to talk
with me in private. He told me at the time that he was coming to
discuss my daughters. I thought this would be a valid reason for
him to need to talk with me, because my ex-wife and I had
consulted him for IVF treatment at his clinic, when we were
having trouble conceiving a child in the early years of our
marriage.

It turned out that I was not working on the Tuesday morning, so
I arranged to pick him up from the Comfort Inn at 09.30 a.m. I
was in fact late arriving and didn't get there until around 10.10
a.m., but I had called him to inform him of this. He was very
formal and businesslike when I met with him. He told me that
he had got some paperwork for me. I asked him if he'd prefer to
go somewhere else to talk, as I wasn't working, but he insisted
that he wanted to go to the hospital and talk in my office. I
reluctantly agreed. We arrived at the hospital around 10.30 a.m.

Once inside, he soon became agitated, and demanded that he see the morgue where my daughter Gabrielle's body had been stored, before her removal to the funeral home. I asked him why, and that was when he told me that he was the biological father of my daughters. I didn't believe him of course, and still don't now, especially in light of what followed. I was unwilling to take him down there, as it is against hospital policy, and I didn't see how it was necessary. He broke down and stated that he would leave me alone as soon as he'd seen inside the morgue. I should never have agreed, but I did, as I wanted to be able to end our meeting as soon as possible, and believed that he would be placated by it. Of course I had no intention of taking him into the working morgue, I had already decided that I would take him to the disused autopsy room, as this would not disturb anyone who was working, or arouse any undue suspicion amongst my colleagues. Once we were down there, in the room, I foolishly left the key in the lock, and moved to the centre of the room. As he closed the door behind us, he locked it. It must have been then that he slipped the key into his pocket, I didn't notice him doing it at the time. The time then was 10.56 a.m., I know this, because I remember glancing at my watch, and believe that this was when he took the key from the lock. Seconds later he pulled the gun out of his inside jacket pocket. I was completely taken aback by this, and perhaps now, with hindsight, I should have realised his true intentions. This was when he admitted to me that he had in fact murdered my ex-wife, by forcing her to drink whisky that he'd laced with powdered drugs. He said that he could no longer live with the burden of the guilt that he felt for what he had done. He said that he had murdered her because although they'd had a long running affair, she had never allowed him to move into her house, and clearly had no intention of them ever becoming a couple. It was apparent to me on that Tuesday morning that for many years he had obviously been and still was completely obsessed with my ex-wife. I believe that he was almost certainly delusional, and possibly suffering from a personality disorder, perhaps brought on by the rejection and the subsequent trauma he had suffered. He told me that he was going to kill me. He fired first randomly against the back wall. I believe it was four or five times, but I can't be completely sure about this as he had a silencer on the gun. I think he did this just to prove to me that he had every intention of going through with killing me, and was just stalling. This did mean that I had time to anticipate his next move, so as he turned the gun on me, I somehow managed to throw myself to the ground moments before he pulled the trigger. I believe that he must have assumed then that he had fatally wounded me. I opened my eyes seconds later to see him knelt on the ground to my right.

He had moved forward and was just about level with me. I believe that he was completely unaware of my presence at that time. He was sobbing uncontrollably and his body was shaking violently. I remember clearly him saying that he couldn't live anymore without Sarah, (my ex-wife,) as he placed the gun into his mouth. The barrel of the gun was pointing upwards towards the base of his skull. He then pulled the trigger, taking his own life, before I had time, or the presence of mind to prevent this. Having regained my composure, I checked and found there was no pulse. I then reached into his pocket to remove the key. I was finally then able to free myself from the room and alert the police, which I did at 11.21 a.m., to report the suicide. I confirm that at no point during the incident was the firearm in my possession, as forensic reports will no doubt corroborate. I also confirm that everything I have stated in this testimony is a true and accurate account of the circumstances of Mr Moya's death.

I would like to add that in light of this event, I would ask that the case file pertaining to my ex-wife's death be reopened.

Witness Signature/Date: *ABuchanan* 4/09/2006

Dr. A. T. Buchanan

Officer Present/Date: *CarlOwens* 14/09/06

Detective C. R. Owens

Six Months Later

Alicia took another sip from the tall glass of ice cold Coke that stood in front of her. She was basking in the sunshine on a wide, open terrace, set slightly back from the sidewalk - happy that day, surrounded by her friends. She had remembered just as she'd taken her first sip from the glass, that she had sat at the very same table with Brad, when they had spent that day together. She smiled as the recollection of everything they had done that day filled her mind. She remembered just how perfect everything had been. She flinched then, as she recalled how it had ended, with her so drunk that she could barely stand.

'Alicia,' the bubbly, pointy-faced blonde sitting opposite her suddenly said, thrusting a packet of cigarettes under her nose. 'Would you like one?'

'Thanks Candy,' she replied sliding one awkwardly out of the tightly wedged new soft pack.

'You haven't introduced us to your friend yet,' Candy continued, '*or* told us why we're here.'

'Sorry,' Alicia said a little absentmindedly; she was still remembering that day. 'Right,' she continued, turning to her companion, 'These two here, well this is Candy, who's a total head case, when she's had a few drinks, and this,' she said pointing to the small slightly shy looking brunette next to her friend, 'is Sadie.'

'Pleased to meet you,' Sadie replied.

'And…' Candy said gesticulating impatiently with her hands.

'I'm just coming to that,' Alicia teased her friends further, flicking her hair, and pausing again.

'Well if you don't tell us, we'll just have to ask him ourselves,' Sadie said.

'All right, all right,' she replied. 'This is Brad, my gorgeous boyfriend,' she beamed, bringing her hand down hard on his thigh.

'God couldn't you have thought of something a bit more dynamic to say?' he said, with an embarrassed smile.

415

The girls laughed and looked flirtatiously at him.

'So you've moved out of your dad's house finally then?' Cand continued after a brief pause.

'Yeah,' Alicia replied with a grin. 'Well Brad and I had wante to get our own flat together, but he had to sell his first. Yo know, fresh start and all that, and besides, I didn't like his fla When I went there it was too dark, and well, in quite a bad area.

'Gee thanks a lot! You really are painting a great picture of me he replied in feigned annoyance.

'Oh Brad,' she said nudging him, 'I'm only kidding! But yo have to admit, that place desperately needed a woman's touch.'

'Yeah,' he protested, turning to Alicia's friends, 'That woul probably explain why I didn't get any say in the choice o furniture or colour scheme.'

'Alicia,' Sadie scolded, 'and I always thought it was your siste who was the dominating one out of the two of you.'

She smiled in response, 'Well, just goes to show how wrong yo can be.'

'How's your stepmom?' Candy then asked her, changing th subject.

'Oh she's fine. You won't believe it, but she seems to have gor all Holy Joe on us. It was ever since Andrew was born. I thin it was the miracle of birth that did it.'

'What seriously?' Candy said aghast.

'Well she's started going to church, and she's already arrangin Andrew's christening. Dad's been a few times too.'

'So she's changed quite a bit then?' Candy pressed her further.

'Well I don't think she's changed that much really,' she replie 'I mean she still drinks far too much and is still trying to qu smoking. But no, she's no different, not really.' She paused a the others looked back at her intently. 'Anyway,' she sai wanting to steer the conversation away from religion, as it wa always an awkward topic in company, especially when trying t impress friends. 'I was just thinking Brad...'

'That's dangerous, thinking what?' he said, as he glanced aroun in search of the waiter so he could order another beer.

'Well I was remembering the first time that we came here. D you remember that?'

416

'Yeah of course I do,' he replied, happy now that the waiter was on his way over. 'Anyone want another drink?'

'I'll have another glass of wine,' Sadie said. Everyone else declined his offer, so they both decided to wait until the others had finished.

'That was a good day,' Brad then said with a smile, 'That's one of the last things I do remember. The next thing I knew, I was waking up in a hospital bed, surrounded by my family and a pastor. Then I remember you bursting in looking a right mess.' He looked back at Alicia with a mischievous grin. She laughed and jabbed him in the ribs. He responded by beginning to tickle her and they both laughed hysterically, forgetting almost for a moment that they were in company.

'Sorry, but why are we here?' Sadie suddenly interjected, 'I mean it's great to see you after so long, but you said to me on the phone you wanted to ask us something.'

'We'll get to that,' Alicia replied, 'there's no rush.'

'I mean we can talk on all day after you've told us,' Sadie continued, 'but I just want to know what it is…like now, I can't wait any longer.'

'Well,' Alicia began cautiously, 'We were wondering if you would be interested in a summer job?'

She waited to see their reaction; they looked at each other, slightly bemused, and then looked back eager to find out more.

'A job where?' Candy said.

Alicia looked then at Brad for his approval.

'Well go on ask them then,' he said. 'That's what we came here to do.'

'We're going to buy Jennifer's,' she said, the words suddenly tumbling from her mouth.

'You are kidding me,' Candy replied a look of utter amazement on her face.

'No,' Alicia continued, 'we're deadly serious, we're gonna do it up in time for the summer season.'

'What are you going to call it?' Sadie asked.

'Jennifer's of course,' she answered in a matter of fact tone.

'My God!' Sadie replied. 'After everything that happened there, I mean are you crazy? Jennifer was the one who…'

417

'Yeah we know,' Alicia interjected, 'but the place is well know now. We think it'll make it more of a crowd puller. We'd hav loads of customer's, you know like those goulish kinda peopl the sort that hang around at a road accident. Anyway, we'v been in touch with Jack Thorpe, Jennifer's dad, and he w; delighted at the prospect of us taking it over. He couldn believe it either, he's such a cool guy. After that we felt we ha to keep the name, we wanted to do it for him.'

'Do you really want to attract those kind of people though' Candy asked.

'I'm only joking about the geeks,' Alicia conceded. 'But let face it, that place is gonna be famous, especially when they fir out who the new proprietor is.'

'Well I guess you've got a point there,' Candy relented.

'Well I'm up for it,' Sadie said beaming from ear to ea 'Definitely.'

'Me too,' Candy said, not wanting to be left out. They shook c it, and decided to order the next round of drinks to celebrate.

'What if it's haunted though?' Candy added, in a low whisper.

'I doubt it,' Alicia replied with a smile, 'I think all of our ghos are well and truly laid to rest. Don't you reckon?' she sa turning to Brad.

'Yeah for sure,' he said, 'hey, where's the restroom round here?

'Just inside, first door you come to on the right,' Sadie replied.

'Thanks, I won't be a minute.'

Sadie and Candy began to talk excitedly about Alicia proposition, leaving her alone with her own thoughts for moment. She had suddenly begun to feel nervous agai concerned that maybe they had made the wrong decision, ar that it would be in some way disrespectful to her sister's memor to even contemplate reopening Jennifer's.

In that moment, she thought about her life and was feeling guil that she had moved on and had left her sister behind. She d still think about her all the time. She wondered how she w; doing, she wished that somehow she could speak to her agai just one last time, so that she could make sure that she was happ and that everything was going to be all right.

Just as the thought had passed through her mind, she heard flutter of wings to the side of her. She looked round to find th

418

source of the noise and on the next table, close enough to reach out and touch, there stood a robin, with its mottled brown feathers ruffled and its plump red chest thrust forward proudly. Its beady black gaze seemed to be fixed on her, and as she connected with this tiny creature, she felt a wave of emotion wash over her, immediately followed by a very real sense of complete peace and contentment. She knew then that this was the sign that she had been so longing for, for the past six months. The little bird chirped happily back at her and as it jerked its tiny head sideways, so another bird landed beside it and began pecking at the stray crumbs on the table. A noise suddenly distracted her and as she turned again to look, she noticed that Brad had appeared back on the terrace and was walking towards them with another tray of drinks. His eyes met hers and a radiant smile slowly spread across his face. It was then that she saw her future, and she knew that it was right that she should be looking forward to it, that she was meant to walk tall with him, and that together they would stay to face whatever the future had in store for them.

She turned back to look at the next table, expecting to find that the two robins had gone. To her surprise they were still there, looking up at her quizzically. She smiled in response, amazed at how fearless and bold they seemed, but as she did they suddenly took flight in a flurry of feathers, their agile wings lifting them almost effortlessly, high into the sky. She watched as they disappeared into the sun drenched distance, a new feeling of warmth now pervading her entire being. She was sure then that she would see her sister and her mother again one day, when it was her time, but from this moment forward she was free to live her own life, and she intended to live it to the full.